Void

A Novel

Kris Heywood

Published in the United States by Siskiyou Press.

Library of Congress Cataloging-in-Publication Data
Heywood, Kris
Void/Kris Heywood
2011910429

ISBN: 0615496075 ISBN-13: 978-0615496078
Siskiyou Press
1. Emperor of song—Fiction. 2. Oregon mountain—Fiction. 3. Tyrol—Fiction. 4. Longhaired German shepherds—Fiction. 5. Tabloid bullying—Fiction. 6. Multicultural—Fiction. 7. Celebrity shakedown—Fiction.

Printed in the United States of America

First Edition

Cover Art by Leanne Zinkand, Silverlining Designs

This book is dedicated to the one and only King of Pop.

—*First and foremost, good fiction is distilled truth.*—

CHAPTER 1

THE WHOLE MESS STARTED ON THE DAY I decided to drive out and give Jimmi a surprise ride home from the school bus stop. I hid the truck around the corner from the mailboxes and walked up the county road to where it intersected with the highway. Asa and Marvel, my long-coated German shepherds, followed close behind me. We were early so I led them into a little copse near the bus stop, sat on a log from which I could see the crossing, and made the puppies lie down at my feet, one at each side.

The bus arrived on time. Only two kids got off. The first was a short skinny boy with the pinched face of a weasel. Jimmi came second, tall and slender, honey-brown, his nappy hair needing a cut. Hissing, the door slammed shut and the tail lights stopped blinking. With an exaggerated sigh the bus veered back onto the highway, strained around the next curve, and passed out of sight.

Jimmi started walking downhill before I could get to my feet. And then the other boy gave him a hard shove from behind, making him stumble. "What you do that for?" my son said when he'd regained his balance, sounding more puzzled than mad.

"Cause you're a nigger!" the kid sneered.

"What?"

"You heard me, nigger. Why don't you go back to Zululand where you belong?"

"I live here. I've lived here all my life." Jimmi said, baffled.

"Not much longer, now that I'm here. I'll give you a bloody lip every day till you crawl back to Africa." The kid picked up a rock and threw it. It bounced off Jimmi's shoulder.

"Hey!" Jimmi cried. "Hey, don't!"

To my right, Asa sat up and gave a low growl. Marvel leaned against my other leg, vibrating with anticipation. I said, "Go!" They took off like two ground-hugging missiles, shooting out of the trees and across the road to stand between the two boys. Asa licked Jimmi's hand and Marvel, dead-serious, sat in front of the skinny kid, curling her lip and watching his every move.

"These your dogs?" the boy asked Jimmi, foolishly picking up a stick. Asa, who had the massive head and teeth of a bear, promptly showed him the full length of his canines.

"No," I said from the edge of the copse. "They're mine. Great guard dogs. I think you'll be all right as long as you don't wave that stick around. They're polite unless somebody threatens them."

The boy dropped the stick as if it had begun to writhe in his hand, started to run, and didn't stop until he passed the mail boxes below. As I'd had to point out to our neighbor Kosmo a couple of times, running away from shepherds is never a good idea. Sure enough, Asa started to go after the kid. But Marvel just gazed at me, waiting for a command. "Stay," I said, and they both did.

Jimmi dropped to his knees and wrapped his arms around their necks for a vehement hug. In response they licked his ears with devotion. Then he slipped off his pack and spent an inordinate amount of time retying a shoe lace. Finally he glanced up, his hazel eyes hostile. "You were spying on me," he said.

Lately, he'd been getting unaccountably touchy. "Don't be silly," I replied, nice and easy. "I had no idea there was anything for me to spy on."

Angrily he pulled loose the other shoe string and retied it, too. "Why did you come to walk me home, then? I'm not a child."

I nodded downhill. "I brought the truck. And some cookies. Who was that boy?"

"How should I know?" His tone was still rough. "I never saw him before. He was bugging me all the way from town. As if I'd done something to him." His eyes said, *And it's all your fault.* My fault for raising him near a town that was ninety-nine percent white, so that no matter where we went together we couldn't help standing out. That fact had made me unusually protective. Lately, he'd started to chafe under it.

I said, in an effort to keep things light, "Something must be wrong with him then. Want me to give you a ride to school tomorrow?"

"You leave too early."

"We can eat breakfast at the co-op."

But he wasn't willing to let go of his resentment at having me be a witness to his humiliation. "How many times do I have to tell you that I don't like to eat breakfast," he replied in a tone so belligerent that it made my hand itch.

"As many times as I have to tell you that you need food energy if you want to do well in school," I replied impatiently, sick of that particular argument. "I heard that on the days you leave home with an empty stomach you're at the candy machines by ten." I could tell from the scowl spreading over his face that it was something else he didn't want me to know about.

At that moment a black Rolls Royce with dark-tinted windows came around the bend, cruising slowly up the highway. It stopped at our crossing. We moved to the side, expecting the driver to turn onto the county road, but the car stayed where it was. The rear passenger window came down. A man with porcelain-white skin stuck his head out, his long, tied-back black hair gleaming blue in the weak winter sun. Aviator sunglasses obscured half of his face but I recognized him by the red jacket he was wearing and his perfectly shaped ears.

"Gorgeous longhairs," he said in a breathy voice. "I love those black and red coats. Where'd you get them?"

"The male's from Vienna," I told him. "The female from Frankfurt. Same age, exactly."

"You breeding them?"

"Maybe next year. When they're full grown."

He stepped from the passenger door. "Are they friendly?"

If he had waited for my answer I would have said they were not. But he was already crouching, running his fingers first through Marvel's coat, then Asa's. To my surprise both dogs wagged their tails. Lightly.

The pale, soft spoken man straightened and said with a tentative smile, "I'm a new neighbor. From down below. I bought a place that used to raise cows. Do you have a card?"

"Pardon?"

"You know. A business card. So I can get in touch with you. About puppies."

"I didn't bring any," I said, silently vowing to have some made at the first opportunity.

He patted around on his jacket until he found a small note pad and a pen. He clicked the pen. "I'm thinking litter mates. A boy and a girl." He gave a rueful smile. "Some old dog bit me when I was little and I've been scared of them ever since. I think it's about time I got over it, wouldn't you say? Yours seem extra nice. And steady. Kind of lean, though. I could feel their ribs."

"I'm keeping them on the thin side." I said. "Less stress on their developing joints and bones. German shepherds make excellent companions. Gentle but protective. And they're great hiking partners."

His smile grew more certain. "That settles it. What's your number? I'll give you mine as soon as I'm moved in."

I stammered my number. He scribbled it down. Then he put the implements away, rose, and offered Jimmi his hand. "Hi. I'm Ari. When I come back from California I want to invite you and your mom down to my place. For a movie and popcorn. What do you say?"

"She's not my mom," Jimmi told him, giving a timid shake.

Ari dimpled. "Oh? She looks like she ought to be."

A flood of gratitude washed through me. Most people only noticed our color difference and agreed with Jimmi. We watched Ari climb back into the Rolls. It turned onto the highway. He waved out of the window, his smile now full blown. His teeth were as perfect as his ears. After the car disappeared around the next bend, Jimmi cried, "I don't believe it! Ariel Jordan! Here! In the backwoods of Oregon!"

I said, "He must have bought the pasture land down by the creek. No wonder I haven't heard any cows mooing lately."

"He took our number!" Jimmi whirled his pack, dancing in an exuberant circle. "And he's got a TV!" Trust him to think of essentials.

"Probably won't be around much," I cautioned. "He does have that fabulous spread in California, remember? The one with the zoo."

Jimmi stopped, awestruck. "Oh my God! What if he'll . . ." Then he shrugged, reining himself in. He slipped on his pack, looked straight at me for the first time that day, and allowed a genuine grin to cross his preadolescent face.

"He might lose our number," I said. "Find himself some puppies elsewhere. Be too busy to call."

Then Jimmi actually put a hand on my shoulder. I couldn't remember the last time he'd condescended to touch me. "You know what I'm thinking?" he asked.

"What?"

"Could be you were right about him. And everybody else was wrong."

He was referring to the report I'd helped him write about Ariel Jordan for a class project last year. The one *I* had done all the research for. The one his classmates had openly ridiculed, making him feel ashamed of openly supporting his scandal-plagued idol. "Of course I'm right," I said. "No doubt in my mind."

There never had been. After all, Ariel and I had practically grown up together. Even if he still didn't know my name because I hadn't thought to introduce myself—or owned a single business card. But both omissions could be easily fixed the next time our paths crossed. If they ever would again.

CHAPTER 2

I WAS THINKING ABOUT ARIEL JORDAN WHEN I woke up the next morning. About how his dad had named all eight of his kids after angels, even the girl. About Ariel's voice soaring above the voices of his six brothers from the time he was tall enough to hold a microphone. About that amazing face of his, both trademark and curse, depending on whom you asked.

I left Jimmi sleeping and slipped on my clothes. The three dogs burst from the cabin as soon as I opened the door. Then they exploded down the forest trail without a flicker of hesitation although yesterday's fragile green end-of-February landscape had unexpectedly been transformed into desolate winter during the night.

"Damn!" I muttered, frowning at the snow and my sneakers before changing into my bulky red moon boots. Then I flipped up my coat collar and clumped after Asa, Marvel and Racket moments before all three dogs reappeared to find out what had delayed me. As usual Marvel was running circles around the other two. They stopped to sniff at the boots I'd had no occasion to wear since the first week of December. Then the two shepherds started their favorite keep-away game.

Snapping and snarling, Marvel dove for Asa's feet, a move he countered with blood curdling growls and horrific teeth gnashing. When they tired of the wrestling match they reared and fenced tooth to tooth. Racket, the Chihuahua, zipped around them at breakneck speed, yodeling in the shrillest tones he could conjure until I finally yelled, "Enough!" in the fake male bass I adopted whenever it was necessary to startle my pack to its senses.

Instantly the shepherds came to my side, heeding the advice of their genes. But Racket, who firmly believed my occasional attempts at discipline had nothing to do with him, buzzed ahead on his delicate fawn legs, waiting for no one. Following at a more leisurely pace I bent low to evade snow laden branches slumping over the trail and tightened my coat's Velcro wristbands against the chill.

At the abandoned cabin, the shepherds stopped and chewed snow as if it were vanilla ice cream, licking their muzzles with appreciation. I glanced up the rotting stairs to the treacherous porch and shivered, recalling the last time Jimmi and I had stepped inside for a quick look around. Once this had been the best little house on the mountain, with its wraparound porch, the jaunty, steep angled roof, the solid, hand carved front door. But nature, in the process of reclaiming what was hers, had sent hordes of wood rats to nest on the stove top, in the oven, and inside the walls from which they'd torn chunks of pink insulation, using the debris as their toilet.

Past the cabin the trail took a sharp left onto a logging skid that led to the top of the ridge. I could see Racket's dainty footsteps swerving off the path straight to the draw. Just as I turned uphill the Chihuahua came streaking out of the bushes, tailed by an incensed, determined coyote. Stretching his utmost Racket homed in on me and jumped into my arms. The coyote kept coming until it noticed that I wasn't a tree. Then the beast smoothly swerved uphill and out of sight. Before I could find my voice to yell "No!" the shepherds, as soundless as the coyote, went in pursuit.

A second coyote emerged from the gully in support of the first, chasing after Marvel and Asa. Outraged, Racket wiggled out of my arms and hurried to join the battle somewhere above. I froze, remembering my landlord Barret's horrible tale. Some years ago, his beloved Golden Retriever had strayed a few yards too far from his fancy cabin one evening and was surrounded by a bunch of coyotes. They tore him to pieces before Barret could stumble toward them.

A picture of the slaughter had lingered in my mind ever since. It was why I began straining up the snowy incline, shouting in the hope that the sound of my voice would drive the coyotes away. It had worked once before. Just last month I'd come out of my cabin early one morning, heading for work, when I heard the heart-rending death cry of a fawn somewhere nearby. His mother and herd panicked and ran off, leaving him alone with his attackers. The fawn's scream went on and on. I hurried toward the sound, my shouts interrupting the kill. The screaming stopped. Barret, who'd come running to the rescue from the opposite direction, stepped out of a clump of bushes looking grim.

"Don't go in there," he warned. "You don't want to see what they did to the little guy. The kindest thing for us to do is to leave him alone so he can finish his dying."

I wasn't about to let a couple of coyotes rip the throats out of my naïve puppy-dogs. Jogging uphill in my cumbersome moon boots, dodging sagging branches, shoulders hunched to keep snow from sliding inside my collar, I used muscles I'd forgotten I had. The dogs were waiting for me on top of the ridge, strangely subdued. Racket's small haunches quivered. Asa and Marvel were gazing toward the far off lookout, from which the coyotes yipped a clear warning before they returned to the draw. I scooped up Racket, holding him tight. "I bet you found their cave and stuck your nose in it," I told him. "You're lucky you caught them unawares. Now they'll have to dig a new den for their pups somewhere else."

The horizon behind the lookout was molten scarlet, setting dark clouds ablaze. I walked on, my boots sinking into virgin snow. When I saw a brown blur in my peripherals I hastened to grab at both shepherds' collars, forcing them to stand still.

A great stag pranced down from the neighboring height, crossing the ridge ten yards before us. Powered by thick muscles rippling under his pelt he moved as if he were rolling on wheels and carried his magnificent rack like a crown.

"Leave it. Sit," I said sharply when Marvel began to yearn after the buck. Asa cringed, flattening his belly onto the snow as if the chastisement were meant for him. But Marvel made a leap for freedom. I yanked her out of the air. That the buck aimed for the same draw into which the coyotes had disappeared was his own business. Keeping Marvel out of harm's way was mine. Most likely the coyotes would consider the buck unstoppable anyway.

I leashed the shepherds, carrying Racket in one arm. Together we climbed the last slope, inhospitable under deep drifts. We passed a stand of scraggly scrub oaks and were aiming for my little conifer friend when I almost stepped on the first buttercup of the season, peering out of the snow.

"Last snow, first flower," I said, bending to feather a finger over the velvety petals. They reminded me that on the mountain no winters were the same twice in a row.

I freed the shepherds, put Racket on the ground, and straightened, pressing my knuckles to the small of my back. He was heavier than he looked. The trail under my feet was slippery red clay soil bleeding through scoured white. A sudden gust snatched my breath away. I leaned into the cold wind, feeling it tug at my scarf. It loosened and fluttered behind me, a lavender banner. On impulse I spread my arms wide, wishing I could lift like a kite. But only the scarf sailed away. Asa stepped on it as soon as it touched down, giving me a chance to retrieve it. He left a red-clay paw print on the glossy silk.

Jimmi and I had first noticed the little conifer five years before. The sapling had only been knee high then. That spring, March had turned unbearably hot, killing wildflowers the day they emerged, browning the grass as soon as it greened, curling the leaves on deer brush to wither and drop before the month was over. The little conifer had been severely gnawed. Half the bark was chewed off and the main branches, including the crown, had been snapped.

We wired the branches together, painted a sealant on the wounds, and lugged a gallon of water uphill every morning. For two years we kept the baby tree surrounded by protective fencing and promised him he would grow up to be a giant. From his seeds would spring a future old growth forest, reclaiming the stripped hillside and restoring its God given splendor.

Now the little ancestor-tree's snow covered branches swayed wildly in the harsh breeze, almost as if he was waving at me. "Wind is good for you," I told him. "It'll make you stronger." Touching the slender trunk, I could feel sap striving up from the roots. Gently, I brushed the snow off each drooping branch, then gave the trunk a firm shake, releasing a cloud of cold diamond dust. Relieved of his white burden, he stood taller. He had already outgrown me.

Above us the entire sky was on fire. Pink cloud oceans roiled, their breakers foaming scarlet and orange. "Look up there. Just look!" I told Marvel. She did, enthusiastically wagging her tail. But Asa only glanced at the clouds for an disinterested moment, finding nothing the least bit edible in them. I knew without a doubt that Ariel Jordan would have loved this sunrise as much as I did. Glancing toward the configuration of boulders topping the hillside, I saw it transformed into Archangel Ariel's throne, covered with glittering snow.

I lay flat on my back beside the ancestor-tree, getting out of the wind. Racket made himself comfortable on my thighs, trying to wiggle underneath my warm coat. "That's the trouble with snow," I told him, wrapping him in the lavender scarf. "At first it looks and tastes good, but in the end it always turns to slush."

I gazed at the kaleidoscopic changes happening in the cloudscape above me until the colors waned to gray. "No yellow overcast either," I told Marvel who loved listening to me. "That means whatever's up there will come down as rain and wash the snow away."

No telling what the roads would be like this morning. It made me appreciate the dependable old four-wheel drive Toyota pickup I'd bought last September. I called her Efi. She was made to handle whatever the sky could spit out. The only thing wrong with her was that the gas gauge was stuck on the half-way mark. I was careful to top off the tank twice a week.

Cold, wet, and happy, my crew and I trouped homeward. The shepherds played some more of their war games until they scented a herd of black-tailed deer hiding in a manzanita thicket directly below. Cutting toward them, Asa and Marvel split the herd apart. Does hopped out in every direction, flicking stubby black tails and bounding away as silently as the big puppies chased them.

I considered the hunt a good ending to our hike, for the herd seemed to enjoy the exercise as much as the dogs. From the does' powerful jumps I could tell they were nowhere near their best stride. The shepherds fell farther and farther behind. Soon they lost interest in the uneven contest and labored back toward me, tongues pulsing.

"You get to lounge by the warm stove all day while I'm off earning our dinner," I told them. The shepherds liked taking turns on Asa's easy chair, but Racket the burrower preferred wiggling under the baby sized sleeping bag inside his box.

Sides touching, the puppies flowed ahead on the trail, as awesome as the stag and the molten sky. I let my eyes feast on their matched steps and synchronized souls.

MUNCHING on apple slices and raw almonds later that morning, I engaged the locknuts on Efi's front wheels, then climbed in the cab next to a sleepy Jimmi and started the engine. It turned over at once. I had called Barret just before we were leaving the cabin, asking, "On the way out do I put it in low drive or high?"

With a loud yawn Barret said, "You woke me up for that? High drive of course. Low drive's for off-road stuff like mud flats. Just keep your speed steady on those hairpin curves."

I thanked him for his expert advice but when I hung up my gut urged low drive. As usual I ignored it, deferring to male opinion instead, convinced that any man's technical savvy was bound to be better than mine. Besides, Barret had owned an elderly 4X4 pickup for years while I'd never driven Efi in real snow before. The week after Thanksgiving didn't count—the accumulation had been no more than an inch.

In front of us the road fell, leveled, and fell again. We passed Kosmo's old camper to the left, Stu's cabin up high at our right, the parking lot below it. I had a split second glimpse of Barret's house, downslope. There were no footsteps in the snow nor was smoke curling from anybody's chimney. Then came the long climb to the top of Ridge Road. The tires cut through the white stuff as if it were whipped cream, making me feel invincible. Efi maneuvered well until she came to a drift.

Although we negotiated it perfectly, at the next curve the back tires started spinning and slid to the outer edge of the road. Jimmi gasped, clutching the dashboard. I tried to ease the tires out of the groove they had cut. The engine revved and strained, protesting loud enough to awaken all three of our neighbors. Then I got Efi moving again—only to have the wheels slide right to the brink.

"Oh help!" Jimmi said, his eyes wide.

I rolled down my window and peered out. The left rear wheel was half off the edge. One little mistake and Efi would tip down a slope so steep that even the deer detoured around it. And if by some chance she didn't smash into a tree on her way down she would hurtle straight for Barret's cabin below.

"Climb out, Jimmi. Real slow," I said. "Don't slam the door. Stand by the ditch." For once he did what he was told without arguing first.

I turned off the engine, set the emergency brake, and got out to consider our options. After inspecting the truck from all sides I decided it was definitely time for us to call upon Barret's male expertise. I was glad I had already roused him once. It would speed his reaction time when we came pounding on his door to break our bad news.

CHAPTER 3

"DON'T SAY ANYTHING ABOUT ARIEL JORDAN," I cautioned Jimmi on our way to Barret's front door. "The man needs all the privacy he can get." Barret's two portly black Labs barked from inside the kitchen, announcing our arrival before I could knock. Barret, whom his renters surreptitiously called "the Bear," opened the door and wedged himself into the gap. He was looking shaggier than usual in wrinkled long johns, his fuzzy but thinning dark hair disheveled, his gray-streaked beard askew. Holding a mug of steaming coffee, he slitted his eyes to signal his annoyance with our untimely visit.

"We're stuck!" I announced before he could remind me that he hated to be disturbed before ten. "The pickup slid to the edge."

He took a leisurely sip and gave a careless shrug. "No problem. Weather report calls for rain. Just leave it sit overnight. You'll be fine by tomorrow." His dogs pushed their noses out from between his legs, wanting Jimmi to pet them. When he did, they slobbered all over his fingers until he shoved his hands in his pockets.

"Jimmi has to go to school," I reminded Barret. "And I have to get to work. You know I'm indispensible."

"Maybe you are and maybe you aren't," Barret said, unmoved and unmoving. "But I bet Jimmi wouldn't mind a mini vacation."

While I worked to keep a frown from crossing my face, the dogs squeezed outside, brushed past me, and rolled in the snow, barking with glee. Barret's face lit with an indulgent smile. "Look at those fat babies go!" he said, still barring the door.

"Cute," I allowed, knocking the snow from my boots. "If you don't want to help us will you at least let me use your phone to call a tow truck? A tow couldn't cost more than eighty or ninety dollars. I'll have to take the money out of the rent, though. It's due tomorrow but with the added expense I won't be able to pay it till next week."

It worked. He opened the door wider, stepped aside, and said, "Aw, Silvi. Don't you know I was only kidding? You guys come on in while I finish getting dressed. That's one thing I've noticed about you, Silvi—you can't take a joke."

"And you can't make one." I stomped through his cramped kitchen and stood by the living room window, blindly looking out while I grappled with my irritation. Behind me I heard Jimmi scrape a dinette chair away from the table and plop himself down. "I like school," he informed Barret. "I get to hang out with my friends. There's nothing to do up here except watch TV. And we don't have one." Just a year ago my boy spent his winter weekends sledding down the road on his Flexible Flyer. I used to have to drag him inside for our meals. Lately, he'd been wasting his spare time rooted on his bed. What the heck was Barret thinking, encouraging my boy to play hooky? At his impressionable age.

While the Bear shuffled off to his new indoor bathroom to get dressed, I stared at the porch banister, reminded myself of the first iron-clad rule I lived by, and recited it under my breath: "Don't rile a moody landlord unless you've found a new place to live and all the papers are signed!"

"What you say?" Barret asked, sticking his head around the door jamb.

"You've been bird-watching?" I gestured at the binoculars sitting on the banister, which, I now realized, was dry and had recently been swept clean of snow. By Barret, who slept in even on weekdays. "What's there to see except crows and blue jays this time of year?"

"You'd be surprised." He came out wearing overalls and stooped to lace his steel-toed work boots, his face flushing pink. "Well, let's get to it. If we must," he grumbled, putting on his coat. "I'll carry the snow shovel. Silvi, you take the rake. Jimmi, see if you can handle this." He handed the boy a glazed doughnut. When everyone knew Jimmi wasn't supposed to eat anything with sugar.

I gave an imperceptible headshake, signaling him to refuse it.

"Thanks," he said. And took the first bite staring defiantly into my eyes.

KOSMO the hunk stood waiting for us outside his rickety camper, his head wrapped in a peacock-bright turban. All through last summer he'd worn a brown crocheted cap, even when the temperature rose past one hundred. I assumed his hair was the same pitch-black as his wildly arched brows. If he had hair. I was beginning to wonder.

"Guess you got stuck, huh?" he said, rubbing an unshaven jaw. "I'll help you dig out." He grabbed the rusty broad bladed shovel leaning against the discolored vinyl siding.

"How altruistic of you," Barret growled at the taller and much younger man. "Unless you were planning to ask Silvi for a ride." He forged ahead. Jimmi raced past him on his long coltish legs, no doubt feeling the first effects of a sugar rush. He threw himself onto Stu's empty, snow covered parking lot, stuffed what was left of the doughnut in his mouth, and started a snow angel. To our right, Stu was skidding down his steep cement walkway, carrying his one and only winter coat and a gardening spade.

I walked beside Kosmo, noticing deep shadows under his languid gypsy-dark eyes. His clothes smelled of skunk. It was Stu who had clued me in last autumn. "That's marijuana, Silvi. Kosmo moved up here to grow weed. In our bushes. I'm sure Barret suspects although so far the juvenile fool's been careful to cover his tracks."

"Are you? Going to ask me for a ride?" I asked the juvenile fool, wondering what would happen to Barret if Kosmo planted another crop this year and the sheriff found it. On Barret's land.

"I *was* going to flag you down," Kosmo admitted. "Must have dozed off at the critical moment. Your slide is my reprieve."

We fell in behind Barret. Framed by his dogs, he wagged his snow shovel at the approaching Stu who looked like a young Johnny Depp. Stu grunted something that sounded like "mo'n'n" and jumped over the ditch onto the road. Leaning the spade against his hip, he slipped on his frayed down jacket, which sported several patches of duct tape. While he struggled with a stuck zipper I took stock of his longish unkempt hair, his sculpted but sleep-drenched features, his scuffed plastic sneakers.

"Hey, mon," Kosmo said. "Kind of early for you, isn't it?"

"Yup," Stu replied unenthusiastically. When Kosmo made a half-hearted effort to catch up to Barret, Stu turned to me and my boy, saying in his slow, deliberate voice, "Hi, Jimmi. Hi, Silvi. Thought I'd get some exercise to warm me up. My fire died during the night. The cabin's as cold as the inside of an ice-chest. Here, Jimmi, something for you from the restaurant. Catch!" He tossed Jimmi a sandwich baggie filled with after dinner mints, smiling at the boy's startled "Gee, thanks!"

"Jimmi, save them for later!" I said. "We're eating at the co-op, remember?" Naturally, I'd have to buy him a sugar-free equivalent before he'd let me pry the mints out of his hands.

Lowering his voice, Stu said, "Hey, Silvi. If I help dig out your truck can I catch a ride to the highway? How did you get it stuck anyway? Did you forget to put the wheels in lock?"

"I did not. Where's your car?"

He searched his pockets for a tissue, then blew his handsome straight-bridged Italian nose. "I parked it out by the highway. At two o'clock in the morning. That's when I decided a long slippery walk in deep snow—without a flashlight—was bound to be more fun than wrestling with two ice-cold metal tire chains. In the dark."

I shuddered, remembering similar hardships. "Can't say I blame you. Why do you think I finally bought a truck with four-wheel drive? All those chafed bleeding knuckles. Coat sleeves drenched in tire muck. Are you going to put on the chains and drive your car up here? Now that you can see what you're doing?"

"No way. I forgot to take my box of restaurant leftovers home, is all. My cupboards are bare. It was a lousy night for tips. Good night for mints but I'm getting kind of tired of sweets."

Ahead, Barret threw a snowball for the dogs. It fell apart upon hitting the ground. Kosmo, a few steps to his rear, made a bigger, firmer ball. It flew past the Labs in a powerful arc. When they chased after it Barret glared back at Kosmo, yelling, "Get a move on, people! I'm only shoveling out one tire."

Kosmo, who disliked being prodded, stopped walking and waited for the rest of us to catch up. I said in a low tone, "If he can't get my pickup unstuck you guys can help me put on my chains. They're still sealed in the original box."

Stu said, "No way, Silvi. I'd rather walk to the highway."

"I'm with you on that one." Kosmo's teeth flashed white. "I can always hitch a ride with some rich chick driving a SUV. Hitch with me, Silvi. I'll look more trustworthy with Jimmi and you at my side."

I said, "It would help if you took off that turban."

"Why? Something wrong with it? It's keeping my ears warm."

When we arrived at my disabled truck Barret was already scraping snow away from his tire. We busied ourselves with the other three while Jimmi dug an icy clump out of his boots and the dogs sat and watched. The moment all four tires were clear Barret leaned his shovel against a tree and looked at me sternly. "You should have put it in *low* drive."

"I would have," I sputtered. "If you hadn't told me to put it in *high*."

"I did?" he asked as if this was news to him. Then he chuckled. "See? That's what happens when somebody wakes me up from a sound sleep!"

I started to point out that he'd been bird-watching in his long johns when I phoned. But his face immediately began to harden, so I said meekly, "I'm so sorry. I promise to never wake you again."

Jimmi tittered but Barret flashed me an appreciative smile and made himself comfortable in the driver's seat. Then he turned the ignition and eased the wheels away from the abyss. Efi climbed smoothly up the rise and out of sight.

"Too cool!" Jimmi said, racing after the truck, the Labs at his heels.

"You've got to hand it to our landlord—he has all kinds of nerve," Stu muttered, collecting our tools and depositing them next to Barret's shovel.

"Yeah." Kosmo's nostrils flared with distaste. "It almost makes up for a few of the Bear's lesser qualities."

"You had another run-in with him?" I asked as we walked uphill together.

His wild brows knitted. "Let's put it this way—he likes to jerk people around and I don't like to be jerked."

"Watch it, Kosmo," I said. "He also likes to kick people out. I've seen plenty renters come and go. Don't get on his wrong side unless you have someplace to sleep tonight."

"She's right," Stu said, nervously looking ahead.

Kosmo tugged at my long braid in what he seemed to think was an endearing manner. "I could come sleep at your place. He'd never evict you. It's men he can't deal with." I yanked the braid out of his hand.

"Forget it," Stuart told him. "You know Silvi's a devoted celibate. It's the one thing she's religious about. If Barret can't shake her from her convictions what chance could you possibly have?"

"None!" I patted Kosmo's well-muscled shoulder to soften the rejection. "Besides, you're barely twenty. End of discussion."

He threw up his hands. "Okay, okay. I was just—"

"—joking?" I finished for him. "You and Barret must have gone to the same humor school."

He stopped short. "That's it. One more crack like that and you'll have to *beg* me to get in your truck."

"So long, old man." Stu took my elbow, steered me around Kosmo, and murmured, "Good thing I already have a wife or I'd be near as big a pest as him."

I wiggled my arm free. "Heard from Grace lately?"

"That's what I want to talk to you about." Up close Stu's breath smelled of toothpaste. Or mint chocolates. "Stop by on your way home. I've got a proposition for you."

"Ha! Thought so," Kosmo huffed close behind us. "Hypocrite!"

"Eavesdropper!" Stu countered. "Snoop!"

"God," I said, sprinting ahead. "If only I'd put it in low. I could have avoided two bickering kindergartners and a landlord who thinks I owe him a favor." I mouthed the second rule I lived by: "Never sleep with your neighbors, especially horny bachelors who think it would be convenient if the only female living nearby were available to them whenever they've run out of bed partners."

Efi was idling on top of the rise. Jimmi sat on the open tailgate swinging his feet and Barret was leaning against it, self-satisfied arms crossed over his broad chest. "Hey, Silvi," he grinned as I came closer. "I have to go out of town for three days next week. Starting on Monday. Could you   "

"—come feed the dogs while you're gone? Well, I owe you, don't I?"

Ignoring my ironic tone, he said sweetly, "Let them out in the morning and put them in before it gets dark, okay? Say—aren't you going to thank me for saving your truck?"

"You're my hero," I told him. "But are you sure three days of free dog-care are enough for your good deed?"

With a casual shrug, he crossed his feet too. "I decided to let you off easy this time."

"I couldn't have gotten out of this one without you," I had to admit. "Unless I'd gone ahead with the tow truck. My usual pet-care fees are thirty dollars per day. What do you know? I think I'll just about break even." I offered him my hand. "It's been great doing business with you."

"Isn't it always?" he said, stepping forward to shake it, his slate-blue eyes twinkling. He gave me a hug. I could hear him chuckling into my hair.

"Careful," came Kosmo's barbed voice from behind us. "The lady has principles."

Barret dropped his arms, his eyes turning frosty. "One of these days . . ."

"Right," Kosmo drawled. "Whatever."

The two men stared at each other, neither willing to be the first to blink. I patted the tail-gate. "Coming, Kosmo?"

Barret stepped away, Jimmi crept inside Efi's rubber lined truck bed, and Kosmo followed after him. Stu made himself comfortable in the cab on the passenger seat. I wiggled behind the steering wheel, gave Barret a good-bye wave, and adjusted the levers he had changed to accommodate his shorter legs. Making sure the gear was still in low drive, I took off, watching him stare after us in my side mirror. "I tried to warn Kosmo," I told Stu. "He's a dead duck."

Stu sighed. "Yeah. I know. Thing is, I'm afraid Kos has principles too."

I risked a quick glance at the rearview mirror. Behind the sliding glass windows separating the cab from the canopy I could see Jimmi furtively unwrapping one of the chocolates. Kosmo sat just inside the tailgate, facing the abyss—straight backed, cross-legged, upturned hands on bent knees. His thumbs and index fingers were forming small circles. His eyes were shut, his lips moving.

If he was praying to keep his leaking blue-plastic-roofed sanctuary it was too late.

CHAPTER 4

PET-SITTING WAS MY LATEST CAREER choice. It was infinitely better than pouring myself into nylons and working in an office all day. I liked being my own boss. Besides, I had all the right qualifications and was not afraid to list them on my flyers.

- *Utterly reliable.*
- *Experienced.*
- *Committed to the total wellbeing of your pet.*

These days I had a waiting list and no longer needed to advertise. The only drawback was that I had to deliver what I promised even after an unexpected blizzard.

I took Kosmo to the plaza as he requested, bought Jimmi the promised breakfast and a power bar in exchange for what was left of the mints, dropped him off at his school, and drove to Lillian's house. She had flown to California for a few days, leaving me in charge of her six dogs and five cats. When I pulled into her red-brick driveway, Rosy the Chihuahua started yipping the alarm from the living room window before I could set the parking brake.

Unlocking the front door, I was greeted by a shrill chorus of canines. They included Rosy; Dolly the white miniature poodle; Speedy the beagle; and Kiska the goofy and endearing elkhound. Paco, Lillian's shaggy gray-furred rat terrier, stood on her best recliner with a challenging gleam in his eyes while in the background, peering at me from the hall, the paraplegic Phoenix gave an expertly delivered, heart-rending cry.

I hastened to peel off my coat and held it before me like a truce flag, but Paco threw himself at me anyway. Waving my makeshift shield at the relentless terrier, I barely managed to keep him away from his favorite chew-toy—the toe ends of my shoes.

"Go back on your chair!" I ordered in my most commanding tone. But it wasn't until I reached up to the top book shelf for treats that he withdrew, with a great show of reluctance. He knew from past experience that I would not give him his share unless he minded me first. I passed out six bits of desiccated liver, the last one to little mixed-breed Phoenix who was still looking at me through the slats of a baby gate. I lifted him over, taking care not to turn my back on Paco.

As soon as I put Phoenix on the slick living room floor he scuttled toward the deck, dragging his paralyzed hind legs. I slid the patio door open and watched all six dogs file out. Then I gave the obese diabetic cat Feebee her daily insulin shot, armed myself with a roll of paper towels, liquid enzyme cleaner, and a plastic bag, and dealt with the usual overnight "accidents." Next I replaced every strategically located piddle pad and sifted through the litter boxes to remove whatever cat poop the dogs had considered inedible. Finally I poured kibble into everyone's bowls.

While the animals ate I called the principal of Jimmi's school to describe the scene I'd witnessed at the bus stop the previous afternoon. "I will certainly look into it," he said, sounding almost as angry as me. "The boy's family just moved up from the Bay Area hoping small-town living will straighten him out. Let me call his mother and talk to the driver. I'll get back to you later. If the boy does it again we'll kick him off the bus for a while."

After a short incredulous pause I said, "I don't want him to have a *chance* to do it again. Not even once."

The principal gave an exasperated sigh to let me know he didn't like being put on the spot, said "I understand," in an irate tone, and severed our connection without saying good-bye. Jimmi was the only African-American boy in his school. This wasn't the first incident the principal and I had discussed. It probably wouldn't be the last. Sometimes I suspected he was secretly hoping Jimmi and I would just keep our mouths shut and suffer in silence. Or quietly disappear. But as I had explained to my boy several times, I considered us social pioneers. His school needed him exactly because he was different. And the town needed our familial configuration for its own mental health. *Trail-blazing is hard,* I'd told him, *but necessary. What we're going through will make living here easier for other kids like you and other parents like me.*

I hung up and joined the dogs in the snow-covered backyard for a quick ball game and a few minutes of rough-housing, careful to stay clear of pickle-puss Paco. Although he was absolutely devoted to Lillian he had no love for anyone else, be they canine, feline, or human. Once the dogs lost interest in our game I walked around in a squat searching for and picking up droppings. That done I lifted Phoenix back into the hallway where he made himself comfortable on a large folded quilt. The cats resumed their naps. Before I left I passed out a second round of treats and promised to return in the afternoon to do it all again. The neighbor across the street got paid for giving the dogs their evening bathroom breaks and tucking them in.

On warmer days I often brought Asa and Marvel along and took them to the dog park in between jobs, not wanting to neglect them just because I had to take care of other people's pets. Racket was content to curl up in Asa's chair while we were gone.

My next stop was the private cat sanctuary. Its owner had fled to Hawaii two weeks ago for some much needed R&R. I spied half of the fifty-odd cat inhabitants through the storm door. They were sitting patiently in the extravagant hall, waiting to be fed. Turning the key in the lock, I drew one last fresh breath, then rushed through the house sliding open windows and patio doors.

I spent an hour on feeding the felines—upending cans into a giant bowl, measuring and mixing the exact proportions of a recipe tacked onto the refrigerator, passing out fifty saucers. Then I sifted through twenty litter boxes and wiped up unspeakable messes. Finally relocking the storm door behind me, I sucked in precious crisp winter air and appreciated how well I was being paid for this assignment. Two more days, four more feedings, and then *I* would get some rest and recuperation.

I looked forward to my next job—the apartment with the two bunnies. They had a room of their own complete with chewed base boards and gnawed chair legs. Their litter boxes were easy to clean, and except for occasional poop-pearls their floor stayed immaculate. I took a couple of baby carrots and apple slices out of the fridge, set them on the counter to warm, and made myself comfortable on the floor, opening the bunnies' favorite fairy-tale book.

Velvety black Morris cuddled against my right thigh. Fluffy white Myrtle cuddled against my left. As soon as I started reading their bunny eyes turned thoughtful. While they were listening their whiskers twitched contentedly and their long ears moved like rotating antennae until I came to ". . . and they lived happily ever after. The end." It was their cue to give slow full-body stretches and cast meaningful glances at the counter. I passed out the snacks and watched them start nibbling on my way out.

Around noon I drove to the co-op for hot soup and a roll. The morning fog had given way to serious rain. It was melting a variety of creatively attired snowmen on front lawns along B Street. To celebrate the weather shift I bought myself a tall yerba maté along with a six-pack of almond biscotti, bagging the more sensible soup for supper that night.

Before picking up Jimmi from school in mid afternoon I swung by Lillian's house again to give Phoenix another chance at the yard. His injured spine kept him from climbing stairs. He could drag himself outside easily enough but he could not come in again without my help. I stayed with him until his business was concluded, then carried him inside, not noticing that I had stepped in something smelly hiding in the wet grass. It left smeary tracks over half the living room's hardwood floor.

"Oh, shit!" I said, kicking off the offending shoe. "I hate last minute snags!" It was when I was at my most vulnerable, still bending over after I had gently lowered Phoenix onto the hall floor, that I felt sharp little rat terrier teeth embedding themselves in my shoeless big toe. In reflex I jerked my foot high in the air. Paco came up with it, hanging on with nothing but an outstanding set of canines. No amount of shaking could dislodge him. I pried his jaws apart, yelling his name. He dropped onto the floor, blinked a couple of times as if awakening from a particularly pleasant dream, and wagged his tail before reclaiming his favorite perch on the arm chair. From those heights he barked at me with a self-satisfied gleam in his eyes. I'd made his day.

I told him, "Lucky for you I'm wearing thick woolen socks. Hardly felt a thing. So there."

He heaved a sigh of utter fulfillment, curled himself into a shaggy ball, and prepared for a nap. I spent ten extra minutes with paper towels and enzyme cleaner during which the terrier did not stir once. When I counted heads and passed out the final treats of the day I pretended he was invisible to me, but from his smirk I could only conclude that he already considered himself paid in full.

Luckily all three of my customers were returning on Friday afternoon. And Jimmi was planning a sleepover in town at a classmate's. He wouldn't be back till Sunday evening. Thus I was looking forward to a lovely, long, uninterrupted, childfree weekend at home—and I knew just how to spend it.

On our drive up the mountain I only had to ask Jimmi to turn down the volume once. The rain had cleared Old Siskiyou Highway, the county road, and even the dangerous stretch of Ridge Road on which I'd come to grief in the morning. On the radio the weatherman predicted more rain during the night and throughout the next day.

As I unlocked the kitchen door I could hear the puppies whine soft hellos from the other side of the gate that kept them confined to the living room. But Racket sang his usual lusty, high pitched welcoming song. Jimmi clattered upstairs to dive onto his bed and listen to Chuck Berry. I ignored the dogs to bring in a boxful of my dwindling firewood, changed into a dry sweat suit, and only stepped up to the gate after Racket ceased his head-splitting yodeling. The puppies sat calmly, gently swishing their tails, their eyes bright. "Are you as glad to see me as I am to see you?" I asked them, letting them into the kitchen so they could watch me prepare mine and Jimmi's dinner. There wasn't much to it, that night. I poured the store-bought soup into a pot, set it on the stove, and butter-fried four slices of bread in my biggest cast iron skillet. Then I pushed the retrieval button on the answering machine.

The first message was from my mother in Vienna. "Silvia?" she said. "*Bist du da?* Are you there?" She waited for me to pick up as if I was a recalcitrant child intent on snubbing her betters. "Pick up!" she demanded when I didn't respond. "Answer the phone!" There was a long pause while she waited for me to do what was right. Then she said, "If you're really not home I guess I'll have to try again tomorrow morning. Six o'clock. Your time. *Auf Wiederhören*!" She'd disrupt my yoga session but that couldn't be helped. Overseas calls were too rare to ignore.

The next message was from Dorrie who lived in Key Largo. I pictured the pier in the evening, the tourists milling to catch the best show in town—sunset. "I've got some great news I'm dying to tell you," she crowed. "So call me back the minute you hear this."

Counting three hours ahead, I judged that as usual I'd be interrupting her dinner.

"Guess what!" she said after swallowing a succulent bite. "Some man wandered into our gallery today. At first I thought he was your average bored tourist tired of spectacular sunsets because he did the usual vacant eyed browsing. But when he came to the wall where I'd hung your paintings he stopped with his mouth hanging open. Thunderstruck."

"Yeah. Sure."

"Seriously, you need to quit putting yourself down, Silvi. He stared and stared, walked up so close to the picture of the abandoned cabin that his nose just about brushed the canvas, then backed all the way to the counter. 'Oregon, right?' he said, looking from it to the one you did of those flowering bushes and that patch of Red Indian Paintbrush. 'Near Ashland,' I told him. 'Made by one of our most popular artists.'"

"Uh huh," I said, cringing at the hyperbole. She always got verbose when she had red wine with her dinner. Or when she had a guilty conscience.

"Well—you *will* be one of our best artists if I have anything to do with it," Dorrie insisted in a raised pitch. "Anyway, he pawed through your greeting cards, went to the door, and stared at the abandoned cabin again. 'How much?' he finally asked.

'Priced as marked,' I told him. He nodded and walked out. It's something that happens a lot in a gallery. People want good art but don't want to pay for it. But this guy came back an hour later with a handful of hundreds.

'I'll buy both paintings and a set of those cards—provided you supply me with the artist's address so I can write her a note. Of appreciation,' he said.

I told him, 'That's confidential. Just hand me the letter. I'll pass it on.'

'Sorry,' he said, turning to leave. I mean, we're talking three thousand dollars getting ready to exit. So I gave it to him. What's the harm? We have *our* address splashed all over the internet and national art magazines. And anyway, he wasn't exactly shifty-eyed."

"Did you give him my mailing address or my street address?"

"Your mailing address of course!"

I could live with that—it would certainly be easier to rent a new mail box than a new residence if the guy should decide to pester me. "Promise you won't give it to anyone else," I told Dorrie. "Ever again. Not my phone number either. You know how I am about my privacy."

"Obsessive. But okay—I promise."

"A complete stranger! A walk-in!"

"Cash, Silvi! And we're not even taking a cut. Though we will for the next batch now that you're a professional. See, I told you it would work. Now just send me two more paintings to plug up the gaps. Special delivery. We're still at the height of our season. This place will be dead in a couple of months."

Dry mouthed, I asked, "Did you say three thousand? It's got to be a fluke."

"A trend, you mean. Go with it, why don't you? Opportunity is knocking. Let it in for a change."

"As long as it doesn't come in the form of some demented stranger. What's his name? Where's he from?"

"That's the funny part," Dorrie said. "I asked for *his* address so I can put him on our mailing list, and he said he's in between. Whatever that means. If he had paid by check I'd be seriously worried. But with cash, who cares? Listen, maybe he'll send some business your way—and I'm not talking poopy litter boxes and dogs with foul breath. There could be a fulltime career in this for you!"

I recalled the exact moment that morning when I had opened the cat sanctuary's storm door to eye-smarting ammonia. "Maybe you're right. I'll paint two new ones for you, but they'll have to be acrylics. I like to let my oils cure naturally." What I didn't tell her was that I had a whole stack of oil paintings in my living room at that very moment, none of which I was willing to part with quite yet.

"I don't care what medium you use as long as they're good."

"All right then. And you can still be my best friend. Too bad you're so far away."

"Whose fault is that? How many times have I offered you and Jimmi our spare room until you find a place of your own?"

"On your over-built island? Suburbs crowding the shore? In eternal sunshine? Remember the time we came for a visit, two years ago?"

"At Christmas. Sure."

"I was sleeping in a hammock in your back yard. Without a blanket. Wearing nothing but a t-shirt and shorts. And I still woke up sweat drenched. It convinced me I'd never survive your summers."

"You could get used to them. I did."

The soup was boiling. I lifted the pot off the burner. "You can't drag me away from this mountain. Where would I stow my two-and-a-half dogs and uncountable cats?"

"I told you before," Dorrie said, getting critical. "You have—"

"Too many animals," I finished for her. "Absolutely. For Key Largo, that is. Well—soup's done. We've got to eat." There was no point in continuing our conversation once she switched to her lecturing mode. Did she really think I'd give up my critters and mountain for her?

I'd sooner be dead.

Chuck Berry was still wailing upstairs. His guitar riffs made my feet itch. I gyrated around the kitchen a couple of times before calling Jimmi to dinner. He clattered down his stairs, snatched up his plate mumbling something about homework, and retreated back to his room. I wound up eating at my desk, a Margaret Atwood novel propped at a comfortable angle, surrounded by three faithful dogs who loved me even though I wasn't offering them a single bite.

CHAPTER 5

I STARTED MY PEACEFUL YOGA ROUTINE at five in the morning. In the dark. The phone rang while I was doing my favorite posture, the plough. By the time I'd eased myself out of it and groped for the receiver, the answering machine had kicked in. My mother said, "Silvia? *Schlafts du noch*?" It was a typical Mama question.

I fought the impulse to tell her, "Of course I'm still asleep and not even your phone call can wake me." Taking the receiver to the mat, I made my voice as cheerful as I could so early in the morning, saying, "*Hallo*? Mama? *Wie geht's*?"

"*Ach ja.* An early riser. Like your father." She gave one of her meaningful sighs. "How's the weather in Ashland? We had such a good week in Wien. Until yesterday. It snowed all night. Clearing the walkways this morning I tried to imagine myself on Ischia, floating in a hot thermal pool. But by the time I went back inside my nose was blue and dripping like a faucet."

"Papa couldn't shovel the snow? Does that mean he's still—"

"Not just 'still,' Silvia. He's worse. Absolutely no energy. A constant fever. The doctor thinks it's some rare kind of virus. Nothing he prescribed so far has made any difference. I'm frightened. Papa's been asking for you. He wants me to arrange for an airplane ticket. How soon can you come?"

I did a full leg stretch, pressing my face against my knees and letting the wires hum. Eventually I said, "We've been through all that, remember? Jimmi's school is still in session. I can't just whisk him off to Wien. And I can't cancel on my steady customers. I advertise total reliability. Besides, I have no one to watch my own animals." Straightening, I crossed my legs, arching my spine until the top of my head rested on the mat behind me. It was difficult with only one hand.

"Your dogs are more important to you than your own Papa?" my mother gasped. "He's made out a new will. He wants to explain it to you. In person."

What did they expect me to do? Abandon my puppies? Hire one of my unreliable neighbors to come feed three dogs and an army of cats twice a day for a month? The woodstove iron-cold? Water freezing in my plastic pipes? "They're at a delicate age," I reminded her, not for the first time. "You wouldn't leave toddlers alone for a month. Dogs will go bad if they're not properly guided and socialized. Especially guard dogs like shepherds." I segued smoothly into a one-legged stretch.

"Really, Silvia! You have too many—"

"It's my life," I told her. "They're my family."

"What nonsense. *We're* you're family. Your old room is empty. A waste. Papa would be glad to help you get a good office job. Your sister would too. As for Jimmi, my goodness, he's not even your own flesh and blood. Surely someone—"

"That someone is me. I promised his mother. He is my son."

"Yes, but he does have a living *father* somewhere in California, doesn't he? In an emergency—"

"Never!" I said flatly. "He goes where I go. Besides, my passport is expired. And I promised to paint two new pictures for that Key Largo gallery I told you about. The first two just sold. Isn't that nice?"

In the ensuing silence I shifted into the back-twist, corkscrewing my spine, and felt my muscles relax.

She sniffed. "I don't understand how you can be so disorganized as to let your passport expire. You must apply for a new one at once. You'll need it for the funeral."

"Don't say that. Don't even think it," I cried even though I knew full well that exaggeration was a specialty of hers. "Where is Papa, anyway? Let me speak to him please."

"Napping. Shall I pass on a message?"

"*Ja*. Tell him to get up and do something that makes him feel good. When was the last time he went to the farm? Why don't you take him? It'll be beautiful up there in the snow."

She cleared her throat. "You know I swore never to set foot on that place again. And he's too weak to drive."

"Erika can take him."

"She won't. Your sister's on my side in this."

I switched the phone to my other ear as if that would improve the conversation. "Tell him I . . . I . . ." Neither of my parents had ever been demonstrative. *I love him* sounded pretentious in our lilting Austrian dialect.

"You what?"

". . . wish him a speedy recovery. And remind him that all the men on his side of the family lived to be old. So will he."

"You really don't want to understand, do you?" Mama sounded genuinely bitter. "Thank God I have Erika."

"I'm glad she's such a great comfort to you," I said. And meant it. "You two have always gotten on so well. You and me, on the other hand . . ."

"If you made more of an effort—"

"That thing with Papa will turn out to be a false alarm. I'm certain. Please don't borrow trouble. And call me next month. Okay?"

She sighed again, this time in defeat. "Ja. In April. Hopefully your passport will be fixed up by then. *Servus. Auf Wiederhören!*"

"Bye-bye!" I pushed the disconnect button, carefully set the receiver on the nearest shelf, and felt my whole body contract like a giant fist. My mother hadn't said one word about the paintings I sold. She'd changed the subject instead and wound up talking about her favorite daughter again. The one who didn't fall short.

For solace, I shifted back into the plough and stayed in the pose for several minutes. Coming out of it with my legs straight up on the air, I imitated Mama's voice. "What!" I had her say with genuine enthusiasm. "Two paintings. How wonderful. I always knew you could do it. Your father will be so proud."

AT FIRST light I made a trip to the outhouse, wrapped in my bulky down coat. It started raining again when I returned to the cabin, harder than it had during the night. A cold wind blew downslope. "Sorry, no *w* this morning," I told the dogs from the landing. I'd realized months ago that they considered the word *walk*, spoken aloud, to be a firm commitment no matter what context I was using it in. For a while I got away with spelling it out but they caught on fast.

Now they glanced at my feet to see what shoes I was wearing. Marvel reared up to press on the gate latch with her left paw while hooking the other around one of the slats. The gate sprang open. Both dogs wedged their noses through the gap, hopefully wagging their tails.

"Can't," I said. "It's raining. We're staying put."

Their tails drooped.

"Shall I distract you?" I asked them. After a dramatic pause, I said, "Bones." Grinning, Marvel dove for Asa's front legs. "If you're good," I amended. They sat, waiting. I brought out three foul-weather bones, the third Chihuahua size, reluctantly cut down by my protesting butcher who swore I was trying to make him amputate a finger on his meat saw.

Measuring the bones with his eyes, Asa chose the largest. Marvel was satisfied with the middle-sized one. Racket, understanding Asa's inborn greed, carried his booty to his box, crawled under the sleeping bag, and sealed its opening with his rump.

"We'll go in the afternoon. If the sky clears," I promised them silently, remembering how Marvel's ears had twitched the last time I said the word *go* out loud.

I started the porridge, warmed up ground chicken necks for the animals, passed them out in scientific proportions, and called upstairs, "Jimmi! If you want me to give you a ride you better get ready." When the oatmeal was done I mixed in cream, cinnamon, and maple syrup and sat eating my portion at my desk while reading the last chapter of my book, glad of the heat radiating across from the wood stove.

After Jimmi ignored my second wake-up call, I set my biggest alarm clock to go off in five minutes and put it on the top stair, where it ticked like a time bomb. Then I went out to scrounge through my wood pile for the last, unsplittable piece of madrone to keep the fire going throughout the day, opened the damper, tossed it onto the coals, and got dressed for town. Hopefully, I had enough wood to last till the weekend. And then I'd have to fine-tune my chain saw and cut down the nearest dead trees left standing. Getting firewood was a time consuming, back-straining chore.

When the alarm went off it gave me a start. Even the dogs looked momentarily stricken. Upstairs, zombie feet lurched across the room. The alarm stopped clanging. "Good morning," I yelled cheerfully. "Now that you're up, stay up."

THE only way I could get Jimmi to eat his oatmeal was to carry the bowl out to Efi for him and plop it onto his lap before I zoomed down the first rise. Driving by Stu's cabin, I saw him waving frantically at me from his porch. I pulled up next to his oxidized orange Honda.

"Keep eating," I told Jimmi before climbing Stu's quaintly curving walk. He met me halfway. We ducked inside his woodshed to get out of the weather.

"I asked you to stop by on your way home yesterday," he reminded me tartly.

"Your car wasn't here. And it was raining."

He nodded toward his cabin. "Well, can you come in now? For a minute? So we can talk? I've got a nice fire going."

In the absence of Grace, Stu's cabin was not my favorite place to be. "One minute," I conceded, following him in. He swept a stack of National Geographics from the nearest chair. I examined its lopsided legs and declined, preferring to lower myself onto the rim of the claw-footed bathtub that stood between the kitchen sink and the stair-ladder leading to his sleeping loft.

Stu sat on the chair, bracing his feet on both sides to keep it from swaying. Then he ran all ten fingers through his spiky hair, making it stand on end. "It's Grace. She called out of the blue. We haven't spoken since last time she was here. That's when she told me I lived in a pig sty and she didn't like pork. She said I was welcome to call her as soon as I cleaned up my act. I couldn't, so I didn't. It's way beyond me, Silvi. Not that I haven't tried. Trouble is I don't know where to begin." He waved his hand in a limp circle.

"Who would?" I scanned the columns of dust-covered books and magazines, piles of soiled laundry, dirty dishes stacked from one end of the counter to the other.

"*You* would," he said, making it sound like a plea.

I let it pass, waiting for more. Grace was a nurse. A couple of years ago she went off to work in San Francisco. When she first signed on with the registry there she drove home once a month. Gradually her visits grew further apart and shorter until they were reduced to an occasional call around holidays. I expected her to snag an upwardly mobile doctor before too long and send Stu a sheaf of divorce papers.

"She asked me if I cleaned up my act yet. Naturally I said yes. Then she said that was good because she was planning to drive up this weekend. With a friend."

"Girl or boy?"

He frowned at me. "Not funny! She's trying to impress some new woman buddy of hers who thinks living in a funky cabin in the Oregon woods is the ultimate cool."

I knew the type. She'd want to be driven around to the tourist attractions. Get cheap tickets to a couple of Shakespeare plays, sold out or not. "Sorry. Jimmi and I have other plans."

His face fell. "You want a divorce on your conscience?"

"Yes. Considering the alternative."

"Aw, Silvi!" He put on a disconsolate look. "I'm willing to deal."

"What? An outdated set of Funk and Wagnall's?"

He tipped back his chair. "One full cord of split and well-seasoned madrone." He knew it was my favorite kind of firewood. It burned hot, steady and clean, leaving almost no ashes. With my last piece smoldering on the coals, all I had left were odd lengths of misshapen fir.

"While you clean out my sty I'll take the entire cord back to your place and—check this out—stack every piece against the wall right outside your door."

I jiggled my keys, just for show. What was there left to consider? By tomorrow night I'd be so desperate for dry seasoned wood I'd strike a deal with the devil. "Not on my pickup," I hedged, feeling my gut clench because I was about to lose a big part of my precious weekend. "You'll have to borrow the Bear's farm truck."

He beamed a relieved smile at me. "Done. I have to borrow it anyway. For a dump run. Two loads should do it, what do you think?"

I scrutinized the room. "At least. When will your houseguests arrive?"

"Saturday evening. They're staying for an entire week. If I live through it."

It wasn't until I was back in Efi, buckling the seat belt, that I cursed myself for giving in so easily. I'd just traded away a day's worth of painting. For dead wood. Then again, how far would I get with cold tubes of paint in a frigid house, wearing woolen gloves?

Glancing over at Jimmi, I saw that his bowl was suspiciously empty. I got out, circled Efi until I found where he'd ditched the oatmeal, buckled up again, and started for town.

CHAPTER 6

IN THE AFTERNOON I WITHDREW THE RENT MONEY from my checking account, asking the teller for three hundreds and one fifty. Later I idled Efi on the ridge top, rolled the bills into a tight tube, and stuffed it inside an empty vitamin container. Often Barret was not at home when I arrived with my offering.

Today was no exception. All four of his junkers, including the current favorite, a blue Subaru Brat, were parked in front of the Manor. But I received no response to my knocks. I hid the vitamin bottle behind a carton of Soy-Chocolate ice cream in his freezer. Then I browsed his living room desk for writing material to leave him a cryptic note but could find neither a blank piece of paper nor a pen that actually worked. Turning to leave, I noticed Barret's new birding binoculars still sitting on his balcony banister.

The rain had stopped around noon. By now half the clouds had blown away, allowing the sun to peek through at odd moments. It was casting patterns of dappled shade over the slush streaked hillsides. The temperature had gone up, making it easier to believe in the return of the first songbirds than it was during yesterday's unwelcome snowfall.

Some impulse made me peer through the lenses. As I expected, tree branches obscured most of the view. But when I pointed the binoculars down and to the left there was one bare patch I might have missed had it not been for blurred movement.

I adjusted the focus whereupon, to my astonishment, I captured the faraway image of two very odd "birds." One was a tall and willowy Madonna with flaxen orphan hair flowing artlessly over her shoulders. The other was a plump rosy cheeked cherub. My best guess was that it wasn't the cherub Barret was spying on from his drafty balcony.

Once, in a talkative mood, he'd confessed that he was only attracted to women who were blonde, young, svelte, tall, and unattainable. His shrink explained he was unconsciously trying to counterbalance his overbearing Jewish mother. It proved to be an incurable condition. "It's the 'unattainable' part that's most vexing," he'd complained. "Once I go after a woman and she makes the mistake of throwing over her current partner for me, she suddenly loses all appeal no matter what she's willing to do to keep our relationship going."

As I watched, Madonna and Child became obscured by a shivering conifer branch somewhere along the way. Then, unexpectedly, a big red metal blade with pointed teeth attacked the magnified branch. I put the binoculars back on the railing and looked downslope to where broad backed Barret stood facing a tree, his pudgy hands gripping the long handle of a pruning saw. His arms were raised so high that his ever present black baseball cap slid from his tilting head, exposing a baseball sized bald patch above his sparse ponytail.

In an effort to improve his balcony view he'd already littered the ground around him with freshly cut branches. I started to give him a shout and a wave but thought better of it. He would not have appreciated a witness to his secret obsession.

*

I COULD tell Jimmi was home as soon as I got out of the car. That blast coming out of his window—could that be *gangsta rap?* But as I stopped to listen all I could hear was his Chuck Berry tape. When I got to the kitchen I yelled, "Jimmi! Turn it down!" Then I left a message on Barret's voicemail informing him that I'd put the rent in the usual place. "His life is his business, my life is mine," I told Asa as he rose to his full height, resting both of his huge front paws heavily on top of the living room gate and smiling a welcome at me. Marvel whooped, took a quick look to check if the latch was still securely fastened with the spring lock, and stuck her slim muzzle through the bars as far as she could, her eyes alight with a question.

"Absolutely," I replied. "Just let me go in the closet and change." I never wore city clothes on our walks—the mountain forest was unforgiving, slashing new coat sleeves even faster than old. Over the sound of a caterwauling guitar I called upstairs, "Jimmi—I'm taking the dogs for a double-u. Want to come with us?" His answer was to turn up the volume. He was wearing that old boombox out.

Changing within hearing distance of the dogs was an involuntary audio strip-tease. They sighed when I kicked off my town shoes, moaned while I unbuttoned my blouse, and whimpered as I wiggled out of my skirt. Their enthusiasm increased at the soft swoosh my windbreaker pants made when I stepped into them. The hum of the zipper fastening my matching jacket took them right up to the edge of their self-control. But they saved their wildest applause for the sound of my feet cocooning themselves into my black rubber boots, celebrating my reemergence with yips that could easily have bested a whole tribe of coyotes.

By this time even Racket had become infected by their doggish enthusiasm. He squeezed his small tan shape between them, out-yapping them both. "Are we ready?" I asked, whereupon they hurled themselves at the front door. Installed to open outward, it burst wide as soon as I undid the latch. All three dogs dashed down the path that led to the abandoned cabin although the shepherds quickly returned to perform their self-appointed duties—Asa escorting, Marvel scouting in wide circles to make sure all was clear. Racket, who felt no compulsion to include himself in the guarding, followed his own inclinations.

What came next happened so swiftly that my mind couldn't quite process what my ears heard and my eyes saw. Somewhere ahead Marvel gave an startled yelp. It was followed by a loud crashing noise in the underbrush. Then something big broke onto the trail and headed in my direction.

A buck?

Asa froze at my side as the brown deer bounding toward us stretched into the improbable shape of a sleek tawny nine-foot-long mountain lion who abruptly changed course when he was only an arm's length away. I had a stunning close-up of pinned back ears and huge powerful hindquarters coiling like springs as the cougar hurled himself down the slope.

Marvel, who had morphed into a snapping she-devil, was hard at the beast's heels. Her fur standing on end, she brushed past my knees to dive for the same manzanita thicket the cougar had escaped into. If my reflexes had been a bit faster I could have grabbed her bushy tail the split second it was within reach.

Empty handed, I yelled "No," clutched at Asa's collar, and shouted, "Marvel, come back!"

From what little I recalled a cougar usually jumped on his prey's back from above, catching it unawares. Then he pinned it with his monstrous claws while his fangs bit through the jugular. Although a fast sprinter he tired quickly when forced to run. Once cornered he turned to fight for his life. There was no doubt Marvel would lose if she succeeded in running him down.

"Marvel! Come back!" I yelled again and again, hardly daring to take a breath between pleas. There might be an instant once the cougar found refuge on an oak big enough to hold his full weight— one instant when Marvel could wake from the predator-spell she was under before she became prey. And in that moment my voice would reel her out of the lion's reach a heartbeat ahead of his pounce.

Asa understood the consequences for his sister almost as fast as I did yet he strained to join her in what could only become shared doom. Keeping a tight grip on his collar, I bellowed "Marvel! Marvel!" until, miraculously, she appeared on the path, subdued, huge eyed, fur standing on end.

With a grateful sob I hastened to snap on their leashes. I dared not think what had happened to Racket, dared not wait for the situation to shift yet again. But then he came running from the direction of the abandoned cabin, nose down, following the cougar's spoor.

I snatched him into my arms before he could head downslope. "This is no time to push your luck," I told him. "Or mine. This walk is now over!"

THE NEXT morning I left the dogs locked in the house and carried a spade to the draw. As I suspected, the mountain lion had chosen it as his killing field. A nearby seasonal creek filled with snow melt attracted small herds of deer. Over the years the stream had cut deep into the hillside so that they had to climb down into the cut to drink. All the cougar had to do was belly up to the edge of the bank and leap down on his victim while the rest fled. I counted three decaying corpses partially buried under leaf mold. A fourth, lying fully exposed, was still fresh.

Most likely Marvel had surprised the lion over his latest kill, rushing at him while he was unprepared for combat. I couldn't decide whether I should let the cougar keep the fresh carcass, in which case he'd hang around for a while, or bury it along with the others in the hope he would wander off to less contested sections of his vast territory. In the end I buried only what stank and elected to walk my dogs elsewhere until he chose to depart.

I WAITED for Jimmi to come home and started him on his math homework. Then I drove the dogs out to the county road. It was usually traffic-free until the high valley's commuters returned. That gave me enough time to walk the dogs safely on the brink of civilization where wild things only roamed after dark.

I parked across from the upper strip of mailboxes and led the dogs down the sandy roadway, crossing a vast field and backtracking before the forest could touch us. The dogs were eagerly investigating new smells along our route. I was pleased with the occasional glimpse of a glamorous super cabin built of logs or finished with redwood siding. These dwellings were usually lodged behind a picturesque cluster of trees at the end of some long, curving driveway.

Our high mountain valley had recently been discovered by the Bay Area's affluent who bought the land cheap, tore down existing structures in far better shape than the one I called home, and erected those more to their liking. The three old cabins Barret owned up on the ridge had become an anomaly, museum pieces without historical value. One day soon people like me would no longer walk on the valley's three roads—nor would anyone else, for this new breed of mountain dweller went nowhere his SUV could not go.

Thus I was awed to encounter two pedestrians lingering at the lower strip of mailboxes. One was a tall, slim, flaxen haired woman, the other a rosy cheeked child with fair locks who was barely old enough to stand upright. The woman had a hand in the rustiest mail box but hastily retrieved it to lift the child out of harm's way when Marvel and Asa trotted up to investigate.

"She's not used to dogs. We've never had one," she said, smiling at me. "Hi. I'm Violet, and this is my sweet Lavender. We just moved up here last week."

I stopped and shook hands. "I'm Silvi. You must be on what used to be Ralph and Edie's land." It was the only piece visible— through binoculars—from Barret's balcony. Ralph and Edie had lived happily in a tight little cabin on the far side of the creek for a dozen years until they'd saved the cash for a big addition that they proceeded to build by themselves—with Ralph hogging all the important work while he turned Edie into his fetch-it-girl and chastised her for every mistake he made. Once the last nail was pounded they decided to split. She fled to Alaska, he to the Mexican hillsides, and their newly renovated house stayed unoccupied. Until now.

"Still *is* their land," Violet said. "We're just renting the place, trying to get rid of the accumulated spiders and mice and the rest of the little squatters."

I introduced my four-legged hiking partners. "It's a long way back on foot with a baby on your hip. You still have that rickety bridge going across?"

"I pray every time I drive over it—and squeeze my eyes shut whenever my boyfriend does." She gave a careless laugh. "Last night we had a fight and Clyde took himself and his funky truck out of here, leaving me stuck with no wheels. I decided to get the mail out of sheer boredom. Oh-oh. Lavender, no!"

The little girl grunted, a meditative look in her eyes. Violet wrinkled her nose, carefully setting her onto her feet. The shepherds approached Lavender's rear end with deep interest.

"Darn," Violet groaned. "I didn't think to bring a spare diaper. How stupid of me. The long walk just doubled. She's hard to carry even without poop in her pants."

Unable to suppress an urge to be helpful I offered to drive them home in the Toyota. "With the windows wide open, if you don't mind."

Violet looked relieved. "Sounds good to me. We just finished baking some brownies. I could make tea. It'll nice to talk to somebody besides Clyde for a change. And maybe we could get Lavender used to your puppies."

As I walked uphill to get Efi, part of me was eager to make a new friend. Another part already regretted losing my treasured privacy and, worse, landing in the middle of something messier than just a soiled diaper. By accepting Violet's invitation I'd be expected to issue one of my own. It would bring Madonna and Child up to the ridge, onto Barret's land, and near his lair. Where they were bound to be noticed by the passionate bird-watcher, with binoculars or without.

CHAPTER 7

EARLY ON SATURDAY MORNING I SIFTED through my stack of nature snapshots, pulling out the two I wanted to use for the paintings I promised Dorrie. I had taken the first one on a misty April day three years before. It showed a weathered fir stump. What was left of the severed log rested companionably beside it. The stump sheltered a lush cluster of ferns, the small conifer sprout in its center dreamily biding its time. A carpet of moss spilled from the stump's winter-softened lip onto the ground.

It was the picture of the old not only protecting the young but nurturing it with the very fiber of its being. While the log—which had once been a tree wide enough for three men to embrace—decayed quietly into compost, the stump birthed and reared new life. One day the sprout would outgrow its cradle and sink its roots into its own past, entwining with ancestor molecules in a chain reaction that reached back to the first forest and forward to the last.

The second photo captured a tableau of flowers down by the county road. After driving past it several times, I'd finally stopped to study the unique design. To the right was a wild rose bush with pink blossoms. One vibrant creeper, covered with bright buds, bowed toward the patch of deep purple vetch on the left, which had sent runners into the air to meet and embrace the vine. In the exact center of this two-toned arch one single wild sunflower was thrusting skyward, its gold-and-brown face turned to the sun.

The striking pattern had not been repeated since. And now that Jimmi was staying at his friend's and the morning sun flooded my living room my hands were aching to translate the memory onto canvas. If only I hadn't made that rash promise to Stu. If only I hadn't needed another cord of wood. But although the weather report promised a mild day, the next cold spell was already blowing down the coast from Alaska.

THE FIRST thing I did on arriving at Stu's cabin was to wake him from a sound sleep. The second, after I'd convinced him to unlock the door, was to elbow past him and open every window in the room. "Your place smells like there's a skunk living under the floorboards," I said, going toward the stair-ladder and contemplating the closed trapdoor above.

He got there ahead of me and barred the rungs with his bedraggled body. His clothes looked slept in; his cheeks were unshaven. For some reason, those grooming errors made him look even more handsome than usual. "I'll take care of everything up there," he said, brushing stair dust from his grubby shirt sleeves. "You concentrate on the living room and the porch."

"Porch?" I said with a groan. "I don't remember us discussing the porch."

"Do you have any idea how hard it is to collect a full cord of wood?" he countered. "First you have to find dead trees. Then you cut them, saw them into rounds, drag them on and off the truck, split the rounds into wedges, stack the whole bunch and let it air-dry for a year to get it seasoned just right. As if that weren't backbreaking enough, now I have to move the whole pile again. To your place.

Into the truck. Out of the truck. Stack it against your wall. Believe me, you're getting the better half of our barter."

"Now you've got me feeling sorry for you," I said drily. "Why don't we just leave the stack where it is?" I started to leave. "I'll buy myself an extra cord from some poor wood vendor in town and you'll scrub down your own cabin. Here's a pointer: throw out everything that isn't nailed down. Ciao, bambino."

Nimbly, he arrived at the door before me, holding up his hands. "Silvi, Silvi, Silvi. What we both need is a cup of hot coffee. The civilized brew." He grinned, showing off his evenly spaced teeth. They reminded me of Grace's. I'd almost forgotten what an appealing young couple they used to make.

"All right then." I sat on the rim of the tub and watched him measure and pour. By the time we finished the coffee, we'd hammered out a solid plan for the day. Stu would borrow Barret's old farm truck to deliver my madrone. I would empty the downstairs and porch, throwing everything not specifically exempt into a heap. When he was done delivering the wood he would load the trash onto both trucks for a combined dump run.

"Grace's houseguest gets a spick and span living room floor to sleep on, you get a warm cabin, and I'll straighten the upstairs tonight. Deal?" Stu held out his hand. We shook. He headed to Barret's to drive up the farm truck. Five minutes later he parked it at the bottom of his walkway and came inside for his work gloves. Chuckling, he poured himself a second cup of coffee. "I forgot that the Bear likes to celebrate the first warm spring day in his birthday suit. A grisly sight."

I'd thought so myself the couple of times I caught inadvertent glimpses of the spectacle. "That's why I stay away from his place on hot days. Me, I'm more into celebrating the first autumn rain. With a long walk, fully dressed, minus the umbrella. Come home with my hair and clothes plastered to my skin."

"Hmmm! A vision comes to mind." Stu said, letting his gaze travel down my front.

"Oh shut up." I jerked my thumb at Barret's battered truck. "Focus on your work. And take your innuendos with you."

Back inside, I rolled up my sleeves, tuned his radio to the classical station, and let the music motivate me. By the time the Met's opera broadcast came on I'd pretty much emptied the room. When the last aria was sung I'd cleared the porch, swept a profusion of spider webs into oblivion, scrubbed and dried even the stickiest dishes and greasiest pans, put them away, and left the sink soaking in a powerful bleach solution.

I was sweating and covered in dust. The one thing I'd never been able to get used to about the local climate was the abrupt change from cold to hot. Sometimes the temperature jumped forty degrees from one day to the next. A couple more days like this one and every buttercup on the mountain would shrivel and die.

Although I'd begun the work with distaste the feeling soon gave way to compassion. No one in his right mind would let things get this bad. Stu must have gotten stuck in a long bout of depression while he was holed up in his wintry sty. When Grace left our mountain she took his heart with her. Abandoned, a young man in love with his wife could easily succumb to lead-boned loneliness.

Barret, too, had his dark days, refusing to answer the phone and the door, sitting in his leather recliner and staring at nothing. Who needed a gardener when the grass didn't grow? Or a waiter when tourists and well-heeled townspeople fled to the Baja Peninsula?

That's where I had the advantage. A lot of Ashlanders left their animals behind for somebody like me to tend because it was less traumatizing for them than a month inside a cage at a commercial kennel. But without my three non-judgmental dogs and an argumentative son to welcome me home every afternoon, I might have spent my spare time inert in a chair and staring at the wall too.

Every now and then I caught a glimpse of Stu laboring down the precipitous walkway, first with armloads of firewood, then with bundles of trash. As the heat increased he shed his shirt, then the t-shirt. Finally he came in for a drink of well-water and rubbed a wet washcloth over his face.

"Old naked Bear does have a point," he said, climbing the stairs to raise the trapdoor just high enough to fish for a wrinkled pair of shorts. "It's stifling up here. I'll change in the outhouse." He cocked a brow as he was climbing back down. "How about you? Shed a couple of items, why don't you? Make yourself comfortable."

I looked at the loaded trucks. Barret's was tarped, mine was stuffed to the canopy's ceiling. "I'm perfectly comfortable already, thank you. When you come back from the outhouse I want you to sweep the porch and hose it off real good. I'll be scrubbing the living room floor for the third time, even though I'm so hungry it hurts. Your cupboards are still bare and there's nothing inside your refrigerator fit for human digestion. Clearing out the slimy bits is nobody's business but yours—and definitely not included in our oral agreement."

"Not yet you mean." He offered me his hand. "Let's add an amendment."

I slapped it away. "Let's not. The purple sludge in that plastic tub looks like it used to be liver. According to the label it's been outdated for three months."

"I spaced it," he confessed. "And after it started to smell I was afraid to touch it."

"Too late to throw it away. You'll have to bury it."

The phone rang before Stu could think of a witty reply. I got on my knees, vigorously scrubbing while he picked up the receiver.

"Hello?" he said. "Oh, Barret. Almost. We're fully loaded. Let's see—forty-five minutes to the dump, forty-five to drive back. And I have to borrow a futon in town. I'd say two hours or so. Why? " . . . Oh, I see. That's too bad. He'll have to wait till tomorrow. I'm sorry." He hung up and watched me until I felt self-conscious.

Rubbing a white rag over the scoured floor, I held it up for his inspection. "Now we're getting somewhere—the rag's staying clean."

"Looks good enough to eat off of," he said. "It seems the Bear promised his truck to Kosmo last week. For a hauling job. Barret forgot all about it and Kosmo just showed up to get the key. They had words. Kosmo left in a huff. I—oh, no!" He snatched up the receiver, dialed, waited, and slammed it into its cradle. "He must be on his way to Kosmo's camper to tell him he's got to reschedule.

Damn. Maybe I can . . ." He ran out to the porch, leaned against the banister, and strained to listen.

Puzzled, I followed, wondering why he looked so stricken. I could hear a loud knock on the camper's flimsy door, the creak of rusty hinges.

"Too late," Stu moaned, blanching under his stubbly beard. During the next few seconds the birds stopped their singing and the breeze ceased to play with high-up conifer branches. Then came a thundering "KOSMO!" pronounced as a curse.

"What?" Kosmo grunted from the outhouse he'd inherited after Barret installed a deluxe version inside his Manor.

"Get over here," Barret demanded. "I want a word. Now!"

"Coming," Kosmo squeaked, his footsteps crunching gravel. "Why?"

Like their many previous "words," these began in a civilized tone too low for Stu and me to catch in detail, even when we hung over the railing to glean what we could. The conversation rapidly deteriorated into a shouting match, ending with the one phrase Stu must have been trying to brace himself for.

"—but Stu's doing it too," Kosmo yelled, throwing friendships and confidences aside.

Stu stole a glance at his loft windows, started for the door, and turned back to listen to the rest of the argument.

"Then I'll kick him out next," Barret was shouting. "As for you, I'm giving you the required three days' notice and not one minute more."

"Shove it, slumlord," Kosmo returned, equally loud. "I'm sick of this moldy hole anyway. It's driving me nuts. Mice in the cupboard, leaking roof, mildewed walls—I'd rather sleep in a tree."

The camper door slammed. Barret stalked up the rest of his driveway. "He's coming!" Stu muttered, wildly looking around for someone to toss him the rope that would save him. His eyes fastened on me. He steepled his hands and said beseechingly, "Grace!"

I went inside, picked up the bucket and scrub brush, and climbed the perilous stairs to the loft. Then I pushed up the trapdoor until it leaned against the wall and stood waiting as a pair of leather clogs clomped up the porch stairs.

"Barret. I . . ." Stu stammered.

"Out of my way," Barret snapped, shouldering him aside. When he stood poised on the threshold I had already turned my back to the room. Now I blew my bangs away from my eyes and slowly climbed down the ladder one rung at a time, dragging the bucket along.

"Well, that takes care of the loft, Stu," I said, guileless. "Don't bother to thank me. I did it for Grace." I looked down straight into Barret's stony eyes. "Oh, it's you," I said with a welcoming smile. "Watch out, that floor's still wet. Nice towel."

He glanced at the striped bath-towel he'd wrapped around his middle, black fur sprouting in all direction above and below. "This old rag? It was drying on a branch outside of Kosmo's slummy camper shell. I only put it on because I know how sensitive you are about some things." He considered the rectangle of daylight coming through the open trapdoor.

"I'm grateful." I stepped onto the cabin floor and plunked the bucket down by my feet.

Stu peered nervously over Barret's fuzzy shoulder. "Didn't she do a great job? I'd have been lost without her."

Barret gave him a hard stare. "You got that right. I just went to the camper to write Kosmo a note about the truck mix-up. There were growlights and weedstarts everywhere, even on the bed. It was definitely the last straw. I kicked him out on the spot."

Stu winced. "Where will he go?"

"Who cares?" Barret was still contemplating the trapdoor. "Nobody grows weed on my land, indoors or out. That kind of trouble I don't need." Abruptly, he squeezed past Stu's trim frame and stood on the porch with his feet planted wide. "From anyone. Got it? And bring Grace down to my place tomorrow for some coffee. It's been too long." He tightened the towel, tucking in the end. "Tell her we need her here, why don't you? It's the truth. Grace gave this place class. No reason she can't find work at one of our own hospitals, is there?"

Stu waited until Barret had descended the walkway down to the road. Then he came in and carefully closed the door. "I owe you," he whispered.

"I did it for Grace," I reminded him. "She's the only friend I have who's worth lying for. Don't let us down. Come on, we're getting out of here. I'm desperate for something to eat and I've got company coming in a couple of hours."

A minute later we got in our trucks. Then Stu jumped out again, climbed to the cabin, and groped around in a planter. He found a padlock, brushed off loose dirt, and snapped it shut on the door, rattling it a few times to make sure it remained locked. Obviously, the goop in his refrigerator wasn't the only thing he planned to remove on his return.

CHAPTER   8

I WASN'T EXPECTING VIOLET AND LAVENDER until three. Plenty of time for coffee with Stu at the co-op. I bought an tuna sandwich to split between us. After the first couple of bites we got to talking about our favorite ridge legend. Over time, Barret had supplied us with varies tidbits that made him look good. The less favorable accounts had come from his disgruntled ex-friends, though Stillman never said one word against him. Fitting together as many pieces as we could, Stu and I came up with this story:

Once upon a time there was a young Harvard student named Randy who dropped out of law school in order to live the simple life and annoy his parents. A true trust-fund baby, he bought into a land co-operative other future heirs had started on the mountain. Lithe and lovely blond Liz had come out west with him. She helped him design his cabin. They built it from scratch using the old-fashioned hand tools he'd inherited from his grandfather. They learned to chop firewood, carry water, and grow organic veggies in the communal garden. And were well on their way to living happily forever after. Or so they thought.

Barret, who'd dropped out of Yale's post-graduate program to become one of the founding members, took a special interest in baby faced Randy. That interest didn't stop Barret from coveting Liz. She was flattered by the attention (and no doubt intrigued by the luxurious "Manor," which had running hot and cold water, a spiffy outdoor shower, a snazzy outhouse, and full electricity). All too soon she switched alliances, choosing the seemingly world-wise older man. True to form Barret turned cold and distant the day she moved in with him.

It wasn't long before she asked Randy to take her back. But Barret, figuring that ending the relationship ought to be his prerogative, not hers, threatened to have Randy expelled from the land co-op if he let her return to his bed. Before Randy could sort things out Liz flew east to embrace a more civilized life style. The ambiguous note she left behind promised that the man willing to sacrifice his counter-culture principles for her could win her for life. That turned out to be Randy. He proceeded to give up all that he loved to follow her to New York and love her.

Barret decided to feel doubly betrayed. Some badly drawn clause in the land agreement stated that anyone who dropped out of the co-operative automatically forfeited his section to those who stayed. Barret lost no time selling Randy's share to an outsider named Todd Mittendrin.

This spiteful act backfired when Todd promptly brought in a line of heavy equipment to dig into the slopes. His plan, as it turned out, was to create a mountain-top suburb, widening and paving the co-operative's private dead-end road and using it as the future settlement's main thoroughfare.

Barret and friends succeeded in blocking the road as the first bulldozers rolled down from the ridge top. Chaining themselves together and then to road-side trees, they created a living barrier. It defeated the equipment operators who were forced to backtrack to the county road. Infuriated, Todd took the hippies to court, battling for the unconditional access he insisted Barret had promised him. After Todd lost he smashed all the windows of Randy's pretty new cabin and propped open the doors, inviting beasts and the weather to take their toll.

"The Bear went on to scare off his other buddies," Stu said, finishing his coffee. "Including Stillman. Then he claimed they'd abandoned their plots. You have to hand it to the guy—he's got a huge supply of what New Yorkers call *chutzpah*."

"What about Randy and Liz?" I asked. "Do you think they're still living happily ever after?"

"I don't know and there's no use asking Barret," Stu said. "The minute anyone mentions Randy his eyes glaze."

For a while Barret kept the "forfeited" cabins empty, taking turns living in each before deciding he liked the Manor best after all. Since uninhabited forest dwellings speedily attract pests he chose to become a landlord.

"That's where I came in," I told Stu. "My rustic hovel was seriously overrun by critters. The cats chased off hordes of mice, wood-rats and bats. I swept out the spiders." Randy had been a talented carver. Each of the cabins had something he made, including my scenic outhouse. He'd built a magnificent covered porch for it and installed a solid, hand-carved door with a round window that featured the wooden silhouette of a howling wolf.

The three cabins, erected on piers, had been the only permanent structures on the land; one of the other sites had a lean-to on it, another a yurt. In addition, there were a couple of tipis, a small dome, and a dilapidated camper. All but the camper were dismantled and carried off by their disillusioned owners, leaving no trace except for a few barbeque pits and outhouse holes.

Over the years Barret's bushy pony-tail thinned and became threaded with silver. He mellowed a bit but young men like Kosmo still found some buttons to push and lived to regret it—though not on the ridge. I cultivated Barret's good side by staying out of his way, punctually paying my rent, and knowing when to keep my mouth shut. In return he didn't count the feral cats I took in and came only when I needed help with a major repair.

Engrossed in the tale Stu and I pieced together, I forgot all about my guests until I was driving up the highway. Increasing my speed, I careened around alarming curves as fast as Efi would let me. At last I passed Stu's parking area. A white rear wheel drive Nissan pickup stood in the middle, its doors wide open. The cab was empty. There was a toddler seat on the passenger side. Violet? Out here? When I'd drawn her a clear and detailed map all the way to my cabin?

Suppressing an anxiety attack, I approached the edge of the lot to survey Barret's yard below. There stood the Madonna, one arm supporting the cherubic Child on her hip, the other poised at the front door. Before I could think to yell "Don't," Violet knocked. Barret answered wearing nothing but his black baseball cap. I could hear Violet's nervous high giggle, Barret's deep-toned reply. He invited her in. She shifted the cherub onto the opposite hip and vanished into his kitchen.

As the wood moth is drawn to a flickering candle, so Violet had unerringly found the one place she needed most to avoid, and now moth and flame were beginning their ancient dance. It wasn't likely to end until one was singed and the other snuffed out.

What could I do but drive home, hoping the Bear would have the decency to give her fool-proof directions to my house and send her on her way? I made the promised tea. I poured Lavender's milk. I arranged my whole wheat, fruit juice sweetened cookies on a platter. I sat and read. Until it got dark. Violet never showed.

Long after I'd given up waiting, had sipped the milk and nibbled my way across the platter, Barret phoned to demand my attendance at a potluck he'd suddenly decided to throw. "Tomorrow afternoon," he decreed. "A sort of welcoming party for Grace and her friend. And for our new neighbors, Violet and Clyde. They just moved into Ralph and Edie's place. I'm making a salad and my famous guacamole dip with chips. Stu volunteered the lasagna. I'm putting you down for a bean type casserole."

"But I've already made plans for tomorrow."

"Well, cancel them. They couldn't be more important than this. Besides, I told Violet you'd be there. She came all the way up here to see you this afternoon but took a wrong turn at the end."

I couldn't have put it better myself. "So—why didn't you escort her back here?"

He gave a fond chuckle. "That was the idea but we had such a good chat that we lost track of time. Then the baby turned fussy and Violet asked me to tell you she'll see you tomorrow instead. At the party. She's bringing the dessert."

I almost blurted, "She *is* the dessert!" What I actually said was, "When do you want me to come?"

"At two. Sharp. Bring something delicious." It was a definite order. We hung up but he called me back a minute later. "I almost forgot—I got a call from Todd Mittendrin. Seems somebody recently bought the piece up on Strawberry Hill."

My chest tightened. On our mountain, change of ownership was seldom good news. "The land with the little green house on it? Facing the freeway?" I sometimes caught glimpses of it when the oaks were bare, from the skid trailing down Strawberry Hill. But the house was always visible to anyone driving down the pass from California during daylight if they knew where to look.

"That's the one," Barret said. "Apparently the new owner's got big plans. One of them is to rape the surrounding forest. Todd thinks some of the trees tagged for cutting are actually on *his* side of the property line so he hired a surveyor to stake out his boundaries. You might run into the guy on one of your walks. He'll be around for most of the week. And don't forget our arrangement on Monday. Feed my pups first thing in the morning and when you put them in for the night. Nothing could be simpler."

After he hung up the second time I tried to think of a cheap, tasty dish I could make with material on hand. I came up with cornbread and black bean chili. Then I pondered how I might rescue what was left of my weekend and cobbled together a plan. I'd stay up all night. It was the only way I could fit everything in.

I could boil the beans while I was sketching. And mix together the dry ingredients for the cornbread before I started preparing my canvases. Take the dogs for their constitutional earlier than usual tomorrow. Maybe up to Strawberry Hill for a peek at the green house. Our regular route past the abandoned cabin was still off-limits because of the cougar.

I'd chop the veggies and set the chili to simmering upon our return. Start painting the mossy stump and the ferns. Around noon I'd take Asa to town in my weekly attempt to socialize him. Afterward I'd bake the cornbread and then join the potluck—briefly— leaving as soon as I decently could. Continue working on the stump-painting until Jimmi got his ride home. Warm some left-over beans for our supper. These days he seldom wanted to spend time with me anyway. It had something to do with his age. Maybe I could paint quietly through half of tomorrow night without disturbing his sleep. Just the paints, the brushes, the canvas, and me.

IT WAS still dark when I stomped past my outhouse the next morning. I shone the flashlight along the trail to make sure I wouldn't trip into the big hole Randy had once dug close by, on what had been his first chosen spot for the privy. Halfway through his labor he was stopped by a vein of large rocks on one side and an abundance of arm-thick roots on the other. He had to start all over again, this time a dozen feet or so nearer to the cabin. Whatever cover he had put on the aborted hole had disintegrated long ago.

Early-spring tree frogs were already singing in the woods. The previous evening one of them had climbed a fence post in the dog yard to sit on the cross brace of the gate. The fragile green frog, the size of a quarter, looked newly minted.

The dogs stayed right at my heels, especially Racket who might have sensed coyotes nearby. We followed the switchback until we reached the plateau from which Randy and Barret used to peer through their telescopes on clear country nights. They called it Stargazer Hill. I paused to take in a panoramic view of jagged crests, the Siskiyou Pass, Greensprings. It was still dark enough to mistake the occasional car lights descending from the top of Highway 66 for floating UFOs. At least that's what I'd done on my first night on the mountain.

Climbing through a large plot of poison oak I raised my hands high to keep them from brushing against the scraggly branches of what Barret jokingly called his secret poison oak garden. Over the years I'd learned to respect the plants for what they were— placeholders anchoring unstable soil until something bigger could root and take over the business of keeping the dirt from running off with the rain. This early in March the noxious shrubs were still bare but in August they would become the heralds of autumn, turning an unrivaled hot-pastel pink.

The rest of the slope was given over to scrub oak, each weather gnarled tree decorated with badly healed scars left from limbs breaking off. Many of the trees were dead standing but sometimes the worst wrecks decided to sprout new leaves for no reason at all.

Ask a child to draw a mountain and he'll most likely produce a steeply pitched triangle with a sharp tip. In truth, there was level land on top of those crests, with gentle rises and falls and comfortable land bridges connecting summit to summit. Keeping my breathing steady, I focused on the height above us, letting it draw me toward it.

The slanted fields my trail was crossing reminded me of the rolling alpine meadows of my father's Austrian farm, although even the healthiest green of my Oregon mountain could never rival the deep satisfied tints of Papa's Tyrolean Alm.

A twenty minute climb brought us to the highest point of the westerly peak. The first of three, I had named it for the patches of tiny wild strawberries growing all along the skid we were about to descend on the far side of the top. "Are you my shadows today?" I asked the dogs. They were still sticking close. "You know this part. Run, puppies, run!" Asa and Marvel galloped downhill but Racket remained at my heels.

The shady skid we were on was crowded with juvenile conifers and stayed lush all summer long. In a few feet we would round the first bend to a spot where wild rosebushes grew so close together that I would need a stick to push aside their thorny vines. I found a good one, long and stout. But when I reached the place with the brambles I saw that they were no longer there. I stared stupidly at the ground, which was littered with freshly cut vines and conifer boughs.

Cut by whom and for what? To widen the trail? No one ever came up here except for me and the dogs. And then I heard the sound of pounding metal echoing across the slopes. Hammers? On Strawberry Hill? Before I could determine what direction the noise was coming from, Marvel began to bark. I could tell by the lilt in her voice that she'd discovered a skunk. I hurried to catch up so I might pull her away from her find before she got sprayed. She would consider the skunk's defensive maneuver an act of aggression and would punish the misguided bushy tailed beast whom God had given no other options.

There she was, around the next bend, face to tail with the small black and white creature who was pressing himself against a downed log not ten feet away from his burrow. Still barking, Marvel ignored my imperative whistles. When I was almost close enough to catch her she lunged at him and got sprayed in the face for her troubles. Incensed, with her eyes squeezed shut, she dragged the skunk away from the log by his tail. I tackled her, made her let go, and sat on her until she stopped struggling. The skunk recovered and slapped his feet challengingly against the ground. Then, having no alternate plan, he aimed his rear end and sprayed again, engulfing both Marvel and me in a cloud of oily droplets that made me gag. Wisely, Asa and Racket had moved off a respectful distance.

My skin and throat burning, I called Marvel a stupid bitch, put on her lead, and dragged her away. She rolled on the ground and scrubbed her face against patches of moss, trying to wipe off the foul odor.

"Hey! You!" a man's voice yelled from somewhere off to the side. Turning, I glimpsed the distant green house below, half obscured by naked oak branches and by a huge backhoe. Two men were standing beside the machine. The tall, dark haired one wore a blue-and-cream all weather sport jacket, the shorter man an unbuttoned black overcoat over a charcoal gray suit. I wondered why they were here so early on a Sunday morning. Perhaps the guy in the suit was on his way to church and was stopping by to give orders to the other one, probably the backhoe operator.

Both men were looking up in our direction. No doubt they had been alerted to our presence by Marvel's maniacal barking. The man in the suit cupped his hands around his mouth and yelled. "You and your fucking dog are trespassing! Get him off my land now or I'll shoot the bastard!"

In all the years I'd lived on the mountain, no one had ever talked to me in that tone. Growing up in the Alps, I had the crazy notion that mountains belonged to everybody. And that if you did meet someone on the slopes you said a friendly hello and went on your way.

Shocked by the man's blatant hostility, I barely registered his stocky good looks, the mustache, the short blond hair. His backhoe operator said something I couldn't hear and abruptly moved away. Then the stocky guy jumped on an ATV, revved the motor, and steered the machine toward us. I decided not to stick around to see if he actually carried a gun.

The dogs and I rushed to the nearest thicket on the downslope side of the skid, slipping and stumbling into underbrush until we lay on rotten leaves, well hidden. Soon the motor was idling on the path directly above. I held the dogs tight. We didn't get on our feet until I heard the ATV driving away. That's when I noticed my scraped wrists, snagged hair, bramble-torn sleeves, and the skunk cloud still clinging to Marvel and me. Worse than any of these minor inconveniences was knowing that our pursuer considered us low life trash good for nothing but target practice.

We stayed in the safe forest following the curve of the slope and came out of the trees close to where we had seen the great stag. Marvel started rolling again, trying to wipe herself clean. Asa copied her moves as if he'd been sprayed too. My eyes were still tearing but I was unwilling to give up and run home.

"Hell no, we won't go," I muttered under my breath. "We came to see the madrones and no gun toting vigilante is going to stop us."

CHAPTER 9

WE FOLLOWED THE TRAIL TOWARD THE CENTER
peak. Its apex was covered with a thriving conifer forest so dense
that it was impossible to find an open space from which to view
Emigrant Lake. Even though I'd walked these trails for half of
forever, it wasn't until the end of last May that I'd stumbled upon a
hidden path winding around the east side of this particular peak.

The path had been aglow with lavender, Indian Paintbrush, wild
roses, and a long lane of white raspberry blossoms. They were the
reason I'd christened the peak *Raspberry Hill*. I had taken the vision
home with me and put it on canvas at once, but hadn't sent the
finished landscape to Dorrie until the fall, along with the portrait of
the derelict cabin. There was no use hiking up to the lane now. In
March the path was a desolate place.

Today I noticed something different about the peak. Five
hundred yards to my left some kind of machine had made a gash
from the meadow below all the way to the forest above, where it
vanished among the trees. Squinting, I could just about make out

that the edge of the forest was not as thick as it had been. Somebody had been messing with my mountain, but I would have to investigate another time; if I stepped out in the open now I might be spied by the man at the green house. Besides, that kind of detective work required the cover of night and a discreetly aimed flashlight.

We turned to the right, heading toward the lookout, and Marvel stood at attention in front of our first buttercup, giving me a significant look. "Flower," I said. She cocked her ears and padded ahead, stopping a bit farther down the path, where six more yellow blossoms were pushing out of the soil. "Yes. Flowers," I repeated. "Buttercups." Then I pointed upslope. "Little ancestor tree." She ran to lie down beside him and waited for us to catch up.

Our favorite conifer looked satiated with rain. "You're still the best looking thing on this hill," I told him when I arrived, admiring the way his uppermost branch had trained itself to become a new crown after the original one was mutilated beyond repair. "In a couple of years you'll be tall enough to poke at that oak leaning over you," I went on, joining Marvel on the damp ground. "Then I'll have to trim its branches to give you more head-room." Until then the oak would shade him from the merciless summer sun. Closing my eyes, I could see a century into the future to where the ancestor tree, now with a fabulous girth, towered above his flourishing offspring.

From the conifer our trail took a sharp right toward the third peak. I called it Blackberry Hill because the front part of the pinnacle was covered by blackberry vines. Two giant madrones took up the other half. The peak was a good fifteen minute walk away. Asa and Marvel surged ahead to play at their favorite rain-water filled pit. Similar pits dotted these hillsides at regular intervals. Mittendrin had them dug back in the days when he thought he could divide these wild slopes into lots complete with two car garages.

Our bare bellied, water shy Chihuahua continued to trot at my heels. And then I noticed the shadow of a hawk brushing across the trail directly in front of me. Looking up I saw the bird itself, sailing, every feather detailed in the first beam of the still hidden sun. Soon the hawk was joined by a second and a third. Silently all three passed overhead, dipping first one wing then the other, swooping low, looking for prey. Before long there were seven hawks circling above us, each with a different flight plan but all of them keeping pace with Racket and me.

I tilted my head until my neck grew weary. Then I supported the nape with one hand, stretching the other toward the birds, still staring. Something inside me worked my throat, letting loose a primeval raptor call that soared to meet its kin.

In response they tightened their loops. Stretching my arms wide I turned in place, making a loop of my own. The pups, who had returned upon hearing my hawk cry, gleefully chased around me in the opposite direction until I felt like a living gyroscope. I had to embrace a tree to keep from falling. Squeezing my eyes shut, I saw a myriad of circles inside my lids, each with its own direction of spin.

When I opened my eyes again Marvel was already dashing back to her pit. Deciding to impress us by jumping over its entire length, she flew across like the legendary Strongheart himself, not realizing until she was at the halfway point that her trajectory was too low. For two, three seconds she tried running on air. Then gravity claimed her, plunging her into the icy water where she did a couple of brutal somersaults before staggering out at the far end. She didn't shake herself until she was close enough to give me a cold shower.

I wiped my face dry and looked up again. The hawks were still there. They escorted us to the madrones and then drifted into the blue. The same sun beam that had highlighted the hawks was gilding the trees' boughs and illuminated a myriad of small, crisp leaves. I ran my hand over the base of one trunk, rubbing off flaking bark to expose the new skin underneath. It would darken gradually to match the trunk's coppery hue.

I lay on the ground and considered the great limbs above me. Where three of them joined I imagined building a platform beneath the shimmering canopy. One stupendous branch, growing horizontally to the edge of the clearing, was perfect for a rope swing. How would it feel to pump out over the top of Blackberry Hill under a leafy roof?

One day I might get good enough to paint the power of *treeness* and the magic of emerald light. Until then I was content just to see the glistening leaves, touch cool madrone skin, and feel liquid energy surge under my palms.

Stargazer Hill, the three peaks, the hawks, jewel-green tree frogs and galloping puppies—it was for these I tolerated the primitive cabin, a peevish landlord, my occasional feelings of impotence. I was a willing part of the mountain and everything on it. Nothing my landlord said or did mattered as long as I could come up here and have this.

CHAPTER 10

I DROVE LEISURELY DOWN THE WINDING HIGHWAY, glancing back at the truck bed after a particularly tight curve to make sure Asa was still comfortable on his quilt. Conifers framed both sides of the road, the sun illuminating their crowns. Efi was the only vehicle as far as the eye could track.

I passed a hitchhiker, feeling the usual moment of guilt for deliberately ignoring his raised thumb. Now that the early morning commuters were gone I was probably his sole chance for a lift. But I had a firm rule against picking up strangers. Keeping him in sight in my rearview mirror, I wondered where I might have seen him before. And then Asa began to bark in the odd pitch he used strictly for Kosmo. I reversed up the incline.

Indeed, that's who the hitchhiker was. Kosmo had cast off his peacock-green turban to finally reveal what he'd been cultivating under it for most of the year—a thick crop of black dreadlocks that made him look like a Somali war lord. As soon as the truck got within smelling distance of our old neighbor Asa threw himself against the canopy windows with ever increasing fervor.

"Hey, mon," Kosmo said, backing away. "Is the doggy secure? Won't break out the cab window, will he?"

The fact that Asa loved to terrorize him was his own fault. One day when Asa still had his milk teeth we'd encountered Kosmo near the abandoned cabin. Asa started a puzzled, tentative bark, unsure exactly how he ought to proceed. If Kosmo had petted him and called him a good dog all would have been well. Instead he turned and ran off as if Satan himself was after him, leaping up the nearest oak. It convinced Asa that, in this game, he was a force to be reckoned with. No wonder he found it delightful and wanted to play it again every time he got a whiff of the man.

Rapping on the rear window, I yelled, "Asa, knock it off." Then I got out to open the passenger door. "Ignore him," I told Kosmo, who was staggering under the weight of an overflowing back pack and a large bloated duffle. "That's quite a load. I'll put it in with Asa as soon as you're safe in the cab."

He made himself comfortable on his seat and said, "I left most of my junk in the camper for Barret to haul off to the dump. Pay-back for kicking me out."

Over the months I'd only gotten a couple of glimpses at the disorder inside. Barret would hate having to deal with it, but if he asked for my help, I was prepared to give him a loud and impossible to misunderstand "No!"

I heaved the luggage in back with Asa and reclaimed my seat. Kosmo smiled, producing a couple of winning dimples. "I'm glad I get to see you one last time. This is good-bye. I've decided to put my body on the line—or rather, out on a limb. I'm joining my tree-sitting buddies in a grove of old growths."

"Tree-sitting? That's good work," I said. "I like people with principles."

He shifted, looking for the safety belt. "Yeah. I guess our slumlord did me a favor. I was dithering and his little tantrum helped me make up my mind."

I fished around the gearbox for my sticky first gear. "Speaking of favors. I think you owe one to Stu. You squealed."

Kosmo had the grace to blush. "A slip of the tongue which I regretted immediately after. Tell him he can collect any time."

We passed a new mailbox, a gleaming super deluxe model. "Isn't that the box for the green house on the other side of Strawberry Hill?" I asked. "I heard the sound of hammers on my walk this morning."

"Dawn to dusk," he confirmed. "That little bitty shack is morphing into a million dollar villa. I worked there a couple of weekends until they clear-cut that incline above the house."

I switched to second gear. "Did they replant?"

"Too cheap."

"A million dollar house on the bottom of a denuded slope—that's not cheap. It's stupid."

Kosmo scratched his scalp. "Not a seedling in sight," he said, checking his fingertips. For dandruff? Lice? "Most likely the entire thing will come down on them in one gigantic mudslide during the winter rains. Which is exactly what I told the new owner."

I wondered how or if one washed dreadlocks. Especially when one didn't have a faucet to call one's own. "Stocky blonde guy? In a suit? With an ATV?"

"A shiny *new* ATV. This guy's a big time California developer by the name of John Gierig. Aiming to spread his poison in our midst now that he's run out of bargain-type land to fuck over in the golden state. He showed up to inspect our work, so, as a favor, I took him aside and advised him to reseed the incline. It's ugly as sin. A glaring gash visible all the way from the freeway pass by any motorist turning his head due north."

"And?"

"He asked me what my name was, said he didn't need unsolicited advice from a drifter, and told the foreman to fire me at the end of the day. So I quit. On the spot."

"Reminds me of someone," I said, slowing for a dangerous curve.

"Yeah, but at least Barret's got a real heart under *his* crud. This guy's a spoiler, Silvi, and I'm glad I won't be around to see what all he spoils. I know his kind from Southern California. A whole mountain range, pure wilderness—one year it belonged to the wildlife, the next it was studded with fence-to-fence houses, every natural tree gone, the soil imprisoned under tons of cement. That's why I came up here. Should have guessed it would just be a matter of time before the developers followed. They can smell a buck a thousand miles away. And I'm not talking stag."

"Even if you're right, what can he possibly do?" I said, feeling uneasy. "After the trouble we had with Mittendrin every piece of land on the mountain was designated a tree farm. Only one dwelling allowed on each, owner occupied. We're lucky we got grandfathered in because our cabins were built before the land use change. Another thing—there's no water up there, which is why Barret didn't build his Manor on Stargazer Hill like he wanted. Best scenic view but bone dry."

Kosmo raised one dramatic black brow. "I told you, this guy's nothing like Barret. All I'm saying is—watch out for the mountain. I was going to trek farther north but, funny thing, I couldn't think of a single place I want to live that isn't biggering with Bay Area refugees. Which is why I'm making my stand."

"I didn't know you had it in you," I said as we merged onto 66. "I'm going to have to admire you from now on."

He gave a royal wave. "Tell you what—I'll let you buy me a soda next time we meet."

"Deal," I said. "When's that?"

He gave a nonchalant shrug. "Whenever."

I dropped him off in the middle of town then circled around to the co-op, parked in the shade of a tree, and fastened the pronged collar high on Asa's neck, getting him ready for our usual Sunday constitutional along Main Street. Although he had graduated from obedience class with top marks and regularly impressed passers-by with his impeccable heeling, Asa was apt to forget everything he'd ever learned the instant he glimpsed a male dog.

We walked past the post office and turned toward the plaza. Asa considered the green space in the middle a safe zone along a road rife with motorized vehicles, bikes, skateboards, and plastic-shopping-bag rattling pedestrians. I took him to the grass and sat beside him, my back against a tree. An elderly couple, holding hands, paused to admire Asa's deep chest, his short, perfectly sloping back, his strong hind quarters. "A magnificent dog," the husband said. "We still miss our last shepherd."

I smiled, nodded, and watched them walk on. It was one of those mild pre-spring days during which townies came out in droves to saunter along the sidewalks, half of them prematurely wearing shorts. It seemed there were couples everywhere, holding hands and looking content if not downright happy.

It was depressing.

I used to long for that kind of commitment. But, excepting Stillman, I was too adept at choosing the wrong guys. These days I put my faith in dogs. They were far more loving, less complicated, and vastly more trustworthy. Nonetheless, sitting there I ached with the absence of something that could have been good. Yet no matter in what direction I looked no soul mate was coming toward me with a glad smile and outstretched arms.

All at once the leash jerked as Asa lunged at someone who had foolishly stepped up behind me. I tightened my hold but Asa had enough momentum to drag me backwards toward a tall man wearing sunglasses and a leather jacket. Dark and handsome, he looked like every young girl's dream—a dream I had learned to spurn long ago. He was somewhat ragged around the edges, his hair overgrown and graying a bit at the temples, his leather jacket worn, his boots dull and scratched. As Asa refined his slavering, teeth-gnashing trick, something inside of me cheered him on.

Stumbling out of biting distance, the man snarled "Control your dog!" and walked off.

"Don't sneak up behind me, then!" I said to his receding back when it might have been more prudent to admit I was sorry. Passing townspeople frowned, suspecting Asa of being a dangerous dog and me of being an irresponsible owner. "You're making us unpopular," I muttered, yanking him to my side. Why couldn't he be more like Marvel who strolled along Main Street with aloof dignity, bothering no one?

When the negative attention had eased I rose and pulled Asa into a heel. He moved magnificently, his chest out, his head up, his gait satin-smooth. We caught some admiring glances. One woman stopped and said, "That's a beautiful dog you've got there!" I was beginning to feel better.

Outside the Black Sheep restaurant a young, very tall African-American stood waiting for his lunch date. It was Con Conroy, a talented Shakespeare Festival actor. He stretched a tentative hand toward Asa. "Nice dog. Is he friendly?"

In answer, Asa snapped at Con's fingers with all the delicacy he used when dispatching bothersome wasps.

Conroy hastily withdrew them. "Guess not."

"I admire your work," I told him, partly because it was true, partly to apologize for my rude canine. "You're getting better with each season."

Conroy smiled, dog forgotten. "I love what I do."

"It shows," I said with a jab of envy. Asa was sniffing suspiciously at the two stone lions on either side of the pub's red-painted entrance. Only eight months before he'd been certain the lions were monsters. I could still recall his initial double take, the puffed fur, his desperate leap past his own fear trying to get the fiends before they got him. To the chuckles of meandering tourists.

Marvel once had a similar reaction to the huge teddy sitting on a bench outside the chocolate store. At the tender age of six months she'd thought it her duty to chase the stuffed bear out of town.

Outside the Bakery Café we encountered the first dog of the day. It was a grizzled Golden Retriever, tied to a lamp post while its owner was drinking coffee inside. Asa's ruff rose momentarily but smoothed once he realized "it" was a female. But when we approached Bloomsbury Books, Asa finally got what he wished for. A white mini-van, parked at the curb, began to rock violently to the sounds of bloodcurdling snarls, yowls and shrieks coming from somewhere within. Then two harlequin Great Danes raised their huge heads, gnashing over-sized fangs against a half open window. Asa sprang at them just as I realized that his leash was wrapped around one of my legs. The leg jerked out from under me. I fell flat on my butt. My cap flew off. I fought the impulse to retrieve it, keeping a tight hold on the leash with both hands.

Snapping and cursing, Asa dove for the van's immaculate paint job. Still sitting on the sidewalk, I drew him back inch by inch. Beige high heeled shoes, smelling of new leather, stopped beside me while their owner clamped the cap back on my head. Before Asa could decide this was an act of aggression, I squeezed a hand over his muzzle, hissing "Leave it!" until he desisted.

The van at the curb continued to tremble. The Danes still slavered. Then a frail elderly man hobbled out of the bookstore, leaning heavily on two canes. Locking his knees, he shook the canes at the van, yelling, "Down Caesar! Down Lear!" Immediately the two giant heads withdrew. All was quiet. The old man turned and went back into Bloomsbury's. Asa sat, looking deflated.

As I tried to get my legs back under me, someone tossed a piece of jerky at Asa's feet. He gulped the tidbit without chewing. "Good boy," a man's voice said. Briefly his big hand hovered in front of my face. "Up you go." I squinted into bright sunlight and recognized the man with the sunglasses and leatherjacket we'd met at the plaza. Before I could protest that I didn't need help he was pulling me onto my feet. "Your little guy needs some serious obedience training," he said. "Very important for shepherds. He could have dragged you out in the street. In front of a moving car."

His lecturing tone made me want to counter with *what business is it of yours,* or *fuck off,* but all I could produce was an inarticulate stutter. Snatching my hand out of his, I pivoted the way Asa and I had come. He heeled beautifully all the way down the street. I hoped the man was watching.

Still, I was glad when Asa and I reached Efi. He jumped easily over her tailgate and I locked the canopy hatch before he could swing around. Then I retreated to the co-op for a yerba maté and a fresh baked cinnamon roll. Sitting alone at a table for two by a window, I browsed through discarded sections of the Daily Tidings. Every now and then I raised my eyes to glance distractedly through the glass, watching shoppers come and go. And waiting, though I couldn't have said for what.

CHAPTER 11

LAST YEAR I GAVE UP MY SEX HORMONES. It was on the day I stumbled into the rear office of my gas station and saw one heavy equipment calendar too many. A sweet young thing with D-cup breasts was sitting on a tractor with her legs spread apart, prepared to hold her position for the entire month of May in order to encourage an increased interest in farm machinery.

There was freedom in knowing that I didn't have to make myself look attractive anymore. I began to wear baggy clothes and kept my face and hair unadorned, fading into the background of any gathering as effectively as if I'd slipped on the habit of a nun or a Muslim woman's burka.

I liked it that way.

I eschewed parties unless I was forced to attend. They were the playground of couples and those who longed to join their ranks. Unattached singles, especially celibate ones, had no place at such gatherings. Barret's potluck would be no exception.

That's why I walked across his yard wearing a loose washed-out shirt over the shabbiest jeans I owned, wondering how long I would have to stay and pretend to enjoy myself. The exit from such gatherings often presented a problem, too, since the first person to depart could start a trend that did little to endear her to the host. Thus I usually soft-shoed out of sight and kept going.

The white Nissan Violet had come in yesterday was parked intimately close to Barret's open front door. I could hear her high-pitched giggling from somewhere within as I stepped over the reclining forms of the Labs. One was blocking the entrance from the outside, the other from the inside, neither giving the slightest sign that they were still among the living.

Barret's kitchen was remarkably tidy. Even the counter was unnaturally clean. Entering the living room, I saw that his idea of having this potluck in order to get closer to Violet was not going according to plan. She had brought Clyde with her. They were sitting on the couch, hip to hip. Little Lavender was pressing herself against their knees, playing with a baby bottle filled with orange juice.

"Oh, it's just Silvi," Barret said when I made my unassuming entrance. The social smile he offered me stopped short of his eyes. They appeared wounded.

"Hello, everybody," I said cheerfully, wishing I could just turn around to leave as quietly as I had come.

"Oh hi," Violet replied as I set my offerings on the table. Then she told Clyde, "She's the one with the German shepherds."

"Pleased to meet you," Clyde said, though his eyes instantly dismissed me. "I hear you're an old-timer here." He pushed his gold rimmed granny glasses up a long, sharp nose. The rest of his face was hiding behind a shaggy beard and hippie-long hair.

Although he belonged to a later generation than Barret or me, I doubted Clyde had ever been anything but staid. What on earth was Violet doing with someone like him? Pulling out a chair, I sat and practiced my small talk. "I moved up here soon after the land co-operative . . . dissolved." I told them. From the relieved smile spreading across Barret's face I could tell that he approved of my euphemism. So I continued with, "I've outlasted a decade of drought and seen tenants come and go at dizzying speeds. It's the silence that breaks them, and the long drive to town."

"Not to mention snowdrifts and ice-slick curves," Barret put in. "After a winter storm the roads can be impassable for days. And in summer we can never be sure the cabins will still be standing when we come home from work. A couple of forest fires got uncomfortably close."

"But spring's gorgeous up here," I added. "Especially once the oak leaves unfurl. How do you like cabin life so far, Clyde?"

He touched his glasses again. Behind them, his eyes were expressionless. "I think it's kind of primitive," he admitted. "I'm spending whole days doing piddling things like splitting firewood."

"Hardly piddling around here." Barret said, amused. "Wood's worth its weight in gold. Sometimes we have to heat until June."

"June!" Clyde cried, alarmed.

"At least." Barret was warming to the topic. "Hey, Silvi— remember the miner?"

The miner had become part of ridge legend. "I never met the guy," I told Clyde. "But I have to think about him every time I walk across my kitchen floor."

Barret leaned back in his blue leather recliner, savoring the recollection. "The miner had a wife, three little kids, no phone, and two Dobies so vicious none of us dared go anywhere near his place." He chuckled. "Then after a hard snow the whole bunch of them suddenly departed. On foot. We didn't realize till the following week that they were gone. And we couldn't understand why they had left in the middle of a cold snap until we went up to the cabin. He'd run out of firewood, you see, so he'd pried off all the inside wallboards and half the support beams, sawed them into pieces with a handsaw, and burned them in his stove to try and keep the place warm. When we walked in there the place had become unglued. The floor was buckling and every wall was leaning in a different direction. It looked so lopsided our mouths literally hung open. We managed to save it from caving by no more than a hair, but for a while there it was touch and go."

In the real world, the "we" had mainly consisted of Randy and Stillman, who had built the cabin himself, thereby depleting his bank account. That's when he decided to go off to work in Alaska for a year. Barret offered to find a reliable renter. The only one who had applied was the miner.

I said, "The kitchen floor still buckles."

"And always will," Barret grinned. "But then, you knew that when you moved in."

"Oh God, that poor miner must have been desperate," Violet said in a high pitched voice, wrapping her arms tightly around Lavender. The little girl squirmed, drooling juice onto Clyde's pants. He heaved a long suffering sigh and scooted away, dabbing the spot with a napkin.

"The guy was cracked," Barret said, displeased with her interpretation of events. "Any one of us would have been glad to loan him some wood if only he'd asked. My guess is that he was too lazy to cut a full winter's worth while the weather was still decent. And after he'd been disassembling the cabin from the inside for a while, he woke up one day and noticed that the roof was about to cave in. Coward that he was, he waited till the middle of the following night before making his getaway. He made his family walk off the mountain with him, Dobies and all. Owing three months' rent. He ditched his snowed-in jalopy. Never came back for it. We wound up towing it to the nearest wrecking yard."

Stillman had left behind a new, tight little cabin and come home to a wreck. And after he and Randy rehabilitated it, Barret had some miniscule disagreement with Stillman and nursed it into a feud. Eventually he shut off the water and power to the cabin and squeezed Stillman out of the land co-op and off the mountain. The following year it was Randy's turn.

A long time later, Stillman and I started dating and he came to live with me in what used to be his own cabin. Barret greeted him like a long lost brother. That's when Stillman told me life was too short to hold grudges. Turned out he was right.

"Obviously that miner believed you weren't going to help him," Violet said, bouncing Lavender on her knees until the little girl stopped fidgeting. "It's hard to be stranded in the middle of nowhere. A couple of days ago, when Clyde got mad and took himself off overnight, the farthest I got without wheels was our mailbox."

"You have a phone, don't you?" Barret went to his desk, wrote on a sticky pad, and slapped it down on the coffee table in front of her. "Here's my number. Next time he leaves you stranded, give me a call. I'll take you anywhere you want to go. That's what neighbors are for." He sounded kind and righteous at the same time.

Clyde's eyes hardened behind the polished lenses though he forced his lips into a bland smile. Tittering, Violet peeled off the page with the number and slipped it in a pocket.

Barret grinned smugly and asked, "Need help with your wood, Clyde? I've got some discards you can take home with you if you want. You're renting a prime piece of land—five flat acres right next to the creek. I own a hundred and what you see outside my door is the only flat piece I've got except for Stargazer Hill. Whenever our well quits I can't even flush my toilet, let alone wash my hands. All you have to do is dip a couple of buckets."

"Wells can quit?" Clyde asked. "You mean, a person could turn on his faucet and nothing comes out?"

"Happens every summer," Barret said placidly. "Right, Silvi?"

"Yep. I keep a dozen water bottles under my sink for emergencies. I've learned to get by on one gallon a day. Sponge baths, dishwater and dogs included."

Violet and Clyde stared at me, shocked.

"Me, me!" Lavender squirmed toward a bowl filled with corn chips.

Barret put some in a napkin and deposited it tenderly on Violet's lap. "Here, munchkin. Eat all you want."

Lavender grabbed a tiny pink handful and tried to stuff it into her mother's mouth. Violet dodged, laughing. "Mommy eat," Lavender insisted.

Violet extracted one chip from between the baby's chubby fingers, chewed, and said, "Mmm! Thank you."

"Ack ooh," Lavender repeated.

Barret asked, "Is she always this cute?"

"Not really," Clyde said. "You should see her when she wakes up."

"Who, Violet?"

"She's worse."

"He's joking," Violet said, giggling. "Aren't you, Clyde?"

"No I'm not." He frowned at the stain on his pants.

I couldn't help thinking he was a square peg in disguise. Walked into a costume shop and rented a counter-culture outfit complete with long hair, beard, and John Lennon glasses, laid-back attitude included. Except that it wasn't as firmly in place as he wanted people to think. I suspected that under all that improbable hair he was hiding a weak chin or donkey ears. My hands itched for some scissors.

Outside, gravel shifted, then laughter spilled through the kitchen. Grace appeared in the doorway. She ran light footed to Barret and gave him a hug. "I've missed your sweet face," she said in her melodious voice. "You look exactly the same."

"Not you," he replied, his eyes softening. "You're prettier every time you come."

She laid her cheek against his newly trimmed beard. Her long dark hair spilled over his shoulder. "I want you to meet a special friend of mine. Zora."

A human sized Stellar Blue Jay had come in behind her. Sharp black eyes darted around the room, coming to rest on Lavender. While Barret made introductions Zora homed in on the couch, worn flip-flops slapping her heels. "Hello, little one," she cooed. "I bet you'd like one of these." She dug in her blue muumuu and came out with a lemon-yellow sucker, which she dangled enticingly in front of Lavender's face. "I always carry a few spares."

Lavender dropped her chips, but Clyde snatched the lollipop before she could grasp it. "Lavender doesn't eat candy," he said loftily.

The little girl tried to shimmy up his arm, crying, "Me! Me!"

Violet pulled her into a hug. Cheek to cheek, they were very alike—milk skinned, white haired, two pairs of pale orphan eyes filming with tears. Violet asked brightly, "More juice?" and slipped the bottle's nipple into Lavender's outraged mouth.

Zora wagged a finger at Clyde. "Spoilsport! What harm can one little sucker do?"

He let his eyes track over the muumuu. "Plenty."

"I said one, didn't I?" Zora chortled. "It'll be a while before she has to worry about a waist-line like mine."

"With any luck she'll take after her mother," Barret said amiably, playing the good host. "Grab a chair."

Zora pulled one out from the table, shook it a few times and slammed it down hard. "Did you get your chairs from the same store where Stu bought his?"

Grace grinned. "She made the mistake of sitting in the wrong chair last night. Stu said *Not that one* too late."

Barret looked at me, lips quivering. Suppressing a grin, I said, "I *told* Stu it belonged in the dump."

"It does now," Zora supplied gaily, joining in our laughter.

"I'm glad you could come to my party on such short notice," Barret said. "We're having a nice lull in the weather. A couple of days of grace."

"More like seven." Grace sat down beside Violet. "According to our best sources that lull will last for a week—but just in case it won't we brought winter clothes. Here comes Stu with our offerings."

The handsome young man who stepped into the room hugging a brown paper bag bore no resemblance to the unkempt neighbor I spent most of yesterday with. Clean shaven, with expertly shaped hair, a well ironed shirt and slacks with sharp creases, he could easily have been mistaken for Grace's twin brother. He had the same finely wrought face and high coloring. Setting the bag on the table, he extracted two bottles of wine. "Grace's." Next he showed us a dish of lasagna. "Mine." Then he pulled out a tray sealed with plastic wrap. "Lox and cream-cheese bagels from Zora's favorite Haight deli."

Barret jumped up for a closer look. "Wow, these are the real thing. Obviously not from around here. Mind if I—"

"Go ahead." Zora lowered herself gingerly onto the uncushioned chair. "That's what they're for."

Bagel in hand, he insisted on trading places with her. She sprawled appreciatively on his comfortable recliner while Barret, just as appreciative, positioned his chair in front of Violet, sitting so close that their knees practically touched.

Dimpling, Grace said, "We also brought a package of disposable cups in case it turns out Barret still owns no more than two coffee mugs, one of which holds his toothbrush."

Violet clapped a hand to her mouth in mock horror. "Was that the one you gave me yesterday? No wonder my tea tasted funny."

Zora clapped. "Two mugs. A minimalist. How precious!" She flopped her arms over the recliner's sides. "Why are you all nibbling on chips? Stu, open the wine. Dish out the food." She padded her middle. "There's room in here for everything on the menu today."

"And then some," Barret said under his breath. She tilted her head and drilled him with her sharp black eyes. He shrugged, rising to prepare the first plate. "A little of everything, Zora?"

"I don't do 'little'," she said. "Especially when everything looks this good."

He piled on the chili, cut a generous slab of cornbread, another of Stu's lasagna, and topped it all with a heap of salad.

"Perfect." She kicked off the flip-flops, angled for the matching footstool, and plopped her bare feet on it before nestling the plate on her lap. Her feet were surprisingly small and well-cared for, the toe nails painted cherry red. Stu gave her the first tumbler of wine and she held it up to the light streaming in from the window. "Thanks for insisting I come, Grace. You were right, this mountain's special. Just look at the view. It makes up for that paper-thin futon Stu put on his living room floor for me."

"A back breaker, huh?" Barret said. "We'll soon fix that. I have an air mattress I keep for the occasional guest. You're welcome to use it. We'll make Stu puff it up."

Zora gave him a grateful smile. "Have another bagel. Have two."

I sat with my back to the wall while Stu poured me some wine. Like Zora, I let the light turn it golden. The window framed the mountain chain on the other side of our high valley, its crest heavy with conifers. Taking a sip, I let my eyes settle on the two women sitting on the couch. Violet and Grace looked nothing alike. But they were equally lovely although one was moon-pale and willowy, the other petite with an exquisite hourglass figure. Their combined radiance, shining on Barret, transformed him into a romantic swashbuckling pirate missing only bandana and eye patch.

I savored my first bite of lasagna, sighing with satisfaction. The food on the table was a celebration of colors: black beans, golden corn, tomato-red lasagna under melted white cheese. Barret's salad, in a clear glass bowl, offered a palette of purples and reds mixed with cool shredded greens.

A luxurious feeling was wafting through me. Could it be that pasta really was an aphrodisiac? I dropped my fork and, bending to retrieve it, felt pheromones swirling all around me. In fact, the room was thick with them, attracting, colliding, hovering. Looking for a chink in my invisible burka.

"Don't look at me," I thought at my empty glass. "I'm an estrogen drop-out. Immune." Perhaps the wine had been more potent than it looked. I scraped my plate clean and recklessly cut myself a huge wedge of Violet's apple pie. It was better than any sex *I* could imagine.

Lavender nibbled from Violet's plate, yawned with her mouth full, and curled up between her mother and Clyde, who awkwardly brushed a stray curl out of her flushed face.

"I envy you guys," Grace told him. "You're on the best property in this valley. Stu and I once dreamed of buying that piece. First thing I was planning to get was a wood-burning hot tub. I loved imagining us sitting in it naked surrounded by snow drifts while fat flakes danced down from the clouds."

"Neat," Violet said. "Let's get one, Clyde—as soon as our ship comes in."

"My ship," he corrected with a tight smile.

She waved her hand dismissively. "Whatever. Why don't you buy the place? It would be a good investment for you."

"There you go, spending my money again."

"What money?" Barret asked. "Did I miss something?"

Violet sat up straight, clasping her hands around her crossed knees. "Oh, didn't I tell you? Clyde's going to be an heir—any day now."

"Not if you can help it." Clyde brushed his mustache with a finger tip. "You'd spend my entire capital in a week." He turned to Barret and explained. "My dad and I are already setting up a financial plan—we'll invest the whole bundle, see, and I'll live on the interest."

Zora licked her spoon. "Maybe I can help. I know a good investment broker. How much are we talking here?"

"Two hundred and fifty thousand."

Zora considered her spoon. "That used to be big bucks. Before the average house started going for half a million."

"Yeah—but Violet's right," Barret said. "Around here land's still a great value. I hear the three hundred acres behind Ralph and Edie's are up for sale. Now there's a piece I wouldn't mind buying, if for no other reason than to snatch it up before some developer does. It's got a derelict farmhouse on it. And cow pastures. The creek runs through the entire length of the land."

I kept my mouth shut.

Zora played with her spoon. "How much?"

He gave her an indulgent smile. "More than the likes of us can afford."

Zora looked at Grace. "Can I see it? Do you know how to get there?"

"All we have to do is follow the draw down till it levels," Grace replied.

"Okay then." Resolutely, Zora took her plate to the table. "Let's do it. Right now. Who wants to come? A little exercise before dessert will do us all good." She considered Barret. "What about you?"

He shrugged. "Sure, I'll go. But I wouldn't advise you to wear those." He nodded at her flip-flops. "And certainly not the tent you've got on."

"Even I know that," she said. "I brought jeans and sneakers. Will they do?"

"With socks. On account of the poison oak." With a quick glance at Violet, he asked, "Who else wants to come?"

She, Grace and Stu decided to go too. I had nothing to say.

Lavender had fallen asleep with her head on Violet's lap. Gently, she lowered it until the toddler's cheek pressed against the upholstery. Then she rose and stretched a hand out to Clyde. With a loud yawn, he slumped against the backrest. "Count me out. I've had enough exercise for today, thank you very much. I'll stay with the baby."

Barret positively brightened. "Excellent. Then you can brew us some coffee. Put on some music. Make yourself comfy."

Zora helped herself to a big piece of pie. "I guess I better hike up to my suitcase to change. Don't start without me. I'll be right back."

Barret waited until the slapping sound of her flip-flops had faded before telling Grace, "She's a trip. Where on earth did you meet her? She's too fat to be a nurse."

"Her father died in my hospital. She was practically living in his room toward the end. She loved to hear me talk about Oregon and our cabin. It gave her something to focus on. Peace, she wants. And lots of green."

Barret finished his wine and dabbed his beard with a napkin. "But can she afford it? Even a shack on A Street costs a king's ransom these days."

Grace looked at Stu. "Didn't you tell him?"

"Tell me what?" Barret asked.

"That she's worth more millions than you have digits to count with. She said she can't make a dent. The more she spends the more pours in."

Clyde jerked upright, eyes wide. "Are you serious? I don't believe it. She doesn't look rich."

"Damn," Barret said cheerfully. "Too bad she's the spitting image of my mom, down to the last frizzy curl. Definitely not my type." With a quick glance at Violet, he added, "Besides, money isn't everything."

Clyde snorted. "Says who? Not Violet, you can be sure. Is there a . . . Mr. Zora around someplace?"

Grace frowned. "Not yet. But when she finds the right guy she'll snap him up in a minute. She's a woman who makes up her own mind—and when she does, watch out! She'll be the best neighbor you and Violet ever had. If you get lucky."

I cut myself a second helping of pie, wrapped it in a napkin, and soft shoed to the kitchen to deposit my dirty plate in the sink. Then I tip toed outside, carefully stepping over the sleeping Labs. Treading quietly over shifting gravel, I didn't dare pause until I had rounded the bend of Barret's driveway. There was a bank of clouds moving in overhead, gliding fast on the breeze. I could see a dragon in them, a galloping dragon with great wings and a long crocodile tail. He was being chased by something dark and vicious that I couldn't quite make out. I almost collided with Zora on her way back, studying the same clouds. She looked extraordinary in her oversized jeans. "Do you think it'll rain?" she asked.

"Probably not. These clouds aren't dark enough."

"You're leaving already?"

"It seemed a good time."

She tugged at her waist band and discovered she'd forgotten to zip herself up. "Your friend Barret," she said, trying to pull in her stomach to take the strain off her zipper. "Is he spoken for? You and he aren't—"

"Definitely not!"

"How come?" She put her hands over her heart. They were as dainty as her feet, down to the last cherry red finger nail. "He's such a teddy bear. A Russian Jewish teddy bear. Straight out of Fiddler on the Roof. Is he free?"

I thought of Violet who probably had less of a hold on Clyde than she realized. In fact, I suspected that the moment his ship did come in he'd step right out of his costume and walk away in a pin striped suit, swinging a briefcase and leaving Violet and Lavender behind counting pennies. According to Barret's self-confessed pattern that was the moment the moon maiden would lose her attraction-power for him. So I answered warily, "Not even he knows the answer to that."

Zora pulled her shirt out of the waist band and attempted to fluff it over her hips. "Good," she said. "I'll help him sort it out." Then she marched resolutely down to his house.

CHAPTER 12

JIMMI CAME HOME JUST BEFORE DARK, already fed. Wisely, I didn't ask with what, since he had no friends who did not consider hamburgers and fries the ultimate meal. He fell asleep easily, giving me a few more hours of uninterrupted work. When the phone rang it was already after midnight. Afraid it might be Mama with bad news, I picked up the receiver. But there was no answer to my first "Hello?"

I repeated, "Hello—who's there?"

Still nothing, although the line was alive. I distinctly heard someone breathing before the disconnecting click but thought nothing of it. Sometimes people misdialed and were too rude to say "Excuse me."

Five minutes later the phone rang again. And again I could hear heavy breathing. I was about to hang up when a man's rasping voice said, "I want to talk to my son."

My blood chilled. On instinct, I unplugged the wall jack and sat, wondering how Leroy could possibly have found my number. It was and had always been unlisted. He didn't know anyone I knew. Except Dorrie, but she promised she'd never . . .

Most likely, he was high on something and would forget he called after he crashed. Or rethink his options. Next month it would be Jimmi's thirteenth birthday. It was more than twelve years since Crystal brought him to me. Her face had been so discolored and swollen that I hardly recognized her when I picked her and the baby up from the Greyhound station. She stayed until her wounds healed, though her right eye still looked bruised when she asked me to keep Jimmi. Her plan was to fly to New York and start a new life before she'd send for him. Along with her son, she left me a notarized power of attorney in case of emergencies. Like a fool I let her go, glad she was finally strong enough to turn her back on Leroy, with his crafty schemes, caustic power plays, and violent fits of jealousy.

It wasn't until Jimmi's first birthday that I heard from her again. Well—not exactly *from* her. About her. First by way of one of her Brooklyn neighbors, then from the New York police. She'd taken a bottle of pills and there'd been no one who cared enough to check on her until long after her heart stopped beating. She left a suicide note and a testament. In the first she asked me to keep Jimmi away from his father, "so he can't ever screw with my baby's head the way he's been screwing with mine." In the second she bequeathed him to me. I hired an attorney to make it legal. Of course I never mentioned to him that I knew anything about the boy's father. I didn't want Leroy to have the opportunity to introduce me—or Jimmi—to his favorite yo-yo games.

Crystal and Dorrie had been my best friends at the Art Institute in San Francisco. After we dropped out each of us headed in a different direction—Crystal to L.A. with Leroy; Dorrie to model fashions in New York; and me up into wine country and eventually to the mountains of Oregon. We kept in touch. In fact, Dorrie was peeved that I was the one Crystal named in her will. But Dorrie was kind of wild for a few years until she settled in Key Largo and got married. Maybe Crystal hadn't thought she was steady enough to raise a child.

Suddenly I didn't give a damn that it was three hours later on the East coast. I plugged in the cord, dialed Dorrie's number, and let it ring till her voicemail came on. Then I hung up and called again. And again. Until she answered, sounding slurred and more than a little annoyed.

"How come you gave my number to Leroy?" I demanded.

"Silvi? Is that you? What are you talking about?"

"Leroy. He just called. You're the only one who knows both of us and has my number."

She had the grace to admit her sin, though she seemed to think having been tipsy on red wine during their conversation was a good enough excuse for breaking the trust between us. "He stumbled across our website," she stammered. "Cried on the phone. Said he had a God-given right to know his own son. And he does—no matter what you think. People change, you know. Besides, he can't find you just from the number, can he? How long were you planning to keep on lying to Jimmi, anyway? A boy needs to know his natural father."

"There's nothing natural about Leroy!" I said. "You had no right!" And then I slammed down the receiver and unplugged the cord for the rest of the night. I'd stick it back in before I started my yoga session—in case Mama needed me. The Leroy I remembered never woke up before noon. I resolved to call the phone company at eight to request an unlisted number. Until it was in place I'd keep the phone unplugged and tell Jimmi there was something wrong with our line.

Even though I knew I wouldn't sleep for the rest of the night I couldn't make myself pick up my brushes. How could I send Dorrie more paintings after what she had done?

How could I not?

I WAS tired when I took the dogs for a walk. Didn't even notice I'd led them past the abandoned cabin and the draw until we were halfway up the skid. Didn't notice the clouds overhead either until the light dimmed. I raised my face to find out why it was getting darker and was ambushed by a vehement cloudburst. Supersized drops pummeled me, drenching me in an instant. There was no walking in it.

Racket had disappeared, as usual. Marvel and Asa were at my side, sopping wet, looking questioningly up at me. I sputtered "Come," turned and ran down the already slippery skid. Rats or no rats, we were going to shelter in the abandoned cabin until the downpour stopped.

The warped front door had somehow slammed shut. While I was wrestling with it Marvel perked her ears, growled, and leaped to the back of the wrap-around porch. When Asa and I hurried after her she was already pushing at the kitchen door at the far end. A moment later she was inside, barking *treed*.

Something big was in there and she wasn't about to let it get away. I hoped it wasn't the cougar. Peering into the gloom, I saw her on her toes snarling up the counter at a pair of shabby brown boots. They were occupied by a tall dark haired man wearing jeans and a scuffed leather jacket. He shuffled his feet as far from the edge as he could and said in a pained voice, "Lady—call off your dog!"

Strangely enough Asa was not interested in aiding his sister. Instead he sat next to the counter grinning up at the man's face and salivating as if he expected something good to drop. Such as beef jerky.

"What are *you* doing here?" I said, dragging Marvel away.

"Same as you. Sheltering from the storm." The man jumped gracefully to the floor, which didn't seem quite as dirty as it had always been.

"Don't tell me *you're* the surveyor Mittendrin's hired!"

"Okay. I won't."

Marvel was sitting quietly now, watching his every move. He threw her a bite of jerky. She ignored it. Asa snapped it up. The surveyor eyed my coat and my chattering teeth. "You're wet clear through. I guess neither of us is going anyplace for a while. Why don't you peel off that coat? Here, put on my jacket. I've got another one in my bag."

Marvel kept watching his hands. Her ears stayed erect. Asa sat beside her, touching his hip to hers, the tip of his tail wagging slightly.

I took off my soggy coat and slipped on the soft leather jacket, toasty from the man's body heat. There was a roll of thunder from somewhere nearby. We didn't normally get thunderstorms in March. Lightning slashed across a black sky. I glanced at the stove. The stick nests were no longer on the burners, but the kitchen still smelled rat-waste sour. "I'm going to sit on the porch to watch the storm," I said, stepping outside. "You can come if you want."

"Don't mind if I do," the surveyor answered, following us out. That's when a very wet Racket rushed him and bit him in the shin. The surveyor stumbled backward, holding onto the door jamb. "Lady," he said wearily. "Call off your dog."

"Racket!" I cried. "Poor baby, you're soaked!" Racket released the leg and shivered. I wrapped him in my wet coat. The surveyor rummaged in his bag and pulled out a blue-and-cream sport jacket and a rolled towel. He pushed my coat off the Chihuahua, wrapped the towel around him, and handed him over like a special delivery package, taking a momentary interest in my paint speckled hands. "The name's Paul," he said, slipping on the sport jacket. "Looks like I'm going to be around for a few days."

"Right. So I heard." I folded the ends of the leather jacket around my shivering bundle. "We'll watch for you. Asa likes chasing men up trees but I think that as long as you keep your pockets full of jerky he'll listen to reason. Marvel can't be bribed, though. She makes up her own mind about things—especially men."

I sat down on the porch floor, glad the roof above us was not leaking. Marvel lay at my feet, Racket made himself comfortable on my lap, and Asa sprawled close to my right. Paul sat cross legged at my other side, near enough for me to smell his scent, a pleasant mixture of aftershave, toothpaste and soap. The rain remained savage. Lightning needled across the black clouds.

"This used to be a nice looking cabin." I knocked on the wall behind me. "Well-built. It's a shame it's been empty so long. Mittendrin keeps the doors open on purpose because he wants it to rot." A bright bolt flashed across my field of vision. An instant later thunder clapped angrily overhead, so loud and close both Paul and I jumped. Racket burrowed under the towel. Even Marvel and Asa looked a bit taken aback.

"The framing's still solid," Paul said when we'd recovered. "I've been checking the studs. The roof's okay too, though moss is prying at the shingles. If someone were to clear out the critters and their debris, scrub everything down real good and patch up the damage they caused . . ."

"Which someone?" I scoffed. "You can't mean Mittendrin. He lives in town, in a mansion. Besides, my landlord won't let him drive back here. Ridge Road's strictly private, and it goes right by Barret's house. He put a gate on top of the rise after Mittendrin brought in the bulldozers. It hasn't been locked for years, but if Barret saw somebody driving through without his permission he'd lock it in a minute. How did you get back here, anyway? Where did you park?" I took a good look at Paul's blue-and-white jacket, then shifted away from him. "It was you I saw with John Gierig when he threatened to shoot Marvel. You do get around."

He ran a hand through his dark hair. That's when I noticed it wasn't even the slightest bit damp. "It's what surveyors do," he said lightly, smiling. "I lost no time telling John his remark was way out of line."

"Yet you let him come chasing after us on his ATV." I pushed at Asa to give me a couple of extra inches of space and scooted off a bit farther. "And it was you who snarled at me on the plaza. You don't like dogs either. Just like Gierig."

Calmly he said, "I don't like *unmannerly* dogs. Especially when they try to take a chunk out of me."

I dismissed his remark with a wave of my hand. "Asa puffs himself up so no one will suspect that he's nothing but a big softie."

Paul wasn't smiling anymore. "I had a couple of German shepherds myself not too long ago. Nobody cuts them any slack. If you love your dogs you've got to discipline them. No excuses."

A new volley of thunder cracked right overhead. The awful sound arrived simultaneously with a sizzling spear of white light. I waited for the ground to stop shaking, then I took off the leather jacket, laid it on the porch floor, and got up to leave. "I'd rather drown in the rain than get lectured by some fool who doesn't know what he's talking about," I said frigidly, unwrapping the towel. I tossed it on the leather jacket and stalked to the corner, clasping Racket to my chest.

"Hey, look, I'm—" Paul said. I didn't pause to hear the rest.

The dogs and I ran all the way home, Asa and Marvel gleefully dancing around me, a much subdued Racket at my heels. By the time we reached our clearing the rain was already diminishing. The clouds split, exposing a slash of blue. And then a full double rainbow appeared in the blackest part of the sky, its four ends shimmering against the wooded slopes on the far side of our valley.

I almost wished I'd stayed on the porch so I could have pointed it out to Paul. "Look up there," I told Marvel instead. She glanced at the sky but it wasn't awe I saw in her eyes—it was benign, loving patience; she was humoring me.

The red light on the answering machine was blinking when I walked into the kitchen. I'd forgotten to unplug the phone after yoga. Luckily it was Mama who'd called and not Leroy. There was a real note of panic in her message. She wanted to know if I had done anything about my passport yet. Maybe I would. Today was as good a time as any to get my pictures taken and to fill out the form.

Putting on some water for our oatmeal, I called upstairs, "Jimmi, time to get up!"

I could hear some sort of creaking although he did not respond. When I climbed the stairs to repeat my clock trick I saw that Jimmi's head was under the cover, which moved up and down. Rhythmically. As I stared, fascinated, his head emerged, eyes puffy, cheeks flushed, an earphone wire protruding from the nearest ear.

"Stop sneaking up on me!" he screamed. "Get out!"

I threw up my hands. "Okay. Okay. Please get dressed. It's been raining. I'm taking you to the bus stop."

"I'm tired of you barging in here!" he howled. "I want a door! An honest-to-God door I can lock whenever I want!"

"Dream on," I shouted back. "I want something even bigger—a room of my own. But we're both out of luck."

AFTER the bus took him away I drove back home, went upstairs, and peeled back his futon. There, on the box spring, a strictly forbidden gangsta rap CD was lying on top of a couple of porn magazines. He must have borrowed both from his friend at the sleep-over. Pulling off his sheet for the Laundromat, I found a damp stain in its center.

Weak kneed, I stared at it and wondered what the hell I was supposed to do next. As soon as my legs steadied I put everything back the way it had been—even though I longed to at least make up the bed—and tossed a clean, folded sheet and pillow case on top of his cover. Then I measured the opening at the bottom of Jimmi's staircase. With some thick old-fashioned drapes from Goodwill, a few two-by-fours and a sheet of half-inch plywood, I might construct something that would give him at least the semblance of privacy. It was high time.

CHAPTER 13

THE INFAMOUS RANDY WOULD HAVE BUILT and installed the door in an hour. It took me all day. I used some of the scrap lumber stored under the house, old gate hinges, the only sheet of plywood that was not warped, and leftover poultry wire. In the end my creation served its purpose but it wasn't exactly a work of art. At least Jimmi didn't think so when he did a double-take after he came home from school.

"What you do that for?" He fingered the wire panels on either side of the plywood door. "It makes my room feel like a chicken coop. Or a cage."

"It's for privacy. Yours. The fencing will let the heat rise up the stairs yet keep out the cats. And look—the door only latches from the inside." I showed him the eyelet and hook I'd screwed into the wood.

He grimaced. "Other boys have real doors and real walls. And even real door knobs. You know—the round kind you can turn from either side?"

I was beginning to feel underappreciated. "We'll get heavy drapes to block off the top of the stairs. It'll muffle the noise and the light from down here you're always complaining about."

He rolled his eyes. "Gee! You don't have a clue how real people are supposed to live, do you?" Stepping to the inside of the door, he hooked it, locking me out, and clattered upstairs.

"You still have to come down to eat when I say," I called after him. "But you can set your own alarm from now on." He didn't answer. Seconds later his boombox came on extra loud.

"Jimmi!" I yelled. "Turn it down!"

No reaction. I unplugged the extension cord that went from the kitchen to his room. There was a moment of silence. Then he said in a husky voice I hardly recognized, "Other boys have electric outlets in their walls."

"Other boys don't live on top of a beautiful mountain," I replied.

"Lucky them!" He sounded contrite and resentful at once. "If you plug me back in I promise to keep it low."

One of his two major ambitions was to be a normal boy with a normal family in a normal house in a normal town. It conflicted sharply with the second one—of getting pierced, tattooed and shaved bald, moving to a big-city ghetto, and becoming a member of some street gang called "Crypts" or "Bloods."

I sat at my desk and started a list, writing, "Goodwill—drapes. Passport pictures. Groceries. Canvas roll. Mailing tubes?"

My first acrylic was done. I'd start the second one tonight, although I still hadn't forgiven Dorrie. The phone company had promised to switch me to the new number in a couple of days. I was bound to lose business because of the change. Former customers would be unable to get in touch with me.

I started another list—of everyone I knew who should get the unlisted number. On the bottom, I wrote "Dorrie???" And then I thought about Ariel Jordan who would have no way of reaching me since he didn't have my address and I didn't have his number.

The thought triggered an unsettling sense of loss.

MARVEL and I were walking through town at noon the next day. She'd spent the entire morning lounging in Efi while I took care of seven miniature ponies and one stubborn Billy goat. My back was sore from mucking, feeding and watering. The tender March sun felt good on my shoulders and on the tight muscles in the small of my back. Marvel held her head high, creating an exquisitely sloping curve from the back of her triangular ears to her bushy tail. While she stopped at every tree we encountered and at each building corner, analyzing scents, I studied my new passport pictures. I was trying to feel some connection to the tired face and pulled-back brown hair of the stranger looking out at me with glum eyes. It wasn't until I held the pictures upside down that I finally recognized myself. Not that it mattered. Hardly anyone would ever glance inside my new passport whether I used it or not.

I'd parked Efi on the street running alongside Lithia Park, and as a special treat I walked Marvel there via the wooded path behind the plaza, on the far side of the creek. The ground was covered with shredded bark and leftover autumn leaves. There were even blackberry vines crawling up the bank. The only trouble with the trail was that it ended much too soon.

After Marvel led me to Efi I helped her in, poured some water into her stainless steel dish, and gave her a final hug. I was in the process of locking the hatch when someone behind me said,

"Hello, Silvi. We meet again."

Marvel wagged her tail once, in recognition. I turned to see Paul stopping on the sidewalk behind me, wearing his boots and his leather jacket. He was almost a foot taller than me; I hadn't noticed that fact at the abandoned cabin. The color of his eyes hadn't registered either, probably because of the gloom. They were a rich sable brown.

"Done surveying for the day?" I asked.

He rested a hand on the hatch window, letting Marvel sniff at his fingers through the grill. "I had an appointment with Todd Mittendrin," he said. "And now I'm looking for a good place to eat lunch. Any suggestions?"

I hesitated. "How about the Greenleaf? It's warm enough to sit on the upstairs balcony. It'll be quiet because the festival season hasn't really started yet."

He looked toward the plaza, considering. "Why don't you come eat with me? My treat."

Since I had intended to get a bite anyway, I decided to take him up on his offer and made one of my own. "I'll buy our desserts. Marionberry pie. So tell me, how do you like Mittendrin?"

He fell into step beside me. "I get the feeling he's tired of owning that steep piece of wilderness. Doesn't like any of his neighbors. Can't develop the property. Won't put any money toward building a proper road from a different direction, especially now that he's on the outs with Gierig. I wouldn't be surprised if he'd grab any halfway decent offer."

Right away I thought of Zora. "Hey," I said, "I know someone who's looking to buy."

"Actually, so do I." He looked at me sideways. "And I'd appreciate it if you didn't mention that the land might be available. If he thought two people were interested he'd up his price."

"That he would. But how much can he get if Barret won't give the buyer access?"

His face grew opaque. "Good point."

We settled at a table next to the railing. A good-looking young waiter wearing a pencil thin mustache, a stylish t-shirt, and designer jeans brought two glasses of water and our menus. Paul ordered coffees, sipped some water, and watched the waiter leave before he said, "I'm so glad I ran into you. I was feeling bad about yesterday."

"Oh—that." Uncomfortable about my part in the little fiasco, I quickly asked, "Did you see the double rainbow? Wasn't it spectacular?"

"A sight to remember. I hung your coat under the porch roof to dry. I can bring it over if you'd like."

I let the words hover between us and fade away.

By the time our coffees arrived we had agreed on lentil soup and chicken salad sandwiches. As the waiter wrote down our order I asked him to bring our two servings of pie right away. "Hot. With vanilla ice cream. I like eating my desserts first."

Paul laughed. "So do I. Once I satisfy my sweet tooth my stomach's less likely to get impatient for the rest of the meal."

"Good strategy," the waiter said. "And it sure takes the pressure off me."

IT WASN'T until I was done with my pie that I asked Paul, "What happened to your German shepherds? Are they dead?"

Although I couldn't point to anything in his face that actually changed, I felt an immediate sadness emanating from him. His eyes shuttered. He took his time chewing the last bite of his crust and chased it down with the dregs of his coffee. Then he said, "My wife took them. Along with everything else."

"I'm sorry. I shouldn't have asked."

"It's okay. Maybe talking about it will help me get used to it." He clutched at the table, then willed his hands to relax. "She took the house, the cars, our two girls, and the dogs." He aborted an effort to smile. "I can deal with the break-up. I can't deal with the way the dogs looked at me when I left them behind—or the fact that our daughters deliberately chose their mother over me."

"It's none of my business," I said. "But was there a man?"

He nodded. "My . . . business partner. Apparently, after all the years my wife and I spent together I was getting too predictable for her. Or was it too trusting? And you? I don't see a ring on your finger. Are you single . . . and free?"

My first impulse was to tell him to quit prying. But then I realized I had absolutely no reason to be coy. "The man I loved drove down the mountain on a cold morning two years ago," I said without inflection. "Somebody was driving up on the wrong side of the road. People will do that on those spiraling curves. Stillman veered to the shoulder and lost control. The car slid over the edge. It got stopped by a big tree before it could bullet down an unending incline, but he wasn't wearing a seat belt. Snapped his neck. He was going to town to buy me some flowers for my birthday. Turned out, I bought some for his funeral instead. I haven't celebrated my birthday since."

Paul had paled. He put his hand next to mine. "Stillman? An unusual name."

"He was an unusual man."

"Was he . . . from around here?"

I moved my hand to pick up the water glass, then put it down on another part of the table. "One of the original members of the land co-op. Barret eeked him off the ridge long ago. We started dating, and soon he moved in with me, into what, ironically, used to be his cabin. Most likely he would still be alive if he hadn't."

Stillman and Jimmi had really hit it off. If anything, the accident affected Jimmi even more than it did me. Although he claimed he didn't care, right after the service. Said it out loud in front of everybody. And hadn't been the same since.

"Let's talk about something else," I told Paul, silently wrestling with the sinking feeling that came over me whenever I was made to remember. "Did you see any sign of the cougar while you were surveying?"

"The one who killed that deer in the draw? I'm pretty sure he's gone." He tried for another smile. This time he succeeded. "If the weather holds, will you let me come for a walk with you and your dogs tomorrow morning?" His voice was almost eager. "Show me your favorite places? That is if Asa doesn't chase me up a tree."

How many times lately had I wished for someone who'd witness an awesome sunrise with me? The sight of a regal stag? Seven circling hawks? "We're early risers," I said. "If you're at the abandoned cabin when we walk by, sure, come along. We'll see how it goes."

I was taking a sip of coffee, noticing the waiter approach with our tray. Then a group of young boys appeared directly below us on Calle Guanajuato. One of them was taller and more slender than the rest. And darker. Without a backpack. No textbooks, no folders. At noon, with the middle school on the other end of town. I set the cup down hard.

"What is it?" Paul followed the direction of my gaze. "Someone you know?"

"It's Jimmi. Playing hooky." I leaned over the railing.

Paul hauled me up again, gently squeezing my arm until the waiter was done unloading our lunch and had gathered the dessert plates. After he was out of earshot, Paul murmured, "If you humiliate the boy in front of his truant friends he'll never live it down."

He was right, of course. I put my hands on my lap under the table and clamped them together until it hurt."But he's always *loved* school!"

"He's getting to the age when friends are more important than anything else. And looking cool is even more important than friends."

I watched Jimmi and his buddies heading toward Main Street. Half a minute later they appeared on the path Marvel and I had so recently walked along. If Jimmi's nose had been as discerning as hers he would have found the trail of our scent molecules, which no doubt still lingered in the creek dampened air. Watching the boys disappear behind secretive bushes, I had to admit it was a good place for truants to hide, hang, and do nothing. Or worse. My Jimmi, who'd been thoroughly impressed with the "Just Say No" campaign sponsored by the police department last year.

"How come you know so much about boys? When you raised girls?" I asked Paul.

He chuckled. "Believe it or not, I actually remember being one. And before everything fell apart I was a Big Brother. My favorite little brother looked a lot like Jimmi. Full of rough edges. No idea what was happening to him once the hormones started to stir." He picked up a wedge of his sandwich, considered it, and asked, "Does he belong to a friend of yours?"

"He's my son of course. Why else would I get so bent out of shape?"

I waited for an incredulous look, an insensitive, stupid remark.

He said, "He lives in that isolated little cabin with you?"

"Obviously!" My tone was sharper than I intended.

He raised a hand as if to calm a spooked dog and then asked, in a casual tone, "Why don't you bring him along on our walk tomorrow?"

I gave a derisive snort.

"Stupid question," he said. "He sleeps in, right? Won't get up until your voice reaches dangerous levels. Sleepwalks through breakfast. Spends all of his time locked in his room, only comes out for his meals, but only if you make him. Has a boombox earpiece fused to his ear. Listens to the wrong kind of music. Loud."

I couldn't help laughing. "You sure have him pegged. Me too." I could see flashes of skin through the bare branches. "I don't know much about teenage sons. I was a good mother to him when he was little, but things have changed. Since Stillman . . . Sometimes I don't recognize Jimmi anymore." I found myself tilting toward Paul, but only with motherly interest. "What would you advise me to do about this?"

"Nothing," he said, taking another bite of his sandwich.

"Nothing?"

"Except eat your lunch and then go on with your day. Calm down, think it through, see him in the best possible light. And still— say and do nothing. You ever play hooky as a child?"

"Once," I admitted reluctantly.

"What emotion does the memory hold?"

"Guilt. Anger." My mother had dragged me to school and shamed me in front of the teacher and all of my classmates.

"What do you think was more detrimental to you—missing school or being made to feel bad over it?"

It still hurt. "You really think sticking my head in the sand is a better approach?"

He shrugged. "Some boys get through this period quickly and come out stronger. Some never come out of it." He looked at his watch. "Does he like sports? Football?"

"And break a bone? We don't have health insurance."

"Soccer, then. Baseball. Basketball. Get him tired and keep him tired. Let the coaches talk mean to him. You just offer him cookies, milk, and a sunny smile when you pick him up from a workout."

It seemed so simple, almost as if I'd solved the problem already. "Next fall I'm letting him sign up for all three."

He scanned the check, then pulled out his wallet, and put down the correct change. "I've got to drive to Medford right now, research some land use records. I'll see you at daybreak tomorrow. The weatherman's predicting clear skies."

I finished my soup and wrapped my sandwich in a napkin. "I prefer a good cloudscape, myself. But I'm glad I ran into you. I wouldn't have seen—and then again, it makes me wonder just how long he's been—" I glanced at the check, counted out the money for my order plus the two desserts, put it on the tray, and gave him back the amount he overpaid.

He picked up my bills and deposited them in front of me. "I said my treat."

I pushed them toward him. "Thank you very much, but I always pay my own way."

"Of course," he said smoothly, adding a generous tip to the tray before sliding the excess into his wallet. "I'll be sure to keep it in mind next time I invite you to a meal." He offered his hand in truce or as a good-bye, I couldn't tell which. "Remember, ignorance is bliss. For Jimmi and for you. I'm glad we had this opportunity to talk. What are you going to do with your afternoon?"

I stretched and got to my feet. "Play with a litter of Siamese kittens. Take a slew of hunting dogs for a long stroll and throw balls for them in the dog park until they collapse from exhaustion. I'm a pet-minder."

"Now that sounds like fun," Paul said, standing so close that I could smell his special clean scent rising out of the jacket. "Can I walk you back to your truck? It's on my way. I'm parked near the playground."

Strolling beside an agreeable-looking man my own age, in companionable silence, was something else I'd had no practice in lately. It put a bounce in my step for the rest of the afternoon. It wasn't until I was on my way up the old highway that I realized he knew my name even though I'd deliberately withheld it when Marvel cornered him inside the abandoned cabin during the rainstorm.

CHAPTER 14

I WAS CRUISING PAST STU'S PARKING LOT when I saw a memorable sight. It was Zora, jiggling down the steep cement path from his cabin, waving both arms at me, flesh rippling. I braked, staring in awe.

"My agent just called," she bubbled. "I got the land I wanted." How could this be? Hadn't Ariel Jordan's deal gone through, after all?

"The three hundred acres?" I said, not quite able to hide the disappointment I felt.

She gave me an odd look. "We never could get to it. The creek makes a deep vertical cut at the stretch we tried to cross, every inch of it covered with brambles. Then there's an impenetrable wood on the other side, and the farm fence behind it is topped with barbed wire. Ford Knox couldn't be harder to break into. And after all our useless exertion, it turned out to be sold." She brightened. "But I found something I like even better, right across from the lake. The asking price was too high, but we made them an offer they couldn't reject." And of course she had the cash to back it up. Must be nice.

"There's a pond," she said proudly. "And a spring. And a drafty old house that the realtor called a rustic chalet."

"Well! Congratulations!" I meant it. Better her than one of those shark toothed developers, any day.

"I feel like celebrating tonight," she went on. "Want to come?"

"What do you have in mind?"

"Stu suggested the Standing Stone. There'll be a live band. I'm inviting everyone I met at the potluck. My treat. Stu says they start playing at eight thirty, so we should order by eight. Is that too late for you?"

"I'll make an exception," I said. "Just don't ask me to dance."

She looked at me as if we had not been introduced and she planned to keep it that way.

"With men," I added drily. "I never learned how."

"Oh!" She gave a relieved chortle. "For a second there I thought . . . Not that there's anything wrong with two women . . . I mean, after all—I've lived in San Francisco for years." Her cheeks turned crimson. As if to distract me she peered into one of the steel-mesh encased canopy windows. "It looks like a lion's cage. What have you got in there?" She rapped on the canopy. Marvel growled softly and sat up.

Zora squealed, "A dog! Stu said you had two fierce shepherds. He won't let me go anywhere near your place. But this one's a pussycat. What's his name?"

Marvel stared at Zora in wonder.

"This one's a she. Fierce with *men*," I corrected. "Because we don't have one of those. Meet Lady Marvelous, aka Marvel. Asa the Great stayed home today, lounging on his favorite chair."

Foolishly, Zora pressed her nose to the outside of the mesh. Marvel flicked her big ears. After a long, soul-searching moment she put her nose against the same spot from the inside.

Zora cried, "She likes me! Don't you think?"

"Absolutely. You're the only person I know she's ever touched noses with—other than me. Well—I've got chores. See you at eight. Thanks for the invitation."

Zora stepped away, hugging herself. "*I* could get a dog," she said. "My dad never let me. But now I finally can." She stretched her arms wide. "I can do whatever I want!"

A scary phrase coming from the lips of a new heiress.

Nevertheless, I wished I could say it too.

THE PHONE started to ring when I was just outside the kitchen door. By the time I was halfway across the room Jimmi was already coming down his stairs. The only reason I got to the phone first was because he had to fumble with his door latch. I jiggled the receiver to break the connection, held it to my ear, and said into the mouthpiece, "Hello? No, I'm sorry. I'm not interested." Then I hung up and asked casually, "Any other calls come in, Jimmi?"

He took a package of Grahams off the shelf. "No. But one of your crazy cats must have played with the cord while we were gone and accidentally unplugged it. I put it back in for you."

"I'm afraid we've been discovered by a new generation of telephone solicitors," I said. "It's getting to be annoying. I'm thinking of asking the phone company for a different number." How ironic that I, who detested liars, was turning into one myself—although for a good cause. But wasn't that a generic liar excuse? I unscrewed the peanut butter jar for Jimmi and brought the grape jelly out of the refrigerator. "Zora invited everybody out to dinner tonight. Want to come?"

He smeared a thick layer of peanut butter onto the crackers. "Grace's weird houseguest? From San Francisco? And the rest of your lame ducks friends? No thanks. I'd rather do homework. Can I turn up my boombox extra loud after the old folks are gone?"

"If you keep the windows closed. And remember that dogs and cats have highly sensitive ears."

He slathered on jelly and stacked the crackers onto his plate like a multi-layered sandwich. I filled a large tumbler with milk and set it on his bottom stair. He put the plate down next to it, waited for me to retreat from the landing, locked the door from the inside, and went upstairs with his snack, humming a jaunty tune.

Smiling, I ran twenty raw chicken necks through the electric meat grinder, pureed the rest of the *B.A.R.F.* diet's ingredients in my blender, mixed it into the grind, and dished out precisely measured portions for each of the waiting beasts. The shepherds gulped theirs from stainless steel bowls. The cats ate daintily from individual saucers. Racket, yowling in anticipation, received two heaping spoonfuls, which he swallowed in two bites. After they licked their bowls clean the shepherds devoured one raw chicken back each. Racket nibbled on a wing tip. Since the day I'd switched from prepared pet food none of my charges had needed a vet. The barf diet was worth every minute of bother and mess.

PROMPTLY at eight I stepped inside the Standing Stone and skirted the crowd waiting for tables. For some unfathomable, quickly regretted reason I'd decided to do honor to the special occasion by wearing a dress. My legs felt naked even though I was wearing disgustingly clingy pantyhose. I found Zora in the rear, surrounded by the rest of her guests at a table overlooking the dance floor. They were already eating. Across the aisle eight elderly men in identical maroon jackets and black slacks coaxed mellow warm-up sounds out of their instruments.

The Easy Valley Eight were a arthritic, aching-joints kind of band with a surprisingly lively beat. Years ago, their first gig in the brewery-restaurant had been so popular that they were invited back once a month. It was an event worth waiting for. Every table was filled with laughing, chatting people ready to eat, drink, and dance.

"Silvi!" Zora waved me to the vacant chair beside her. "We came a bit early to make sure we'd get a large table. Go ahead and order. Price is no object. We're ready for refills anyway." She hailed the waitress who came swinging her pert ponytail to replenish their micro brews and bring me a menu.

After scanning it and the plates on the table, I decided on the lamb shank. Zora had peeled off her dark blue everyday muumuu for a similar garment in powder blue, with a matching velvet bow in her frizzy hair. She looked more like a big chested, oversized Stellar jay than ever, especially when she let loose a raucous laugh, which she did whenever anyone looked at her.

Violet was sitting on Zora's other side, furtively picking red grapes from her pizza and replacing them with the overflow of olives gathered on the rim of Clyde's salad plate. "Where did you put Lavender tonight?" I asked her.

"Our neighbors have two daughters," she explained, tucking a strand of white-blonde hair behind one of her pretty shell ears. "They brought a video for Lavender to watch. They were helping her pop corn when we left. Lavender was glad to trade us in for the night."

"Less rules," I agreed, recalling Jimmi's experience with the very same girls not too long ago. "She'll fall asleep on the floor." That's how I often found him after a date with Stillman, his head resting on children's books, both him and the napping girls surrounded by spilled popcorn.

Perhaps Barret caught a glimpse of my memory, for he leaned across the table, genuine concern in his eyes. "It's your birthday today, isn't it? Are you all right?" It was he who'd told me about the accident, who took care of Jimmi while I forced myself to make the necessary arrangements, who cried at the memorial as I stood at his side dry-eyed and numb.

Everyone looked at me, my new friends puzzled, my old ones with overpowering solicitude. "Oh, birthdays . . ." I said with a careless shrug. "I stopped counting. How's your bird-watching coming along, Barret?"

He pulled in his head at the low blow and concentrated on excavating a fishbone from his broiled salmon. I willed my eyes to stop prickling and wished I'd stayed at home by the stove to finish reading the latest Kate Wilhelm mystery I'd checked out of the library.

Zora's bright jay eyes jumped from Barret's face to mine. Before she could ask a nosy question, I said, "So, Zora. When are you planning to move into your drafty chalet?"

She pulled a long list out of her purse. "Not until the last of these items is checked off. Weatherproofing is my first priority. And good cross fencing. I want horses and cows—and goats to keep the brambles down."

"Wow," I said. "Are you sure? Taking care of livestock is a lot of work."

She waved my misgivings away. "I'll have a farm manager to run things. And cowboys. That's what money is for. Eventually I hope to find a congenial architect to build some sort of big organic home for me near the spring."

"Facing the lake?" I said. "How nice." The usual dream house routine. Another fancy, oversized estate disrupting the natural lines of our slopes.

My lamb arrived with a bottle of *Löwenbräu*. I took a long, thirst quenching sip. If my mother persisted I'd soon have occasion to sample Bavarian beer on the other side of the Atlantic. Although, come to think of it, she'd be more likely to push an Austrian *Heurigen* wine. Wiping foam from my lips, I allowed myself to relax and said, "Here's to you and your drafty chalet, Zora. And your scenic view of Emigrant Lake. And your spring. And your pond."

"That pond will draw all kinds of wildlife, don't you think?" she said eagerly. "It'll be fun watching the little creatures drink. I bet there'll be plenty of birds around, too." She turned to Barret. "It seems you and I share a passion for them. We could go birding together. At dawn."

Barret gave me a dirty look. "Dawn?" he said with distaste.

Grace speared a piece of lettuce onto her fork. "I'm staying an extra week. Just to see how things shake out."

Stu put a proprietary arm around her shoulders. "I'm trying to get her to stay for good. She's going to put in applications at our hospitals."

Grace raised her brows. "Providing?"

"Providing I get some kind of useful employment. With a regular paycheck." He sounded subdued. A regular paycheck would thwart his acting ambitions. I dipped my first bite of lamb into port gravy and added a dollop of mashed potatoes. "What you need is a few good Shakespeare Theater connections."

"Don't I wish," Stu sighed, scanning the faces around us. "Meanwhile, waiting tables in here might not be so bad. This place has become popular with the theater crowd. Maybe I'll hear about the next miniscule acting job up for grabs."

"Foot in door," I said. Then the band began their first tune.

The most serious dancers were occupying the tables nearest the dance space. An elderly couple in their eighties got to it first. They looked as if they'd perfected their moves over sixty shared years. Although the wife's coiffure resembled an iron helmet she still knew how to wiggle her hips. Her partner, who seemed to suffer from a fused spine, compensated with fancy footwork.

Stu pulled Grace to her feet. Her black hair spilled down naked tan shoulders over a back that tapered beautifully to her small waist. As soon as they reached the dance floor they fell into an easy joined rhythm, both ideal representatives of their genders—the kind of couple the world cheered for and schemed to keep together.

Although she was a second generation Honduran and he came from an all-Italian family, they could have passed for identical twins, she abundant in estrogen, he in testosterone. They grew up on the same block, Grace told me once, and were classmates throughout most of their school years. One day their hormones spoke and they listened.

Glancing past them, I noticed dreadlocked Con Conroy on the sidelines, leisurely checking out the tables until his gaze fastened on me. Crossing the room in quick, long-legged strides, he came to tower over me, but it was Zora's hand he reached for, not mine.

"All right!" She jumped to her feet. "I'm ready to boogie."

Soon they were the center of attention as she rocked, rolled and bounced, her breasts swinging from side to side like bass bells. Con wove his agile body around her, tossing every one of his dreadlocks, ebony skin glistening, sweat stains spreading over his shirt.

Her dancing shoes matched the powder blue of her dress and the velvet bow, which was already askew and hanging by a thread. When it finally fell, unnoticed, all eyes were preoccupied with what might be shimmying under her dress. Each energetic spin caused its seam to rise higher and higher until we could see extra large, old-fashioned black lace garters decorated with little powder blue bows. Everyone in the restaurant seemed to find them mesmerizing. What fascinated me, just as it had at the potluck, was the diminutive size of the shoes. They were embracing the dainty feet of a slender woman encased in a great wealth of flesh.

Barret wiped a napkin over his beard. "Talk about rare birds! I hope she won't try to drag me to the dance floor next!"

"After Con Conroy? You've got to be kidding!" I said, forgetting that he was my landlord and prone to hold grudges. "I like her I-don't-give-a-damn attitude. I hope it rubs off on some of the rest of us."

"I hope not," Barret said. "Two of her could drive a man like me out of town permanently."

"Aw, come on, honey," Violet was purring beside him, trying to coax a reluctant Clyde out of his chair. "All you have to do is shuffle your feet. There's nothing to it."

Clyde gripped his plate. "I'm still eating my curry."

"Silvi will watch it for you. It'll keep."

He pushed her away. "Find somebody else to bother, why don't you."

Barret raised his hand as if to volunteer, but he was too late. A stocky man wearing a well-cut gray suit and a fancy cowboy hat stood in front of Violet, inclining his head.

"Howdy, partner," Violet said, taking his arm. As they headed into the fray I had the uneasy feeling I'd seen him before under less pleasant circumstances.

Barret watched them begin to dance. "That's John Gierig," he muttered. "A man who stops at nothing." He helped himself to a swig of beer from my bottle, then wiped a sleeve over his lips. "He came to my door today while I was eating lunch and stuck a huge check under my nose, already made out to me. Claimed he and his wife just happened onto our dead-end road and instantly fell in love with my property. She insists nothing else will tickle her fancy. It's a technique he's famous for. He used it on old Tillie, who had some of the best pasture land on the east side of town. Up to her neck in debt, barely hanging on to the farm."

He took another swallow, glowering at the dance floor. "Dear John held out the same kind of check to her and she took it. Instead of building the dream house he supposedly promised his wife he put in a subdivision. Backyards the size of postage stamps."

Barret dug in a pants pocket and pulled out a business card. "He gave me this after I told him no go. For when I'm ready to change my mind, he said. Then he asked if I know a woman living nearby who owns a big shepherd sized dog. I told him I didn't know one who didn't. Was he talking about you?"

I nodded. "He caught us trespassing on Strawberry Hill early this morning. Marvel barked at a skunk. It got his attention."

Barret wrinkled his nose. "Did you get sprayed? So that's what I've been smelling! I thought it was Zora's obnoxious perfume."

Although I'd washed my hands and changed my clothes after I came home, I hadn't shampooed. Grabbing a handful of my hair, I sniffed and said, "*Could* be skunk. Or horse manure. Or a whiff of Billy goat essence. Let's call it musk." As close as I sat to Paul at lunch today, he hadn't said a word about it. He must have impeccable manners. Or an impaired sense of smell.

Down on the dance floor, Violet's long straight hair glowed. "That dance should have been mine," Barret grumbled. "Look at how clumsy he is." Indeed, Gierig was stumbling, driving an errant elbow into Stu's ribs. Grace stopped moving and stood rigid, staring at the man with the cowboy hat. With an apologetic smile, Violet pulled Gierig away. Then she showed him the right way to dance. "She's good," Barret told Clyde. "Light on her feet."

Clyde picked yellow rice kernels out of his biblical beard. "A good singer, too. That's how I met her. She was the lead singer in a hillbilly band."

"Bluegrass?" Barret chuckled, delighted.

"If you want to call it that. She broke up with the band leader and the band, both. Lavender's his. Or so she claims."

Then and there, I decided Clyde was an undesirable neighbor. Surely Violet deserved someone better. I nudged Barret. "Why don't you ask her to dance once this set's over? After Gierig bruises a couple of her toes she'll think you're Richard Gere."

Grace was still standing, seemingly oblivious to Stu's cajoling. At last, shaking her head, she pulled away from him and fled toward the restroom. Stu stayed behind on the dance floor, his arms sinking to his sides. Gierig gave a small self-satisfied smile.

"So," Barret said to Clyde. "Hear anything about your impending inheritance lately?"

Clyde adjusted his glasses. "Negotiations are moving along. Why do you ask?"

Barret nodded toward Zora. "Think merger. I'm guessing she's sweet on you. Go for it."

"Yeah?" Clyde said, combing his fingers down the full length of his beard. "Yeah! Why not?" He tossed down his napkin and went to the dance floor to tap on Con Conroy's shoulder. Good-naturedly, the actor stepped aside. Just as good-naturedly, Zora switched partners and tried to coax Clyde to unbend. Con returned to our table, stopping in front of my chair. "Don't I know you from somewhere?"

Grinning, I quoted, "'Is this dog friendly?'"

He got it almost at once. "The shark toothed shepherd! You don't have him hidden under the table, do you?" He rapped on the top, rattling the plates. Then he lifted the table-cloth and glanced at my knees. "Care to dance?"

I pulled the cloth down again. "I'll take a rain check. You look beat."

He wiped sweat off his forehead. "It's all that late night rehearsing. I didn't get to sleep till morning. But you're on. Next time." He wove his way through the crowd, brushing past Stu who came to reclaim his seat.

"What do you suppose got into Grace?" he asked. "Indigestion or mood?"

"Grace doesn't have moods," Barret and I said at the same time. I continued with, "Must be something she ate. She may be a while. There's a long line at the restroom."

Stu played with his congealed steak, chewed listlessly on a braised slice of red pepper, and pushed his plate away. "I'm going out to the car for a smoke. In case she cares to ask."

Pheromones were certainly rampant tonight. But with my knees safely tucked under the table I felt immune and contentedly finished my dinner, washing it down with my beer. On the floor, Zora tolerated Clyde until a replacement arrived. It was the eighty-some-year-old husband whose spine had loosened enough for a rollicking jitterbug.

Clyde watched from the sidelines until the music stopped and Gierig disappeared into the crowd. Then Clyde and Violet returned to the table together. She drained her water and asked Barret, "The man I was dancing with—do you know who he is?" He grunted a yes.

"Seems like a nice guy," she said.

His face fell, but then the band started a slow tune, and he seized his moment and led her onto the floor where they melded together, cheek to cheek, moon maiden leaning against a gruff brown Bear scenting honey.

Zora bounced back to her chair. "Gosh, I'm hot." She sat, fanning herself. "I think I must have lost five pounds down there. Time for dessert." She waved to our pony tailed waitress. "Please, guys, do me the favor and order the most expensive sweets on the menu. I'll have mine topped with whipped cream."

I HAD no trouble falling asleep that night. I dreamed I was slow dancing with a shadowy partner who smelled of leather and soap. Around and around we turned, his cheek against mine. Jimmi stood at the edge of the light, wearing his baseball cap backwards and his pants slung extra low. He was glaring at us.

CHAPTER 15

MARVEL WOKE ME AT EXACTLY FIVE A.M. by touching her nose to my cheek. A few minutes later she blew warm breath on my face but I stayed under the covers, intent on sifting through the hush of the forest for my favorite wake-up call. And then it came, sung by the bird who lived in the great Ponderosa Pine next to the clearing. The melody was so complex that I let him repeat it twice before I finally sat up. By the time I was dressed and outside there was a rim of light at the horizon, outlining lacy black conifers on the eastern range.

Since our recent adventures with wildlife, the ATV, and the surveyor, all three dogs chose to stay close to me on our walks. Thus, we reached the abandoned cabin together. Paul was sitting on the mossy porch steps, waiting for us. His face looked scrubbed, his hair dampened.

Asa bristled. Marvel focused on Paul's hands as if to make sure that he was unarmed. He showed her the three bits of jerky he was holding, then tossed them in front of the dogs. Asa quickly helped himself to his own piece and Marvel's, but before he could snap up Racket's, the Chihuahua took his share under the steps for safe-keeping. Slowly, Paul stood up, showing Marvel his empty hands. "This is my favorite part of the day," he said, his voice congenial but firm. "When everything is fresh again. So. Where are we going?"

I nodded toward the skid. "Up there."

Paul fell in beside me and stayed silent while we concentrated on climbing. After the first few steps the dogs decided to accept his continuing presence. Halfway to the top, I admired a spattering of pale-violet wood stars, their petals curled tight in the gloom. "They weren't here yesterday," I told him. "Some years this part of the forest is full of them." Three quarters of the way up I saw my first royal purple shooting star, thrusting out of the ground beside a half open buttercup.

I feathered the star's delicate petals, still closed. "Too bad you won't be here long enough to see the ridge when it's covered with these, Paul. There are a couple of places where they're so thick that when the evening sun backlights them the whole slope looks like purple stained glass."

Not until we were on even ground did the dogs feel free to spread out—Marvel in front, scouting, Asa behind, guarding, Racket weaving back and forth between them. It was getting rapidly lighter. I glanced at the scrub oak we were passing, noticing new buds forming on its twigs. "Let me tell you what you'll be missing," I said. "After the shooting stars come blue irises, and then cream colored pussies and lilies. Just about then, the oaks leaves unfurl and the ground around them grows knee-deep with purple vetch that stretches across entire hillsides. And that's only the beginning." I nodded toward the forest on top of Raspberry Hill. "I've been meaning to hike up there. Something's happening in those woods and I want to know what it is. We'll take the back route. In case John Gierig is spying from his fancy shack." Still a little suspicious of Paul, I asked, "Is that where you parked your car? At Gierig's? Do you walk in from there?"

"Of course not. There are better places if you know where to look," he said as if it were a definitive answer. I let it go.

The back route brought us near the secret lane I'd discovered last year. On impulse, I decided to show it to him, though I couldn't think why. "We don't usually come this way," I said, leading him toward it. "The west side makes for an easier hike. But unfortunately it's visible from Gierig's house. I've never had to hide from anyone before. In fact, in all the years I've wandered these slopes I haven't encountered a living soul—except once, last November. Marvel found a weekend hunter up here, holding a gleaming new rifle. She tried to run him off. Luckily he had the patience to stand absolutely still, pointing the barrel at the sky until I could get near enough to pull her away."

"Oh," Paul said. And then, "Couldn't you just have called her to you?"

"Not last year," I replied shortly, afraid he would turn preachy on me.

"Does she come now? When you call?"

"Usually."

"Is that right?" he said in what he seemed to think was a impartial tone. "I see." If he meant to imply my skills as a dog trainer were not as finely honed as they ought to have been, he was not mistaken. But then, Marvel and Asa were still works in progress.

"I like that you're keeping them so slim," he allowed, running his hands over their backs. "I can't see their ribs, but I can feel them. That's good."

I shrugged, annoyed that his casual praise mattered to me. We didn't speak again until we arrived at the lane. It didn't look anywhere near spectacular yet. "I wish you could see this place in full bloom," I said, sitting down on the first of two boulders.

He sat on the other one, a few feet away. Mine was cushioned with moss. His was not. "I *have* seen it," he said, fidgeting. Then he looked straight at me. "It's fabulous in May and June. I call it 'Blossom Lane.'"

"Huh?" I said, thinking I wasn't hearing correctly.

He gestured at the curving upslope bank. "That's where big clusters of Giant Red Indian Paintbrush bloom. They look great next to the white raspberry blossoms, the lilacs, and the vetch. I often thought if I were an artist I'd paint the whole thing."

I couldn't make sense of his words. "Are you trying to tell me you've been here before? More than once?"

He leaned close and said slowly, "My full name is Paul Randolph. Everyone used to call me Randy back then." I could tell he was watching for my reaction, but I couldn't decide what it should be. "I didn't say I was a surveyor," he continued. "You assumed it. I didn't correct you because it might have spoiled my plans."

"What plans?"

He grinned, looking elated, though his voice remained calm. "Yesterday afternoon I managed to buy back my land and my cabin."

I sat still, waiting for more. "Go on," I finally said.

"A month ago I would have told you I'd forgotten all about them," he went on. "But then my wife sprang her divorce news on me, and I went to the Florida Keys to unwind and rethink the rest of my life. One day I was browsing through a gallery when lightning struck in the form of a painting entitled 'The Abandoned Cabin.' Right there on the wall in front of my eyes. How could I not have recognized it? I built it with my own hands. Even so, I wasn't absolutely sure till the gallery owner told me the artist lived in Ashland. And then I couldn't keep myself from wanting the picture *and* the real thing. So I decided to buy both."

His face tensed. "Mittendrin and Barret would have made a big fuss if they'd known who was buying the land. One because he hates Barret, the other because he hates me. I paid cash. For the picture and for the cabin. This time I won't let anyone take what's mine."

Some might have called them both foolish purchases, made by a man who had temporarily lost his grip. But then it was his money to waste. "You've been sleeping inside that gritty wreck, haven't you?" I said.

He offered me a wry smile. "Henceforth known as 'Paul's Place.' It was a homecoming, Silvi. Balm for the soul. I cleared the floor, got rid of the rats' nests and the gutted insulation, and have spent the last couple of nights in my sleeping bag on the back porch. I had no idea who you were when Asa tried to jump me in town. Believe me, seeing him and you run into the kitchen was an even bigger shock than getting attacked by Marvel and the Chihuahua."

I looked him over good. He looked back, his gaze steady.

"So you're little baby faced Randy," I said, shaking my head. Somehow, I'd imagined a scrawny, insignificant blonde boy with unkempt long hair and a bad complexion.

He flicked me a relieved grin. "All grown up. Bolder and older. Thank God."

"Don't you think it's about time you told Barret you're here?"

"As a matter of fact, I'm planning to do that this morning. To reclaim my right-of-way. Even though I'm number one on his enemies list." Something in his eyes glinted. "He'll soon notice I'm not as easy to push around as before."

There were two reasons perfectly decent neighbors would feud to the death—water and right-of-way. I had no desire to be in the middle of a range war. Even though I liked Paul a bit more every day and Barret a bit less. Crossing my legs, I accidentally kicked Racket. He let loose his best Chihuahua shriek in response. I held his muzzle shut, listening to the echo and waiting for the hollow sound of a warning shot fired from the direction of Gierig's villa. It didn't come. It could only mean that he hadn't arrived yet.

"Well," I told Paul. "I wish you luck. It would be nice to see the old cabin fixed up." I sincerely meant it, but I couldn't help forming a picture in my mind—of his car driving past my place morning, noon, and night. Not to mention the cars of his friends. Weekend parties. Lovers. All in my face.

Maybe it wouldn't be such a bad thing if Barret refused to accommodate him.

Maybe I didn't want a new neighbor.

"Shall we go on? To the top?" I asked, moving ahead, wanting some distance between us.

"Sure," he said. "I'm right behind you."

AFTER WE crested Raspberry Hill we both gasped and stood stunned. The lush forest we remembered was no longer there. Whoever had clear-cut these heights had cleverly left a rim of trees to give the illusion of wholeness to anyone glancing up from below. From close-by the summit looked like a blood drenched battlefield. The air stank of violence. Gierig's bulldozer had dragged off the tallest, most symmetrical conifers, uprooting and mangling the less valuable trees, mostly crooked oaks and spindly new-growth madrones. Their corpses lay piled like a bad hand of pickup sticks. Gierig's work-crew had been busy.

I said, "I *thought* I saw dozer tracks the other morning." The ground wobbled under my feet until I felt Paul's steadying hand at my elbow. "They must have done this while I was off working in town. Or else I would have heard something. Don't you think?"

A white line had appeared around Paul's mouth. "They were probably finished by the time I hiked in," he said, sounding grim. "It's a sad fact that private landowners can do with their trees whatever they want. And what Gierig wants is to get rapidly richer any way he can. From his point of view trees are nothing but green gold ripe for the plucking. But you have to admit he's clever about it."

My stomach was already clenching, a common failing of mine whenever I entered a state of shock. "Quick, let's get out of here before I throw up." No longer caring if a pair of binoculars was trained on me or not, I hastened off Raspberry Hill toward the barren slope of the lookout, where I sat on fragile spring grass beside the ancestor tree and held onto his narrow trunk as if I were drowning. "Why would any sane person want to destroy that beautiful mountaintop forest? There ought to be a law against rampant clear-cutting. It can't be good for the planet. Aren't you a lawyer? Make one."

He knelt close beside me. "Legislators make laws. Lawyers apply them," he corrected. "Besides, I'm not licensed in this state yet. As soon as I get my place fixed up I'm planning to take care of the legal paperwork, rent a small office space in town, and hang out my shingle." He looked appreciatively at my little tree. "An uncommonly fine specimen."

"But is he on Gierig's land?"

"No, on Mittendrin's. Mine. And I won't cut anything living."

On second thought maybe Paul was just the kind of neighbor I needed.

"Barret doesn't cut down his trees, either," I told him. "Every year a few old ones keel over after the snow softens the ground. He saws them up for firewood and gives us the leftovers." I glanced toward Blackberry Hill. "You own that part, too?"

"Luckily, yes. Gierig's trying to buy the parcel on the other side, though. He'll be furious when he finds out what I've done. I think he was planning to aggravate Mittendrin into selling cheap. To him."

The sky was beginning to blush a transparent rose-pink. I jumped to my feet. "Come on, I've got to see something pretty to cover the picture of that abominable clear-cut that's stuck in my mind. Let's visit the two giant madrones. I know a path that dips from there across the draw and straight to your cabin."

We walked companionably side by side along the trail the seven hawks had brushed with their shadows. "I've often wanted to build something near those madrones," he said. "Not a cabin—there's no water and no access. But some kind of camp. For summer night sleeping."

"A tree house?"

"I'm not about to lug any lumber. A lean-to, maybe."

"What about a rope swing?"

"Now that's a fine start," he said. "I'll get right to it." He was becoming easier and easier to like.

"I'm hoping to paint those particular madrones one day," I said. "As soon as I'm good enough."

"Consider that painting sold."

When we were halfway there, I said, "I don't get it. How did you know I was the one who painted your cabin?"

He captured my wrist and held it in front of my face. "Paint freckles. Paint-speckled clothes. The tennis shoes you had on when we sat on the porch were speckled, too."

As I recalled, I had been wearing my oldest clothes. The coat had permanent dirt stains on the sleeves from hugging the dogs. And more than likely my hair had been uncombed. How I looked on the mountain had never mattered before. I liked it that way. "I'm a scruffy dresser," I informed Paul curtly. "By choice. And I'm not about to change just to spare a new neighbor."

"I don't care *what* you're wearing!"

"Is that so!"

"Absolutely. The scruffier, the better. In fact, I'm hoping to give you some competition in that department as soon as I can get to the Goodwill store. You don't think I'm going to clear out rat turds in my town-finery, do you?" He wagged his eyebrows at me.

I responded with a reluctant smile. "According to Dorrie, you owe me a letter. Of appreciation."

He colored. "Oh, that." Then he stopped and lightly cupped my shoulders. "I appreciate you more than words can say."

I nodded and moved out of reach. "You just saved yourself a first-class stamp." We strolled on in silence, walking on a carpet of bunchgrass still pale from the long winter. The sky had turned golden. There wasn't a single hawk in sight.

DRIVING out later that morning, I saw Paul heading down Barret's driveway, waving at me. I wished I could be a fly on one of the Manor walls during their meeting.

"Who's that?" Jimmi asked, nibbling on his cream-cheese topped bagel.

"An old friend of Barret's." I tossed him a tissue just as he began to covertly wipe a smudged hand onto the side of his seat.

He cleaned off his fingers. "That's the trouble with Barret. His friends all have one foot in the grave."

With a non-committal shrug, I said, "This one looks nimble enough. Hardly a gray hair on his head. He came from Key Largo, as a matter of fact. Spoke to Dorrie in her gallery."

"Dorrie is cool." Jimmi balled the soiled tissue and tossed it onto the floor. "She listens to hip hop."

"But not to gangsta rap."

He gave a pitying hoot. "Not in front of you, anyway. When can we go there again?"

"As soon as rap is dead and buried."

He laughed. "Not in your life-time then."

"Are you sure? I'm figuring on sticking around till I'm a hundred and fifteen at least."

Putting a hand over his heart, he gazed heavenward and said, "Don't you think it's time for you to admit that rap is eternal?"

ON JIMMI'S BIRTHDAY I MAILED off the acrylics I'd promised Dorrie, and when I checked my PMB before picking him up from school there was a brief letter from her inside, containing a check for the two oils Paul had bought. On the spur of the moment I invited Jimmi to the Great American Pizza for his birthday dinner. After a serious five minute discussion on the merits of each menu entry we ordered a giant pizza, half pepperoni and mozzarella, half feta and pesto.

The waitress brought it to our table, still sizzling. Just then, a pallid, awkward-looking man slouched into the restaurant. He was wearing a parka, a ski cap pulled over his eyebrows, thick horn rimmed glasses, a Charlie Chaplin mustache, and baggy black cords that had thinned at the knees. Glancing at us in passing, he seemed momentarily startled. Then he slid in the next booth and leaned over the top.

"Pardon me," he said in a soft voice. "What's all that green stuff on your pizza—creamed spinach?"

When I started to explain about pesto, his mouth stretched to an impish grin, exposing a set of flawless teeth. I knew those teeth. And his wide brown eyes, partially blocked by the glasses, were as familiar to me as they were to everyone else on the planet.

"I'm Silvi. And this here is Jimmi." I reached into my purse for one of my new business cards and handed it over, saying, "I'm no closer to breeding my dogs but I've just changed my number. You want to sit with us? We've got enough pizza for three."

He slid in beside Jimmi. "What gave me away?"

"No one has eyes like yours. No wonder you usually hide them behind inscrutable shades."

At first Jimmi looked puzzled. Then I could almost see the light bulb clicking on inside his head. Staring at Ariel's face, he asked, "Is that mustache real?"

Tugging it gently, Ariel replied, "It's real, all right. Even if it isn't mine." He put a hand on Jimmi's shoulder. "I'm so glad to see you again. I've been getting a bit lonely down on my farm. And my California blood's not used to the climate change yet. It's too thin for your Oregon March weather. See?" He zipped down the coat and showed us his multiple collars. "I'm wearing three shirts and two sweaters and I'm still freezing." After helping himself to a slice from my half of the pizza, he said, "Hey, maybe you and your mom can come visit this evening. I'll show you my game room and my CDs. I brought a bunch of old movies with me from my other house. Have you ever seen E.T.?"

Jimmi thought about it while he pulled off his first slice. "The kid flick that came out before I was born?" He broke a string of melted cheese that was reluctant to separate from the rest of his pizza. "Thanks but no thanks. You got any rap?"

CHAPTER 16

IT WAS GETTING DARK WHEN WE REACHED the turn-off to Ariel's land. He was waiting for us in a beat up old Chevy. We followed him over an accumulation of potholes on a clay road that was hardened by a few days of unmitigated sun. We passed anonymous driveways, unadvertised dead-ends, and went over a bridge built of what appeared to be rough sawn Port Orford Cedar. At last we rumbled across a cattle guard, came to rolling pastureland, and stopped in front of a peeling farmhouse with a packed dirt yard. It was surrounded on three sides by tall, picturesque oaks.

Ariel climbed out of his car, spread his arms in a triumphant gesture and did a full spin. "This has got to be the most desolate house on the planet. Not a single reporter anywhere. No fans. No sightseers. I love it. It's amazing how much work you can get done when you're not constantly interrupted." He pulled out a shiny new key. "I had the locks replaced, but to tell you the truth, I can hardly wait for those puppies of yours. The whole place gets eerie around midnight. That's when I start hearing things creaking and moaning upstairs."

He unlocked his front door and preceded us into the living room, pointing down the corridor.   "The music room's thataway. I had it sound proofed. My equipment gets loud." He showed us a library with a large screen built into one wall, and the game room, lined with electronic arcade games and stacked with toys still in their original boxes. Then he led us to the kitchen. In its center squatted a cumbersome oaken table so heavy that the previous owners, who must have assembled it on the spot, couldn't get it out the door when they were moving and decided to leave it behind.

Ariel pointed to the ceiling. "Three bedrooms upstairs, but only one is big enough to turn around in." Opening a refrigerator jam-packed with food, he asked, "What will you have? Grape juice, orange juice, or coconut water? Sorry, no sodas. I'm trying to stay away from sugar these days."

"So am I," Jimmi confessed with what looked to me like a proud grin.

Ariel put a friendly arm around him. "How about . . . honey-vanilla ice cream in grape juice, Jimmi? It's one of my favorites." He pulled off the fake glasses. "I went shopping at the co-op last night and filled two carts, wearing this disguise. Nobody looked at me twice. It was great." The cap came off next. The moment he freed his gleaming black hair it flowed over his shoulders, framing his face. He was wearing some sort of opaque makeup; without the usual lipstick his mouth was exceedingly pale.

He dropped large scoops of the frozen confection into identical tumblers and filled them with juice, creating white and purple swirls. When he handed two of the drinks to us I could see that some of the fingernails he usually taped when performing had stubbornly maintained their original color. He caught me looking and gave me an ironic smile. I returned it with one that came straight from my heart. His smile widened, giving me another glimpse of his fabulous teeth. He said, "Silvi, why don't you choose a movie for us to watch?"

"God!" Jimmi said. "She'll pick something dopey like *The Sound of Music*."

Ariel did a little dance and sang, "The hills are alive . . . " in a voice so high and pure that I wished he'd go on forever. "Great film. Unfortunately I didn't bring it. Let's take our desserts to the library with us. I packed some of my favorite music, Jimmi. You can pick out anything you want to hear."

The library was sweltering. Even Ariel had to take off his coat. He tossed it onto a chair. "Don't fall over the cartons. I didn't have a chance to unpack everything yet." *Any*thing was more like it.

Jimmi knelt by the stereo, searched through a box of CDs, and inserted his pick. The room filled with rap lyrics. Ariel clamped a headset on Jimmi's ears and Jimmi lay down on the rug and closed his eyes, looking enraptured. Ariel and I sprawled at opposite ends on the couch, his legs straight, mine tugged under, and watched *Raiders of the Lost Ark*. Soon Jimmi started glancing at the screen. A few minutes later he discarded the earphones in favor of Indiana Jones.

JIMMI and I were both sleepy when we drove away later that night. If there had been a road straight upward from Ariel's house to our cabin we would have been home in five minutes. But since there wasn't we had to go the long way around. Jimmi was quiet until we were winding up the dark highway. Then he said,

"God, that was the best birthday I had in my life. You think he did it?"

The question shocked me. How could he have any doubts after meeting Ariel in person? I answered with a question of my own. "Do you suppose for a minute I would have let you go to his house if I thought he did?"

"But everybody . . ."

"I'm not everybody. Neither are you."

It wasn't until we turned onto the county road that Jimmi mumbled, "What he pay him all that money for then? If he didn't do it?"

And I said, "Don't be friends with him if you think he's guilty. Go with your gut instincts. It's your job to decide if you can trust him or not. Nobody else's."

My instincts told me Ariel wouldn't hurt a fly and that his clear eyes and voice didn't belong to a liar.

As I unlocked our kitchen door, a battered note fluttered from the jamb. I read:

> Silvi
> Sorry you weren't home. I'll come back
> tomorrow afternoon.
> Got something interesting to tell you. Maybe
> we can go for a walk.
> See ya
> Violet

"Who's she?" Jimmi asked, reading along over my shoulder.

"A new neighbor. Moved into Ralph and Edie's cabin."

"A new *old* neighbor, you mean." He crooked his back and hobbled through the kitchen on gimpy legs to make his point. "She got any kids?"

"A baby girl."

He straightened, wrinkling his nose. "Don't bother to introduce me. I'll be upstairs doing my homework. And please tell her I'm not the baby-sitting type."

"She hasn't asked you."

"Yet." He poured himself some milk, balanced a flat of Graham crackers on its rim, and fled to his room.

I started to take off my coat and noticed that the house was ice cold. I'd been away from home too long. The dogs were sitting on their haunches behind the gate, waiting to be acknowledged and fed. The cats, rubbing against my ankles, emitted chirrups of distress. "I know you're starving," I told them. "But it's late, the fire's gone out, it's freezing in here, and I'm too tired to start grinding necks. How about some 90% lean ground sirloin, human grade? Just give me a few minutes to warm it first."

I heard Jimmi kick off his shoes. The box springs squeaked. His boombox started to spin a rap album. Sotto voce. I wondered what kind of dreams could come to a boy who had rap grinding into his ear. I dished out to the cats and threw Asa and Marvel six raw chicken necks each. Racket got one. All three dogs swallowed theirs without chewing.

I built a new fire, fed the flames kindling until they crackled with heat, added madrone, and let it burn hot while I got ready for bed. Then I damped the stove down and wished Jimmi a good night. There was no response, not even when I unplugged his extension cord. But when the reticent rapping stopped he didn't protest, which was the best indication I had that he was asleep. I clicked off the lamp, slid between my arctic sheets, pulled the covers up to my nose, and listened to a couple of nearby owls croon a melodious duet, weaving my lullaby.

IN THE morning I decided to change my entire life before I even opened my eyes.

It would start with the word *attrition*. I'd finish the jobs I had already committed to but decline future offers. Between my hoard of paintings, my greeting cards, and Dorrie's check, I could afford to take a few months off from my day job. Stay home. Paint something new. All day, every day.

Ten minutes later I was following the dogs down the forest trail, embellishing my plan. I'd pay somebody to help me set up an internet gallery. Visit downtown business establishments to ask if I could hang some of my work on their walls. Banks, maybe. Restaurants. I could feel a heavy weight lifting off me. Three months of ongoing euphoria. If I didn't sell anything on my own by . . . July? . . . I'd call it quits and pick up the pet-sitting where I left off.

I was in such a good mood, I didn't mind that Paul sat waiting for us on his porch stairs again. Without much ado, he matched our pace, carrying a plank and a coil of thick rope. The dogs seemed to take his presence for granted.

"I guess Barret didn't challenge you to a duel after all," I said. "How did it go?"

He chuckled. "He listened to reason. Admitted he'd rather have *me* for a neighbor than John Gierig. And was blatantly happy to hear that Liz has finally left me. He'll grant me right-of-way if I agree to bring in the lumber for my renovations in small loads, but he made me swear to have the road graded and graveled afterwards to smooth out the ruts."

"I don't believe it!" I said. There was nothing reasonable about Barret unless he sensed it would give him the upper hand in a bargain. "Will you need to borrow my pickup?" Good grief! Whatever made me offer my Efi? The first and only time Kosmo asked to use her I fixed him with a stare so cold he never dared mention the matter again. But I believed Paul was the kind of guy who would not only return her unscathed but would top off the tank even if he'd only used up a fraction of my gasoline.

Maybe he could detect a tone of lingering trepidation in my voice, for he said, "I guess I'd better buy a good used truck of my own. Where'd you get yours?"

"Out of the Nickel. How about a trade? You help me with the internet gallery and I'll help you bring in a load of lumber, just to get you started." It seemed a reasonable bargain; I had no idea how much work it was to set up a website.

"Deal," he said. "We'll design it together—but today we're putting up this here swing." He shook the coil of rope at me.

"At the madrones?"

"Indeed. If all goes well I'll let you have the first turn."

With a jolt of pure joy I said, "Now you're talking!"

Once we got to the trees it took us a while to measure the ropes so that the swing would hang straight. And then I discovered the one thing even better than watching a spectacular sunrise: swinging toward gilded clouds from the top of a peak.

VIOLET showed up just as I was leaving to fetch Jimmi from the bus stop, so I stayed home. He'd have to walk up. The weather was fair and a little exercise before lounging on his bed for the rest of the day could only be good. The weasly little bully was no longer on the school bus. Rumor had it his parents had transferred him to the Waldorf school hoping the staff there could straighten him out.

Violet carried a cinnamon topped coffee cake into the kitchen, limping because Lavender was clutching onto one of her legs. Taking one look at the enthusiastic dogs greeting them from the other side of the barrier, she said, "Could we stay in here? I think Lavender wants to play with your kitties today."

Lavender let go of the leg and crammed four fingers in her mouth, staring at tiger-striped Max. He was the first cat bold enough to approach her. Pointing to him with a tiny, spit moistened finger, she squealed, "Kee-ee ca!" Then she knelt down beside him, timidly patting the top of his head. He flattened his ears but decided to stay.

I pulled out a dinette chair for Violet. "Why didn't I hear you drive up? You must have a quiet engine."

"I wish." She put the cake on the table. "I parked over at Barret's. He said I wouldn't make it back this far in Clyde's puny truck."

"Yeah. This section of road stays lousy till June." What the heck had she been doing at Barret's *this* time? Luckily, she decided to fill me in while I brewed our tea.

Making herself comfortable on the chair, she said, "I haven't seen you since we were at the Standing Stone. Clyde and I left soon after you did." She laughed, tossing her hair back. "Halfway up the highway we had a fight about who was paying too much attention to who, and before I knew it he got so mad he stopped the truck and ordered me to get out. He took off peeling rubber and left me standing in the dark. I started walking toward home, hoping he'd come back for me once he calmed down."

I poured. She picked up a spoon, squirted it full of honey, and stirred it around in her cup, saying, "But then Barret came along and offered me a ride. To his house. Girl, how that man talks! We didn't get to sleep till four in the morning. Your new neighbor knocked on the door early and woke us up. Randy, Barret called him."

"Where was Lavender all that time?"

She batted her lashes. Without mascara they were as flaxen as her hair. "At home with Clyde, of course." She squeezed more honey onto her spoon and flicking her tongue over it. "Asleep in her crib. As it turns out, he *did* come back for me, after all. And couldn't find me. Wondering what happened to me kept him awake for the rest of the night. Served him right too." Her wide-spaced eyes looked like pale blue glass marbles. "I went home right after breakfast. But when this Randy guy came I was still at Barret's, upstairs, in his bed. Don't look at me like that."

"Like what?" I pulled a knife out of the utility drawer and concentrated on scoring the coffee cake.

She gave a demure giggle. "He slept on the couch. Downstairs. Honest. But anyways, the trapdoor was open so I heard every word those two were yelling at each other."

Calmly I cut the cake into squares and put the first one on her dessert plate.

"Okay," she said, picking a glob of caramelized sugar off the top and pushing it into her mouth. "To be fair, it was only Barret who yelled. And Randy shut him up fast enough once he mentioned that the surveyor found out that your cabin is actually on the wrong side of the boundary line. Randy said that bit of news could stay between Barret and him as long as he got his right-of-way. So don't tell Barret I told you, all right? He forgot the trapdoor was open and assumed I had slept through the racket they made. And I didn't correct him. Anyway, I just thought you should know about the boundary line. Us renters have to stick together, don't you think?"

"You mean to say Barret's been collecting rent from me for twenty years under false pretenses?" I said, a whirlwind of conflicting emotions racing through me. Good God, by rights I should have been under Mittendrin's thumb all this time. Without any right-of-way whatsoever. Good thing Todd never realized. "And did Randy offer some proof?"

"The surveyor's written report. I could hear the papers rattling. I didn't get a look at him, though. For obvious reasons. Is he nice? He's getting divorced."

Thus was gossip born. "Could be," I said shortly. "I don't know much about him. No—not true. I know *nothing* about him."

"But you've seen him, haven't you? He said he's seen *you*."

"Briefly," I said.

"Good-looking?"

"Not my type."

"Mine?"

"That depends on whether you think Clyde's handsome."

"I don't. I used to think he was nice, though. Not anymore." She lifted the cup to her lips. It clattered when she returned it to the saucer. "So. How about you and me going for a little walk? You could show me where Randy lives. We could say hi."

"He's not there." I took a sip of my tea. It was bitter. I added some honey and said, "His cabin is uninhabitable. I'm sure you'll run into him sooner or later though. Maybe at Barret's now that they're friends."

"I wouldn't exactly say they're *friends*." Violet giggled again. "I don't know what Randy ever did to him, mind you, but Barret's voice was still frosty when Randy left. I didn't come downstairs till half an hour later. By then Barret was all smiles. Men!"

Lavender was sitting on the floor surrounded by cats of every hue and pattern, lining up to be petted. She was purring right along with them. All but Max scattered when Jimmi stomped in. "You promised to pick me up at the bus stop!" he complained, looking sweaty. This from a boy who had chastised me for doing just that a week ago.

"Sorry," I said, unmoved. "It didn't work out today. Want some of this coffee cake Violet made? It's delicious." I introduced them and put a square on a plate for him. He poured his own milk and sat between us, eating with growing enjoyment.

She gave him a friendly smile before turning back to me. "Seems Clyde and I've got a new neighbor too. On the other side of the barbed wire fence. Some rich guy bought the three hundred acres Zora was interested in. I hear he paid up front. I'm figuring on walking over there with a nice chocolate cake just to make him feel welcome and all."

Jimmi swallowed his bite, washed it down with milk, and said, "I don't think that's a good idea, actually. One of the boys in my class told me the old guy put No Trespassing signs all along the barbed wire fence and sits in his house with a rifle, ready to shoot at anything that moves. Some nut, huh? My friend said the guy shot at his dog. Almost hit him, too. This tastes good. Can I have seconds?"

He had decided.

Violet cut him two more pieces. He thanked her politely and skirted around Lavender on his way to the landing. The little girl was hugging Max as hard as she could, making the tomcat sigh like a deflating balloon. I could hear Jimmi fastening the hook on the inside of his new door. Decisively. Maybe he was afraid Lavender would squeeze him next.

"More tea?" I asked, refilling Violet's cup. "So—did you and Clyde make up yet? Did he tell you he's sorry?"

"Sort of." She measured out another spoonful of honey. "But I can see the handwriting on the wall. And it's not pretty, considering that I don't even own a car. Thank God for Barret. Remember him saying he'll take me anywhere, anytime? Wasn't that sweet?" From the look in her eyes, I could tell she expected the rides on offer would not be entirely free.

CHAPTER 17

THAT NIGHT I HAD TO KEEP REMINDING myself that eight hours of sleep were unnecessary for an adult and that lying awake on an increasingly uncomfortable mattress was almost as good. It was my insecure rental status that kept me tossing from side to side. These days, the difference between having a home and being homeless was incredibly slight. In the morning I was so drowsy that I was already halfway to Paul's place before I realized he'd probably be sitting on his stairs again, waiting. Only, as of yesterday, our relationship had changed.

All of a sudden I had two landlords to be leery of when one had been more than enough. Even if Paul kept allowing Barret to play the role—and thus continue collecting the rent—sooner or later their shaky truce would unravel and I would be a pawn between them. The mouse in their cat-game, getting torn to shreds. My best option was to stay away from them both, following the advice of the ancient proverb, *Out of sight, out of mind.* And heed both of my iron-clad rules.

Thus, I did a quick pivot and took the path past my outhouse up to Strawberry Hill. My skin prickled as we labored toward the crest, knowing here too I was no longer safe. Sure enough, as soon as we reached even ground I heard a cacophony of hammering, shouting, and the distant drone of a backhoe. Right then I welcomed the commotion. It would keep Gierig from becoming aware that we were breeching his inhospitable territory again.

I leashed Marvel, afraid she might rediscover the skunk. A few steps later I received a rude shock. The skid that had been crowded with vigorous young trees and bushes was gone. Erased. In its place was a raw gash running downhill. Along its sides lay heaps of small conifers, rose bushes, and deer brush, all uprooted, smashed, and dying. Native bunchgrass, wild strawberry vines and flowers, all flattened by something big, were already dead. Freshly turned earth began to stick to the soles of my shoes almost at once.

Where the gash leveled and curved, crossing the skid that came up from Paul's place, I saw that the destruction was continuing along the ridge trail for another five hundred yards or so. There, the bulldozer that had been cutting the swath was now busily annihilating my favorite patch of shooting stars. Then the big blade rose and broke a living oak into splintering pieces.

Unnerved by the machine, Racket fled down Paul's skid. I followed, hoping he would bypass the abandoned cabin without alerting Paul. I kept Marvel leashed, but Asa, who was not, forged ahead—down to the bottom of the skid, around the bend, straight up the porch, and to the back door, where he loudly asked for his favorite handout.

"What kept you?" a freshly shaven Paul asked after trailing him back to the stairs. He was wearing a tool belt over his old jeans and holding a crow bar.

"Please don't let us disturb you," I said in a formal tone. "We're just on our way home." And then I leashed Asa, too, and started walking away.

"Wait," he called after me. I stopped and turned reluctantly back toward him. "About your kind offer," he said, matching my tone. "I've made a list of the lumber I'll need right away. Would it be possible for us to bring it up here today? I want to get started on the repairs."

I only had a couple of jobs, both in the morning, but I had planned to spend the afternoon canvassing some banks about hanging my paintings. "Sure," I said politely, mentally crossing off several entries on my errand-list. "It'll have to be before three thirty, though. That's when I'm picking Jimmi up from school on my way out of town."

"How about a quarter to three? I'll make sure all the paperwork's done by then so all we have to do is load—"\

"That will be fine. Sorry, but I have to catch up to Racket. He got spooked by the bulldozer Gierig's sicced on the ridge." I hurried on, but even though I pondered my conundrum all the way home, I still didn't know how I ought to feel about the man who had gone from long-ago ridge legend to recent art patron to possible backhoe operator to leather jacketed stranger to supposed surveyor to new neighbor to secret landlord all in one week.

Tiny Racket was waiting for us on our porch, quaking with fright. I knew just how he felt. All his life he'd been able to count on the stability of our mountain. But now something different was intruding into our idyll every day. I didn't like it any better than he did.

"WHEN are you going to stop treating me like a kindergartner?" Jimmi asked on our drive into town, frowning at the organic whole wheat sandwich I'd put in his lunch box. "All the other kids get to eat cafeteria food."

"Huh!" I said. "Don't hold your breath. I've seen their menus."

"Nobody in the entire school eats this kind of bread. You might as well hang a sign around my neck that says, *This moron is being raised by a hippie chick who lives in the boonies.* It's not fair. All my friends live in Ashland. Our house is too far away for me to invite them over for a quick game of basketball. And for weekend visits."

I didn't much like the category he'd assigned me, but I let it pass. "What about Peter? His mom didn't mind driving you up here after your sleepover, did she?"

"Are you kidding? I told her let me out down on the county road, in front of one of those flashy new houses. I actually started walking up to the front door as if I really lived there, for as long as I could feel her eyes following me. I didn't backtrack until I was sure she was gone."

"Oh-ho!" I said. "So that's how it is." He was acutely ashamed of our cabin. And me. And probably of Efi, too.

"If she and Peter had seen our dungeon, I'd be the laughingstock," he confirmed. "Seriously, Silvi—" Recently, he'd discarded the term "Mom," reminding me that we weren't even related. I still missed hearing him say it. "—Wouldn't it be cool if we could be like everyone else for a change?" He clasped his hands as if in prayer and proclaimed, "I want to live close enough to bike to school. Or skateboard. Walk, even. There's this one girl in my class who lives right on the corner. All she has to do is cross the street. Funny thing is, she's always late. Go figure."

Today, I found the idea of moving away from the calamity overtaking the mountain somewhat appealing. Surely there must be a ramshackle cottage for rent somewhere near his school. With a securely fenced backyard, near some traffic-free path on which I could walk the dogs. But off leash? Never. Ashland had a strict leash law. And the rents in town were easily more than double of what I paid on the ridge. I knew I would lose the best part of myself with such a move. How could I live away from the mountain forest? "It would only work if I could *buy* a house," I explained. "On the outskirts. Next to some pastureland, maybe. Who in the middle of town will rent even the most miserable rat hole to someone with two and a half dogs and a colony of cats?"

He glared. "You have too many—"

"Yeah, yeah," I said irritably, taking a quick swig of my peppermint tea before we came to the next curve, which would definitely require two firm hands on the wheel. "That's not about to change anytime soon, is it? Am I allowed to pick you up in front of your school in the afternoon? Or shall we meet in the back alley so that none of your classmates will see you get into this beat up old pickup and sit beside a woman who's wearing no makeup and puts her hair in a braid?"

"You could cut it short," he suggested. And hastened to add, lest I get the wrong idea, "By a real hair-dresser, I mean. In a beauty shop. You know. Like all the other moms."

In a roundabout way, he had actually called me "Mom." I was prepared to ignore everything else he'd said as long as I could keep that one word. "I am who I am," I told him. It was a great mantra. "I tell you what, meet me on the sidewalk next to the parking lot. Your frieds won't notice me there. I might be a few minutes late. Our new neighbor needs me to haul some lumber for him."

"Who? Ariel?"

"Paul."

"Who's Paul? Where's *he* live?"

"Ah," I said. "The guy we saw walking down to Barret's. The one who knows Dorrie. If you were still going on our morning hikes with us instead of sleeping in you've have met him by now. He moved into the abandoned cabin."

"Gross! Another hippie!" He swallowed. "Funny, he didn't look it. Is he married?"

"Divorced," I amended. "He wants to buy a nice used Toyota four wheel drive pickup. If you see one with a for sale sign in the window, give me the phone number. Or go on over to Paul's place and tell him yourself."

He dropped his lunch box into the extra-cab and rolled down his window. "He got any kids?"

"Two girls. On the east coast somewhere."

"How old?"

"I didn't ask." Too wrapped up in my own problems. I did some quick mental arithmetic. "Probably your age, more or less. Why?"

He gave a painstakingly neutral shrug. "In case. Won't they have to come stay with him in the summer? Poor things. Boys would have been better."

"Maybe," I said, barely suppressing a grin. "Maybe not. From what I hear these girls have a beautiful mother. Paul's not too ugly, himself. You might be pleasantly surprised."

"I doubt it." He gazed up at the sky. "Those look like storm clouds to you?" He stuck out his hand, testing for drops. "God, I'm tired of this soggy weather!"

It was hard for me to remember what a cheerful child he had been up until two years ago.

I SPENT the first couple of hours in the cat sanctuary, feeding the hordes, cleaning cat litter out of clogged trays, smeary poop off the floors, and gooey urine from the bathroom counters. Then I ferried two arthritis-crippled mutts to the dog park, wishing I could have brought my own dogs instead. All these seniors wanted was to lie on the grass and watch everyone else walk around.

After I sanitized my hands, brushed my hair, and scraped dog park residue off my shoes, I tried to get my bank to let me hang a couple of paintings, but perhaps there wasn't enough cash in my account for them to take my proposition seriously. The rest of the downtown banks weren't interested, either. And the galleries were swamped with the work of other fledgling artists. The only one vaguely encouraging was too far from the center of town to do me any good. The tourists liked to confine their meanderings to Main Street. By one o'clock I was ready to quit, remembering a home-truth van Gogh had realized long before me—it's much more fun painting pictures than trying to sell them.

On a silly impulse I parked in front of the fabric store and tried my spiel on the owner, Mrs. Sweeney. Her white hair had the same faintly pink cast as her powdered face, and she smelled of perfumed hair spray, but she had a sweet smile. She suggested I bring in a few of my pieces. If she liked them, she would be glad to display them on the long walls above the store shelves. It was an offer I could not afford to turn down.

Heartened by my success, I went to the library for some new reading material and wandered through the stacks, hoping one of the shelved volumes would speak to me. The one that finally did was in the one-hundred section. Its spine literally stuck out of the shelf it sat on. Strangely enough, it was about witchcraft. Leafing through, I discovered it was a hands-on instruction manual complete with rituals and chants promising me greater control over my own life. There was a chapter on how to attract fame and fortune. Another on attracting your soul mate. Having neither, I borrowed the book so I could begin to improve my destiny while I was eating a late lunch.

The co-op's parking lot smelled of spit-roasting chicken and baked bread. I checked out the groceries first and stuck them into Efi's extra-cab. Then I bought my meal. It consisted of chicken noodle soup, a biscuit, a packet of cranberry-coconut cookies, and a Mate. I chose my favorite window table in the snack area, the one with the bench running along one of its sides. I liked sitting on it because it was varnished mirror-smooth and it was fun running my hands over the gloss. Once seated, I put the biscuit on the soup lid so it could get warm. Then I made a discreet book cover from a discarded section of newspaper and began nibbling on my cookies, sipping my tea, and browsing my ludicrous library find.

Outside, the sky was getting rapidly darker. A sudden gust bent the small trees edging the parking lot. The clouds broke just as a lone shopper jogged down the walkway toward the entrance. Wearing a hooded navy blue sweatshirt over equally shabby sweat pants, he glanced in at me as he darted past the windows and gave a tentative wave. I had no idea who he was.

Behind me, chairs scraped. A couple of tables were dragged to and fro. When I looked up from my book I saw a committee of Happy Campers sitting with their heads close together. Males and females alike had those dingy dreadlocks that always got me thinking—guiltily— about parasites, scissors, and a pesticide laden shampoo.

One of them was Kosmo, dressed in an army surplus camouflage outfit. I didn't recognize him until he gave me a nod, detached himself from the anemic girl at his elbow, and came to stand at my table. Black medusa ropes coiled over his shoulders.

"You want that soda I promised you?" I asked, rising.

He gestured me down again and said, low voiced, "Not today. We're having a tree-sitters' strategy meeting. Heading for that grove of old growths I was telling you about. BLM's planning to have them cut down tomorrow. Want to come?"

I put the book on my lap under the table. "Thanks but no thanks. I have domestic obligations."

He helped himself to a cookie. "Excuse noted. About the favor I owe Stu—it just so happens I've got a friend who has a friend who knows someone at Shakespeare who thinks he can get Stu a teensy part as understudy for a couple of bit roles. You never know who'll break a leg around here."

"Hopefully not you," I said while he wrote a phone number on a corner of my napkin. "As long as you don't fall out of your tree." He tore off the corner and presented it to me with a flourish. I stuck it in my shirt pocket. "Do you tie yourself to the branches before falling asleep?"

"Funny you should ask. The question's on our agenda." He glanced at the colorless girl who was openly staring at us. She looked away. He smiled like someone who is aware of risks lying ahead but is determined to plough on anyway. "The next time you see me will be in the newspaper, under 'arrests.' Don't bother bailing me out of jail, though. We're planning to clog the system."

"I wish you the best," I said sincerely. I had great respect for anyone who followed the path of civil disobedience so I wouldn't have to. "Hey, guess what John Gierig is doing to the ridge. You guys should—"

"Sorry," he said, already moving away to rejoin his comrades. "After years of smoking homegrown grass I can only handle one problem at a time."

I liked the honest assessment of his diminished mental capacities. Pulling the book out of hiding, I opened it at random and found myself reading the directions for one of the spells. It had to be performed while kneeling on the floor, sitting on one's heels, in the nude, flanked by color-coordinated wax candles and matching incense. The latter must be tossed over one's shoulder at the end of each stanza. If everything was done properly the chant was guaranteed to attract the perfect mate. Skimming the rest of the chapters, I saw that each category of spell required a different color of incense and candles. I scribbled the ingredients on what was left of the napkin.

Outside, two squealing women were running through the rain, holding their purses on top of their heads. One of them was petite and wore a stylish, light-weight coat. The other woman, though not much taller, was well rounded and wore a cobalt blue muumuu. I snapped the book shut, slipped it into my bag, and knocked on my window when they were near enough to notice. They rushed into the store and soon stood dripping before me, bringing with them fresh misty-cold air.

"What kind of soup you got there?" Zora asked, dabbing a wad of tissues over her drenched but still frizzy curls. "Chunky chicken noodle? Point me to the pot!"

While she and Grace loaded their trays I bolted the rest of my cookies, afraid they'd make me share. But when Zora came back with her tray I saw it was not only loaded with soup, mashed potatoes and gravy, a roast chicken drumstick and thigh, cornbread, coffee and an oversized chocolaty muffin, but also with her own packet of cranberry-coconut cookies. She pulled the soaked muumuu away from her skin before settling across from me. Grace had bought a small salad and a crusty roll. She slipped off her wet coat, exposing a still dry, conservatively cut beige dress. She was wearing sheer nylons.

"I don't know," she sighed, sitting with her back to the room, buttering her roll. "I've left my resume at every hospital in the valley. They're all swamped with applications. It doesn't look like anything's going to come through anytime soon. Zora made an appointment with a psychic for this afternoon hoping to find out how Barret figures into her near future. She wants me to get a reading, too. Maybe I will. I could use some divine guidance right about now."

Zora pounced on her mashed potatoes first. There was something endearing about her unabashed appetite. She actually ran a finger over the rim of her plate to get every last drop of the gravy. Then she looked directly at me. "What's up with Violet? Every time I'm anywhere near Stu's front window, she's either driving down or up Barret's driveway. In Clyde's truck. How come he lets her? More to the point, how come *Barret* lets her?"

I wasn't about to get in the middle of that discussion, particularly since Violet herself was just then hurrying toward the entrance. "Don't ask me. Ask her. Here she is." I rapped on the window and Violet pressed her nose against the outside of the glass in response, crossing her eyes. She came to join us with a slice of poppy-seed cake and a cup of black coffee, taking the chair next to Zora. "Hello stranger," she said to her. "Did you move to your new place yet?"

Zora savored a bite of her muffin before she said, "They're still working on it."

"When can I see it?" Violet asked. "Are you going to have a house warming party?" When Zora merely shrugged, Violet addressed Grace. "Poor girl!" she said. "Your little place must be so congested with a guest and all. How can you stand it?"

"I can stand it better with Zora than without her," Grace replied shortly.

Violet gave an exaggerated sigh. "Lavender's been whining since she woke up in the morning. And all Clyde wants to do today is listen to jazz and smoke weed. I was feeling so stir crazy by the time we ate lunch that I put Lavender down for a nap right after she finished eating and took off. We do need some groceries. What's up with you guys? Or am I interrupting a ridge-only conversation?"

"Not at all," I assured her. "We're just having the usual rainy day gathering. The co-op always gets crowded in bad weather." True enough, every table was now fully occupied, and the drone of voices and low laughter managed to drown out the ceaseless overhead drumming. "But rain or shine, I've never come here without meeting at least a couple of people I know."

"You know him?" Zora said, indicating the guy with the hooded navy sweat jacket. He was standing by the coffee machines now, looking our way. When he saw we had noticed, he beckoned to me shyly. It was that gesture that helped me recognize him, even before I got close enough for a good look at his eyes.

"I just finished my new song," Ariel murmured, drawing himself a three-quarter cup of maté. "Now I'm in the mood for some goodies. A bachelor can never have too many snacks in the house.

How about you and Jimmi coming down for supper? Help me eat some of these." He gestured at the stack of fancy organic vegetarian TV dinners in his cart. "It's no fun eating alone."

"I wish I could," I said with genuine regret. "But I promised to help somebody haul lumber this afternoon."

He added a long string of agave to his cup and topped it off with half-and-half. "And Jimmi?" he asked, giving the drink a good stir.

I'd been wondering about Jimmi myself. He was always crabby after school, and he hated the rain. It did make living inside a forest seem almost funereal. "He'll be delighted. You want to pick him up on your way out of town?" I looked at my watch and at Ariel's half loaded cart. "You'll have to bring him home by nine, though. Tomorrow's a school day."

"No problem," he said with a glad smile.

"And he can't listen to music or watch a movie until he's done with his homework."

"I promise."

"Go finish your shopping. And do me a favor." I gave him my napkin-list of secret ingredients, hoping he wouldn't guess I was planning a session of white magic. In my mind's eye, I was already sitting in my darkened living room, chanting to draw in my soul mate. Alone in the house! Till nine! I held out a twenty dollar bill. "Tell the cashier to ring up my stuff separately. I'll pilot you to the middle school and find Jimmi for you."

Glancing at my table, I found three pairs of intensely interested eyes focused on us. "As soon as I see you heading for your car, I'll come out and start my truck." I shook a warning finger at Ariel. "Nine o'clock sharp." Today, his face was several shades darker than it had been last time we met. He'd even covered over his eyebrows with tan make-up. But he'd forgotten to include his hands. In addition, one of his sock was yellow, the other was blue. "Great outfit," I said. "You look like a bum."

He grinned, taking the twenty. "One of my better efforts. But a drag to put on when I'm in a hurry. And I have to be careful that my voice doesn't give me away."

Or his white hands, or the luminous sparkle in those undisguisable eyes.

When I got back to the others, Violet asked, a bit too offhandedly, "A friend of yours?"

"Sort of." Now I was sorry she was sitting with us. Paul would be here any minute. And she was dying to meet him.

CHAPTER   18

PAUL RANDOLPH, AKA RANDY, ARRIVED a few minutes later, wearing his macho jacket, beaded with rain, and a tight, washed-out pair of jeans. From the way Violet's eyes widened when I introduced him I could tell she thought he looked startlingly good. Unlike me, she responded to his pheromones—by sending out her own. I could actually feel them slamming into his tall, rangy frame. He took a half step back in response. Then he reached for Zora's hand, and Grace's, lingering a tad over Violet's. Mine, he didn't bother to shake at all.

"I paid for everything, Silvi. It's all in a pile and ready to go whenever you are," he said matter-of-factly, sitting on the bench beside me, so close his thigh was brushing mine.

Violet scooted her chair toward him. "Ready for what?"

I explained the arrangement.

"Hey," she said, digging in her purse for her keys. "Why don't we load it all onto my truck, Paul? I was just about to drive home."

"Weren't you going to do some shopping first?" I said, taken aback.

"Shopping?" she repeated, as if the word was foreign to her. "Heck no. I'm done." She snatched her coffee and rose.

But Paul remained seated, his thigh now solid against mine. "Does your truck have four wheel drive?"

"No, it does not," I answered for her. "Or a canopy either."

He shook his head with regret. "Then I'm sorry to say I'll have to decline. It's a sure bet our clay road is the consistency of peanut butter by now. And I've just bought four rolls of fiberglass insulation I don't want to get wet."

Violet nibbled her angelic bottom lip. "But in this rain she'll want to pick up Jimmi, and her truck's only got two bucket seats. Where are *you* going to sit?"

"Duh!" Zora said, breaking into her cellophane-wrapped cookies. "In his car, I assume. Tailgating Silvi's pickup."

I liked her wit. "You can help Paul haul his *next* load, Violet," I said in a placating tone. "Providing he won't need it before June. Besides, Jimmi's going home with a friend today."

She couldn't quite hide her disappointment as she plunked back onto her chair. Through the glass behind her I saw Ariel exiting the store, carrying two stuffed-to-the-brim paper grocery bags. With any luck he'd get them to his Chevy before they disintegrated. I grabbed my canvas satchel and maneuvered past Paul's knees. "I've got to go on a last minute errand. Paul, you want to wait here till I come back or ride with me?"

He rose so fast his knee caps bumped mine. "It was nice meeting you all," he said, "Zora. Grace. Violet—I'll see you again."

I thought he lingered over the final name.

"You bet," Violet said.

I offered her a neighborly smile. "Tell Clyde I said hi!"

Zora snorted and choked on cookie crumbs. Nurse Grace whacked her in between the shoulder blades until she stopped coughing.

On my way to Efi, with Paul ducking through the rain beside me, I wondered what I'd been so huffy about. It wasn't as if I was seriously interested in him, or he in me. Somehow Violet's presence had temporarily changed the chemistry between us. Or rather, her pheromones had. I pulled out, watching in my rear-view mirror as Ariel's rust-colored Chevy lined up behind me.

"Was your wife very blonde?" I asked Paul on our way to Jimmi's school.

"Was and is."

I wanted to say, *As blonde as Violet?* What I actually said was, "That's one thing Barret and you have in common. You're both fatally attracted to blondes."

"Is and was," he replied, a enigmatic smile playing around his lips.

Jimmi wasn't actually waiting for us on the sidewalk out in the rain. But I hadn't idled Efi long before he came running from the direction of the bicycle shed, which had a metal roof. It wasn't until he tore open the passenger door that he realized someone was sitting in his seat. He looked quite taken aback.

Paul offered him a friendly smile. "Hi, Jimmi. I'm your new neighbor. Glad to finally meet you."

"Yeah, right," Jimmi said, sounding dazed. "Where am *I* supposed to sit?"

"You're going to Ari's for dinner," I explained. "Got any homework?"

"Algebra."

"Well, hopefully he'll be better at helping you with it than I usually am." Putting up the hood of my coat, I led him to where Ariel was waiting in the idling Chevy, its windshield wipers squeaking loudly as they slouched back and forth. I held Jimmi's pack while he got in. "Finish your assignments before you do anything else. And be home by nine. Do you think you can guide Ari to our house in the dark?"

Jimmi's eyes shone. "Blindfolded!"

"Hey, Jimmi," Ariel said, digging around in his grocery sack. "Boy, am I glad you're coming over. I'm not used to all this gloomy rain yet. Though I can see that it's good for the trees and all." He passed me a small bag containing my witchcraft paraphernalia. "I slipped in your change. And one of the TV dinners I bought—I hope you like organic enchiladas."

"Thanks! I love them. Drive carefully," I said, waving them on.

If I'd thought things through I might have realized that the Chevy had rear wheel drive and that the clay would be no less slippery on Ariel's road than on mine.

BY THE time Paul and I finished loading his supplies, thick clouds and fog were dimming the afternoon toward a premature evening. We had to scrounge a length of string from the lumber yard office to tie down the canopy hatch. Then I dropped him off at the co-op so he could follow me in his rental car. It was still raining, and noticeably darker, when we arrived on the ridge. While he parked in Stu's lot, I set the locknuts and shifted Efi into low drive. He climbed in beside me and then we moved ahead at an excruciatingly low speed, the headlights stabbing into the dense fog swirling around us.

I stopped at the section of dog fence that stretched from my driveway to the house. Paul unlatched the passenger door. I realized the polite thing would be to offer him tea, but I had no desire to play hostess tonight, especially without my usual built-in boy chaperone. "No point in making you walk home in this weather," I said, rummaging for my groceries and backing out. "Not when the truck's full of your stuff, anyway. So—I'm willing to let you take it to your place, just this once. Can you unload everything first thing in the morning and bring it back by seven?"

He opened his mouth and shut it again. Then he said, "Yeah, sure," sounding puzzled. "I can do that. Thanks."

He took my place, adjusting the seat to give himself additional leg room. I watched him start off to make sure he wasn't going to grind my gears. But I got wet so rapidly that I dashed to the house before the tail lights could dissolve into mist.

MY EVENING of being home alone was . . . enchanting. I ate Ariel's enchiladas, measured out ground necks for the cats, and threw the dogs a meaty bone each. Then I stoked up the stove and peeled off my clothes. After positioning my two contently gnawing canine familiars on either end of the coffee table, I turned off the light, knelt on the floor, sat back on my heels, lit two green candles, and started the first ritual. Tossing green incense power over my naked shoulder, I intoned, "Oh great and mighty Jupiter, your treasures I do seek . . ."

Once I'd sufficiently addressed fame and fortune I switched to blue candles and blue incense to focus on bodily health, outrageous beauty, and eternal youthfulness. Unimpressed, Marvel and Asa finished crunching their bones, stretched out flat on the floor, and proceeded to nap. Racket jumped onto Asa's easy chair, curled into a ball, and dropped his little bone between his refined paws, guarding it first with one eye, then the other. By the time I set up for the evening's highlight—red candles and red incense powder—both of his eyes had remained shut for some time.

The love spells were simple but catchy. According to the instructions, the trick was to emote while saying the chants. With great feeling, I whispered my way through the whole chapter of them. I was just starting on the last one when there was a vigorous knock on the living room door. Shocked, I wondered why the dogs had not sounded the alarm. Then I realized that I was clearly visible through the uncurtained window facing the porch. I dowsed the candles and felt my way through the dark, calling, "Who is it?"

"It's Paul," he replied. "Are you all right?"

The dogs had come up behind me, their cold noses stabbing the sensitive skin behind my knees. They whined a soft welcome as I opened the door just wide enough to stick my face through the crack I'd created. "Why wouldn't I be?" I said in none to friendly a tone.

He was breathing hard, as if he'd been running. "I thought I heard you calling my name. Like you needed me."

"I don't." I narrowed the crack, keeping a firm grip on the door handle. Dark or no dark, being naked that close to a man I didn't really know made me feel vulnerable.

"I distinctly heard—"

"You ran all the way over here in the rain just to ask me that question?"

"Well—actually, I thought we could—"

"I'm too busy to chat. Go home. Sorry about the false alarm. See you in the morning." I shut the door in his face, locked it, and stood by the big picture window, facing the road and hugging a blanket to my chest until I saw his blurred shape streak back the way he had come. I could almost feel sorry for him, stepping into his unheated cabin dripping wet, climbing up to his loft and crawling into a clammy sleeping bag. Probably it wasn't me he was after but the warmth of a fire, a comfortable place to sit near a lamp. Hoping to share a soft bed?

"Think again, Paul," I muttered. "I'm not a charitable institution." Then I returned to my make-shift altar, relit my candles, and tried to recapture the mood he had interrupted.

Repeating the whole love ritual from the beginning, I reached for ever deeper emotions with each rhyming phrase. This time I managed to finish the first stanza of the last chant before I was interrupted again. By the telephone.

It was Ariel. "Hi, Silvi, " he said. "I'm so sorry. We started out to your house but the Chevy got stuck in the mud."

"You're kidding! How far did you get?"

"We didn't make it past the first puddle. And the more I pushed on the gas pedal, the deeper the tires sank into the muck. I'm not the world's best driver. Can you come down and get Jimmi? You better bring some dry clothes. And shoes. He got soaked trying to help me get the car out."

"Why did you have to buy a Chevy, anyway?" I said ungraciously.

"I thought it would be a good disguise," he said with a timid giggle. "Nobody looks at a beat up old Chevy twice, you know? Or the guy sitting inside it."

"Wrong. How many old Chevys have you seen around Ashland? This is Subaru country. I know a place where you get a nice used one with all-wheel drive." I cleared my throat, trying to soften my voice. "I don't have my truck right now, Ariel. I let my neighbor keep it for the night. It's still full of his building material."

"So we're stranded?" The wire crackled while he thought it over. Then he said, "What do you want me to do? Call a taxi?"

"Do you think the driver could find your God-forsaken farmhouse in the dark?"

"Never."

With a sigh, I said, "I guess Jimmi will have to spend the night. If it's all right with you. I'll come for him around seven thirty. Do you have a spare bed?"

"In the guest bedroom."

"Let me talk to him for a minute."

When Jimmi came on the line I gave him strict instructions to finger-brush his teeth, go to his room, and be ready for me first thing in the morning. "With any luck I'll get you to school before the first bell rings."

"Oh, great!" he said.

I had no idea if he was being facetious. I asked, "Did you have fun?"

"Ariel turned the music real loud and we danced. He showed me some new moves. And he wants me to—Oh. Never mind. I'll tell you tomorrow. Good night."

"Happy dreams. Call me if you need me. Promise?"

There was a pause. Then he said, "Sure. But I won't, you know."

"I know. See you soon."

Was I worried?

Only about getting him to school on time.

CHAPTER 19

A<small>N</small> <small>INSISTENT</small> <small>POUNDING</small> <small>WOKE</small> <small>ME</small> <small>FROM</small> <small>DEEP</small> sleep. This time, the dogs did decide to sound the alarm. Unable to pry my eyes open, I just lay there, hoping the din would go away, but then Paul added his voice to the mix.

"Silvi!" he was shouting from the porch. "Emergency! Open up!"

Mouthing bitter curses, I felt my way to my clothes, slipped them on, and unlatched the door. He pulled it wide and burst into the room, wet and disheveled. The dogs did nothing to stop him. "There's a river gushing down the logging skid," Paul gasped, struggling to breathe. "It's washing out my piers. You got a decent flashlight and shovels?"

Even though my tongue would not yet obey me, my hands found a lantern and rain gear. I shut the dogs in and led Paul to the shovels in back of the wood shed. "Is my truck floating away on the current?" I asked while we were jogging toward the disaster.

He tried to laugh. "Not quite yet."

When we arrived at his cabin I could see there was nothing to laugh about. Although Efi was reasonably safe, the nearby path was covered with gurgling dark water. "It's that damn Gierig!" I said. "Did you go check out the ridge yesterday? Did you see what he's done?"

"Not yet, but I'm about to," he said, forging upstream.

Our skid had been swallowed by turbulence. It was sweeping away rotting debris along with every bit of humus and the subsoil underneath. We had to fight our way uphill through the thicket of conifers and brambles crowding the path's sides. I could hear a loud roaring from the direction of the draw.

Once we gained the top, I saw water pouring down the newly created gash. But instead of flowing around the curve the backhoe had made, it was taking the path of lesser resistance: our skid. Essentially, what Gierig's equipment operator had done was dig a riverbed without thinking of the consequences to anyone living below the next time it rained.

Paul shone his light over the turbid crossing, shouting, "We've got to make a dam right here or else my place is going to slide off its moorings. It'll take some hard shoveling with all this water. You ready?"

We positioned our flashlights on a stump, pointing them in our general direction. Then we dragged the heaviest deadwood we could find across the current and began to dig and trench alongside the pieces.

"Gierig's so flipping stupid," I shouted after a while. "He knows squat about this terrain!" He didn't even notice that the upper skid was sitting on top of underground springs. That's why the vegetation stayed green even during hot spells. And now that his lackey had ripped out the trees and scraped away the roots that were holding the soil together, we were the ones who would have to pay for their careless mistake. That new road they were building would flood every time it rained. I stopped shoveling to arch my spine, saw that Paul was farther along with his part of the ditch than I was with mine, and resumed digging.

He adjusted the aim of the flashlight beams. ""I'm going to give him an earful," he yelled. "I'm not an attorney for nothing!"

I'd forgotten to bring my work gloves. Soon my palms blistered, though I barely noticed. What I did notice was that Paul was a determined worker, rarely stopping to straighten his back and not trying to direct me. It was amazing how willing the water was to flow in a new and less damaging direction once we had the dam halfway in place.

When the sky turned gray we decided we'd done enough. Our skid was now blocked off; the flood waters were following the curve, surging along the ridge trail to a dip in the distance from which they rushed downhill toward the draw. "Come on," Paul said, grabbing both shovels and one of the flashlights. "Let's check out the damage below."

Everything stored under his cabin was covered with sludge. Fortunately, old wood rat stick-nests, discarded tires, and quietly disintegrating stacks of ancient lumber had kept the water from completely unearthing the piers—although, in my opinion, it wouldn't have been much of a loss if the whole place had tumbled downslope. "It was all built with salvaged cedar and redwood, from an old barn," Paul explained as if reading my mind. "Rough, sturdy stuff that isn't milled anymore—and would be prohibitive to buy new if it were. Including the siding. If Mittendrin hadn't knocked out the windows and let in the weather this cabin would have stayed good as new for another century at least. Provided the roof didn't leak."

"All right," I conceded. "I'm impressed. Where do you want the building material? I need my truck, but I'll let you keep one of the shovels. In case."

We carried the insulation inside and rigged supports on the covered porch on which we stacked the boards. Paul gave me a grateful hippie-type hug I didn't return. Then I drove home, peeled off everything I wore, and opened the faucet to scrub the dirt off my hands.

But the spigot stayed dry. There wasn't a drop of water in my pipes. No point in reporting my plight to Barret this early in the morning. I'd call him from town. Without missing a beat, I unscrewed one of the glass jugs from under the sink and poured filtered drinking water into a bowl for a quick wash. "Sorry. No double-u," I told the dogs, tossing them the usual chicken necks. The cats got a dose of the finest unadulterated organic ground turkey available at the co-op, mixed with their special vitamin/mineral powder. Then I dressed in my town clothes and headed out to fetch my son, bringing my shovel.

THE HEAVY rain had caused damage on the highway too, overflowing the ditch and runneling across the tarmac along with assorted debris. In some spots the entire width of the highway was coated with mud, slowing me down. I switched to four wheel drive once I reached the long winding dirt road that eventually took me to Ariel's farmhouse.

The Chevy was still stuck. Of course Ariel didn't own a shovel. Probably didn't know how to use one; moving dirt around had never been part of his vocation. Besides, we couldn't spare the time it would take to drain the puddle under the Chevy's wheels. I leaned my shovel against the house in case Ariel might want it later. Jimmi came to the door, looking as drowsy as he usually did in the morning. I told him to climb in, but then Ariel stepped out behind him, carrying an attaché case. He was wearing his parka, a baseball cap angled low, and a nerdish pair of baby-blue plastic framed sunglasses that did a good job of hiding the upper half of his face.

"Is it okay if I ride to town with you?" he said, sounding exhausted. "I hate feeling stranded. I decided to take your advice about the Subaru."

"A *used* Subaru," I said. "Sure, come along. Jimmi, you can sit in the extra-cab or in back of the truck."

"Great choices," he muttered, deciding to squeeze into the tight space behind the bucket seats. That's when I noticed what he was wearing—baggy denims, the seams dragging the ground; a red letterman jacket a couple of sizes too big; a new pair of black penny loafers.

I struck my forehead with one of my blistered palms. "I forgot to bring clothes!"

"I wouldn't have had enough time to change into them," he said. "Anyway, Ariel's letting me keep these. Aren't they cool?"

Neither of them had much to say on the drive, though they were clearly impressed with the high water level in Emigrant Lake and with the flooded fields we were passing. "Does it always rain this hard around here in spring?" Ariel asked when he saw how near to overflowing the creek across from the golf course had become.

I shook my head. "Every year's different. You never know what to expect. Just the way we like it."

I dropped off Jimmi first. He joined a few stragglers who were dashing across the lot hoping to make it to their class rooms before the final bell rang.

"Thanks for letting him come down yesterday," Ariel said softly as we drove on. "We watched the Three Stooges and a very old Woody Allen movie. He laughed till he cried."

I nodded. "He probably told you we don't have a TV."

"Do you want one?"

"Heck no. He's the kind of kid who would stay glued to the set. Used to be our favorite time together was in the evenings when I'd read to him. Lately, he's developed a dislike for books and prefers to get whacked out on music."

"That's one of *my* favorite past-times," Ariel grinned. "But I love books, too. Maybe I can help you convince Jimmi that the two aren't mutually exclusive."

I gave him detailed instructions on how to drain the puddle in front of his house. Then I dropped him off at the lot advertising "pre-owned vehicles." There were three Subarus available for adoption. Ariel could have his pick. "Want me to wait?" I asked as he got out. He declined. "Hey," I said. "Anytime you need help, call me, okay? I'm filled to the brim with free wisdom and priceless advice."

He laughed and waved me on. Before he had a chance to take his first step he'd already been spied by a salesman who was jogging eagerly toward him.

I HAD skipped breakfast. And since I didn't have any jobs
scheduled, I decided to eat at the co-op again. To my pleasant
surprise Grace was sitting at the same table we'd occupied the
previous day, wrapped in her coat. She was nibbling on scrambled
eggs and home fries and working a crossword puzzle. I ordered what
she had, substituting a maté for her coffee. She gave a cheerful wave
as I took my tray over to keep her company.

"How was the séance?" I asked.

"The reading," she corrected. "I don't usually go for that kind of
stuff, but this psychic knew more about me than Stu does."

"That shouldn't be hard since you and Stu have been leading
entirely separate lives for two years."

"Exactly." She pushed the newspaper away and concentrated on
finishing her meal. "Don't get me wrong—I do love Oregon. But, as
it turns out, I love San Francisco more. For one thing, this valley has
a glut of RNs right now. God knows when I'll get a job. Graveyard
shift, most likely. I've made such a nice niche for myself in the city.
I can buy fresh croissants half a block from my apartment. And,
frankly, my germ-free little bathroom beats Stu's outhouse hands
down."

"Bio-toilet," I said.

"Whatever it is, he hasn't cleaned it since the last time I came."

It hadn't been part of my assignment, but probably only because
Stu had forgotten to mention it. "So why are you so happy this
morning?" I asked.

"Because the psychic saw Stu living in San Francisco with me.
Finishing his degree. Teaching."

"So?"

"So he's off right now getting his own reading. And if it meshes
with mine—which it must—he may be open to a little persuasion."

"Oh," I said, remembering Kosmo's contribution. I was wearing
the same shirt I'd worn yesterday. The number was still in its breast
pocket. I fished it out and placed it in front of Grace. "That's the
number of someone Kosmo found who has influence at the
Shakespeare Festival. He thinks the guy can get Stu some parts."

Grace considered the scrap. Then she balled it up, stuffed it in her mouth, and washed it down with some coffee. "This is our last chance—because, frankly, even though we've grown up together and probably will always be close—there's this very cute doctor who thinks I'm wonderful and I don't know how much longer I can hold out."

It occurred to me that she *liked* wearing nylons and pretty city clothes, even though just a few years ago she'd dressed like the original earth mother, maxi skirt and all. "And Zora? Didn't she move up here because of you?"

"Zora does what Zora wants. There's no law against her keeping her California house just because she bought one up here, is there?"

"What did the psychic see for her?"

Grace chuckled. "A tall handsome dark stranger."

"I suppose it's remotely possible she could be talking about Barret," I said, although he was more pudgy than tall, more roughhewn than handsome, and the darkest thing about him was his inclination to be moody.

Grace grinned. "It's what Zora sees when she's looking at him that counts."

From her blue jay perspective? "That reminds me," I said. "Did you guys have running water this morning?"

She groaned. "Another reason Stu and I came to town early. I've lost the knack of living without the basic necessities. And I don't want to have to relearn."

"I was going to call the Bear."

"Stu already did. Woke him up, too. Barret swore in his ear. He said he couldn't do a thing until the rain stopped. That's if it's just another pipe leak. If it's the pump the prognosis will be infinitely worse."

Jimmi wasn't going to like missing out on his daily shower, even though it was a simple out-door contraption at the rear of the cabin. He refused to wash at school because the other boys tended to eye-measure each other's equipment. He didn't like showering at the university pool either, claiming some of the naked men in the dressing room could pass for gorillas.

I stabbed up a slice of potato. "John Gierig," I mused, apropos nothing. "I take it you two met somewhere in the Bay Area?"

Grace blanched and looked around to make sure no one was listening. Then, just as she started to confidently lean toward me, Stu came bounding toward the entrance, his face radiant with a brand-new vision. Obviously, the fortune-teller had given him permission to make a huge life change. Some undeserving, cheap part of me wondered how much Grace had paid her for it.

"Do you know what Gierig has done?" I asked her.

"What *hasn't* he done?" she said quickly. "He's an e—"

"Hi, sweetheart," Stu sang out, striding across the little café to claim the chair between us. "That psychic's a blast! Wait till I tell you what she said."

It's possible I might have been scoffing a bit, because he took one look at me and clammed up. As if a woman who'd spent her previous evening chanting witchcraft slogans was likely to mock a mere psychic prediction. I gathered my dignity, collected my dishes, and announced it was time for me to do some serious shopping. Bottled water was at the top of my list.

DRIVING home an hour later, I noticed that Paul's car was still parked in Stu's lot. For some reason, I found that fact oddly pleasing. The rain was holding steady. If anything, the clouds seemed thicker than before. On a good summer day my cabin usually received four, five hours of direct sunlight. But even then the mountain's deep shadows didn't move out of the clearing before ten and returned by three, forcing me to click on the overhead lights way before dark. They were a poor substitute for natural light, particularly today.

The painting I'd been working on seemed to have acquired a mournful cast. I took if off the easel, dragged out my old pieces, and lined them up along the walls, trying to decide which I might bear to part with for the fabric store exhibit. Just thinking about relinquishing them brought on a bout of separation anxiety because my paintings were as much a part of me as my arms and my legs. I felt the compulsion to interview prospective buyers to make sure they would provide my spiritual offspring a good home.

It wasn't until I went to the kitchen to try the faucet—still dry—
that I noticed the red button on my answering machine was patiently
blinking. I tapped it, hardly recognizing the frail old-man's-voice it
coughed out, calling my name. It belonged to my father. "I need you
to come, Silvia," he was saying. "Now. I'm wiring you money for
two round trip tickets. If you order them early you'll be booked by
the time your passport arrives." Then he switched to an uneasy
whisper. "You've got to get me out of here. These women won't let
me go to the *Reherlberg*. I want to die there, like my father and his
father before him. Call me the minute you know your itinerary.
Servus. And good night." It seemed to have taken him an awfully
long time to hang up.

Realizing I'd run out of valid excuses, I crumpled onto the
nearest chair.

What would I do with the dogs?

CHAPTER 20

I WENT TO PAUL'S PLACE TO TALK to him about my predicament but he wasn't there. The rain-drenched mid morning light made it obvious how much of the surrounding forest floor had been swept away, leaving only the rocky bones. In the gloom the inside of his cabin was bleaker than ever. He'd scrubbed it without getting rid of the musty odors. A black sleeping bag was airing on the loft banister. Looking in vain for pen and paper, I noticed just how little he had brought with him, this man who'd given up a lucrative practice after his law partner stole his family away.

I tried his ancient brass faucet. It was as dry as my own. No window glass. No heat. If he'd chosen to burrow in this hidey-hole hoping to heal himself with hard physical labor he'd come to the right place.

Back home, I spent an hour making detailed lists. Then I crammed five of my best paintings into the extra-cab and onto the passenger seat, spread a couple of old quilts over the truck bed, and loaded the puppies. At Stu's lot I wrote a short note to Paul, inviting him for lunch at the Greenleaf, sealed it in a clear plastic bag, and stuck it behind one of his wiper blades. Halfway down the mountain I realized he was unlikely to see it if he planned to stay home.

In the fabric store, Mrs. Sweeney, her pinkish white hair swept up in elaborate beauty shop curls, placed my canvases in a methodical row against a white-washed brick wall, stood back, and scrutinized each. Her eyes sparkling behind a homey pair of bifocals, she said, "The tourists will love these. This is the kind of Pacific Northwest nature that keeps them coming to the Rogue Valley year after year." She straightened with some inner determination. "I want them all. An exclusive." Following her gaze to the bare stretch of wall above her shelves, I wondered how many tourists would frequent her shop on a lazy pre-play afternoon. She initialed each entry on my inventory list and signed it. I gave her Paul's cell phone number and told her he would act as my agent while I was away. It was a rash promise since he knew nothing about the arrangement as yet. But for me, this day, by necessity, had to be full of presumptions.

I recognized Ariel by his parka and horn rims. He was at a checkout stand in the co-op, transferring a cartload of groceries onto the conveyor. "Where are you going to put everything?" I asked, putting a light hand on his arm in greeting. "Your refrigerator's overflowing already."

He grinned, clearly pleased with himself. "I've got a walk-in pantry to fill. And plenty of room in my freezer. You never know how long you're going to be stranded by foul weather around here. Besides, I love shopping. Or haven't you heard?"

Actually, I had—although, according to the tabloids, it was mostly for the new toys he liked to bestow on a few select young friends. "I trust you bought a car?"

He gave an eager nod. "Come on out to the parking lot with me and I'll show it to you."

I got my usual maté and a sticky bun, and followed him to the gold toned Subaru Legacy I'd parked next to. It was as fancy as a used car could possibly get without being new. "Good color," I said.

"It won't show the dust. And it's dependable enough so you can drive it down to California next time you go."

"Uh-uh," he said. "For that I'll take a plane. I'm a lousy driver. Too many mountain passes and curves on the freeway for me—I'd doze and go right over the edge."

I had a glimpse of Stillman's crashed VW hung up in a downslope tree. "That's a nice option," I said, swallowing a resurgence of cold desolation. "And a real time saver, too." The moment Ariel opened the Legacy's hatch, Asa reared in Efi's truck bed and started barking. "Quiet, Asa!" I told him at once.

Ariel peered through the mesh. "You brought both of them?"

"We're going to the dog park." On impulse, I added, "Why don't you follow behind us? You can help me throw balls." Minutes later, the Emperor of Song was shooting a tennis ball out of my blue plastic thrower and Asa sped across the grass to catch it. Marvel, who had no passion for this particular game but loved to run, stayed easily at her brother's side as he brought back the first ball in exchange for a second.

"They've got awesome gaits," Ariel said, pulling up his hood to ward off the rain, although it had eased. "Totally smooth! I bet you could keep a glass of water on their backs when they're trotting without spilling a drop. God, I wish I had my own two puppies already. I'd take them on tour with me. They'd help me relax between shows."

"Where would you keep them while you're onstage? In a hotel room? What if the maids let them out and they got lost?"

"I'd hire somebody to mind them. But I'd take long walks with them, and they'd sleep with me. I'm good with animals." Asa dropped the second ball at Ariel's feet. He stuck it onto the thrower. "Outside of art and music, animals are what I love most in the world. Them and kids. That reminds me—I need to talk to you. About Jimmi." He wiggled the loaded thrower. Asa hurled himself into the air, capturing it in his maw and tearing it out of Ariel's grip. Marvel gave a sharp bark. Asa hastily dropped it.

"Sorry, Asa." Ariel retrieved the thrower and threw a beautiful curve ball clear to the opposite fence. The dogs leaped in pursuit.

Ariel held out his palm to the sky without catching a single drop. The rain had finally stopped. "I would love to invite Jimmi to come to my California ranch with me some weekend. You, too. I'll show you my elephants." He pushed back his hood and scratched at his hairline. "Jimmi wants to go on tour with me this summer. See something of the world. We'd travel by private jet. I usually rent a couple of hotel floors. I'd take good care of him." From the way he was standing I could tell my answer would matter. In a way, maybe it was even a test to see just how much I was *really* willing to trust him.

"Jimmi's at a precarious age," I pointed out gently. "Who'd be providing the light-handed, steady supervision he needs while you're off doing day-time rehearsals and evening performances? Your puppy minder?"

"Come with us, then. With the dogs."

"Thanks for the invitation," I said. "But I had an emergency overseas call this morning. My father's very ill. Jimmi doesn't know it yet but we're about to fly to Vienna. In fact, we may not see you again for a month."

Quickly, he put a supportive hand on my arm. "Oh, Silvi! I hope he gets better soon. You could both join me later. It's a long tour."

"I hate traveling. Even to Vienna." I finished my sticky bun, licked honey-goo off my fingers, and threw Asa's next ball, feeling a twinge in my shoulder. "I've just rearranged my life so I can stay home and paint full time. I hate having to give it up again."

With a tone of wonder, he said, "You paint? What kind of stuff?"

I told him about my upcoming exhibit. He said he'd check it out. I congratulated him on his car. Before we parted company he wrote down a phone number. "It's my mother's private line. She'll know how to reach me. In case you change your mind."

I stuffed it away. "Does that mean you won't be here when we get back?"

He shrugged, offering me a lopsided grin. "You never know in my business. Things come up. I just don't want us to lose touch. Sorry about your dad."

He started to put his arms around me. I managed to catch a whiff of his intriguing cologne before I made myself draw away, aborting the consoling embrace. He dropped his arms to his sides. There was an awkward silence. Then he offered me a smile instead. "Things have been tough for you. I'm sorry."

Jimmi must have told him about Stillman. "I come from a non-hugging culture and family," I tried to explain. "It's a handicap hard to overcome."

"A daily embrace is the best multi-vitamin there is," he said. "Doctors should prescribe hugs instead of aspirin." Then he walked away across the turf. Asa and Marvel escorted him to the gate and stayed inside, watching him climb in his car. They didn't come back to me until the golden Subaru was out of sight.

MY PROPOSITION to Paul was simple. He needed a decent place to live while he was remodeling, and I needed someone to stay in my house and take care of the animals while I was gone. Since there was no one else I could trust to do this for me, I wouldn't even consider going to the travel agency for plane tickets unless he and I had a definite deal.

Before the waiter could arrive with our soups Paul said without hesitation, "I'd be delighted."

"Even though you may not have running water?"

"Oh, we'll have water." There was a hint of steel in his smile. "Barret doesn't like paying for professional help. He'll futz around and around, hoping whatever's wrong will fix itself. I'll make sure he stays on top of it. In the old days the pump quit on a regular basis until we upgraded it. Time for some infra-structure renewal projects, I'd say."

Crushing my whole wheat crackers, I strewed the crumbs on top of my soup. "I keep filled jugs under the sink. Emergency drinking water. I've never left Asa and Marvel before. But they know you. And I believe they're beginning to trust you."

"I'll take them on lots of hikes."

"They'll like that." There was a loud crash from the restaurant's kitchen area. We both turned toward the noise. "A stack of dropped plates," Paul guessed.

We listened to raised voices, one scolding, the other contrite. I said, "The cats are happy to be left to themselves as long as you feed them regularly. You'll have to run the meat grinder. I'll show you the whole routine. And—oh—about my paintings . . ." I told him about my deal with Mrs. Sweeney.

Then he mentioned stomping up to confront Gierig. "He always comes in the mornings to check on his hired help. I took him to see the damage. In one stretch, his bulldozer had strayed onto my land. I showed Gierig where I'd flagged it. He's scrapping the whole road and starting another one farther away."

"Is he going to fix the damage he's done to the skid? Replant trees?"

"He said nature will take care of it. Eventually."

"Did he apologize?"

"He lost no time pointing out that what he does or doesn't do on his private property is no damn business of mine. I doubt the word 'sorry' is part of his vocabulary. But at least he knows we're on to him. "

He jiggled his water glass, staring at the melting ice inside. "I've been thinking. I need some kind of office space in town so I can start getting established. Someplace where I can keep my files, build a clientele, plug in my computer. I can create your web- site from there while you're gone."

"I'll give you an itemized list of my entire stock of paintings. With snapshots."

"No problem. I'm setting up an email account for you, too. And when you get back from Austria I'll help you buy a good laptop and show you how to access your sites."

"I'll pay you, of course. For everything."

He patted my hand. "You helped me dig that dam. That more than makes up for the web stuff. As for the pet-sitting, I'm doing that strictly in exchange for a warm bed to sleep in every night. Favor for favor. That's how being neighborly works. Besides, I miss living with dogs. And just think—I'll get to lounge in a regular armchair after dark and read books. Under an electric light bulb. What luxury. Feels like some kind of promotion to me."

The waiter brought the roast beef sandwich we'd decided to split. I took my half off the plate, pushing the rest toward Paul, including the chips, dill pickle slices, and parsley. "I brought the puppies so you guys could hang out together some more. Just because they've seen you on the mountain a couple of times is no guarantee they will be friendly in town. They get more touchy in social settings. Like me. How about a walk on the loop road? All four of us, together."

"They'll be leashed?"

"Of course."

"Do they pull?"

"Only when they see something exciting."

"I'll hold Asa. I think he already likes me."

WE PARKED at the round old reservoir close to the falls. I leashed Asa and Marvel before letting them jump onto the road. They sniffed thoroughly up and down Paul's pants and along his shoes until they had satisfied themselves that he was the same man they knew from the mountain. But when I handed Paul Asa's lead, my proud canine protector sat down at once, making himself heavy as a black-oak burl. No matter how hard Paul jerked and cajoled, Asa refused to be budged. "Silly dog," I said, exchanging his leash for Marvel's. "Here, walk her. She has more common sense. And no male ego."

Marvel watched the transfer with interest, but when Paul began to pull her ahead, she gave a low, chesty growl. "Oh, go on, Marvel," I said. "We'll be right behind you." Asa rose to catch up to his sister. I yanked him to heel. Marvel looked worriedly back us. Paul tugged lightly. She showed him her teeth. At his next tug, she snapped at his forearm. Paul gave a sharp exhale, tossed the leash back to me, and dabbed at his wound. "Don't fret," he said. "She didn't even break the skin. It was meant as a warning. As far as she's concerned, I was trying to steal her."

He offered the back of his hand to Marvel, who sniffed at it with great caution. "She's a bit shy. And who can blame her? We've never even had a proper visit inside your house. A dog's loyalty lies with the person who feeds her. I promise you we'll be vast friends by the time you come home again." He offered her a piece of jerky. She left it lying on the road. Asa gulped it without the slightest compunction.

Paul was right of course. He'd knocked on my door twice; neither time had I invited him in. "If you come tomorrow at five you can watch me prepare their evening meal," I conceded. "Then we'll sit and have tea. With Jimmi."

The dogs had no objections to walking beside him as long as I was the one in charge of them. Paul pointed to the sprinkling of fancy mansions on the hillside above Granite Street. "Most of these weren't here twenty-five years ago. And the surrounding forest was denser and healthier. I can't get used to the new look."

"What do you mean?"

"Brick and cement swallowing what ought to be generous yards. You know how long it takes to dust and vacuum these monstrosities? It's a good thing the people who own them can afford housekeepers to do the dirty work for them. I bet each one of these houses has five bathrooms. At least. "

He got that right. Though one of my customers had nine. Another had three separate kitchens. "It's precisely these kinds of newcomers who will hire a high priced attorney like you," I said drily. "In fact, without the Bay Area refugees a lot of the locals would have been forced to move up to Portland to make a living. Do you know what Ashland's three major industries are?"

"There's the university, of course—but Shakespeare's got to be number one," Paul guessed.

"Right. And if you can't get a job with the festival or the tourist trade it generates there's always elder care. Ashland has become multi layered. After the hippies came the punks and new-agers. The yuppies. Gays. Happy Campers. Then the seniors took over and stabilized the town. They've been a good influence, economically and culturally. Have you noticed how many silver haired couples you can find strolling along Main Street, holding hands? Sometimes I envy them."

He contemplated the hillside again. "I liked it better the way it was."

I tousled his well cut hair. "You've changed, too. From hippie to yuppie toward brittle boned senior."

He laughed, leaving his hair standing on end. "I liked being a hippie best."

I patted it down for him. "Did you have a beard and a long pony tail?"

"Long*ish*. And I didn't have enough whiskers for a good beard back then. The one I tried to grow made me look like a milquetoast."

"Will you grow one now?"

"Nope. And no pony tail either. I've become the clean-cut type."

"It suits you. I've always considered all that bushy hair a disguise. If you shaved off Barret's he'd look as pinched and sour as he acts."

When the road forked I took the ascending part. "My dream house is up there. I love to just stand and watch it from outside the gate and pretend it's all mine. Not that I could ever afford it."

I didn't mind the steep rise. It was worth it. First came the fenced rolling pasture. A white horse and a brown one, grazing. Sometimes they ran side by side, tails high, making me catch my breath. Then came the orchard. Mostly apples, some cherries and plums. Probably pears. The graceful stone house stood well away from the road, down a nicely curving lane. Nestling against the hillside, it was surrounded by trees. With skylights for every room. A wrap-around porch. And a separate artist's studio, mostly glass.

"Behind the studio is a path leading right to the watershed," I said, leaning over the fence to touch the velvety noses of the approaching horses. "I've seen a couple of teenage girls ride these horses up into it. That tall tree on this side of the studio is a baby Redwood. There's a pond on the other side, and a big willow you can't see from here. Once when the property was between owners I walked down the lane and looked around, imagining what it would feel like to be the next occupant. A piece of mountain a stone's throw from town. Jimmi would love it."

In my mind's eye I could see him on the pasture, romping with the dogs. I could picture us riding up the trail. Sometimes I wondered how much money Papa was leaving me in his will. And if it might cover the required down payment. It was a futile exercise since I didn't even earn enough in a year to pay the property tax.

Paul stood as transfixed as I. "If there are any drawbacks I don't see them. How often has it been for sale?"

"Twice since I discovered it. When people get old they don't want to do a lot of outside chores any more. Spouses die. Marriages break up. Oops—I'm sorry." For the first time I wondered what kind of house he'd lost along with his wife. And what dream they'd shared together.

He raised my chin. "Don't be," he said. "I'm not anymore." And then he kissed me.

DRIVING home, I felt compelled to keep touching my lips. It had been my first kiss since Stillman. Had I known Paul's intent I would have pulled away, although there'd been something almost brotherly about his mouth brushing mine. And yet, my lips tingled. I'd thought they had died with Stillman.

I could have invited Paul to the house this afternoon. But that much socializing made me tired. And I had to sit down with Jimmi and explain our traveling plans. To that end I brought home a large pizza to soften him up. According to the middle school principal he would have to take the rest of this school year's homework to Austria with him and enroll in summer school after we returned, neither of which would go down well. I will forever blame myself for vacillating before launching into my speech when we sat side by side at the table. Because he used my guilty silence to start a speech of his own.

"This reminds me of when we had pizza with Ariel. Remember?"

As far as I knew my short-term memory was still intact.

"You should check out his music room. He dances in there. Mirrors all along the wall so he can watch his moves from every angle."

"Yes," I said. "I hear he's a good dancer."

"A *great* dancer. He showed me a video of his last tour. God, you should have seen the fans screaming and fainting. And the stuff he does onstage—"

"I've seen pictures."

"Next time we go down to his place I'll ask him to show you that video." He busied himself with a slice and started his next sentence with his mouth full. I raised a finger. He chewed and swallowed, then said, "He invited us to his California ranch. And he wants me to come on his world tour. In the summer. It'll be better than a year's worth of geography lessons."

I wiped my hands on a napkin just to give myself a few extra seconds. His eyes were aglow with enthusiasm; what I had to say would douse that ardent light. "I'm sorry," I began. "You can't."

His smile became fixed. He waited.

"You are only thirteen."

"Almost fourteen!"

"Not by a long shot. Face it, you're too young to fly off without me."

"He said you could come too."

"We're going on a trip of our own. To Vienna."

He stared.

"Pap*a* called this morning. He's dying. I've already reserved our tickets. We're leaving in a couple of days. I'm not sure for how long."

I watched his eyes cloud. "I'm not going," he said.

"We have no choice."

"Grandmam*a* hates me."

"She's not a warm hearted person," I admitted. "But we're not flying to Vienna for her sake."

"When we were there before she looked at me like I was a shit-fly on her kitchen wall. Once, she picked up a fly swatter. I was sure she was going to squash me with it."

"We won't stay with her. Pap*a* wants me to drive him to the *Reherlberg*. And keep him company until—"

"Okay then. I'll come with you if I can go with Ariel afterwards."

"This isn't a bargaining session." I'd get to the homework and summer school part another day. Preferably when we were half way across the ocean.

He bit his lip. Then he said, "I'm not coming and you can't make me." He reminded me of Asa dragging his butt on the loop road.

"You can't stay here without me."

"Then I'm staying with Dorrie. In Key Largo. At least I won't have to worry about her chasing after me with a fly swatter."

"Grandmam*a* didn't. You only thought—"

"She's got mean eyes. You can't make me do stuff anymore. I'm almost as tall as you are. And probably stronger."

I fought the impulse to give him a couple of resounding slaps. "Go upstairs!" I ordered, jaws clenching. "Fast!"

Whatever he saw on my face convinced him to comply at once. I held in my tears until I got to the outhouse. I had no idea what to do next.

CHAPTER 21

AT THE MEDFORD AIRPORT PAUL WAITED until Jimmi had to use the restroom. Then he wrapped an arm around me and drew me as close as I would let him. Momentarily resting his cheek against the top of my head, he said, "While you're putting distance and time between us, think about you and me, together. Try to get used to the idea. Okay?"

I didn't know how to respond. Or how to feel. But I didn't pull away, mostly because I liked the combined scent of his warm skin, leather, and soap.

"Call me when you're ready to fly home so I can come pick you up," he went on. And then he released me. Our moment was over. Jimmi came out of the restroom and followed me to the gate. With each step I took away from Paul my legs felt a bit heavier. I held our tickets out to the stewardess, then changed my mind. "Wait for me," I told Jimmi, going back to where Paul stood watching. "Here," I said, holding out the keys to Efi. "You can use my pickup while I'm gone."

He seemed startled. "Are you sure?"

"It's the least I can do. To repay you for your kindness. You can haul up more lumber." He still wouldn't take them. So I said, "If I can trust you with my house and my animals I can trust you with my truck. She's in good shape. Except for one thing—her gas gauge doesn't work. Keep topping her off and you'll be fine."

He looked at me funny. "What's her name?"

"Efi."

He took the keys. I felt lighter walking away from him the second time.

JIMMI didn't say a word on our flight to San Francisco. He occupied the window seat like a straight backed Prussian soldier, eyes narrowed, chin thrust forward, never once looking out of the air plane. After we landed we whiled away the time before his connecting flight was called by wandering in and out of airport restaurants. I plied him with a cheeseburger and fries, pizza, and a couple of extra large colas. Sugar-free. "I hope you'll have a wonderful month with Dorrie," I said. "Eating shrimp and watching dreadful TV. I'll call you as soon as I'm back. You know I love you, Jimmi. I always will."

He looked past me to some unfathomable distance without betraying the slightest emotion; I did my utmost to keep from showing how much it hurt.

I watched his plane until it disappeared into the overcast.

ON MY own flight I sat in the window seat that should have been his, knowing I was moving away from everything I loved. There was an invisible elastic band connecting me to my life on the ridge. It stretched and stretched beyond the point of endurance. A stocky man with a prominent nose who looked like an Arab was sweating and fidgeting in the center seat. Beside him the flesh belonging to an overweight middle aged woman spilled over the armrest, boxing him in. I gave him plenty of room at my end, wondering if he had the ingredients of a bomb in his shoes and wishing I had drawn up my will.

To distract myself I pulled out the little book of poems and parables Ariel had written, which he presented to me this morning when he brought Jimmi home. He'd given Jimmi a consolation prize for missing the tour—a basket overflowing with music and films. It was me who'd called Ariel, asking if Jimmi could spend our last night in Oregon at his house. I knew it was bound to be a more pleasant arrangement than having him in the cabin with me; I couldn't trust myself not to shout at him every time he made a sarcastic remark.

The book had a young, dark and radiantly beautiful Ariel on the cover, embraced by magnificent arch-angel wings. He was wearing a flowing white shirt, his mouth open in song. He looked happy. On the fly leaf, he'd written, *To my dear friend Silvi, with love, so she'll know what kind of person her puppies will live with.* He'd signed his full name with a flourish. I leafed through the pages, enjoying the many stunning photographs inside. After I finished reading his simple first poem I realized that everything I'd suspected about him was true. His soul was as pure as a child's.

From the little writing I'd done I knew that it was easier to compose a complicated sentence than a plain one, especially for an adult. His parables, like good fairy tales, went straight to the heart. It didn't take long for me to discover why he'd bought a farmhouse in the backwoods of Oregon; he loved forests as much as I did.

The Arab had stopped fidgeting. He was shamelessly reading along. "I have always adored Ariel Jordan," he said. "He is America's best export. A world wide good-will ambassador. Admired by all cultures." His accent was slight. I was unable to guess what country he was from.

"Ariel Jordan!" the fat lady exclaimed in a rich baritone. "That pedophile? You can have him. And keep him, too."

I wanted to tear out her mouse-colored bob clump by clump. "A genius," I said with some heat. "Slandered and underappreciated in his own country. Like Mozart, whose corpse, if I remember correctly, was wrapped in a sack and tossed down a paupers' mass grave."

"How dare you mention both names with the same breath!" she cried, leaning over the Arab's protruding belly to deliver a scowl.

I glared right back. "Mozart was wrongfully accused of fondling some of the young girls he was tutoring. By a rumor mill no less vicious in his century's Vienna than our tabloid industry is today. Those who listen to gossip mongers must share the blame."

With a hiss she stabbed her summoning button, heaving herself upright just as the stewardess arrived. "This *person* has been highly offensive," she declared loudly, pointing to me. "I demand another seat, preferably at the other end of the plane. Until I get it I shall stand in the galley." And off she lumbered, stiff kneed and stiff hipped. Arranging her features into an apologetic smile, the stewardess followed.

The supposed Arab held out his hand. "*Mateus Simao Marco*. Of *Lisboa*. We are well rid of her. She made me feel like a canned sardine." I gave him my name. We shook with all the enthusiasm of reunited old friends. "A prophet often excites great passions," he said. "In those who understand him it is enthusiasm. In those who do not it is hate. If you don't mind—when you are finished reading, could you let me borrow your book?"

"Of course."

"Good. Meanwhile—I must make myself more comfortable, now that I finally can." He moved into the aisle seat, reclining the backrest. Folding his hands on his belly, he stuck his elbows out on both sides, gave a relieved sigh, and closed his eyes. He slept while I read through the rest of the book. After dinner I handed it over, listened to a piano sonata, and slept myself, not waking until we circled over Heathrow. Mateus Simao Marco and I shook good-bye. Not liking queues I stayed in my seat until he and everyone else had debarked. On my way into the terminal for my connecting flight I realized he had not returned the book. I raced to catch up to the other passengers, saw him blend with the crowd, and ruthlessly barreled after him, grabbing onto his jacket and holding out my hand. "Give!"

He flashed me a discomfited smile. "A wonderful dedication. One of a kind," he explained as if that would fix things.

"Addressed to me, not you!"

He pulled the book out of his briefcase. "Take good care of it. It will be a collector's item one day."

I snatched it away and showed him my back, but as I walked toward customs I wondered at his choice of words, for copies of Ariel's book would surely always be available at any good bookstore. And the endearing inscription could mean nothing to anyone but me.

The elastic band tied to my heart grew ever tighter on the last part of my journey.

PUDGY Mama was wearing her gray Loden outfit reserved for special occasions, and Erika had on a salmon pink knit dress that hinted at her curves in a most becoming, though still lady-like fashion. Sensibly they'd decided to wait for me at the Vienna terminal's luggage retrieval area. Erika was holding a small bouquet of prickly white roses that I could only smell since she didn't offer to help carry my luggage. Mama, who'd brought me a box of her favorite pralines, didn't hand them over until we were settled in the Peugeot.

"I'm so glad you found other accommodations for Jimmi," she said from the front passenger seat without looking at me. "He would only have been in the way."

Ignoring a stab of annoyance, I asked, "How's Papa?"

"We left him sleeping. That's all he does these days. In fact, he's in no condition to be moved. You'll have to forget his hair brained scheme of dying on the farm. He can't even walk down the hall without one of us at each arm. You will see that soon enough. Then perhaps you'll help us convince him to stay put. He'll last longer that way."

"But taking him to the farm is the only reason I came!"

"Nonsense. Erika and I have planned some small outings for us. I hope you packed a couple of nice dresses. Your traveling ensemble is nothing short of atrocious. Old jeans and t-shirts might do on a mountain, Silvia, but this is the city. For the opera, you can borrow one of Erika's gowns."

"We're not the same size," I reminded her as if she didn't know perfectly well that I was a head taller. "And I didn't come here to be entertained."

"Your school chums want to see you. And I have tickets for next Sunday's concert. Mozart. You've always loved Mozart."

Word by word, minute by minute, her expectations were winding a silken cord around me. I'd forgotten how good she was at this genteel fencing. How she'd pricked and pricked at me when I was a teenager until I'd blow up, always at fault but magnanimously forgiven. What I liked best about Asa and Marvel was that they never said anything at all. Jimmi, though he used to be an unremitting chatterer, shut up the minute he turned eleven and hadn't said much since. Stillman had been an good fit for his name.

When Erika dropped us off in front of the house I was ready to withdraw to my room, pleading a headache to give myself an hour's peace. But first I had to look in on Papa.

"I don't care if he's sleeping. I won't make a sound," I told Mama, who was blocking the entrance to the sickroom while keeping a congenial smile on her face—a smile that did not quite reach her eyes.

"I'll go in with you," she finally said, brooking no argument. She opened the door to drawn-curtain gloom, ominous dark furniture, and spent air. Papa stirred, trying to sit up in bed.

"Silvia?" he asked in a tremulous voice. "Is that you?"

I went to plump up his pillows. "I came as soon as I could. Here, let me help you." Wrapping an arm around his emaciated shoulders, I wedged enough padding behind his back to support his sitting upright.

"I beg of you, do not excite him," Mama murmured from the doorway.

He looked at her out of hollow eyes. "A moment alone with my daughter. If you please."

She came to straighten his covers. "There is no need. I thought we could—"

"If you please," he repeated, staring at her until she slumped.

"I'll make coffee. Erika and I have baked a torte. Five minutes?" she said, reluctantly fitting herself through the doorway.

"Ten!" he said firmly as she began to close the door. Then he whispered, "See that she's gone."

I did. She was just outside, leaning against the wall. We exchanged another uneasy smile. "I don't want coffee," I said. "Do you have herbal tea?"

Her mouth pursed. "Perhaps a packet of stale camomile from the last time you came."

"Good enough. But not now. And no torte. I need to lie down for a while." She gave an impatient toss of her head. "Don't be absurd. You've rested enough on the plane."

I crossed my arms. "Let me be the judge of that."

"I will expect you in the parlor in ten minutes. Wearing a decent dress," she said, walking away to the end of the hall. Seething, I stayed at the door until she went into the kitchen. Then I sat on the edge of Papa's mattress.

He clutched my wrist with unexpected fervor. "Quick, get me out of here while I can still totter. Every breath I draw in this house is a breath lost." He pulled off his covers to show me the sweat suit and tennis shoes he was wearing. "I'm ready to go. Josef is expecting us."

"Right now? But I've just—"

"Socialize later. On your own time." He dangled a set of car keys. "Take the suitcase I've packed. It's under the bed. But ease me onto the passenger seat first. Don't talk to them now. You know how they are."

I was beginning to recall unpleasant details of Mama's talent for managing people. Even reluctant ones. It helped me propel his skeletal frame away from the kitchen and parlor toward the rear of the house. We made our escape to the garage from there, Papa mostly dead weight. Luckily, Erika had left the garage door open. I assisted him onto the seat, gently closed the passenger door, and went back for our luggage like a thief in the night.

The Peugeot's engine was exceedingly quiet. And there was no treacherous gravel to broadcast our departure. Papa's head sagged after we'd rounded the first corner. "You remember the way?" he murmured.

"Of course."

"You haven't been on the *Reherlberg* for a long time."

"I've looked it up. On my map. Here." I pulled it out of my purse. "Already opened to the right page." I put it on the dashboard and stopped the car. "Do you want me to recline your seat?"

"Please."

As I searched for the appropriate levers, I noticed for the first time how yellow his face was. "What did the doctors say you've got?" I asked, stroking his hot, wasted cheek.

"Terminal exhaustion." He put his thin fingers over mine and then dropped his hand as if just that small gesture had exceeded his strength. "There's no medical cure."

"I'm sorry." I shook my head, giving a rueful laugh. "I can't believe we're running away from home." Neither Mam*a* nor Erika would thank me for our abrupt departure when it was all over and I returned the car. But with any luck I wouldn't be around them long enough to feel the full force of their well-practiced displeasure.

CHAPTER 22

THE ONE THING I HAD IN COMMON WITH MAM*A* was that I, too, hated long distance driving. I only did it for exceptionally compelling reasons. Pap*a's* last wish fit into that category. But driving toward Tyrol was stunning enough to render my sore rear end, tension headache, and fatigue insignificant.

I stopped to buy coffee and snacks. Pap*a* wanted neither; I insisted he at least keep sipping water. Hour by hour it became clearer how serious his condition really was. If he had died right there on the passenger seat I would not have been surprised.

The granite-peaked giants to whom we drew ever closer were etched in my soul. Although I had no conscious memory of the route, something inside of me, taking over, guided me steadily toward the *Reherlberg*. And the whole time I was driving, heavenly choirs sang about the sanctity of the Alps from the car radio. It was like being in a gothic cathedral. Nothing in Oregon could compare.

At last Pap*a* stirred, needing a bathroom break. I helped him into the next roadside *Gasthaus*, maneuvered him in and out of the WC, and, propping him on a chair in the dining hall, fed him a bowl of hot, brothy soup. Afterwards, at the register, I found a display of chocolates of a brand I had never seen before. Fumbling, Pap*a* pulled out a dark chocolate bar filled with almonds and blueberries, and a milk chocolate bar filled with hazelnuts and raspberries. He insisted on paying for them himself and cradled them on his lap after I helped him back into the Peugeot.

While I buckled myself in he read the label out loud. "*Guggermukken Schokolade. Von dem Tirol. Einmalig.*" He gave a proud chuckle. "Guess who makes these."

"I'm too tired to guess."

"In that case, break off a piece. Let it melt in your mouth. Guaranteed to raise your energy level."

I followed his suggestion. The chocolate was peculiarly delicious with an intriguing aftertaste. Less than a minute later colors grew more intense; all at once I felt light and free, glad to be alive.

"Contains a secret combination of revitalizing herbs," he explained. "Cooked up by a small home based outfit. You can't get these in *Wien*. Yet." A radiant light spread over his features and stayed as he napped. I demolished both bars square by square, taking only the tiniest nibbles. They were gastronomical arabesques. Discovering Pap*a*'s stack of Mozart CDs in the glove compartment, I played them while admiring the abundance of spring flowers on the rising meadows we passed. It was mere chance that the last phrase of the Requiem faded when I rolled to a stop in front of the *Trüffelhof*, our ancestral home.

Josef looked just the way I remembered, with short chestnut curls and lucid green eyes. The moment they fastened to mine I felt the years dissolve and saw, superimposed on his shaved, adult face, the dear features of the boy I had always considered a brother. He'd grown into a fine man, broad shouldered, slim hipped, and tall.

Together, we half-carried Pap*a* through the house to an addition that hadn't existed the last time I came. Facing south, it was full of windows letting in the sun. Pap*a* protested the light hurt his eyes, so Josef helped him onto a bed in the adjoining chamber, drawing white linen curtains but keeping the windows ajar. He covered Pap*a*'s legs with a duvet. "The *Muatal* is off in the woods looking for morels," he told him, his voice tender. "She can hardly wait to get at you." The *Muatal* was what he had always called Soferl, his mother, in an unfailingly loving tone.

With a wan smile, Pap*a* folded his hands over his chest like a corpse laid out in a casket and closed his eyes.

Josef took me to a big bedroom on the ground floor of the main house. "I would have recognized you anywhere," he said, dimpling. "Except that your hair's tidier now." He tugged playfully at my braid. "Why don't you lie down for a while? I'll keep my eyes on him till the *Muatal* gets back. I'll call you when we're ready to eat."

I was glad to stretch out on the mattress. A few feet away my mottled reflection yawned at me from an oval wall mirror. A grouping of old photographs in silver frames stood on the top of the dresser. I'd seen them before, except for the studio portrait of Soferl. This must have been the bedroom Pap*a* occupied on his summer visits. I picked up each frame in turn. Grandfather and Grandmother in their wedding finery. I had never met her; she died before I was born. Infant Pap*a* in his lacy christening gown. A snapshot of the three of them, taken with a box brownie. A Polaroid of Pap*a*, Mam*a*, Erika and me. And that recent enlargement of Soferl's face, showing every wrinkle, crow's foot and silver strand without taking away any of her inherent beauty. Unlike Mam*a*, she wore no make-up but had managed to age with grace.

On the long wall behind me hung a dramatic landscape of the mountain scenery surrounding the *Trüffelhof*, masterfully contrasting misty greens with roiling black clouds and jagged white granite peaks. On the opposite side hung a sunny sketch of the front of the farmhouse or *Hof*, complete with artfully stenciled wall decorations, geraniums crowding the windows and balconies, a wide open front door. One of my early works, framed and preserved by a doting grandfather. I pulled apart the lace curtains and unfastened the window. Cool, spicy air, containing whiffs of cow dung and pine sap, streamed into the room. Along with it came the whisperings made by breeze ruffled conifer boughs, and the peaceful blending of measured bird song. Lying back down I wondered why Josef hadn't brought Pap*a* to this pleasant room and why he hadn't taken me to the little one that used to be mine.

One summer, a couple of years before I was born, Grandfather, a gentleman farmer and esteemed regional painter, rented out the vacation house at the end of the road to a Viennese banking family. Luise, their chubby teenage daughter, dutifully accompanied her parents on walks through the woods and to the *Hof* in the evenings to chat it up with my grandfather and Pap*a*, who was using his break from the agricultural college to whitewash the outside of the house.

Later Mam*a* would claim she instantly fell in love with him; I suspected she simply got bored with the company of grownups. The fact that Pap*a* had an understanding with Soferl, the farm manager's daughter, did not deter Mam*a* in the least. I could well imagine the push-and-pull that went on all summer long. By the end of August Mam*a* had won. She did it by gleefully announcing that she was pregnant with Pap*a*'s child. Case closed.

Grandfather lost his investment in higher education along with his son. Pap*a* followed Mam*a* to Vienna, switched his major to finance, his career from farming to banking, and assumed the life she prescribed. Soferl stayed behind, quietly married, gave birth to Josef, and helped her father and husband run the farm while Grandfather went on painting his favorite aspects of the *Reherlberg* and the rest of Tyrol.

With a great show of heartiness Mam*a* accompanied Pap*a* to the *Trüffelhof* every summer, insisted on occupying the best bedroom in the house, and kept her eyes not only on toddler Erika and baby Silvia, but also on young married Soferl.

Eventually Pap*a* had to assume additional responsibilities at the bank. His yearly trips to the farm became a much criticized inconvenience. I was too young to know why, but the last time Mam*a* came along she had a big row with Soferl. Mam*a* demanded that she be dismissed. Pap*a* refused to oblige her. That's when Mam*a* took herself and Erika off the mountain and declared they would never set foot on it again.

That year Pap*a* insisted I stay on at the *Trüffelhof* with him until September. Mama allowed me to spend my subsequent summer vacations there for Grandfather's sake. The old man was delighted that I had inherited some of his artistic ability and we often drew and painted together, though I hardly remembered what. Then he died. Even though Josef and I were best friends, after the funeral Mama declared that she was tired of smelling cow dung on my clothes and forbade all future visits.

She could wheedle, she could cajole, she could threaten, but she could not prevent Papa, who had inherited the property, from continuing his yearly treks. Once she even found a buyer for it. But although, for the sake of peace, he allowed her to dictate most everything else in his life, in this he held firm: he had promised Grandfather to keep the farm in the family and so he would. That commitment was a constant source of friction between my parents while I grew toward my teenage years.

Mama decided what my food preferences should be; what I must wear and study; what kind of novels I could read and boys I could talk to—and what kind of career I had better make for myself in the family's banking business. But her best piece of work was convincing me that I had no artistic talent and that my drawings were worthless. To prove it she threw away any I left lying around.

Papa saved me the only way he could think of. He enrolled me in an art institute on the other side of the world. That's how he lost me.

I left Austria in a teenage rage and did not return except for one brief visit. Jimmi came with me—but I soon vowed never to subject him to his grandmother again. It was why I did not force him to come with me on this trip. Indeed, my initial half an hour with her had already brought out the worst in me. How lucky for Erika that she was so much like Mama; otherwise, she would not have been able to stand her either. And how lucky for Mama that Erika helped her establish a united front. Poor Papa—they had given him no respite. No wonder he insisted on his yearly time-outs on the *Trüffelhof*. They were the only reason he had lasted this long.

IT WAS Soferl, still slender, her thick gold and silver hair put up in a braided coronet, who summoned me to the kitchen. There she donned heat-proof mitts and took a golden delicacy out of the oven. "April-fresh asparagus and morels, both homegrown," she said.

"Transformed into my special bread pudding. With Emmenthaler. Josef's all-time favorite dish." It smelled inviting.

He grinned, putting the finishing touches on a simple salad featuring radishes and a variety of baby greens. "From our own hothouse," he said, placing the glass bowl on the table.

"What hothouse?" I asked, promising myself to take a good look around first chance I got.

"Part of the annex. The indoor garden and our sun room are vast improvements. They make the winter and early spring on the mountain almost pleasant. You're lucky we're having a mild spell right now. But it won't last."

I said, "I've only ever been here in the summers. To get away from the city heat." Josef and I used to climb up to the hut that was Soferl's residence on the Alm, where she had begun to tend our cows from June to September. We'd bring her news and supplies, sleep over, and descend the next morning, Josef carrying fresh churned butter and I bundles of rare herbs that Soferl instructed me to hang from the *Hof's* rafters.

According to Pap*a,* autumns on the *Trüffelhof* were rife with golden light and red leaves, the nights growing ever colder. The winters were cruel, depositing a snow cap on the steep roof and a white collar half-way up the outside walls. The cows stayed in the stable then, chewing their cud, contentedly mooing while their keepers mucked, spread fresh straw, forked down hay from the loft.

Soferl cut the mushroom pudding, depositing a piece on my plate. The first bite proved addictive. Josef passed me the salad, lightly grazing his knuckles against mine in the process, evoking an agreeable sensation. "I'm not a fancy-salad maker," he apologized. "Hope my plain oil and vinegar dressing is okay with you. I did dice in some chives. The snow was slow about melting this year. The soil in our outdoor garden is still too wet to be worked."

"I've seen pictures of the kind of snowbanks you get around here," I told him. "What do you do all day when you're stuck inside? Besides cleaning up after the cows."

Josef and Soferl looked at each other, amused. "We mend everything that broke during the year," he said. "From socks to axe handles. I do maintenance on our machinery. And since your father and I built the annex we make cheeses and chocolates for the tourists."

I asked, "*Guggermukken Schokolade*?" No wonder Pap*a* had looked so proud.

Soferl poured some *Veltliner* into our goblets. "To make us self-sufficient, he said. In case he—"

After an uncomfortable silence, I said, "I hear his doctors have given up on him. How long has he got?"

She shrugged. "As long as he wants."

"What do you mean? He came here to die."

"In Vienna he wouldn't last out the month. Up here he's got me, my herbs, and tranquil surroundings. You'd be amazed what a difference they make."

"I would be amazed if they didn't." I held my goblet against the nearest candle for the simple pleasure of seeing the white wine shimmer in its soft light. "Mam*a* is a born warrior. It's hard on the people she loves."

A vertical groove cut into Soferl's forehead. "Short list!" she said before taking a deep breath to iron the crease out again. "Tomorrow Josef will procure a wheelchair for your pap*a*. We'll make it your job to push him around. Take him to visit all his favorite places. I'll do the rest. If he's still with us in June I'll get a couple of strong men to put him on one of our Haflinger horses and lead him up to the Alm with me and the cows. All the energy of the mountain radiates out at the heights."

"And if he won't let you?"

She gazed at the dark window, her pupils widening. "Then this really *will* be a good place to die." Changing the subject to my life in America, she proceeded to ask a bunch of questions about Oregon. Most of my answers included Jimmi and the dogs.

Then Josef said unexpectedly, "Do you think you could be happy here? If you lived with us all year around? Could Jimmi?"

To be honest, I would have had to say that Jimmi definitely could not. As for me, I didn't have the faintest idea. But before I could voice my response, Soferl held up her hand. "Have mercy,

Bua. She only just got here." She gathered the dishes, smiling at me. "You're still exhausted. Go to bed. And leave your pap*a* to me tonight. Everything will look better in the morning."

A few minutes later I slid under my covers and thought of Jimmi pedaling Dorrie's bike across the island to the shore, and of Asa and Marvel gazing anxiously out of the cabin's living room window listening for the sound of my footfalls. After I sank into sleep I dreamed I was inside their grief laden puppy souls, joining their endless wait.

CHAPTER 23

FOR A LONG TIME MAMA PRESSURED PAPA to have a phone installed at the *Trüffelhof* so she could reach him on his vacations any time she chose. He told her stringing a line up from the inn would be too costly. Besides, he didn't drive all the way to the top of a mountain just to have the world follow him.

When the road was passable a truck came to collect the day's milk and deliver the mail. Taking care of the lifestock was our most important and time consuming task. That's why Soferl and I made a deal—she would dedicate herself solely to Papa's care if I agreed to take over most of her chores. There were plenty. My milking skills were exceedingly rusty that first dawn, but soon I remembered the rhythm of it.

In the dusky stable Josef and I stumbled from cow to cow, taking the full buckets to our dairy. He led the cattle and the two flaxen-maned horses out to the field while I strained the milk. Then we cleared the stall floors, adding the collected muck to a large pile hidden behind the barn where it slowly disintegrated to become fabulous garden soil. It was good work, making me pleasantly tired. Afterwards I stood on the stone terrace appreciating the crisp air and admiring the breathtaking vistas before me, glowing with colors. During that first week I lost track of man-made time. Every day was a drop of forever.

As soon as Pap*a* was able to sit comfortably for a while Soferl bundled him into the wheelchair and pushed it onto the terrace to let him soak up the sun. Pulling up a stool, she sat close by. They talked in low tones, sharing childhood memories and laughing at past exploits. She read a poem to him and—of all things—a fairy tale. When it was time for her to start cooking she gave him over to me.

I pushed him through the downstairs, out the front door, and along the road past the vacation rental, now permanently occupied by two brother who were taking care of paddocked herds of goats and sheep. "They are taciturn mountain bachelors," Pap*a* explained, "shy of outsiders—especially pretty women from across the ocean who speak with an American accent. I doubt you'll see much of them unless you wheel me into their kitchen unannounced." He asked me to take him up a gentle incline and turn the wheelchair, giving him an unobstructed view of the farm.

"One day soon all of this will be yours," he said proudly, scanning the voluptuous slopes and the benign, ever present granite watchers crowding overwhelmingly close all around us. "It's in my will. You must promise me to always take care of Soferl and Josef. This is their home."

"Of course it is, Pap*a*," I answered. "More theirs than mine."

"Your grandfather wanted you to have this place. I was saving it for you, Silvia. I knew one day you'd come back." I wasn't about to remind him what it was that I had come back for. "The annex started out as a separate bungalow for Soferl, after Walter died," he said. "That's when it looked like Josef was about to get married. He was engaged to a fellow student at the agricultural college but in the end the girl decided our *Hof* was too isolated for her. That was years ago." He chuckled. "He came back full of ideas for improving the farm. I aided and abetted each one."

"Such as boutique chocolates?"

"*And* extraordinary goat chevres, not to mention our pungent sheep cheeses. All popular with the tourists. If he cared to Josef could get rich producing the stuff."

"Why doesn't he?"

Papa smiled with affection. "He says all he wants is a comfortable living. Myself, I suspect he just loves to make something extra fine now and then the same way you create pictures."

I pushed him around and around in the chair, humming a slowed version of Strauss' *Frühlingsstimmen*. Papa conducted limp wristed, humming along. His eyes seemed less sunken, less bruised. "Take me up higher," he said. "Soferl is making chicken stew and dumplings. From scratch. It'll take a while." I hoped she'd plucked an old hen ready to die.

We did a lap of the entire circular road. As I maneuvered him back down the rise, he murmured, "Odd that you never got married either." Not so odd after witnessing my parents' version of wedded bliss.

"What was Walter like? As a husband," I asked.

He thought it over. "Never raised his voice. If something bothered him he'd just leave the room until he'd mastered his emotions."

"Neat trick." I wondered if Josef had inherited his father's admirable self-control. "Were Walter and Soferl in love?"

Another pause. I'd met Walter, of course, though he always seemed to make himself scarce in the summers. Off visiting relatives when the cows were safely on the Alm with Soferl. Until her father died and he had to take over full management, doubling his chores. "They appreciated and respected each other," Papa finally said. "It's more than I can claim for your mother and me."

Odd answer. With the sharp ache of a scab freshly torn I thought of Stillman again. And then of Paul, wondering where we might possibly be heading. But he seemed a million miles away.

THE NEXT day Soferl showed me how to drain Papa's lymph system. Thereafter I helped her do it every day. It required a light touch and lots of patience. She'd concocted an elaborate get-well regime, including her medicinal herbs and massages, taking care never to overtax him. He was always extra tired after their sessions and slept more than he was awake, especially in the beginning. But by the end of the third week the yellow parchment stretching over his hollow cheekbones had begun to turn baby-pink.

Still in the wheelchair, he joined us in the kitchen, sitting at the table and watching us chop and stir. He even ate with us though Soferl gave him a special diet. While Josef and I cleared and washed dishes she sat with Papa, poring over stacks of old photographs and helping him paste their favorites into a new album. They exclaimed over how young and foolish they'd been and how cute Josef and I were as toddlers.

It wasn't until the kitchen was empty that I pulled the album to me and leafed through it, following Josef's growing-up years. He'd been a striking baby with long dark curls and large eyes, the chiseled face full of intelligence and good humor. Whenever he and I and Erika were in the same photo it was always my sister who seemed the unrelated stranger, and Josef my kin. She had become a young replica of Mama, and Josef a tall, dark and male version of Soferl. I saw nothing of Walter in him, and nothing of Papa in Erika. For a moment I fancied myself Soferl's biological daughter, Josef's true sister. It was a gratifying thought.

The next morning when Soferl wheeled Papa in to breakfast he brought with him a studio portrait of Grandfather along with some yellowed newspaper clippings. A man of his time, he'd let his beard and eyebrows grow shaggy. "Even if no one told you he was a fine arts painter you'd know just by looking at him," Papa said fondly. "I loved reading by his feet when he was outdoors at his easel." He gave me a yellowed section of newspaper. "A detailed report about his last exhibit, in Zurich. Most of his paintings have long since dispersed all over the world. But inside his painting room . . . Soferl, where's the key to the atelier?"

She riffled through a deep drawer until she found a long-stemmed key. He fondly examined the medieval scrollwork on its handle, then pressed it in my hand and said, "The works he couldn't bear to part with are up there. It's time you climbed to the third floor to examine the evidence."

Laboring up the stairs, I remembered how sometimes Grandfather would shut himself up for days on end, spending the nights on a folding cot. Soferl would bring a tray full of food, set it in front of the atelier door, and take away another, laden with dirty dishes.

My memories of Grandfather came into sharp relief as soon as I entered his studio. The cot was long gone, the tubes of paint caked, the brushes brittle with age. But the color on every canvas leaning against the wall or affixed to it shone as vibrant as if it had been applied only last week. We were passionate about the same subjects though his were local to the Tyrol and mine belonged to Oregon. Like me he loved plants intertwining, glowing patches of wildflowers, intriguing skyscapes. He loved the play of light upon shadowed land, translucent purples and fresh greens and clean blues, the golden sheen of autumn, misty spring rain, thunderous rainclouds hanging low over the slopes.

No wonder he could not bear to let these paintings go—he'd imbued each with part of his spirit. This, then, was the hidden treasure of the *Trüffelhof*, a private art museum, a window through time. And whatever talent he had painted them with he had passed on to me. It was my true inheritance. I needed no other.

I stayed inside Grandfather's favorite room for a long time, examining brush strokes, the subtly applied light, his daring vision. At last I went back to the ground floor and held out the key. Pap*a* shook his head. "Keep it. For as long as you're here. Understand, the paintings are worth a small fortune. But, like the *Trüffelhof*, he wanted them to stay in the family. For you." He smiled. "How do you like the atelier? He paid a lot of money to have the extra windows and the skylights put in. Leak-proof. Josef makes sure they stay that way. After I'm gone you can—"

I had to laugh. "As far as I can see you don't seem in an awful hurry to go anywhere. How do you feel?"

He cocked his head as if listening to some far-off melody. "*Ach*," he said. "I seem to be hungry. Is that a good sign or just Soferl's irresistible cooking?"

I WENT for my usual walks at first light, missing the dogs and envisioning their delight with this landscape, the surrounding green rolling meadows, the manicured forests kept clear of deadwood and shrubs, the well built graveled road circling the land. Here, there were no mountain lions or bears to contend with, nor poisonous snakes and pesky mosquitoes. It was a thoroughly tame place—if you didn't take into account the surly weather.

Even so, Josef didn't think I should be walking alone. I was glad of his company, particularly since he was good at finding a different route for us every morning. "How come you're not married?" I asked head-on.

He chuckled. "Haven't gotten around to it—yet. I'm used to being footloose. Besides, not many of the girls I meet at country dances are interested in living this high up. And those who are I wouldn't want to be snowed in with all winter."

"But seriously," I persisted, "don't you have any neighbors with eligible daughters looking for a lifetime partner?"

"These days most farm girls are pining for some office job in the city where all they have to do is sit and walk their fingers over a keyboard. How come *you're* not married? Don't you have any single male neighbors in love with you?"

Stillman and I hadn't needed wedding rings to know we belonged together. Our shared lives were plenty comfortable without them. He cooked for us while Jimmi did his homework and I painted. Stillman loved playing his guitar in the evenings. That's when Jimmi was learning the alto recorder and then the flute. They'd improvise together for hours. Jimmi never talked about needing a TV back then. But with rings or without, Stillman would have wound up just as dead in the end.

"I do have one new neighbor," I admitted. "Divorced. He's taking care of my dogs." I didn't mention the numerous cats, who actually—all things considered—would hardly be noticeable in a big farmhouse like the *Trüffelhof* and the attached cow-warm stable, the cozy hayloft, the huge barn. Of course, I'd have to charter a plane to transport my multitudinous brood—an alternative I couldn't afford. "His name's Paul," I said. "He seems nice."

"How long have you known him?"

"A month?"

"Oh?" He looked relieved. "Barely more than a stranger."

"When I arrived in Vienna," I said, "I was sure Pap*a* had some sort of terminal cancer."

"You should have brought him to us sooner."

"Mam*a* and Erika should have, you mean."

"They would rather have watched him die than deliver him into the *Muatal's* hands," he said with a burst of anger.

I stopped walking. "If he goes back he will."

"He's not going back."

We stopped at the rim of the upper forest and sat on mossy boulders looking down upon the faraway *Hof*. The peaks were shrouded. It started to rain. Just off to one side, half-hidden by trees, were misty paddocks holding goats and sheep, the blurred outline of the vacation house barely visible through the branches. "I used to count the months and days until June," he said, pulling up his jacket hood. "I thought you would keep spending your summer holidays here with us until we were old enough to get married. Instead you stopped coming. No letter. Never a word of explanation." He tore a patch of moss off his boulder and shredded it to bits. "When I asked the *Muatal* she said it was because your mam*a* didn't like farms."

Feeling cold, I zipped my coat to the chin and turned up the collar, regretting that I had left my silk scarf in my chamber. "Didn't they have a fight? Pap*a* took Soferl's side. Mam*a* never forgave him."

He shrugged. "That was before your pap*a* had the indoor toilet installed. The way I heard it, your mam*a* fouled every chamber pot one day and ordered the *Muatal* to empty and scrub each one. The *Muatal* reminded her that she was nobody's maid and gave her directions to the outhouse."

I gave a mirthless chuckle. "Mama wants people to grovel as a sign of their affection. Which is why I live on the other side of the world."

He looked at me. "As far as she's concerned, this *is* the far side of the world."

I shook my head. "Not far enough." The drops were getting heavier, wobbling on my supposedly water-proof shoulders before sinking through the coat's fabric. Rising, I pulled at my sticky jeans. "I shudder when I think of what will happen when I return the Peugeot. I'm sure she's rehearsed some piquant conversations between us. Or should I say *accu*sations?"

Our return route took us past the spot where Papa and I had done the Strauss waltz. I caught a movement in the goat paddock, off to our right. A slender, shadowy shape enveloped in a raincoat was squeezing out of the paddock gate, carrying a bucket.

"Do your shy middle aged bachelor assistants wear ankle-long skirts?" I asked.

Josef watched the figure walk toward the small house. "They did mention that one of their sisters was coming to help them with some serious spring cleaning." He fashioned a bullhorn with his hands and shouted a greeting. The figure froze. Josef waved. She darted to the front door and disappeared inside. "Look at that!" he said, disappointed. "She must have inherited the family shyness gene. I wonder if I can coax her out of it with a bar of our best *Guggermukken Schokolade*."

CHAPTER 24

Soferl came running as soon as we entered the *Hof.* "Quick," she said. "Sepp lurched down to the lower meadow when I wasn't looking. And collapsed."

The three of us hastened to the terrace and from there downhill to where Pap*a* lay like a wet bundle of laundry, his face an unearthly pale. He opened his eyes when Josef pulled him into a sitting position. "Rubbery legs," he groaned. "Slope's steeper than I thought."

I helped Josef get him to his feet. Soferl put a Loden cape around him and then, between the three of us, we dragged her shivering patient to his bed.

"Obstinate man," Soferl grumbled after we'd lowered him onto his mattress. "Worse than a baby." While Josef undressed him she sent me to the kitchen to fill two hot water bottles. Through the heavy metal door leading to the stable I could hear the cows restlessly mooing. Pap*a* was completely covered by his duvet when I returned to the sick-room, the only proof of his presence his shock of silver streaked curls.

Soferl pointed to a bowl of gruel on the nightstand. "I went to
the kitchen to make him his breakfast. When I came back he was
gone. I couldn't find him anywhere in the house." She'd had the good
sense to step into her rubber boots before starting an outdoors
search. Rain clinging to the meadow grass had soaked my cloth
sneakers and the socks inside them. Josef, though he'd at least worn
leather shoes, wasn't faring much better.

We hurried to change out of our wet clothes and took care of the
cows whose teats were heavy with milk. The pleasant warmth inside
the stable soon thawed my icy hands though the first few cows
complained bitterly when I touched them. I got wet again
transporting muck to the steaming pile behind the barn. I knew this
kind of rain—it would go on for days, veiling the farm and its
environs in heavy fog, the temperature falling by the hour.

Throughout the morning Soferl brushed, padded and slapped
Papa's pasty skin. Around noon she asked us to put him in a tub of
warm water because his temperature was refusing to rise. We took
turns supporting his head. As the bath cooled we added hot water.
His submerged naked body looked insubstantial.

"I thought he was getting better!" I said, not realizing until the
words were out of my mouth how thoroughly I'd believed Soferl's
assessment of his condition.

"He was. Is. A week ago he couldn't have walked across the
room by himself," she reminded me. "Of course there'll be setbacks.
He's full of toxins. That's why I've been massaging him. To move
them through." The bath was scented with a pungent herb that made
my throat tingle each time I inhaled. When Papa's head sank to his
chest she put smelling salts to his nostrils. He startled awake, his
face flushing bright red. The color ebbed away leaving his cheeks
rosy.

"A little nap," he whispered. "Then I'll be good as new."

"Let's hope so, old Sepp," Soferl said, signaling us to draw him
out of the tub. "I've spent a lot of time on you. I'll thank you not to
sabotage my efforts again."

He gave a weak chuckle. "A thimble of Schnapps might perk
me up. Or a cup of mulled wine."

She blotted him with a large white terry towel. "Mulled porridge, you mean. Piping hot." Tugging the duvet up to his ears, she nodded at me. "Silvia, you sit on him till I come back. And keep everything below his nose under the featherbed. "

I waited for her to close the door before asking him, "Are you getting warm yet?"

He gave a muffled sigh.

Sitting on the mattress, I said in a scratchy voice, "I was beginning to suspect you got me to fly over here under false pretenses. I kind of liked the idea." I tried to clear my throat, but only managed to tighten the knot wrapped around my vocal cords. Then some dam inside me burst, making my chest heave. Next thing I knew my arms were draped around him pinning him under the cover while I flooded his cheek with my tears.

Over the lonely years I'd spent away from him he'd become less and less real to me until at last he and Mama and Erika were nothing but fragmented memories. Even after I came to Vienna and saw what a wreck he'd become I'd struggled to keep my emotions at bay. Why should I resurrect old feelings when by his own admission he was getting ready to die? It was only now that I realized how much his ongoing life actually mattered to me.

"Maybe you're right," he said, clumsily patting my arm. "Maybe I just wanted you to come see what you'd left behind. Why do you think you moved from California to the top of an Oregon mountain? Because you were missing this place. It's your true home, Silvia. I was deprived of seeing you become a woman but I had the privilege of watching Josef grow into an exceptionally fine man. You two were always so much alike. Still are. There's no one in the world as right for you as he is. Don't waste another minute. Start being happy. Tonight. And shout it out loud in the morning."

With his hand on my shoulder, what he wanted seemed not only possible but preordained. Before I could speak again Soferl reappeared with Papa's porridge and her own dinner plate. She gave me a handkerchief. I wiped my eyes.

"About time you let yourself cry," she said approvingly. "Josef's putting together a little supper for the both of you. Go get it. I'm eating with Sepp."

In the kitchen Josef had poured a deep-red *Zweigelt* into two goblets, leaving the bottle handy for refills. Between the wine and our plates stood a pencil-thin vase containing a half-open long-stemmed red tulip. It was framed by two golden beeswax candles. "To drive off the gloom," he said, lighting the wicks. I sat with my back to the cook stove, glad of its glow, and drank a long swallow for courage.

"Told you the weather wouldn't last." He raised his glass. "*Prosit*." Then he pointed to the open faced sandwiches on my plate. "I thought it was about time you had a good taste of our renowned cheeses. That creamy one is a mild chevre. And the dark one is a very sharp sheep cheese. I hope your palate is equal to it."

Neither of them was anything I'd ever get in a store, even the fabulous co-op. Topping generous slices of buttered, home-baked bread, the cheeses were a taste sensations on par with my previous sampling of Josef's best *Guggermukken Schokolade*.

I ate every slice on offer, finishing my wine. "You were born in this house, weren't you," I said. "Have you ever considered living anywhere else?"

"Never." He refilled our glasses. "I'm one of those few fortunate ones who know exactly where they belong. To me the *Trüffelhof's* more than a farm. It's who I am."

"You ever wonder, with Pap*a* so sick and all, what might happen to it once he dies? If Mam*a* gets—"

"He's not going to die. And she won't get it. Sepp told me about his will. The *Trüffelhof* and everything else on top of the *Reherlberg* is solidly yours."

"And if *I* die? Then Erika will inherit, and that's as good as Mam*a*—"

"Worst comes to worst I'll buy it from her. The *Muatal* and I have laid by, you see. I could buy it from you. But that's not how your pap*a* wants it. And it's not how I want it." He put his hand on mine. "None of us live forever. I might lose control of the farm truck next time I drive down to the inn. There's a couple of hard curves that often ice over. But at least I'd die knowing that I've lived a good life and have put my stamp on this place, on this mountain. Every year the *Hof* gets a bit more livable. Your pap*a* calls it our ongoing project. What have you got on your Oregon mountain that compares to all this?"

"Not a thing," I said honestly. "My little cabin is modeled more along the lines of Soferl's Alm hut. Rickety and mean, especially in inclement weather."

He chuckled. "I bet. Insulated?"

"Poorly."

"Electrified?"

"Only the downstairs. Somewhat."

"Indoor bathroom?"

"Not now or ever."

"You own it?"

"Can hardly afford the rent."

"And that new neighbor feeding the dogs. His house is better than yours?"

I chuckled. "A valiant ruin begging to be knocked down."

He refilled my glass. "There's a school bus comes as far as the inn. In the winter Jimmi could board in town if he wanted. Or study up here. In a few years he'll be going off to some college. I recommend mine. Afterwards he could come back to us and fiddle with anything he likes. Think up new projects."

"He's brown."

"It's a nice color."

"A lonely color around here."

"Unless you're color-blind. To my mind everybody should be. It would eliminate half of all wars. Getting rid of religions would eliminate the rest."

"That's good," I said. "Unless you're religious."

"I'm not. In that way. And I'd never dream of imposing my beliefs on anyone else."

"Jimmi's too old to be made to move without his consent. He refused to join me on this trip."

"To *Wien*? I would have, too." He raised his glass. I raised mine. He went on with, "All I'm saying is let him spend a summer with us. Let me show him everything I love about the place."

"At present he's an oppositional adolescent who hates my guts."

"Not enough homegrown salads. Low on the feel-good vitamins. Does he like horses? I'll teach him to ride the Haflingers."

I didn't have the heart to tell him that the only thing Jimmi was prepared to like was gangsta rap.

Josef held my hand tighter as if afraid it might fly away. "This thing we have between us. How much longer are you willing to pretend it isn't there?"

I blinked. "Brotherly love?"

"Brotherly, my foot. Deep-down soul mate kind of love. One kiss will show you the difference." He leaned close, his pupils dilating, deliberately exposing his heart. I valued the courage that took, for mine had long since learned to be guarded. "We belong together," he insisted. "You know that. As husband and wife." His lips parted. Mine tingled with anticipation.

There was a loud crash from the hall door. It was Soferl, whose plate had slipped out of her hands and shattered to pieces. Her face was stark white. "No," she whispered. "You can't marry."

Josef's mouth tensed. "You . . . object?" he asked, incredulous. I tried to pull my hand out of his but he bore down harder, watching his mother slowly pick up the fragments as if trying to give herself time to think.

"Yes," she finally said.

"Why?"

She went to the garbage pail, stepped on the pedal that opened the lid, and dropped the shards inside. Then she returned to the door, closing it as if afraid someone in the hallway might overhear. At last she sat down across from us, clasping her fingers and addressing her crossed thumbs. "I never thought I would have to say this but now there's no way around it. Forgive me, Josef, Silvia. You see, you really *are* brother and sister. Half, anyway."

I couldn't take in what she was saying. Josef shook his head as if trying to clear it. Then he released my hand.

She sighed. "Sepp has no idea, to this day. But Walter knew. You see, at the start of the summer during which your mama stole him away, Sepp and I had a spat. While I was waiting for the courage to tell him I was pregnant your mama sprang her news first. What could I do but keep silent? When the truth would have destroyed other lives besides mine?"

For a long time nobody spoke. Josef, having so much more to swallow than me, sat like a statue, staring at the nearest candle flame.

A confusion of images swirled through my mind. Thoughts. Equations. Readjustments. "Papa is asleep?"

"Resting."

I jumped up. "I have a feeling he'll rest much better once he knows the truth. I'm going in to tell him. Right now. Unless you'd rather do it yourself."

Soferl's eyes were moist and pleading. Josef's swam in tears. I took their hands. "Don't be afraid to give him the greatest gift he could have imagined. He's missed out on so much. There's not a moment to lose."

I pulled them to the annex, one on each side. In the sickroom I flipped the featherbed off Papa's nose and clapped until he opened his eyes. "Papa?" I said cheerfully, hoping to convey that we were the bringers of good news. "Soferl has something to tell you." I made her sit on the bed, pushed Josef into the nearest chair, and took the one in the corner. For several second I was almost sorry, for I knew without a doubt that I was about to lose my life-long status of favorite child. But it was worth it just to see the look of wonder and delight that presently spread over our papa's face.

I FELL asleep feeling relieved and happy. There was no reason at all why, in the middle of the night, I should have found myself in a bad dream. In it, Jimmi was standing with his back to me and would not turn around when I said his name. Instead he walked off as if I had not spoken. "Jimmi," I kept calling after him. Still he walked, getting ever smaller and darker and moving farther and farther away. When he was only a dot on the horizon I heard the sound of desolate weeping and realized it was coming from me. Then Marvel's lean face shot toward me out of nowhere, filling the screen of my mind, her eyes huge and pleading, sending through me a shockwave of pain that made me gasp and jerked me into a sit.

I clicked on the light, packed my bags, and sat in the dark until morning.

ONCE HE realized I could not be persuaded to stay Josef insisted on driving me from the Alps to the Munich airport, where I told him to let me out at the curb. He idled the car, gripping the steering wheel. "You're not coming back to us, are you?"

"Not anytime soon," I admitted. "You have each other. Jimmi has no one but me. He needs me. In Oregon. The *Trüffelhof* could never work for him. And as much as I love it—and all of you—I love him more. He must come first."

Josef held me against him, cheek to cheek. It was a strange sensation, for his skin felt like an extension of mine. Watching him drive away, I could see his longing to get out of the city, away from the flatland, back to his mountain.

THE FIRST flight I was able to book was scheduled to leave in late afternoon. This gave me plenty of time to call Key Largo. No one answered the phone, so I left a message for Jimmi, asking him to get ready—I was coming home and so was he. I had even worse luck calling my own number. The phone rang and rang without the machine kicking in.

As the hours dragged I calmed my rising anxiety by reliving Soferl's bedside confession. It had rallied Papa at once. "You should have told me long ago!" he cried.

She'd blushed. "I was too young, too hurt because you allowed yourself to fall for Luise's wiles. And after she announced she was pregnant it was too late. Then Walter said he would have me, but only if I promised him the baby would be raised as his own. We fudged some dates to make it credible. In case you asked."

"One lover's quarrel plus two proud hearts equaled long, wasted years!" With a regretful laugh he took her hand. "I have a secret of my own to confess. My dear wife threw it at me after a particularly bitter argument the year after Silvia was born. It is that she was already pregnant when she and her parents came to occupy the vacation rental—and that they'd known all along." He stuffed a couple of pillows behind his head and beckoned Josef to sit next to Soferl. I leaned forward in my chair, unwilling to miss a single word.

"If I could have taken Silvia with me," Papa went on, "I would have gotten out of the marriage right there and then. But Luise made all the usual threats—no custody, no visitation rights—so I stayed. Particularly since she had taken an instant dislike to the daughter who resembled me; I was the child's only buffer."

Lest I should feel left out, Papa invited me to sit on the other side of his bed. The four of us weighed down the mattress, which started to sag alarmingly. "Summers on the *Trüffelhof* were my only solace, my dear Soferl," he said. "You hid yourself on the Alm and Walter usually found pressing business elsewhere but little Josef was always glad to see Silvia and me, and I loved the way the kids took to each other. Watching them play was almost like seeing you and me grow up all over again."

Soon Soferl insisted we leave him alone to rest. I was feeling pretty tired myself—a good, joyful tired, even though I understood very well that Papa was going to change his will to include Josef. It was only right.

JUST before my flight was announced I called the cabin once more. Still no answer. I counted back eight hours—or was it nine? Most likely Paul was out taking the dogs on their morning hike. I would try him from San Francisco. Pacific Coast Time.

When I did, a woman answered. At seven in the morning. "Violet?" I said, perplexed. "Is that you?"

"Oh hi, Silvi. How's it going?" she asked sleepily, as if it were perfectly normal for her to pick up my phone.

"I'd like to speak to Paul," I said.

"He isn't here right now. Want me to pass on a message?"

Reluctantly, I asked her to give him the time of my arrival so he could pick me up. She said she would. But when I got to the Medford airport he was not there.

CHAPTER 25

I WAITED INSIDE THE TERMINAL FOR ONE MISSPENT hour before realizing Paul was not going to appear. Phoning home produced no results. With growing unease I dragged my luggage onto the next bus to Ashland and got out at the southern tip of town, futilely dialing my number from a pay phone. Then I called a taxi.

Forty minutes later my cab stopped at Stu's lot. The cabbie took one look at my access road and refused to drive on, claiming the ruts would break his axle. I paid him a twenty five dollar fare and watched him drive back toward the county road, stirring up dust, before I proceeded to drag myself and my baggage homeward.

The red clay under my feet was already stone-hard. Amidst the cracks were deep ruts made by heavy truck tires during the last rains. The grooves had baked in the sun and would remain until Paul kept his promise to Barret and brought in a grader.

Shiny new leaves on nearby brush were half covered with clay dust. Obviously it hadn't rained for a while, nor was there a single cloud in the sky. By the time I managed to reach the third churned-up rise I was bathed in sweat, the suitcase bumping my right shin, the carryon's strap biting into my opposite shoulder. At last the old cabin stood before me, looking even shabbier than I remembered. The only vehicle in the driveway was my lonesome Efi, filmed with red dirt. The dog yard was empty but I spied movement at the big living room window.

It was Marvel, sitting on top of my desk just inside the glass, staring out at me as if she didn't quite trust her eyes. Then she did a double take, gave a yip, and disappeared from view. A second later she was barreling down the ramp that led from the dog door to the yard. Asa was right behind her. They were much too thin. Making odd noises half snore and half purr they pressed themselves against the fence, their hip bones jutting out of rumpled, dull fur. Every rib showed.

I dropped my stuff and let them out of the yard. They threw themselves at my feet, convulsing with joy. I ran my hands over the big hollows where their flanks had been. "God!" I said, hugging them both. "I'm sorry I trusted him. I should never have left." But if I hadn't Papa would still be in Vienna more dead than alive and neither of us would have found out about Josef.

The dogs followed me into the house through the unlocked kitchen door. Three sad-eyed cats were sitting on the table around a saucer piled high with ground necks. They took one look at me and dove for cover. "Kitty, kitty!" I said. "It's only me coming home." They did not respond.

The countertop was brutally clean. So was the sink. The freezer, which should have been near empty by now, was still crowded with chicken parts. An excess of thawed, bleeding necks languished on the refrigerator shelves giving off an unpleasant odor. I pulled out the pinkest looking bunch, unzipped the baggie, and threw necks to the dogs until each of them had devoured six. Then I tried the faucet and was relieved to find it was working though what poured out looked like tea. But that was probably because the water at the *Trüffelhof*, spring-fed, was so much clearer than anywhere else.

I hadn't heard a peep out of Racket. He didn't appear when I called. He wasn't hiding anywhere in the kitchen. Nor was he under my bed in the living room, in the closet, beneath my desk, or in the cat yard. Returning to the kitchen, I finally noticed that the saucer on the table was swarming with ants. Paul had taken the trouble of setting it on a plate filled with water but some cat had dropped crumbs, making a land-bridge for the invaders. One of my written instructions to Paul had been that the cat food was to be kept out for no more than thirty minutes lest it attract vermin. I found one part of the saucer's rim not yet crawling with the marauders, heaved it, them, and the carrion into a plastic bag, sealed it, and dropped it into the freezer. A good number of ants were already crawling up my hands and wrists and disappearing inside my sleeves. The phone rang as I was brushing them off.

It was Barret. "Welcome home," he said gruffly. "That your cab I saw driving out? I thought Randy was supposed to pick you up from the airport."

"So did I. We must have got our wires crossed." I stared at the answering machine, noticing that someone had turned it off.

"Didn't he know you were coming today?"

"I'm not sure. When I called home from San Francisco Violet answered the phone and I told her—" I lowered myself onto a stool, biting my lip.

"Violet doesn't have a phone anymore," he said, his voice turning frigid. "It got disconnected."

"Of course," I mumbled. "Sorry. Jet lag. I guess I'll walk on back to the abandoned—uh . . . I'm sure there's a good explanation. For everything. Bye." I hung up, staring at the receiver in horror. For one vital moment I'd forgotten the sensitive political climate up here. "Come on," I told the dogs, marching outside. "We're taking a walk."

BEFORE the abandoned cabin came into view I could hear Violet's silvery laugh and Paul's throaty reply. We passed her dirty white truck and a metallic-blue, more recent version of Efi. It was a Tacoma, polished to a high gloss. The dogs stopped at the bottom of newly made stairs. I climbed to the porch, stepping around empty spaces where rotten boards had been ripped up and not yet replaced with new ones, and made my way around the corner to the back. Violet was sitting on the porch floor, leaning against the wall at the same spot I'd occupied during the rain storm that had been followed by double rainbows. Lavender was bouncing on Violet's thighs, playing with her mommy's lank hair. Paul stood bent over his saw horses wearing torn jeans and a sleeveless undershirt that showed off his muscular arms. He was unclamping a board, a rip saw by his feet.

From somewhere inside the cabin came a shrill yip, a scrabble, and then a very fat Racket charged through the doorway. He threw himself at me, yodeling in the highest registers he could reach, his terrible Chihuahua voice drilling through my ears straight to my brain to trigger the beginnings of a migraine. I snatched him up and clamped one hand over his grinning muzzle while trying to contain his frantic wiggling with the other.

Paul had turned toward me, arms dangling. "Silvi!" he said as if seeing a ghost. "Is that you? How did you get here? Why didn't you call?"

"I did," I said, keeping my voice bland. "From Munich. And again from San Francisco early this morning. Violet answered. Didn't she pass on the message? She said she would."

Violet tittered, pressing Lavender's winsome cheek against her own. "Oh gee—I guess I was still half asleep. I thought you were talking about *tomorrow*, Silvi. I was going to get around to it. Honest."

"I see," I said, glaring at her. "Well—after I waited at the Medford airport for over an hour I figured out something was wrong. So I took a bus and a taxi." I shifted my glare to the other perpetrator. "Paul, I do want to thank you—very much—for taking such *good* care of my animals, even though the shepherds look half dead. On the other hand, Racket certainly seems extremely well-fed. Don't let me disturb you. I was just on my way up to the ridge."

Paul took a step toward me anyway, tripping over his saw. In an effort to right himself, he grabbed at the board. It crashed to the floor, taking one of the sawhorses with it. Ducking as if to ward off a blow, Violet clutched Lavender tight to her bosom.

Still holding Racket I went around the corner to where Asa and Marvel sat, strangely subdued. "Come," I said, stomping down the stairs. "We're leaving." When I strode toward the skid, they slunk so close that their noses kept bumping the outside of my knees.

From the porch, Paul was yelling, "Don't go up there by yourself! Let me come with you!"

I pretended not to hear.

"Silvi!" he cried again. "I need to explain—"

I stopped him with a very polite "Don't bother. Everything's crystal clear." Racket peered over my shoulder and whined. Trying to get back to Paul? Ingrate.

"There's something you should know," Paul tried again. "Please!" He undid his tool belt. "I'm coming with you."

"No you're not!" I said sharply. Then I tried for a neighborly smile but couldn't quite get my lips to soften. "Stay where you are. With your new girl friend. Congratulations. I think." And on I went, fueled by outrage and disappointment, my formerly confident puppies cowering at my heels, my formerly slender Chihuahua struggling to ditch me in favor of an untrustworthy fool who hadn't kept his promise to carefully measure out precise Lilliputian portions each day.

Hiking up the denuded logging skid, I spied a few long-stemmed tiger lilies and columbines hiding behind trees. But up on top the blush was off the season. My favorite early-spring flowers had long since wilted away, making room for ordinary bachelor buttons, wild sunflowers, and swathes of vetch that were not nearly as deep purple as they had been in past years. Racket had grown heavy in my arms. Judging him safe from Paul and his own worst instincts, I put him down. He shuffled ahead, listlessly sniffing at the shriveling sky-blue petals of a Hound's Tongue and at a stunning, ultra-marine grass bell shining in a dry patch of weeds.

On the long flight from Munich I had yearned to make my pilgrimage to Blossom Lane. In my mind's eye I'd seen it beckon on the easterly slope with its long rows of lavender, white, and pink blossoms, and the puffy orange-red orbs of Indian Paintbrush that Paul had promised would cover the steep slope behind them, every bloom surrounded by contentedly buzzing bees.

If memory served, Paul and I had made a date to enjoy this expedition together. A long time ago. *While you're putting distance and time between us, think about you and me, together. Try to get used to the idea. Okay?*

Oh, well. It wasn't as if I needed him by my side. Not on a hike, not sitting across an intimate restaurant table, or at home sharing my bed. Thank God I'd learned to be self-contained. Thank God I actually *preferred* being alone. Except for those all-too-brief years with Stillman, loneliness had been my mantle of choice. I'd shucked it off temporarily to help Pap*a* but it had hovered on this hillside waiting to embrace me again. It was a good fit.

Sitting on *Trüffelhof's* orderly terrace, I had longed to be in wild Blossom Lane, surrounded by a hodgepodge of colors and entwining brush. I'd arrived not an instant too soon. The way the sun was bearing down on the hillsides even the miracle of my secret lane couldn't last much longer. Studying the heights of Greensprings, I saw that the tender green that had covered its sheer slopes when I left had already shriveled. Ashlanders liked to pretend it was real grass but it was only a spindly crop of weeds not meant to last out the season. Dying away, it had exposed such large patches of seared earth that the invasive blankets of vetch could not begin to cover them. Already I missed the juicy Alpine meadows on the *Reherlberg*, never anything less than resplendent between spring's snowfall and autumn's.

I followed the deer trail toward the lane. The first baby madrones, guarding its entrance, were about to come into view. And then I stood dumb, staring at an obscene mound of stones burying my paradise. Baby madrones, infant firs, long rows of lavender, raspberry, and wild rose bushes—all crushed under this incomprehensible avalanche. Not one Giant Red Indian Paintbrush had survived.

Faint with shock, I sat hard on the ground before I could fall.

Ever solicitous, the dogs nosed my cheeks. I warded them off, rubbed my eyes, looked again. The rocky heap stretched from the top of the peak across Blossom Lane and buried a good part of the remaining bits of forest farther downslope, wantonly crushing every tree in its wake. Why?

To get the answer I clawed my way to the top. It was gone. Some gigantic blade had sheered it off like the thin end of a soft boiled egg. It had taken nature millennia to form the peak and centuries to produce a thriving forest on it, but a bulldozer had managed to convert the whole thing into barren moonscape in just a few weeks.

The machine had left one tree standing, perhaps because the operator was partial to ancient gnarled oaks. Or maybe he'd used that last tree as a convenient measuring device, for the undisturbed bit of soil the oak clung to had become an island whose surface was ten, fifteen feet above the rest of the jumbled moonscape. Around this island, every layer of decomposing leaves, needles and twigs had been scraped off the summit. The hungry dozer blade had also taken the sub soil underneath, pushing it all over the edge. The only thing left of the peak besides that desolate oak-island were smashed sheets of bedrock.

The migraine Racket's shrill welcome had triggered was now stabbing at my right temple. Feeling nauseous, I massaged the side of my head while circling the rim and peering down at what looked to me like the aftermath of a war. The sun glared on each discarded stone of the ruins.

I WAS ready for an explanation. Obviously Paul knew exactly what Gierig had been up to. Retreating, the cowed puppies and I descended the skid toward the abandoned cabin. We hadn't gone more than halfway when the corpulent Racket put on a burst of speed and barreled around the next curve. His whole hungry life I'd carefully measured out every bite I put in his bowl to keep him lean because, in my opinion, nothing was uglier than an obese lap dog. One quarter cup of ground meat and one little skinned chicken neck or wing tip was our daily compromise. No wonder he preferred Paul's portions. How was a Chihuahua to know that every pound he gained would lead him toward shortage of breath, diabetes, and a failing heart?

Damn you, Paul Randolph. I only thought the words, but someone below was shouting them out. "Damn you, Paul! Fucking Randy! I was willing to let bygones be bygones, but, hell, you had to go and do it again!" Barret. "Why is it that you can't find your own partners?" he raged. "Why do you always have to steal mine?"

In my eagerness to hear every word Barret was spewing I stopped watching my step, tripped, and fell headlong down the trail. As the ground rushed at my face I thought, *Don't stretch out your hands!* Too late. They were already breaking the fall. Something inside my right wrist snapped. I lay stunned, then scrambled to my feet picking bits of bark out of my palms. My right arm was beginning to throb. Racket, who'd made a U-turn when the Bear started shouting, reappeared to reclaim his rightful place in our tribe.

"Let's go home," I whispered. If there had been an alternate route to my cabin I would have taken it. But the underbrush in this part of the forest was too dense for me to even want to attempt passage. There was nothing to do except tiptoe past Paul's cabin hoping the fracas would stay contained to the back porch.

" . . . forget about the oral agreement between us. Consider it broken. By you," Barret was yelling. "Part of our deal was that you'd get the road fixed after you messed it up with your confounded hauling. I see you decided not to take that obligation seriously."

Paul's answer was too low and reasonable for me to understand.

"Not soon enough to suit me," Barret growled in reply. "Which is why I'm giving you twenty-four hours to get off the ridge. If you thought . . . "

We skirted the two pickups, now joined by Barret's unwieldy farm truck. Trudging out of earshot, I nursed my hand, the dogs so close beside me that I was afraid of tripping again. An engine started. Wheels spun. "Come on!" I hissed, diving behind a thicket. Clyde's truck shot past, a white faced Violet at the wheel, a teary eyed, unstrapped Lavender hanging on to the open passenger window. As soon as they were out of sight we hurriedly returned to the path, my single objective to barricade myself inside my cabin before the men could bring their quarrel to me.

CHAPTER 26

FIGURING I WAS SAFE UNTIL I HEARD ANOTHER engine, I went through the house collecting Paul's things, including his shaving kit and clothes. I packed everything into empty boxes and put them out on the porch in a patch of shade. The accompanying note, painfully scribbled with my bruised right hand, read:

Dear Paul,

Thanks again for helping me out. My father seems to be getting better. He insisted on giving you this medley of handmade chocolates in appreciation. Please accept the enclosed check for the pet-minding. Since I'm not feeling well, I'm going straight to bed. We'll talk another day.

Silvi

Another day? Like hell!

NOT feeling well was an understatement. My arm throbbed, my head pounded, my stomach threatened to roll over. It was not the homecoming I had expected. I duct-taped a linen sheet over the window that was facing the porch, lay on my bed, put my good arm over my face to block out daylight, and shut my eyes.

The first one to knock was Barret of course. He did it in his usual no-nonsense way, the indignant landlord demanding overdue rent. I ignored him. "Silvi!" he boomed as if he were planning to oust me along with Paul just for having been cordial to my new neighbor. He rattled the handle. The latch strained.

Asa barked a deep warning. Marvel gave a menacing growl. I threw the covers over my head and lay still until Barret stalked off. Then I thanked the dogs for their assistance.

By the time Paul parked on my driveway the clearing lay in late afternoon shade. No doubt the *Guggermukken Schokolade* under his pile of clothes had long since melted into a gob. What was it to me? I stuffed my thumbs into my ears to muffle the sound of his knocks and his plaintive "Silvi? Silvi!"

Asa started to wag his tail but Marvel backed away from the door. Racket dove out through the pet door and ran to the gate, squalling. Eventually the footsteps receded down the porch steps. A car door opened. Several minutes later the footsteps briefly returned and receded again. The unctuous Tacoma whirred away.

I didn't stir until the pain in my wrist got so bad I was forced to rummage for ice. Cracking a freezer tray one-handed, I crushed the cubes in my blender, poured them into a plastic baggy, wrapped it in a towel, and applied it to my arm, keeping some out to put on my forehead. I went back to bed.

Barret called first. I let the machine take the message, only half listening to his belligerent tone. Paul called much later. I scrambled up to the landing so I wouldn't miss a word. He wanted to know if I'd seen the note he left on my porch. And he explained that in my absence he'd rented a small office in town where he was now planning to spend the night. He hoped I'd feel better after a good sleep and threatened to stop by in the morning. Click.

I was quite sure I wouldn't want to see him then either.

While I was in the kitchen I decided to give Key Largo another try, never mind that it was three hours later at night. This time Dorrie answered.

"I'm sorry you couldn't reach us before," she said, sounding reserved. "We were at the gallery all day. How was your trip?"

"Okay. Thanks for taking care of Jimmi for me. Is he there?"

Dorrie said slowly, "No. He's not. As a matter of fact." She took a ragged breath and rushed on, "Look—I might as well get it over with. Leroy was bugging me on the phone for weeks, so, after Jimmi came—well, I thought it would be a real good time for Leroy to meet his own son."

"You didn't!" I gasped, stunned. "You promised—"

"Let me finish. I felt sorry for Jimmi, okay? A boy shouldn't have to be in the dark about his own father. It isn't as if he doesn't have one. So, a couple of weeks ago Leroy flew in and they hit it off. You have no idea how well—in hindsight I suspect he introduced the boy to pot—or something worse—almost at once. Because Jimmi seemed to change. Overnight. At first Leroy threatened to sue you for child abuse because you kept the boy isolated on an Oregon mountain top. Stunted psychological development, he called it. Then he started to make noises about taking Jimmi back to L.A. with him. He promised to teach him to drive his new black Z around shopping malls before the stores opened. Unlimited access to gangsta rap. A vacation in the hood where everyone was going to be his shade and darker and he wouldn't have to feel different anymore. He claimed he'd send Jimmi to Oregon the minute you returned, but when I called his house an hour ago all I got was a recording saying his number is no longer in service and there isn't a new one."

The kitchen spun. I laid my forehead against the cool wall. "Leroy does heavy drugs."

"He swore he was clean. If I made a mistake it was with Jimmi's co-operation. All he had to do is say no and none of it could have happened. As a matter of fact I did tell Leroy he couldn't take Jimmi to L.A. without your approval. But on Leroy's next to last day they told me they were going to the movies together. They got on a plane instead. If you never speak to me again I can't blame you."

"I *will* never speak to you again," I said. "But you must call me the minute you hear from either one of them. No matter what time it is. Check your phone bills. Maybe Leroy called you from his mother's. If she's still alive. Is she listed?"

"I already tried long distance information. Common first name. Common last. And L.A.'s too big for a needle in a haystack search. But Jimmi will come to his senses. Sooner or later he'll figure things out. All you have to do is wait."

"Thanks for the advice," I said, shaking with anger. "Leroy did a head trip on Crystal. He did one on you. And now he's doing one on Jimmi. Letting a thirteen-year-old drive a sports car. Endless gangsta rap and all the weed he can smoke. When he's at such a rebellious, impressionable age." I clutched the receiver, baring my teeth. "Crystal *died* still entangled in Leroy's sticky web," I shouted into the mouth piece. "And she had a lot more experience with the man's wiles than a clueless thirteen-year-old! I will *never* forgive you!" And then I hung up.

It was the worst night of my life. My wrist hurt, some God was pounding a railroad spike through my right eyeball, and I puked until I had the dry heaves. When the pain got too bad I walked from living room to kitchen and back again, always stopping in front of the phone, willing it to ring. Surely Jimmi would have second thoughts. Surely he would remember how much I loved him, what his betrayal would do to me.

The migraine was worse in the morning. My wrist and hand were swollen to three times their size. Any minute the skin, stretched past its limit, would burst.

I called Stu hoping Grace could give me a medical opinion. Sprain or break? An uninsured visit to the hospital emergency room would cost me at least three hundred bucks. Walking into the Urgent Care clinic would cost me one hundred—not including the X-ray they would insist upon. Or should I tough it out until both migraine and wrist pain retreated? My questions remained mute; no one answered the phone.

I couldn't drive to town in my stick shift pickup with my right hand disabled, anyway—not on those hard curves. Nor could I tolerate the glare of daylight. On one of his good days I might have asked Barret to take me—after all, it was an emergency—but this wasn't one of those days. Calling him now would only invite a barrage of venom, possibly cumulating in an eviction notice, legal or not.

But I was not prepared to get into my hoard of suicide sleeping pills. Yet. So I took the dogs for a walk before the sun could break over the horizon and stab its beams into my eyes. Then I fed my brood, passed out frozen bones, and paced some more. A vile acid was gnawing at my innards, hollowing me. And yet I felt heavier with each shallow moan. Cliché or not, there was no better way to say it—my heart was rent in two. The future was a black pit. Without my Jimmi there was no way for me to go on breathing. The world had stopped. It was waiting for me to get off.

AND YET I lingered. Paul's letter was on the porch railing under a rock, along with my keys. And under the letter was the check I'd made out to him, torn to bits. He'd written,

> *Dearest Silvi,*
> *If you had given me half a chance I would have told you that the whole time you were gone Asa and Marvel refused to eat. They wouldn't come for walks with me, either, not even when I dragged them. Then they'd just flatten themselves on the ground. They spent their days out in the yard, looking down the road, listening for the sound of your footsteps. At night they took turns sitting on your desk, staring out of the window. Racket howled most of the first week. He dug out twice and ran off. Both times I found him up on the highway, just sitting on its shoulder, waiting for you. That's why I started taking him with me wherever I went. Sorry about the*

extra weight. He sucks up food like a vacuum cleaner. And the cats hid the instant I stepped inside the cabin. Wouldn't eat until they were sure I was gone again, and then only a little. And sorry to say, they've been peeing in the house.

I regret Violet's memory lapse. She started coming around soon after you left, telling me her troubles. Her boyfriend walked out on her and left her nothing but that old Nissan. Understandably, she's looking for another situation. And now that she's free, Barret's ardor is rapidly cooling. I keep trying to tell her I'm not interested, but it's not in me to be mean. Certainly, she had no business answering your phone and forgetting to pass on your important message. She had no business in your house, period. I was already working at my place when you called.

I've set up your internet gallery. Next time you're in town I'll show it to you. Meanwhile, I plan to come back for the stuff I left upstairs on Jimmi's shelves. I wish I could have done a better job with your dogs. They're the kind who will lie on their master's grave until they starve to death. Who knew? Not me.

Truly yours,
Paul
P.S.: I meant what I said to you at the airport.

Upstairs, on a shelf, I found a boombox twice the size of Jimmi's, a basket of *Jordan Six* CDs, striped pajamas, and a pair of worn felt slippers. Ariel's latest album was still in the player. It appeared as if no-nonsense lawyerly Paul was a real fan. Unlike me. As I saw it, everything that had happened with Jimmi was Ariel's fault for inviting him to come on tour without asking my permission first.

Grimly, I tapped the play button and was ambushed by an intrusive bass line muffling Ariel's screamed lyrics; I could only understand a few words. Definitely not my type of music. As far as I was concerned he should be singing more ballads, every one of his notes striking clear as a silver bell. Packing up Paul's things one-handed, I put them out on the porch and threw a blanket over the box so the sun would not warp his CDs. Then I loaded my player with Mozart symphonies, turned the volume up as high as it would go, pushed the *repeat all* button, and crumbled onto my mattress.

A WEEK later the box was still there but my headache was gone, although the pain in my hand had become all consuming. Mozart continued playing nonstop. Barret had left a couple of voicemails. I erased them without listening. Paul called once a day, but seemed incapable of leaving a coherent message until his fourth call. I kept them on the machine, to play later. The only message I was interested in hearing had not come in. Jimmi still had not called.

Without him there was nothing I wanted to do with the rest of my life. Not even painting. If no one needed me except for the dogs and cats I had to admit they weren't enough. One dawn, I found myself sitting on my outhouse throne, contemplating Paul's nearby aborted privy hole. It would make a good mass grave. With my eyes wide open, I saw myself leading my magnificent Asa up to its edge, putting Stillman's gun to his trusting head, and pulling the trigger. My brilliant Marvel came next, then the cats, who were sure to be eaten by something once I was gone if I freed them to live in the wilds. Or they'd die a more miserable death of exposure during the winter.

I would leave Racket alive for Paul to adopt. But killing myself and abandoning Asa and Marvel was not an option, now that I knew they would rather die than switch. I'd bury the animals here, cover them up, sneak the Chihuahua into the Manor after Barret went off to work, and leave a note asking him to deliver Racket to Paul. Then I would hike up to the two giant madrones, sit between them leaning against a sturdy red-gold trunk, and swallow my stash of pills.

Afterwards I'd put the gun in my mouth and pull the trigger, leaving nothing to chance. No fuss, no mess.

Coyote fodder.

Tomorrow.

ONE FINAL day to drag myself through, one more night. And then peace. It was all I thought about until that evening. I choreographed the big event in my mind repeatedly, working out details. For the first time since I came home I experienced a sense of release. Finally I had made the only decision I was capable of making and it felt right.

The phone rang when I was sinking toward sleep. I thought I heard Jimmi's voice and rushed to snatch up the receiver. But it was only Ariel, sounding like an embarrassed thirteen-year-old.

"Hi, Silvi," he said, his voice flustered. "I have to leave for rehearsals tomorrow. I thought I'd check just in case you've changed your mind about Jimmi coming along."

"I haven't," I snapped, feeling sorry almost at once. And then I burst into tears, trying to tell him what happened but choking on each word as it came out.

"Hold on," he said. "I'm driving up."

"No," I sobbed. "My landlord's on the war path."

"Then I'm walking," he said. "There's a full moon tonight. If I climb through a couple of barbed wire fences and follow the cut made by your seasonal creek I'll come out near that empty old cabin. I've hiked up to the lookout from there. It takes half an hour. Wait for me, Silvi. I'm on my way."

He hung up and I stood with the receiver in my hand feeling almost . . . relieved. Until I looked around and saw the house through his eyes. Too late to wash the dishes; I'd keep him out of the kitchen. Turning the living room light on high I swept up piles of dog hair and dust with my good hand. Then I dimmed the lamp to hide what was left of the clutter and opened the door to get rid of a week's worth of stale air.

I had to look at Marvel's twitching ears to know when Ariel was coming up my driveway because his step was so light that I couldn't hear a single footfall. Even when he stood at the screen door, his white face reflecting the moon light, the dogs remained strangely quiet. He must have been running uphill; his chest was heaving.

I let him in and they crowded around him. He was wearing a sweat soaked t-shirt, snagged by thorns. Makeup was dripping off his cheeks. I could see the scars at the sides of his nose. They seemed insignificant compared to the stunning symmetry of the rest of his face and those incredible eyes. His long hair hung askew, full of twigs. He wrapped his arms around me in a firm, comforting hug, his hands pressing gently against my back. Hiccupping one final sob, I sagged against him, inhaling the delicious scent rising from his heated skin. I put my head on his shoulder and kept it there until his racing heart slowed to match the rhythm of mine.

CHAPTER   27

"MOZART," HE MURMURED, PRONOUNCING THE Z the American way, like a long and soft s. "Jupiter. One of my favorites."

"His music's the only thing that's kept me going this past week."

"Music will heal you. If you let it." He sniffed the air. "Turpentine?"

"And cat pee," I said apologetically. I could smell it drifting in from the kitchen. Inconsiderate of the cats since they had around-the-clock access to a securely fenced yard of their own.

He laughed and inhaled. "Smells like home to me. Do you know how many critters I've cleaned up after?" Asa and Marvel sat in front of his feet, gazing intently up at his face. He bent to scratch between their ears. "What happened to them? They look like concentration camp survivors."

I explained that they'd refused to eat while I was gone.

"Poor pups. They must have been so lonesome for you." Crouching, he stroked both dogs until they sighed with contentment. Then he went to the canvases leaning against the wall, draped with tattered old sheets, said "May I?" and waited until I shrugged before pulling them off. He brightened the lamp and held each painting up to the light. It spot lit his hands, and while he studied my technique, I studied them. They were not pretty. Nor were they refined. They were the good, steadfast hands of a builder. Then he stepped away from the light, causing it to spill across the floor. I cringed at the piles of dog fur the broom had missed and saw the sparse, thrift-store furnished room as if for the first time.

But he paid no attention to our threadbare surroundings. Instead he focused on my favorite painting—of the lookout at sunrise, the spry little ancestor tree embraced by the oak, both surrounded by early-spring patches of deep purple shooting stars and tiny buttercups, the outline of the jagged archangel-throne etching the sky behind them. "I love what you've done with the light. I want to buy it," he said. "To stare at when I can't sleep. How much?"

I sat on my unmade bed. "Take it."

"No, really," he said. "I like to pay full value. Name a good price."

But he was the kind of guy I wanted to give things to. For free. "I'll be honored if you hang it on your wall," I insisted. "And maybe if anyone asks you can mention where it came from." I told him about the internet gallery. "Until last week I thought I was an up and coming painter. Especially after I saw my grandfather's work. But since Jimmi—" I swallowed. "Painting doesn't mean much to me anymore."

He leaned the canvas against the open door, dimmed the lamp, and sat beside me, kneading my shoulder. "Sometimes your vision turns to ashes. Seems there's not a single spark left in them. An artist without his art might as well be dead. But if you breathe on the ashes they start to glow again." He sat closer, rubbing my arm. I hissed, drawing away, hunching protectively around the hurt wrist.

"What's wrong?" He examined the swollen hand. "Oh, Silvi," he said. "What happened?"

I told him. In excruciating detail. And then he kissed me.

It was only a peck on the cheek but so unexpected that I stopped talking. "I think I can help," he said. "Lie down. Make yourself as comfortable as you can."

I complied, feeling wary. He placed my injured wrist on a pillow, turned off the lamp, and lay beside me. The full moon, shining in the picture window, poured a pool of silver across the painted plywood floor. Ariel's face shimmered. "Sometimes when I hug someone they start to feel better," he whispered, putting his arms around me the best way he could. "Relax. Everything's going to be okay. With Jimmi, too. Don't let that Leroy confuse you with the color thing. Being the same shade as Jimmi doesn't automatically give him dibs. Deep down Jimmi loves you. More than he knows. You're the mother of his heart."

Somewhere between having one of my paintings admired and being called a good mother I had become putty in Ariel's hands. The flood of gratitude washing through me flushed away the last vestige of resentment I'd harbored against him. His cheek, next to mine, was rougher than it looked but radiated a soothing warmth. Greedily I soaked it up. His hands, soft as owl feathers, produced a slight tingling current that I could feel flowing through me as long as I kept my eyes closed. It was like lying on the beach soaking up sun. From somewhere outside, I could hear coyotes yipping.

"Just breathe," he said. "Deep in, long out."

It was a struggle at first since I'd been a shallow breather for as long as I could remember. But pretty soon my legs started to feel as if they were floating away. Part by part the rest of me followed, leaving behind only my breath mingling with Ariel's and the triumphant Jupiter symphony.

A COYOTE, shrieking somewhere downslope, woke me in the middle of the night. The moon had moved away from the picture window. It was now shining through the screen door. I raised my head from Ariel's shoulder, sensing some shadow hovering on the porch just out of sight, creaking down the steps, tip-toeing away. There was the sound of a shrill whimper from the dog yard, the chain link rattling. Then silence. Neither Marvel nor Asa seemed the least bit perturbed. Probably the wind.

Only half awake, I looked to where Ariel was sleeping beside me, his chest naked and mottled, brown on white, the pale patches glowing like backlit spun glass. The sheet twisted around him reminded me of giant wings. They were glowing too. His two-toned skin gave off an eerie radiance as if what I saw—or thought I did— was not a man but a mythical angel.

Remembering all the faces Ariel had worn since we both were children, I realized each one had been exquisite in its own way. The thick white cream makeup that had melted off his cheeks when he'd come inside earlier was now smeared onto the pillow, leaving his face with irregular white circles interspersed with brown dots. He should have looked like a harlequin clown. Instead, he looked ethereal. At that moment I understood how unique he really was. In all the history of the world there was no one else like him nor ever would be.

What exactly was Archangel Ariel's purported role? Protector of nature's balance? Healer? His human namesake certainly proved to be an expert hugger. And my wrist didn't hurt anymore. If that was a coincidence I'd take it.

Ariel's eyes flew open. His first words were, "I'm so sorry. I never meant to—"

I put a finger to his lips. "It's okay. Really. A natural consequence of being close. And you have to admit, it was sweet. No need to mention it again."

Looking searchingly at me, he asked, "Are you sure?"

"Yes."

He nodded, covering himself with the duvet. "I didn't want you to see me like this."

"Like what?" I said. "You're dazzling."

He looked away.

"No, really," I said. "Spots and all. You could never be anything less than beautiful because that's how you are—inside and out." I held up my wrist. "Pain-free."

He cupped my hand as if it was a rare butterfly. "The swelling's down."

"Gone," I said. "And I don't feel sad anymore. Both thanks to you."

"No need to thank me. Thank God. I was just the conduit." He stretched. "What time is it?"

"Middle of the night. The mountain lions are still roaming."

"Lions don't scare me. I'll have to leave you soon, though. I still wish you'd come with me."

But his frenetic world held no appeal for me. I'd make a miserable groupie. "I have to stay and paint my mountain. Now that you're taking my best picture I've got to replace it. When was the last time you were on the lookout?"

"A couple of weeks ago. Why?"

I told him about butchered Raspberry Hill. He couldn't believe anybody would want to decapitate the top of a mountain. I said people will do anything for money.

With a bitter tinge to his voice, he said, "True!" After I described the marvels of Blossom Lane, now gone forever, he wanted me to paint it. "The way it lives in your heart, Silvi. And the peak too. With the forest intact and everything. Large canvas. Very large—big enough for the whole top and hillside. In detail. Take lots of time doing it. You know why?"

"No. Why?"

"Because we get what we focus on. Never mind how." He sounded quite serious. "Make it so real that anyone looking at it will feel they can just step into it and be there. My commission. I'll pay you upfront. There's a huge bare wall in my California house I want to fill with what I love best about Oregon. Put yourself in it too. And Jimmi. The dogs. Wildlife."

He bunched a pillow, turning toward me until our noses practically touched. His dark eyes shone. "I'm really warming to this. I love painting almost as much as I love music, you see. I used to think I could do both but then I realized I wouldn't be great at either unless I could give it my all. And music is my special number one gift to the world." He said it without a hint of vanity or pride.

"Yours is painting. I've been searching for someone like you. I've got a million ideas."

"I've got a million of my own. But I can't possible attempt to put them down onto canvas if you fetter me with your money and expectations. So here's the deal. If it's good, you get it after it's done. If it's not, I'll keep it. Nice and simple."

"Oh, it'll be good. But all right. We'll do it your way." He yawned until his eyes leaked at the corners. "We have a lot in common, you and me. Much more than you know. Can I call you? From the tour? When I can't sleep?"

Rashly, I said, "Any time."

He sat up. "Could you check on my house now and then? You can even stay there if you want. That way it'll feel lived in next time I come. I've had one of those swirly tubs installed. You're welcome to use it—and anything else I've got—stuff in the refrigerator before it goes bad, my music and books, DVDs . . ."

"As long as it's only now and then," I said, "I might do some light dusting." And then we curled up together, two lonely people needing someone to hold. The next time I woke up he was gone. He'd taken the picture and left his house key on the desk.

IN THE morning it was as if my wrist and heart had never been fractured. I decided Mozart was getting a bit redundant and turned him off. Then I attached Ariel's key to my key ring before replaying Paul's messages. The first one informed me that he was coming up to get his boombox. The second said he'd been unable to drive in because Barret had locked the gate. The third, left yesterday, said he would come again after Barret went to sleep, park at the gate, and walk back to my place. If I was awake he'd like to talk. If I planned not to be would I please put his stuff out on the porch so he could quietly carry it away. At the end of every call he left his number just in case.

I opened the screen door to check if the box was still there. It was not. The blanket I had thrown over his belongings was now folded and hanging neatly over the banister. I stepped out to see what, if anything, someone might possibly have glimpsed through the mesh—black night, bright moon, unlit interior and all. Probably plenty if he'd been fool enough to look for more than a second. I wrestled down a feeling of shame. Truth was I owed Paul nothing. But didn't it then follow that he owed me nothing either?

FIVE MINUTES later I was positive that Racket was gone. Training a flashlight on the obscure borders of the dog yard I found the place where he'd dug out. To run after Paul? I suppressed the urge to search for him. Instead I ruthlessly dialed Paul's number although it was not yet five. He answered at once. "Do you have Racket?" I asked without preamble.

"He followed me to my truck." His voice was flat. "There were coyotes nearby, and under the circumstances I didn't think I should be going back to . . . disturb you. So I brought him here. You can retrieve him any time."

Carefully chosen, lawyer-like words.

"No," I said impulsively. "No—I'd rather not. That is if you don't mind keeping him. Since he seems to prefer you."

"He's a bit confused, Silvi, is all. The little apple-head doesn't have the brain capacity of the shepherds. No need to get miffed."

"That's not it. Truth is he's too bold for his size. Sooner or later something big is going to make a meal of him up here. If he wants you and you want him—I'm fine with it. Really. Providing you let me see him now and then. Just to make sure you're keeping him on his diet."

He thought it over. "Ah, Silvi," he finally said. "Since you put it that way . . . okay. Even though I have no plans to abandon my cabin or my land. Gate or no gate, Barret's not going to win this time around. Right now I want him to stew until that gristly old thing in his chest has a chance to turn back into a heart. I'm hoping he'll realize I'm not as malleable as I used to be. Meanwhile I'll have plenty to do here getting my law practice established. And walking my dog."

"All right then, neighbor." I said, feeling contrite. "I've got to drive to town this morning for groceries, anyway. I'll bring you a bag of necks and his dishes. And his little bed. You ought to get an under-the-counter refrigerator. Mine uses less electricity than a light bulb."

"Really?" he said, allowing a bit of animation to creep into his voice. "Bring the shepherds, too. We'll all go to the dog park together. Afterwards we could do a late breakfast. Or an early lunch. Provided you can find a shady parking spot near the Greenleaf."

"My treat. Because I appreciate all you've done."

"Say that again."

"I appreciate all you've done."

"You're welcome. I would do it again in a heartbeat."

I chuckled. "Don't hold your breath waiting. I'm not leaving again anytime soon."

MY HAND was as good as new. In fact, I used it to hold the brush that polished the shepherds' fur to a fine luster, taking out yesterday's burs in the process. The sparkle had returned to their eyes. It intensified when I said, "Get in the car. We're going to town." They couldn't leap up over the tail gate fast enough.

The last thing I wanted to do that clear, promising morning was to drive down to sour faced Barret's house for a gate key. But what choice did I have? He was outside, holding a spade and a pick-ax. Beside him stood a balding red haired stranger with a snub nose and coarse features. They both looked at me as I emerged from Efi.

"Silvi. Where you been this past week?" Barret asked coolly. "I called twice."

"I was sick. Today's the first time I feel like driving out. I vaguely remember you mentioning a lock."

"So I did," he said, his eyes slitting with suspicion. "I had to do something to keep out the riff-raff." He turned to the stranger. "That's where Howie comes in. We're moving Kosmo's camper up to the gate. Howie here will be our gate keeper so that no one foots down here like Violet did yesterday. Very unpleasant."

He relinquished the tools to Howie, telling him, "Make sure you get the ground perfectly level. I'll bring in some cement piers this afternoon, with the gravel."

"Yessir," Howie said, eying me. "Excuse me. Ma'am? Are you driving up to the top right now? Can I catch a ride?"

This was not the kind of man I wanted sitting next to me, even for the shortest of rides. His demeanor was too servile while in the back of his eyes an ill-disguised insolence waited to be triggered.

Reluctantly I replied, "I suppose," although I wished he hadn't asked.

"Give us a minute," Barret told him, waving me toward the house. He let me step in first then closed the door behind us.

"Where'd you find this guy?" I asked, following him to his living room.

"Hitching on the freeway," Barret said proudly. "Just outside of Medford. I gave him a ride and we got to talking. He was broke and homeless. Now he's neither. Isn't that nice?" He threw out his chest as if he expected me to pin on a medal. At his desk he wrote a series of numbers on a stick-it for me. "Memorize them. And don't give this combination to anyone no matter what."

"Aren't you making too much of this? Who'd want it? It's not as if people are lining up to visit us."

"And that's a good thing," hc said. "Would you believe Violet had to nerve to walk down here twice? First she tried to get me to let her move into the camper. Rent-free. When I nixed that, she offered to move in with me instead, Lavender and all. I had the hardest time getting rid of her."

This was the part of Barret he kept carefully hidden under the honey-bear image he liked to perpetuate. It was a good reason for any woman to cut a wide berth. "I heard she was getting desperate," I said. "Clyde left her nothing except that beat up old truck. She's got no income."

"Let her sleep in the truck, then. Or drive it back where she came from. I'm not about to be anyone's meal ticket, Silvi. Things are getting tight, with the camper and Stu's place vacant at the same time. There's just you and me now. Until Howie gets Stu's cabin fixed up. He left a mess."

"Who?"

"Stu. He followed Grace to San Francisco. Didn't you know? Ditched all his junk and wrote me a note of regret. Said I could keep the cleaning deposit. What a laugh! Apparently some fake psychic swore that it was Grace and Stu's combined destiny to live happily forever after in the Bay Area. And off Grace went. Stu dragged his feet for a couple of weeks, probably because he couldn't face packing. Then he caved. Say—you want to earn some extra cash?"

"Forget it," I said quickly. "I'm not cleaning Stu's place again. What about Zora? Is she still around?"

"Unfortunately, yes. She's another one I—"

From outside came a shout of distress, a clatter, a volley of Asa's deep-throated barks followed by Marvel's slightly higher tones. I rushed into the yard to find Howie, gray faced and shaken, backing away from the tail gate, the shovel and pick-ax lying on the ground.

"I was going to put them in back," he said. "Dog leaped at me like a devil. I hate German shepherds. How many you got?"

"I'm sorry," I said, though I was not. "They are guard dogs. And you weren't introduced. You can put the tools in the extra-cab."

He stayed where he was. "After you, ma'am."

Barret was grinning. "Her shepherds are nothing like my Labs," he told Howie. "It's a wonder Asa didn't bite your hand off. Maybe we should chain him to the gate post, Silvi. Wouldn't have to install the camper. We could get by with a dog house."

"I think not," I said. "I need him at my place to keep the cougars away."

Howie swallowed. "Cougars? Like . . . mountain lions, you mean?"

"Yep. You still want a ride? The dogs can't get out of the canopy unless some fool lifts the hatch from the outside. I only ever let them loose near my cabin. They are a great deterrent."

"Yes ma'am," Howie said. "I bet you don't get many uninvited guests, huh?"

I had to open the passenger door for him and pat the seat before he would venture near it. "I don't understand," I said on the drive up.

"If you keep the gate locked, how are people you won't let through supposed to turn around to drive back to the county road?"

He flashed me a gap toothed grin. "I guess they'll have to reverse down that whole long twisty stretch, a ditch on one side, the drop-off on the other. Be kind of hairy, 'specially at night."

At the cabled gate he jumped out and watched me work the lock, which was looped through a thick, short length of chain fastened to the post. I couldn't get it to open for me even though I set the combination dial twice. "What the hell," I muttered at last, yanking the lock in frustration.

"Ma'am?" he said, his eyes brushing down my blouse. "You got to squeeze the thing. Like a titty."

I would have preferred Barret to give me that missing bit of information. In more technical terms.

CHAPTER 28

TIIAT MORNING, WIIILE I WAS GETTING READY FOR town, I noticed the forgotten witchcraft book buried under accumulated junk mail on my desk. It was sure to have accrued a hefty library fine in my absence. In the rush of preparing for my overseas trip I'd confused my intent to put it in the drop box with the actual deed. Now I began leafing through the pages again, marveling at my former gullibility. Did I really sit naked between two candles to perform these silly grade school chants?

Anxious to clear the blot of dishonor from my account I took the book to the library as soon as I arrived in Ashland, laid it on the circulation desk, and mumbled my airtight excuse.

"Oh, yes—the traveling alibi. I hear that one a lot," the gray haired librarian said, presenting me with the delinquent charges. As I wrote her a check something pillow-soft pressed against my spine, then a short plump arm reached around me from behind and picked up the book.

It was Zora, wearing a baby blue muumuu blouse over painted-on jeans. Their cuffs were jammed into a pair of new cowboy boots. "Oh, wow," she said, reading through the table of contents. "I had no idea you were interested in that kind of thing." She hesitated. "On the other hand, if it could help bring around Barret—"

With a grim smile the librarian took it out of her hand. "Would you like to put your name on the waiting list?"

"Don't bother," I told Zora. "The spells don't even work." After the librarian gave me my receipt I steered Zora to a more private corner. "How've you been? Happy with your new place? I'm sorry about Grace and Stu leaving like that. I bet you miss them."

Zora moseyed to a nearby display table covered with donated books for sale. "Not much. To tell you the truth they were constantly bickering until Grace managed to convince Stu to take a giant leap to Haight-Ashbury." She began to turn the books over to browse the reviews. "That's why I moved to my chalet before the remodel was finished. Since then I'm keeping myself busy with rescue work. I haven't had the time or inclination to feel lonely." She explained that she'd started to take in abandoned and traumatized horses. "On the acreage I own, right across from the lake. Cross fenced with a humongous barn and some great big oaks to give them shade. I've been doing a lot of riding lately."

Come to think of it her blouse was a bit slack around the belly. "You're losing weight," I cried.

She grinned, turning sideways so I could admire her new silhouette. "And I've got someone helping me put in an organic garden. Double dug beds and everything. I hired a carpenter to build a full enclosure for it. Like a giant cage. To keep out the critters. Oh, I'm having such fun—only, I can't get Barret to visit me. I've invited him over for coffee, for dinner, for a drink. Nothing. And when I brave his den he doesn't exactly overflow with joy. If the psychic hadn't promised me a tall dark handsome lover I'd find his attitude discouraging."

"He's in a funk," I said. "And when he's unhappy he likes to pass it around. By the way. . ." I looked fully at her for emphasis.

"He's not exactly tall *or* handsome, and in case you haven't noticed, what's left of his hair's been fading for some time now."

"Oh?" she said with a dreamy smile, smoothing the blouse over her belly. It made her look pregnant. "Obviously you don't see him as I do. But honestly—haven't you ever been tempted to—"

"Never. I know him too well. Although I grant you he's good with the charm. Like at that potluck. But even then he had an ulterior motive."

"Violet," she said, her face falling. "The beautiful tow haired Violet. How can I possibly compete with someone like her?" Moving closer she looked around and lowered her voice. "Incidentally, I saw her this morning. At the co-op. It was embarrassing. She went through the checkout before me with an armful of groceries. After they were all bagged and everything her credit card bounced. Then she started to pat herself down for cash and couldn't come up with more than a ten. While she was agonizing over whether she should put back the milk or the bread I slipped her a twenty. I hear that Clyde split, but didn't the jerk give her some severance pay?"

"I doubt he has a generous bone in his body," I said, watching her collect a few of the donated books into a stack. Not one of them appealed to my reading tastes. "Probably only left her the Nissan because it's not worth selling."

She fished in her fanny pack for change, began to count one-dollar bills, and placed four of them on the top book before asking, "If Barret's so hot for her why doesn't he let her move into Stu's place?"

I took another look at her finds. They were mystery novels I'd abandoned in mid-read, probably because I'd scanned the last few pages and didn't like the way the stories ended. "Not a generous bone in *his* body, either. A lot of men hate it when a woman gets needy."

Her bird eyes sparked. "Somebody should give him a good talking to. Appeal to his humanity. God—listen to me. I'm trying to boost my rival. But he has a good heart, I know he does. One that can be unlocked with . . ." She grinned. ". . . lox and cream cheese bagels with a bottle of good Oregon wine."

I had to admire her fortitude. "It's worth a try, I suppose. If you want to go through all that trouble."

"What trouble?" she said. "It's an investment."

BEFORE following Paul's directions to his new office I decided to stop by the fabric store to tell Mrs. Sweeney I had returned. I had to force myself to walk in, afraid I'd broadcast my disappointment the instant I saw my pictures still on the wall. But it was empty.

Behind the counter Mrs. Sweeney hung up the phone and said, "Silvi! Paul just told me you're back. I've got some good news."

"Oh?" I said, wondering why she had taken them all down at once.

"Until an hour ago your paintings were just where you left them." She nodded at the blank spots. "And then a young man came in and insisted on buying all five. He said he was the representative of a firm called Enoch Enterprises. Ever heard of them?"

"Never."

She showed me a business card with a hand-drawn feather underlining the logo. "Me either. A nice looking man even with those old fashioned horn rims. He said their L.A. headquarters needed to be completely redecorated with new artwork. I told him if he wanted additional paintings he'd have to call Paul. I gave him his number."

I felt a keen sense of loss. For some reason I'd expected my work to stay in the Rogue Valley. Within reach. "Did he pay my asking price?"

"To the penny. Mr. Rafael, his name was."

Rafael? Horn rims? "What kind of vehicle did he drive?" I asked, suspicion rising.

Mrs. Sweeney fluttered age worn fingers over her lacquered curls. "I helped him carry the pictures to his car. It was the kind everyone drives around here. A Subaru Legacy."

"What color?"

"Gold, I think. Oregon plates. Probably a rental. Why—did I do something wrong?"

"No, no. Not you." Was this one of Ariel's famous acts of charity or had he meant it when he said he loved my work? It wasn't as if he couldn't afford the prices I'd set. He probably thought they were laughably low compared to what he was used to.

Should I feel grateful or proud?

"I'll have to let it sink in, Mrs. Sweeney." I pocketed the card. "Is it okay if we settle up after lunch? Thank you for giving me the space and your time. It couldn't have happened without you."

THE ONLINE gallery Paul had created for me was impressive. My paintings jumped out at me from a black background. Seven of them, including the two he himself had bought in Key Largo, had big SOLD signs under their extravagant sticker prices.

He'd glanced at me briefly when I walked in but hadn't looked at me since, even though I was sitting beside him. "I just finished adding the signs to the five Mrs. Sweeney handled this morning," he said, keeping his voice sober and his eyes on the screen of his laptop. "Now that you're here maybe we can agree to raise the prices on the rest of them. It's no good to make them a bargain, Silvi. You have to know your own worth."

"Charge whatever you think is fair," I said, tipping my chair backward. "Since you're a disinterested party."

"Is that what you think I am?" he asked softly, placing a hand on the top of my backrest to keep the chair steady, glancing at me quickly and away again. He rose before I could think of a reply, went to the back room, and returned with a camera slung over one shoulder, Racket slung over the other. "I need to post some photos of you," he explained. "I thought I'd take a couple at the dog park. With the hills in the background. And the dogs."

The corpulent Chihuahua grinned at me, showing off his baby-fine teeth. "Bought that refrigerator yet?" I asked Paul, handing over the package of chicken necks.

"You bet." He stared through the plastic at the obscene, naked necks dangling shredded skin and esophagus tubes. "These things turn stinky fast. An obnoxious odor."

"No kidding. My refrigerator reeked when I came home." I'd finally buried the entire bloody mess and wiped the inside walls with baking soda.

"I know," he said. "Believe me, I know."

"Racket likes variety," I lectured. "Kidneys, heart, hamburger, liver. Ground turkey's his favorite. All raw, of course. Along with the necks." I showed him a recipe card. "The magic formula. Got to add these supplements, especially the kelp."

He groaned. "Kibbles would be faster and cheaper."

"But not better."

He studied the ingredients. "Good thing he's so little. A quarter cup? That's nothing."

I put a red plastic measuring cup of that size on the desk. And measuring spoons. "Might as well start you out doing it right. Make up a batch at a time and freeze it in little sandwich sized baggies. Call me if you need advice."

While he took the stuff to the back room I fastened on Racket's collar, feeling bad because I was doing it for the last time. He'd started out being Jimmi's dog until Jimmi developed other interests. There was nothing as cute as a baby Chihuahua, or as full of life. Snapping on the leash I thought in an instant of desolation that now I had lost the boy *and* his dog.

PREDICTABLY, our Chihuahua wooed every human inside the dog park and pissed off every male dog within reach. After Asa and Marvel rescued him from a retaliating Yorkie, Paul snatched Racket up and carried him to the truck, saying, "I'm not waiting until one of the local ruffians breaks his fat little neck!"

By that time it was almost noon. We dropped Racket off in his new digs, then I chauffeured Paul to the plaza.

"Early this morning I parked my truck under the biggest shade tree I could find near the Greenleaf," he confessed. "As a sort of place holder. With the idea that you pull into the spot the instant I pull out. That way you won't have to worry about the dogs getting overheated. Go ahead and stake out a good table while I cruise the Tacoma to the first available sun drenched parking space down the street. The balcony would be nice."

His meticulous planning touched me. I had to admit that both he and Ariel made excellent neighbors even though neither of them was living at home.

NOW THAT the tourists had descended in full force the Greenleaf was crowded. I joined the line of hopeful diners; by the time Paul walked in I was seated on the upstairs balcony as he'd requested.

"You must have had a long walk," I said, pushing a menu card in his direction.

"All the way from the band shell." He dipped a napkin into his glass of ice water and patted it over his flushed face. "I shouldn't have rushed in this heat. The dogs are all right, though. I checked."

We chose salads. Our table was protected from the sun's glare by a wide canvas umbrella. A welcome breeze wafted up from the creek, even though its water level had gone way down since early spring. Leaning over the railing, I remembered the day Jimmi had cut classes to goof off with his delinquent pals. I could almost see him now, through the shrubbery, on the other side of the creek bed. If only I could reset the time.

"You seem down," Paul said after studying me. "Is it your father? Did he—"

Putting my elbows on the table top, I supported my chin on the heels of my hands. "No, no. He's well cared for by people he loves. It's Jimmi." In a wavering voice I told him what Leroy had done, grateful for the genuine sympathy growing in his eyes.

He gave my shoulder a compassionate squeeze. "Any idea where they went?"

I shook my head. "Even if I knew that I couldn't make Jimmi come back, could I? Not if he doesn't want to. And I can't pour money I haven't even earned yet into the justice system knowing I'm going to lose in the end anyway. Teenage boys are usually awarded to the father."

"A good lawyer could fight this and win."

"Win what? If I drag Jimmi away against his will he'll never forgive me. And if he really wanted to come back not even an army of Leroys could keep him away."

"The news must have been devastating."

"It was," I admitted. "By last night I'd made up my mind to make it my final one on this earth. But then a friend called, rushed over, and helped me through the worst of it."

I could see that he understood exactly what parts I was leaving out.

He said, "Then I owe him," and slammed his fist onto the table. "If only Barret would stop being so unreasonable. That locked gate is a serious handicap to any relationship."

"Especially now that Howie's guarding it." I told Paul about the latest development.

"Living in a camper on occupied land without a permit is illegal," he said. "So is not providing a turnaround. I don't suppose Barret posted a warning sign at the beginning of the road?"

"Not that I know of."

"All that just to keep me out? He must really be smitten with Violet."

"Are you kidding? She asked if she could move in with him. Which makes her the last person on earth he wants to see. Or maybe the second to last after Zora."

He grinned. "What could he possibly have against that cute little round barrel?" He made her sound pretty. Maybe they'd make a good couple. He certainly was taller, darker and more handsome than Barret had ever been.

"Zora has a crush on the Bear," I lost no time pointing out. "But he claims she's the wrong shape and coloring to suit him. More to the point, she's available and therefore impossible for him to love. So now he's catapulted into one of his moods."

Paul shook his head and sighed. "For some men depression is a body chemistry fault. He used to pop every kind of recreational pill he could grab hold of. How hard would it be to swallow a couple of effective antidepressants?" He made a gesture as if to wipe the subject away. "I've been saving the bad news for last. Steel yourself. You won't like it."

He pushed my glass at me. I curled my fingers around it. The water was still cold, although the ice had melted. Looking grave, he said, "Since the last time I saw you there've been some ugly new developments with Gierig. I ran into him a couple of days ago. Seems his dear wife has decided she doesn't want to move into the fancy cabin on Strawberry Hill after all. And so, with deep regret, he's forcing himself to put that gem of a house on the market. Along with the building sites he's mapped out on that part of the mountain. But, not to worry, he's bought another hillside nearby, which, he declares, is the prettiest corner in Oregon. It's where he and the wife have decided they'll settle next—for good and all this time. Or so he says. Bearing in mind that this latest parcel too is zoned a tree farm and therefore permitted only one dwelling, owner-occupied. Knowing Gierig, the new place won't suit his wife either, so that he will—regretfully—have to sell it before the paint has a chance to dry on the walls. In the meanwhile, get ready—soon you'll be hearing the sound of another dozer. This one from the far side of Blackberry Hill. Near the giant madrones."

His face swam in front of my eyes. I could feel his hand on mine, which was still clutching the glass. Slowly he guided it up to my lips when what I wanted instead was to toss it over the railing and watch it smash to smithereens on the walkway below.

CHAPTER 29

I LEANED AWAY FROM HIM AND HELD the glass to my cheek, appreciating the cooling sensation. "Isn't he breaking some kind of land use regulation?"

Paul shrugged. "He's a developer, isn't he? A very *clever* developer. Always just a step or two shy of the law, willing to pay a hand-slapping fine." Picking a lemon slice out of his salad bowl he squeezed it into his water until all that was left was pulpy rind. He dropped it on the rim of his plate and wiped his fingers on a napkin before returning his focus to me. "Meanwhile," he said, sounding terse, "Gierig's running for a seat on the city council and doing visible good deeds which he makes sure get reported in the *Tidings*."

I put the glass down hard enough to cause a spill. "So we're supposed to sit back and let him destroy the mountain one clear-cut parcel at a time?"

Paul's eyes glinted at me. "I thought the least I could do was warn the guy who bought the three hundred acres, since Gierig will be cutting upslope from there. But I couldn't discover a phone number for him, and when I drove in on what I thought was his access road I got thoroughly lost. The property is listed to an entity called Enoch Foundation. Curious, that. Especially in light of the fact that someone from Enoch *Enterprises* just bought five of your paintings."

I tried for a modest smile. "It's nice to know there are at least two entities in this valley willing to support my efforts. Even though I was not consulted prior to either sale." I used the napkin he discarded to blot the puddle I'd made and said indifferently, "The Enoch place is just a vacation home. As far as I know it will be empty for the rest of this year."

From the way Paul was staring at me I could tell he smelled something fishy. I supposed lawyers had an instinct for that. I looked past his searching gaze, scanning the nearby tables, wondering if anyone was listening in. Then I recognized a face at the other end of the balcony. It belonged to Con Conroy. He was sitting with three other, vaguely familiar looking men. Con gave a tentative wave and when I waved back he rose to his full height and sauntered across. His dreadlocks were longer, no doubt for some exciting part he was playing this season. I hadn't picked up a program yet nor read a single review.

"How you doing, dog lady," he grinned. "How's your full figured dancing friend?"

"Zora?" I said. "I just saw her at the library this morning. Why?"

He brought out his wallet. "I got a couple of choice tickets to give away for tomorrow's show. I'm fixing to walk over to the Brewery afterwards. The Easy Valley Eight will be on again. I thought maybe I could interest both of you to join me—you did offer me a rain check as I recall." He gave Paul a friendly nod. "Unless you two are a team?"

"No, no," I said quickly. "Just friends. Neighbors, actually."

"All right!" Con pulled out a couple of tickets. "Don't want to be stepping on anybody's toes. Here you are then. One for you and one for Zora. Tell her to bring her best dancing shoes."

I took the tickets, thanked him, and watched him return to his table just long enough to pick up his check. And then, accompanied by the three men whom I now recognized as bit actors with the Shakespeare Company, he swept from the room.

"Darn." I slid the tickets into the back pocket of my jeans for safe-keeping. "And I don't even have her phone number."

"I do," Paul said with a fixed smile.

I was dumbfounded. I must have looked it, for he hastened to add, "I'm in the process of contacting all the neighbors. To make them aware of Gierig's intentions. In case they would like to object. In fact there's a list of their phone numbers and addresses on my desk right now. I was thinking of starting a little neighborhood newsletter."

BEFORE we bought our gelato from the corner café we peeked into Efi to make sure the dogs were still comfortable. They were snoozing. Paul and I took our desserts to the other side of the creek, climbed over large, moss covered rocks to the edge, and sat side by side on a damp boulder, our feet dangling. The babbling water below filtered out tourist chit-chat and traffic noise.

The gelato was creamy though overly sweet. I said, "You put a lot of time into fixing your cabin. I'm sorry it didn't work out."

"I'm not. My *ultimate* plan was and is to finish what Barret and I left unresolved all those years ago. With honor. And to enjoy whatever comes my way in the meantime."

"So—you don't regret buying back your land?"

"I kept Gierig from getting it, didn't I?"

What difference did that make if Gierig was going to carve up the rest of the mountain? A man without scruples and with plenty of money would always hustle to make more.

Paul scraped a smidgeon of chocolate ice onto his tiny plastic spoon and said, "Sometimes the best thing you can do is just wait. Besides, I don't mind living in the middle of town. I can walk to the stores. Maybe I'll buy a mountain bike. Sing in the choir. Take up folk dancing. Join a book club."

All of those things I'd contemplated for myself over the years while living too far away for spontaneous after-hour treats. Yet I preferred my inconveniently located shack; it provided such treasures as a clearing filled with a predawn silence that slowly awakened to a swelling symphony of birdsong; a indigo band at the horizon edged with angular conifer outlines; the surf sounds produced by a brisk wind brushing over the canopy.

"I've never been good at waiting," I said. "In human terms."

Paul's scoops were getting bigger. "Good gelato. Lousy spoon," he murmured, dipping it too deep and breaking off the handle. He extracted the pieces, laid them aside, and started using his finger. "Much better," he said after a satisfying lick, giving me an unnerving, dead-on lawyerly stare. "You want something to do? Take pictures of Gierig's sites. Document everything. Sooner or later we'll catch him in a serious mistake. And nail him."

I RETURNED to the ridge armed with Zora's phone number. Gap toothed Howie was sitting outside the dilapidated camper in a wobbly lawn chair drinking wine from a jug. When I got out of Efi to work the lock he burped and said, "Tha's it. Squeeze 'em." I dropped the cable, gave an insipid wave, and drove through. Snapping the lock shut again from the inside I deliberately kept my back to him.

My answering machine was blinking. I was afraid to push the retrieval button and find out that it wasn't Jimmi who had called. Since Dorrie had told me the bad news I had been indulging myself with a sweet daydream. It mostly came to me between sleeping and waking early in the morning or late at night. It started out with me picking up the receiver to hear Jimmi's breathless voice whispering, "Can you come get me?"

I dialed Zora's number but she did not answer her phone. It rang and rang without the voicemail kicking in. Most likely she was out tending her horses. Feeding them carrots or apples. Brushing their manes. I hung up, aimed my forefinger at the red flash, and pushed. And was immediately attacked by Mama.

In an angry tone she demanded, "Silvia! *Bist du da!*" A short pause. Then, "I'm standing here with a letter that came in today's mail. From Papa. It appears you left him. Up there. With her."

I cringed but wasn't the least bit sorry.

"You could at least have had the decency to return the Peugeot," Mama ranted. "And to explain why you felt you had to steal your father away from us. Neither of you had the gumption to say good-bye."

I obliged Mama by ramping up my feelings of guilt even though my memory of Papa insisting I sneak him to the car was still fresh in my mind.

"Suddenly he's not dying anymore," Mama shouted. "He wants a divorce instead. But why should I be surprised?"

I was flabbergasted. It was the only word that would do. She was right—if Papa was demanding a divorce he must have decided not to croak anytime in the foreseeable future.

"Mountain trash," Mama went on. "The bunch of them. You, too." Here the line went dead. If I was bereft it was only because she wasn't Jimmi. But maybe he'd dialed while she was leaving her spiteful message. Maybe he'd gotten a busy signal and hung up discouraged. Maybe he'd wouldn't ever try again.

I climbed the stairs to his room. It felt empty. Even his grubby boy smells were gone, superseded by Paul's soap and shaving lotion. Jimmi's CDs were still on the shelf, the porn magazines still hidden under the futon. Farther down, beneath his box springs, way back so I had to crawl in after them, were a couple of pairs of his sneakers stretched to the shape of his duck-like adolescent feet. As if he'd just wiggled them out of the shoes an hour ago. I sniffed the insoles. Rank. Nonetheless I hugged the four shoes to my chest because it was the closest I could come to holding him in my arms.

I returned them to their dusty cave, lining them up in a neat row. Pulled out the top dresser drawer, sank my hot face into his multitude of crew socks. Opened the second drawer to shake out his t-shirts. The first one, dyed black, had the words *Jimi Hendrix* stenciled across its front in white letters. It was in the singer's honor that Crystal had named our Jimmi, though she'd added an extra *m*. I'd given up my bedroom to him because it was the only remotely private space in the cabin. The one with the best light, the freshest air. Often I'd yearned to paint up here. One wall was made of salvaged window casements with small panes of glass. Most of them were painted shut. The other wall, above the long shelves, had sliding aluminum frames, the kind with snap-locks and matching screens. I opened everything that wanted to move and felt a cooling breeze brush my arms. "Jimmi," I moaned, suddenly desolate. "Please come home."

Groping on his music shelf I grabbed the first CD my fingers touched and inserted it into his dusty boombox. A moment later a small boy's voice lifted and soared. Ariel, from his early *Jordan Boys* days. "Just close your eyes," he sang in tones incredibly pure. I obeyed, sinking onto the bed and imagining I could feel an indent in the shape of Paul's body beneath mine and under it a much older, deeper groove made and enlarged by Jimmi every night since the day I'd first taken him in.

Around my naked shoulders I felt the caress of a butterfly's wings—Ariel's light, imagined embrace. "I'm coming back to you," the little boy on the CD crooned. "And everything will be all right."

I wanted to believe him, but it was getting harder each day.

LATER I brought the album downstairs to listen to the rest of little Ariel's songs. While I was playing them at top volume the dogs gave a couple of warning whoops from their dusky yard into which they'd fled to escape the loud music. Quick steps climbed the porch stairs. A short rotund figure came up to the screen door, peering in. I invited Zora inside.

"Can you turn that off?" she yelled, hands over her ears.

I pushed the pause button hoping she wouldn't stay long.

"I didn't know you were a fan of Ariel Jordan," Zora said into the sudden quiet.

"I'm not."

"Then how come you're dancing to his music?"

I did a quick spin. "Irresistible beat."

"I'll get my beats elsewhere, thank you," Zora huffed. "I used to like Ariel before he started wearing all that lipstick. Do you think he did it?"

I gave her a cold stare. "Do you?"

"Kind of looks that way, doesn't it? The way he paid that kid off. Where there's smoke—"

"You ever meet him?"

She chuckled uncomfortably. "Well, no. Why would I want to socialize with a known ped—"

I interrupted her with an irate sigh. "I have. Ariel Jordan is the kindest, most loving person I know. With more talent in his little finger than anyone else in the music business. Have you ever looked into his eyes?"

"Of course not."

"Until you do please shut up about him. I'm not interested in hearing regurgitated tabloid fabrications."

Two little tears trickled down Zora's cheeks. "Please," she said, "I came to you for help. Don't you turn on me too."

Asa and Marvel pushed their snouts through the dog door flap. It slapped open and shut twice. Then they guardedly approached Zora to sniff at her crotch. She smiled, wiping her cheeks. "They smell the horses." Pulling the office chair away from my desk, she heaved herself onto it. "I'm getting my puppy right after the work crew finishes installing a kennel at the back of the house. A standard poodle? I hear they're smart. What do you think?"

I grimaced. "You're living in foxtail and sticker country. You need a short haired dog. A Lab maybe."

She grabbed at the desk and wheeled herself toward it so she could rest her elbows against its top edge. "Not if they're as harebrained and lazy as Barret's. I want a dog who can keep up with my riding."

"A Kelpie, then. Short haired, smart, and tough. A dog that thrives in the Australian outback will feel right at home around here."

She wrote the breed name down on a sticky, folded it over, and squirreled it away.

"What kind of help do you need?" I asked. "From me. In the middle of the night."

She glanced at her watch. "It's not that late." Biting her lip she said, "You were right about Barret. He's almost ugly when his face is devoid of that charming smile. Ugly on the inside, too. I went to his house. Without calling first, I admit. That goon at the gate refused to let me drive through. So I walked down to the Manor carrying a basket filled with lox, bagels, cream cheese and wine. Barret wouldn't let me in." She squeezed her eyes shut. "I thought he was joking when he opened the door no more than a hand's breadth, stuck out his head, and told me he didn't feel like company tonight. Then he closed it in my face and pointedly fastened the latch from the inside." Idly Zora arranged the jumble of unopened bills on my desk into a neat pile and continued with, "I put my offerings down on his door step and trudged back uphill. By that time it was getting dark. I asked the goon to please open the gate so I could access the turnaround. He refused. But I'm not about to reverse down that steep grade, night or day. That's why I'm here. Could you—"

"Sure," I said, grabbing my flashlight. "I'll drive you up there. Right now if you want."

She gave me a grateful smile. "In a minute." Then she picked up one of my landscapes, studied it silently, and returned it to its place, saying, "This isn't half bad. When Grace told me you paint in your spare time I thought you were one of those aging hippie chicks disguising her lack of talent by adopting the primitive style. You know—two dimensional, like."

I frowned at my flashlight.

"Sorry," she muttered. "I didn't mean to imply that you're old."

"I'm sure you didn't," I lied politely. "And for the record, I'm not a hippie chick. I am who I have always been. Me. I appreciate hippies because they're accepting of other people, no matter how much they weigh or what color their skin might happen to be. I think we could all learn from that."

WHEN WE reached the top of the ridge my headlight beams found Howie still sprawling in his chair. From the angle his head was tilted, mouth agape, arms dangling, empty wine bottle at his feet, I realized he was in a drunken stupor. We got out and Zora stole past him to her vehicle, which I now realized was a farm truck in worse shape than Barret's. I opened my canopy hatch so I could see what was behind me, climbed back into Efi, slid apart the cab's tinted rear windows, and slowly backed around the camper and up the rutted trail that lead to Stargazer Hill as far as I could without hitting a tree or landing in the ditch. Even so the angle was wrong so that I had to reverse and pull ahead three times before the front bumper cleared the corner of the metal utility shed standing on the other side of the road. I shuddered to think what damage Zora might do in a bulky truck she wasn't used to maneuvering.

When Efi faced the way we had come I eyed Howie again. Incredibly he was still sleeping. I walked past him, opened the lock, pocketed it, and tossed the cable aside. Then I went to Zora's truck and whispered at her rolled down window, "You'd better follow me down to Stu's. His lot makes a much safer turnaround. Go easy on the gas when you start up your engine."

I got into the idling Efi and waited for her. She coughed her engine awake, then revved it so loud that Howie jumped out of his chair, wildly looking around. Zora stabbed him with her brights. He lurched into the middle of the road, arms wide, shouting, "Hey! Stop! Hey!" Zora's truck hopped forward. He jumped out of the way, throwing his empty wine bottle at her tailgate. It bounced off and landed harmlessly in the weed choked ditch.

I preceded her down to Stu's lot, parked a good distance beyond it, and went to where Zora was trying to maneuver into a turn. "Good grief!" she said. "That guy's a nutcase. I feel sorry for you. You have to drive past him every day coming and going. As for me, I'm definitely not heading up here again anytime soon."

I gave her the lock. "Here, toss this at him if he tries to stop you. But if you zoom uphill fast enough I'm sure he'll stay out of your way."

"Gee whizz," she said. "Barret must be out of his mind hiring an alcoholic hobo. What does he need a locked gate for anyway? All of a sudden."

"Barret does strange things when he gets depressed."

"Not much of an excuse," she huffed. "Other people get depressed *without* turning obnoxious!"

I laughed. "From what I hear he's been that way since the land co-op first formed. He was born rich but he renounced his inheritance when he dropped out of his fancy East Coast school. His mother insisted on giving him a small cash settlement as a sort of severance pay. From the day he bought his part of the land with it out of a briefcase filled with one-hundred dollar bills, there was no doubt in his mind that he was meant to be king of this hill. But remember, in his right mind he's a fairly benign despot."

Zora yanked at her steering wheel. "Being born rich is no excuse. It's a handicap. You don't overcome it by bragging, either." The truck hiccupped. The engine died. Zora cranked the starter until it shuddered back to life and then pumped the accelerator. Black smoke poured out of the exhaust pipe.

"Good grief," I said. "Where did you buy this wreck? Is it legal?"

"It's good for hauling stuff. I only use my new Porsche on paved roads."

I couldn't imagine her fitting into a tight sports car even with the steering wheel adjusted to allow for her girth. "Red?" I asked.

She gave a lazy shrug. "Of course. You only live once."

I went to peer down at the Manor. A dark shape was standing in the dimly lighted kitchen doorway. It shouted something that sounded like *shit!* The door slammed shut.

Zora started to pull away. Remembering the tickets, I ran to her window and held them out to her, shouting so she could hear me over the engine noise. "Con Conroy wants you to have these. For his play. Tomorrow night."

She took them, easing up on the accelerator. Tapping them on the window glass, she said. "Why would I need two? Unless you're coming with me."

"Naw," I said. "I've got things to do." Such as waiting for the phone to ring.

"Okay," she said. "Barret's out. Definitely. There are other attractive eligible men around here. Like Paul. You don't mind if I go out with Paul, do you? And give him the second ticket?"

I fought down my sudden, unaccountable dismay. "Con Conroy is taller. And darker."

"And movie-star handsome," she agreed.

"With an excellent reputation," I added. "A brilliant acting career ahead of him. Well liked by the locals. And obviously he admires you even though he doesn't have a clue that you're an heiress. I think he want to get to know you better."

She put the tickets in her ashtray for safe-keeping. "I wonder if he likes to ride. Horses."

"He does have an athletic build," I said. "He said he was going to invite you to the Standing Stone afterwards. For some serious dancing. Why don't you ask him then?"

The truck started rolling again. "Thanks," she said. "Maybe I will."

Standing in the dark, I watched the tail lights disappear around the first curve and listened to the engine labor up the long incline. Hopefully Howie wouldn't insist on heroically flinging himself in front of the moving wheels. The higher the truck climbed the louder the engine roared. Then there was one final burst of speed before it waned down the far side of the mountain.

I COULD hear the phone shrilling before I reached my driveway. *Jimmi.* I ran to the kitchen door and started to leap across the room just as the answering machine kicked in.

"I explicitly asked you not to let *anyone* drive through that gate," Barret snarled without an even halfway polite opening remark. "You broke your promise to me. To your detriment I'm afraid. Because we used to be friends I'm giving you a whole month's notice. At that point I'm changing the gate combination. And I'll instruct Howie to dump anything left inside your shack before he padlocks the doors. Have a good night."

Paul or no Paul, I had always known that Barret was within his rights to throw me out any time he liked. A landlord didn't need a reason for such an outrage. He could even turn loose my animals, chase them away, take them to the pound, or demand that I get rid of them. Over the years he'd had plenty of practice with evictions and had honed them to a fine art. I reminded myself that *I'm kicking you out* was his favorite phrase.

In my worst nightmares I'd often imagined stuffing my prized possessions into the back of Efi along with a perpetual stream of cats, the three dogs, and one boy. I'd drive around in deep snow or blistering heat, looking for some forsaken field or a spot in the woods where the cats would slip away one by one to be eaten by coyotes, and the dogs had to be tied to the bumpers to keep them safe. No water, no food, no shelter, and no future.

But now that my fears were finally turning into reality they rapidly became laced with a huge dose of anger. I dialed Barret's number and coldly said, "Not so fast, Barret. First of all locked gates are not part of our rental agreement. Secondly you can't kick me out because you don't actually own this cabin. It's on Paul's land even though you've been collecting rent from me for years. Third I think you just might have lost your last friend. Good-bye." I disconnected, forgetting how much Barret hated to lose, and that he made an intractable and ruthless enemy.

It would have been so much better if I had just apologized—except in truth I had nothing to apologize for.

CHAPTER 30

I TOOK THE DOGS OUT WHEN IT WAS STILL NIGHT. In the light of a waxing half-moon I could see the faint outline of the path at my feet. We were hiking to the decapitated Raspberry Hill. When we arrived the dark was already fading. I stopped at the island on which the last oak was rooted and took snapshots of the soil the bulldozer had scraped off all around it, leaving raw, layered vertical walls. At the summit's rim I aimed the lens at the discarded slag clogging the slope.

Briefly I considered sending a print to Josef with a caption explaining that in Oregon anyone with money could buy a mountain and do with it whatever he liked. I imagined Josef's shocked Austrian voice echoing my own sentiment: "But it took millions of years to form that mountain, thousands of years to deposit the soil, hundreds of years to grow the trees upon it—how can one person be allowed to destroy all that in just a few weeks?"

Cloaked in lingering night shadows, the dogs and I followed the newly built road that stretched from Raspberry Hill to Gierig's fancy cabin. With careless sweeps the dozer blade had denuded both hillsides abutting the roadbed, crunching every tree within a hundred and fifty yards and collecting the splintered remnants into unsightly heaps. The powdery foot-deep red clay under our feet showed a disturbing number of wave-like imprints left by agitated wood rattlers abandoning old, no longer safe hiding places in search of new.

Noticing a parallel road some two hundred yards below, I attempted to descend an almost perpendicular bank of loose dirt toward it, but soon gave up the struggle to slide the rest of the way on my rear end. Anxious, the dogs stayed on the higher road, their ruffs standing on end. They paced hither and fro, whining softly. Finally they found a section of embankment they judged reasonably secure and scrabbled down after me, causing small landslides with every move. But that angle would be impossible for a tiny wobble-legged fawn to navigate even when nudged by its mother.

The lower road we were now standing on was covered with some sort of sand. I soon noticed three sets of foot prints in this surface. They had been made by a bear and her two cubs. Except for the claw marks their soles looked almost human. The tracks stopped in a place where raspberry hedges used to grow before the bulldozer ripped them out of the ground. The mother bear's footprints went around and around each spot as if she couldn't believe the hedges were gone. The cubs' prints followed behind her in confused circles.

I leashed the dogs, afraid the bears were still somewhere nearby. Mother black bears were notorious for defending their young against all comers. Every now and then the tracks started to veer off the road. I could see marks where the cubs attempted to climb the embankment, clawing into the dirt wall before giving up. A couple of months ago they could have wandered contently across what used to be easily accessed terrain.

Soon the prints swerved down to a third road dissecting the mountain, no doubt continuing their futile search for the ripe berries the mama bear was used to finding this time of year. The third road ran parallel below the other two. Its sides had also been denuded and dirt-banked. Probably Gierig would name his new two lane streets something romantic like "Bruin Lane," "Cougar Court," and "Eagle Trace" in remembrance of the wild country he was destroying with his planned hillside estates.

When his big cabin rose out of the shadows I slowed and stood still, finally realizing why he'd demolished Raspberry Peak. It was for crushed bedrock—a convenient source of the "sand" he'd been tamping onto his knee-deep-in-dust roadbeds.

I studied the cabin's black outline for signs of occupancy. There was a gleam behind a grouping of thickets where someone had attempted to hide a large object from view. It was a dust-speckled white pickup. On cue, the cranky wail of a small child wafted out of an open cabin window. It was interrupted by a womanly murmur and then all was quiet again. I took pictures of the truck, the house, and the clear-cut hillside above it just when the still hidden sun sent its first ray over the top of the opposite mountain chain.

From the newly paved access road winding up from the highway I heard the approach of an ATV. It was buzzing like an crazed hornet. Hastily retreating into the shadows, I wondered if Violet and Lavender were gate-crashers or invited guests.

THE SKY continued to lighten as I stopped by to visit with the little ancestor tree. My firry friend was taller than the last time I saw him. His bright spring-time shoots had already turned a deep summery green. Moving on, the dogs and I hiked to the madrones on Blackberry Hill. I feasted my eyes on their massive boughs stretching skyward. From the edge of the blackberry brambles crowding the southern half of the peak I could see most of Ariel's three hundred acres below us, though the farmhouse itself was hidden behind shade trees. There was no sign of a bulldozer on the forested slopes nor did I hear its obnoxious drone. Not yet anyway.

I hated the idea of documenting the imminent step-by-step destruction. If I had more gumption I would be blowing up Gierig's earth-moving equipment. A bit of environmental terrorism would soon get a mention in the paper and on the TV station, alerting the complacent public.

I CALLED Paul to complain. "How am I supposed to take pictures of the new site if I don't know where it is?"

"Oh, you'll know. Just follow the sound of heavy machinery when the ruckus begins," Paul replied. "Most likely the bulldozer will make a road to the site before doing any clear-cutting. You'll hear the noise all the way to your cabin since there's no landmass between you and that slope."

"I suppose I'll have to start wearing ear plugs. On top of a mountain. In the middle of nowhere," I said, pacing around my kitchen. Then I mentioned Barret's latest phone call.

Paul swore. "Your immunization against landlorditis seems to have run out. Who told you that your cabin is on my side of the boundary?"

"Violet. She was upstairs in his bed when you went to see him that time."

He gave a groan. "You mean she heard the whole thing?"

"Every word. Barret thought the trapdoor was closed."

"Hold tight, Silvi. He'll soon realize that he has no legal power to evict you."

"If you say so. But just in case you come across some little cottage on the outskirts of town let me know. One where pets are negotiable."

If my father had died according to plan I would be getting enough cash for a decent down payment on a small house of my own just about now, but I was glad to have him alive, even if it meant I would soon be homeless. I sighed. "Did you sell any more paintings?"

"Not yet."

It was entirely possible that Paul and Ariel were the only two people in the entire country who liked my work. A dismal thought. "Maybe I'm one of those artists who won't get famous for a hundred years after they're dead."

"Won't happen, Silvi. You've got to stop underestimating yourself. And don't worry about Barret. He'll snap out of his mental health crisis soon. He always does. But if you want I'll check the for-rent ads for you every day."

I STAYED on the mountain for a week. Then, on a very hot day, I had to drive in to collect the forty-pound carton of chicken necks I'd special-ordered. From habit I picked up my mail first, hoping there might be a something from Jimmi. There wasn't. Of the two letters waiting inside my box, one was from Dorrie, the other from Papa. I stuffed them in my purse, planning to read both at leisure inside the air-conditioned co-op.

The store's lot was crowded with a long line of cars idling under the hot sun, each driver waiting for a shopper to leave so they could pull into the vacated slot. I cranked down both windows and punched on the radio, hoping classical music would sweeten my exposure to the merciless light. Far ahead I noticed a police cruiser parked near the entrance. Two officers were just coming out of the store. One was a trim young woman who managed to look sexy in her blue uniform, the other a medium-tall fortyish man with a slight paunch and a matter-of-fact attitude. They were escorting a handcuffed shopper toward the squad car. I was stunned to recognize Violet, her head lowered, the thin orphan hair sliding forward to obscure her face.

Before I could get out of Efi—a dangerous maneuver amidst reversing cars and heat-flushed, irritable drivers—she had already climbed into the rear of the cruiser. Then the woman cop reentered the store, emerged carrying Lavender, and got into the passenger side with her. The cruiser rolled toward my end of the lot, passing within a few feet of me. By then Lavender had discovered her mommy on the rear seat and was holding out her arms to her, but Violet sat hunched over, hiding behind her white-blonde privacy curtain as if it might make her invisible.

For once I regretted not having a cell phone. I had to wait a long time before I could park and rush to the two pay phones on the store's patio. Rummaging through my purse I collected a handful of coins. Usually I lost money in the first booth no matter which one I picked. It was almost as bad as playing the lottery. Today was no exception. I punched in Paul's cell number in my booth of choice but the call didn't go through and the coins refused to drop into the return. I pounded the contraption with no results, moved to the second booth, and tried his number again. He did not answer.

I left a message asking him to liberate Violet. Then I did my shopping, buying a pint bottle of iced yerba maté which I drank in the snack area while reading Papa's letter. Like most people of his generation he had excellent penmanship, each word a work of art.

Dear Silvia,

A lot has happened since you left. I hired an attorney, started a divorce, and revised my will. Soferl and I are now officially engaged—an event long overdue—and soon Josef will be my adopted son. That way we can be sure he'll get his half of the Trüffelhof after I'm gone. Your Mama is bound to contest the changes I've made. To no avail.

Soferl is taking me up to the Alm with her tomorrow. We'll be there for the rest of the summer. Toward that end Josef has concocted a fool-proof harness to keep me on his Haflinger's back. On the high meadows Soferl and I shall dine on nectar and cream every day and I will drink any medicinal teas she's willing to brew. We are getting married as soon as the divorce goes through. If I live that long you are definitely invited to the wedding. And if you ever want to change your mind, you, Jimmi, and your entire four-legged family are welcome to make your permanent home with us. Josef would be absolutely delighted.

With unending love,

Dein Papa

Of course he had no idea just how many four-legged creatures I was sharing my life with and how complicated it had become since the last time we spoke. I wasn't about to tell him any time soon. Nor was I prepared to leave Jimmi behind no matter how long it took him to make up his mind to come home.

Dorrie's letter was much more succinct. In consisted of a sheet of paper on which she had written, *I am so sorry!!! I hope this helps.* The sheet was wrapped around a check for the acrylics. She didn't ask me to send more of my work, which was fine because I would have refused. I kept the check but tore the note and the envelope to shreds and tossed the remains into the garbage. Our friendship had flatlined. We were done.

HOWIE was at his post, wearing nothing but cut-offs. His bare chest was covered with auburn fuzz. He was scratching his belly with one hand while swigging beer with the other, saluting me with the can. I gave a reluctant nod, feeling his eyes on my rear as I fiddled with the lock.

At the cabin the dogs' greetings were subdued. Panting, they led me to their water bowl to let me know it was empty. I carried the bowl to the kitchen sink and opened the valve. Nothing came out. My first impulse was to call Barret and report the outage. Reconsidering, I poured from one of the recycled cider jugs I kept under the counter, watched the dogs lap the bowl dry, and took them with me to the pump house. I was hoping the problem was as simple as priming the pump. It proved to be even less complicated. The valve on the pipe going to my cabin had been turned off. A small handwritten note affixed to it read, *"DO NOT TOUCH!"*

Barret was revving up his nasty-streak against me. Sure enough, there was a message waiting on my answering machine. He announced that he suspected a new leak in my pipes and felt it best to keep the water off until he could get around to playing leak-detective. He kindly suggested I carry containers to the pump house every evening to fill them from the musty, cut-off rubber hose attached to the tank. Until further notice. "Sorry for the inconvenience," he said in a stony voice in lieu of good-bye.

TWO PHONE CALLS interrupted my sleep that night. The first was from Ariel, his voice bashful as he informed me that he was at his California ranch rehearsing for the second leg of his tour. "It's starting to come together again," he said. "The dancers are great. I wish you could see them."

"I didn't know you still had to rehearse if you've already done half of your tour," I said stupidly. "I thought you all would simply get on a plane together and go from country to country with the whole lot set up and waiting for you wherever you land."

"Not for my shows," he said. "There's no live performance till everything fits together flawlessly. Tomorrow the whole stage gets shipped to Munich, which is our first stop. You have no idea how complicated it is. Just between you and me, I hate touring. Things are always going wrong. But there's one lesson my father taught me that I'll always be grateful for. It's that no matter what happens you keep on smiling and singing, not missing a single beat. He claimed *Don't Disappoint Your Audience* was the eleventh commandment. It's amazing how many disasters I've had to smile my way through."

I'd never been to any live concert of his or of anyone else. And lacking a TV I hadn't seen a single one of his music videos. I decided I'd best not mention that fact. "I loved that book you gave me," I said. "I read it on the plane. It's inspiring. Definitely a keeper." I could practically hear him beaming at me.

"Oh, thank you," he said. "I knew you would understand. Listen—I hope you don't mind my calling so late. Did I wake you?"

"Not really," I lied.

"That's one of the problems with preparing for the tours. I get so excited that I can't fall asleep. I try, really I do. I lie in bed and close my eyes but there's a 2,000 watt light shining inside my head. Ideas keep coming and coming and I can't turn them off. Wouldn't want to if I could. All night long I'm jumping up and scribbling them onto paper. I learned the hard way that even the simplest of them will fade by morning unless I leave myself notes. You hear anything from Jimmi? Did he come back yet?"

Immediately my mood darkened. "No."

"Don't worry. He will." The line started to crackle softly. Then he said, "I could ask God to help. If that's okay."

For some reason that quaint option hadn't occurred to me; I was not in the habit. "Well, all right," I replied. "If you have a direct line." To me prayer was a form of manipulation. During a war both sides invoked His blessing and petitioned Him for a swift and glorious victory. Football teams did the same thing. If God were just he'd have to refuse either request or bless both sides. So what determined which of them won? Sheer numbers? Extraordinary fervor? Superior ruthlessness?

Mentally I sifted through the pages of the witchcraft book, wondering if there might have been a spell in it to draw home wayward sons. But I only remembered the failed chants for attracting soul mates.

"Did you start on my painting yet?" he asked.

"I did some sketches. And found a bunch of photos." I explained about Gierig's new project and my self-appointed task of saving the mountain.

"Are you talking about the woods above my place?" he said, sounding worried. "He's not going to clear-cut up there, is he? I don't think I could live with that kind of ugliness."

"We won't let him. One of my neighbors is a lawyer. The one who helped me set up my online gallery. In fact he was trying to get in touch with you—or rather with the Enoch Foundation, to warn you about Gierig. Except he couldn't find your phone number. And he won't get it from me."

"That's because you know it's a secret," he said. "But if you give me his I'll make sure Mr. Rafael gets in touch." Chuckling, he went on with, "About our painting—I'm already finding it soothing. When I close my eyes I can see it inside me. The dense forest that used to be on top of Raspberry Hill. Sunbeams filtering through the branches. A black bear feeding on berries in the darkest part. A few deer peering around tree trunks."

The line began to crackle louder. I missed a few words. ". . . bambies hiding in tall patches of wildflowers," he was saying when the noise abated. "Put me in it too. Surrounded by little kids. All of us wandering through the cool forest together. Add a cherub or two sitting above us in the branches and watchful black ravens with yellow eyes. Put a tawny cougar on the lookout. Just a stream lined silhouette against the sky. Have you been down to the farmhouse?"

"Not yet."

"Check my book cases when you go. There's some oversized photo albums on one of the bottom shelves. In case you need a few pictures of me for the painting. Since I can't sit for you live."

I said, "I think the canvas size just doubled. Boy cherubs or girl? With wings or without?"

He laughed again. "Cherubs have no sexual characteristics. They're not physical beings. Ever heard of an angel giving birth?"

"Never even seen one who's pregnant."

"Exactly. A cherub is a little mischievous angel sprite. Sweet and innocent. With a child's heart."

"Maybe I better send you my sketches before I even think about starting on the big picture."

"No, no," he said. "Not with my crazy schedule. I'll just call you every now and then and we'll talk about it. You still have my mother's number?" The crackling picked up again, this time with a deep drone in the background. ". . . in touch with her from every city. She'll be glad to pass on your message." There was a long pause during which the drone grew louder. Eventually I could hear him say, so softly that I had trouble understanding the words, "I often think of our night together. I'll treasure it always. I could feel our spirits actually blending."

Something like an electric current shot through me, giving me vertigo. My heart started pounding. Against my inclination I admitted, "Me, too."

"The first time I looked into your eyes I knew I could trust you with anything. We have a deep down connection, you and me. As if we've always known each other."

"Yes." It was much easier to admit it in the dark of the night.

"And Jimmi could be one of my nephews," he said. "I mean it. When you go through my photo albums you'll see that some of my brothers' kids look exactly like him. That's why I took to you both so fast. It wasn't really about the dogs at first. I saw Jimmi and you standing by the side of the road. He was glowering at you, making you sad, so I told the driver to stop. How's Marvel? Any sign of her being in heat?"

"Not yet. This wouldn't exactly be a good time for you to take care of two puppies. When you're erecting your circus tent every afternoon and tearing it down every morning."

"Stage," he corrected. "I'd send somebody for them, soon as they're old enough. You better put them in the painting, too. One to my left, the other to my right."

"I can do that," I said. "Since they'll probably grow up to look just like their parents. What age do you have in mind?"

"I leave that entirely—" The drone increased, drowning out his voice. He said something else I couldn't hear. I asked him to repeat it. He did. I still couldn't hear him.

"Listen, Ariel. My phone's acting up," I said. "Maybe some wood rats are chewing on the wires. I'll get it checked. Call me again tomorrow." Then the static got so disruptive that I had to hang up.

I dozed, having pleasant thoughts, until I received the second call maybe ten minutes later. The noise in the wires had stopped. The call was from Dorrie. She was crying. "I'm so sorry," she sobbed. "I was terribly wrong about Jimmi."

All at once I was wide awake.

CHAPTER 31

MY INSIDES CLENCHING, I ASKED, "Why? Did he call you tonight?" He should have called me.

"No," she said. "It was Leroy. A couple of minutes ago. High on something. He said you made a pansy out of Jimmi and the only way to fix him was to take him to a whorehouse. Which he did. Tonight."

"I don't believe it," I stammered. "Jimmi's not even fourteen!"

"Good medicine, Leroy said. To keep him from going queer."

"And? Did it work?"

"Jimmi took one look at the cut-rate whore Leroy bought him and ran off. Leroy had to chase him around the block before he could catch him. He might have hit him at that point; I'm not sure. His speech was kind of slurred. He crowed about the fact that he could still outrun a young boy. And when I tried to wheedle his phone number out of him he hung up. I dialed star 69 but it was unlisted."

I let her cry for a minute. Then I said, "Now do you see why I didn't want Jimmi anywhere near that man, ever?"

That triggered another torrent of sobs. The line began to hum like before. "He'll call you again," I said. "Leroy likes to brag. You're his best audience. Try to get him to let Jimmi come to the phone. And then tell Jimmi I'll help him any time he asks."

The hum became drone. The line crackled. Briefly, I considered giving Dorrie Paul's number. But knowing her, sooner or later Leroy would wind up with it. Paul deserved better than that. Besides, I'd be ashamed to have him find out just what kind of a lowlife Leroy really was.

I told her, "Thanks for letting me know."

She said, "Hello? Silvi? Are you still there? What's wrong with your phone?"

"Beats me," I replied, louder. "I'll get it fixed tomorrow." The crackle grew deafening. When it stopped the line was dead.

I put Mozart on, full volume. Lit a candle. Went back to bed. Stared at the shadows flickering across the ceiling while hot acid dripped from the corners of my eyes, eating identical grooves down my face. Trying to blot my cheeks, I discovered I couldn't raise my hands; I needed to use my entire store of energy just to keep my mind blank. It was the only way I had of making it through the night.

I CALLED the phone company from town early next morning. They promised to send out a repair man the following day. Then I called Barret to make sure Howie would let the man in. But as soon as I identified myself Barret hung up. When I returned to the ridge Howie was not at his post. No doubt mornings were hard on a guy bent on keeping his blood drenched in alcohol. Both Barret's farm truck and the Subaru Brat were still parked in front of the Manor but there was no point in trying to talk to him face to face.

At home I addressed a polite note to him with the exact date and time of the scheduled appointment so he could tell Howie to let the telephone repairman in. Half an hour later I heard the Brat straining up his driveway and away. I walked to the Manor and pinned the note to the front door.

I waited all the next afternoon but the repair man never showed. I had to drive into town to find out why. It seems he'd come as far as the gate but it was locked. No one was around. He was forced to reverse the company truck all the way down steep twisty Ridge Road to where it widened to become the county road. He drove back to town but was willing to come again if I promised to personally escort him past the gate. I apologized for the mix-up and set another date two days in advance.

At the appointed time I drove up to the gate and waited. Howie smirked at me from where he sat in the thin, hot shade of his decrepit camper shell.

Soon the repair man arrived. I got out to work the lock. It wouldn't open.

"What's the matter?" Howie asked. "Forgot the new combination?"

"Yeah," I said, disbelief warring with anger inside me. "I guess I did. Will you give it to me? Please?"

"Sorry," he bleated. "You'll have to ask Barret. He left strict orders for me not to pass it on to *any*one." As if a drunk drifter was more trustworthy than a loyal paying tenant.

"I see," I said calmly. The repair man was frowning. "Just a minute," I told him. Then I got back into Efi, rolled her toward the cable until it tightened against the front of her hood, and pushed on the accelerator until both gate posts started leaning inward. One metal cable fastener snapped, dropping the cable onto the ground.

While I was pushing Howie was yelling, "Stop! Stop!" After the gate popped he said, "You're gonna get it now. Barret will be so mad. Your goose is cooked, lady!"

Ignoring him I asked the repair man to follow me to the cabin. Then I maneuvered Efi to where Ridge Road started to drop toward Stu's place. I expected him to line up behind me. But he didn't. He drove in all right, but just long enough to execute a U-turn, shouting out of his window, "Company policy, ma'am! Call me when your domestic issues are resolved and we'll try again!" Then he drove off the mountain.

Howie gave one shrill hoot too many. I marched right up to him and fixed him with a mean squint, hissing, "Tell your boss I will personally call the sheriff—from town—if he threatens me in any way, shape or form. I have a legal right to access this gate. Any intimidating message he leaves on my door or on my voicemail will be used against him. And if he tries to lock me out of my house I will break a window and climb in."

MIRACULOUSLY the repairman appeared on my driveway the next day, piloted by a poker faced Barret who zoomed off in the Brat before the repairman could climb out of his truck. The man traced the buried wires from my house to Barret's, concluding there was corrosion somewhere underground and a probable break. Fixing it would be a major production. "It'll be a while before we can schedule something that big," he said. "Ma'am."

He wanted a nearby contact number. Even as I was giving him Barret's I already suspected my un-cooperative landlord would "forget" to pass on any message meant for me. Watching the truck drive away I thought how odd a coincidence it was that my phone line should break right after the plumbing developed a leak.

My electricity went out the next day. I stormed to the pump house to check my circuit breaker. It was heavily duct taped to keep it in the off position. The polite type-written note attached to it read,

```
     Silvi,
     Something seems to have gone wrong with
your line. Until I can figure out how to fix
it please refrain from using the electricity.
You're welcome to plug in your refrigerator
and freezer down here until further notice.
Sorry for the inconvenience.
     The Management
```

I didn't want to be part of the tit-for-tat game he was trying to play. Therefore I simply reminded myself that I had done nothing wrong, emptied the appliances, drove them to the pump house, and set them up outside it against the northern wall. After refilling them with my groceries I draped some defunct sleeping bags around them, careful not to block the motors with the thick fabric. Even so I was afraid that trying to keep the food cold at the present 105 degrees temperature would burn them out.

Maybe somebody else would have ripped Barret's notes off the water pipe and the circuit breaker and reconnected the utilities with the flick of a couple of switches, but it would only have escalated our skirmish, possibly ending with guns and bullets. I was already way past my comfort zone; unlike Mama, I was not combative by nature. Paul said it and I had to agree—the only way to deal with Barret when he got like this was to ignore him until he came to his senses.

Meanwhile I'd lock myself in, turn the music up high, and start my Ariel Jordan project.

THE DOWNSTAIRS STEREO didn't have batteries. The ones in Jimmi's boombox must have been weak; Mozart only lasted an hour. Without lights, I went to bed with the birds, acquiescing to the silence of the forest, which was broken only occasionally by a coyote yip or owl hoots. It didn't end until nearby songbirds announced the arrival of dawn. Once the sun climbed over the horizon the scrape of my charcoal pencil on paper was the loudest sound I could hear.

Luckily I kept an emergency old-timey mechanical meat grinder up on the loft. The grinder had a long detachable handle. Cranking it to process twenty chicken necks was good exercise for my arms. The cleanup was another matter. The necks left a thick greasy film all over the gadget. It was a definite eye-opener to see how much bottled water I needed just to wash off the metal parts, my sticky hands, and the congealed sink. But I persevered.

As the days passed I drew sketch after sketch, plotted maps of Raspberry Hill, and wondered how I could get the mountain-top forest and Blossom Lane into the same composition. I'd ordered a roll of canvas so large it would only fit on the wall behind the wood stove. For easier access I took down the stove pipe and dragged the stove to a corner. Then I tacked up the canvas, stood back, and considered my next move. The more I looked the more the vast blank space intimidated me.

What besides summit and hillside did Ariel want me to put in it? Background mountain chains? Brilliant sunrise? How many kids, cherubs, dogs, how much magic? I'd never felt less like a magician. My congested living room made me long for a real high ceilinged studio with leak proof skylights. What kind of art could I possibly create in this broken down shell where nothing worked and my very occupancy was threatened?

In the end I decided to practice by painting smaller versions that fit comfortably onto my easel. There was no rush. No one was looking over my shoulder. Reminding myself that Ariel would be gone for the rest of the year, I allowed myself to relax into my work. I read through his book of poems and fables until I knew them by heart. And then it was almost as if I became him and saw the mountain through his eyes. Time ceased. I returned to reality briefly whenever the cats meowed for their dinners and the dogs scratched on the door expecting their walk.

ONE afternoon a newish silver colored SUV drove smartly up my driveway. A middle aged business man wearing a well cut black suit climbed out and knocked on my living room door. I crept to the kitchen and studied him through a gauze curtained window. He was pudgy, clean shaven, with a baseball sized bald spot in the middle of his precision cut hair.

"Silvi? Are you in there?" he yelled, using Barret's voice. I wondered if my landlord could possibly have an establishment type brother he'd never mentioned. "It's me," the man cried. "Barret. I need to talk to you."

Was this some devious trick to evict me? I'd step outside and then he would slap on a padlock so I couldn't get back in. Opening the kitchen window I asked, "What do you want?"

He turned toward me. "I haven't heard you drive out of here for a while. I thought maybe you were sick or something." There was a note of concern in his voice, making him sound a bit more like the Barret of old.

"Or something," I said. "I'm working on a project."

He nodded, letting his gaze roam to the woodshed, the outhouse, the large Ponderosa pine. "Where's Jimmi? Is he all right?"

"Why are you asking?" After everything he'd said and done I saw no reason to trust him with the smallest hint of personal information.

"Look . . ." He shifted his weight from one foot to the other. "I'm sorry I was so rough on you. Okay?" He wasn't the kind of guy who apologized easily. He must want something big. I waited.

"My father died," he said at last. "I missed the funeral but my mom is expecting me to attend the memorial service." He looked down at his suit. "I promised her I'd look decent for the occasion. She needs me, Silvi."

Trick number one. "You told me your father died a long time ago."

He gave a dismissive wave. "He disowned me way back when I was growing a ponytail and dropping out of Yale. So I disowned him right back. No Chanukah cards, no birthday cards, nothing."

I steeled myself, suspecting he was going to ask me to watch his dogs. But he explained that Howie had volunteered to feed them. "I'm paying him to remodel Stu's place. It should keep him busy till I get back. I gave him the key to the farm truck in case he has to haul in some lumber. You should see him, Silvi—he's a changed man. For a while there he was fucking up but then I gave him an ultimatum and he quit drinking. Overnight." In his missionary zeal he moved a step closer, grasping the railing.

I tilted away from the curtain. "So you think he's trustworthy now?"

"Yes. Well. I would have called you but your phone . . ."

"Out of order? Imagine that!" I rubbed at the dust that had collected on the outside of the window. The slightest breeze wafted it up from the ungraveled driveway.

"You might have noticed that I fixed your other two problems," he said, sounding hurt. "You've got water. You've got lights."

"I stopped checking the faucet ages ago. I go to bed with the birds."

"Howie has instructions to let the phone company in next time they come."

"Why should they?" I said bitterly. "You've chased them off twice that I know of."

He raised his hand as if he was preparing to part the Red Sea. "I'll make the appointment myself this time. Fix it up good. Okay?"

I decided to cut through the preliminaries. "What do you want?"

He looked relieved that I'd called him out. "I want you to check on Howie for me. Make sure he does his job, feeds my babies every day, and keeps their water bucket filled."

"You mean you want me to get close enough to spy on him?" I said, incredulous. "With him and me the only two people up here? Do you have any idea how he's been ogling me? There's no way I'm getting anywhere near that man while you're gone. In fact, I'm keeping my doors locked and my gun tucked in my waistband. Some of my meat's gone missing from the freezer. Chicken backs, for God's sake. He probably wolves them down raw." I started to shut the window.

"Wait," he said, pleading now. I did. He offered me a doleful smile. "Don't do it for me. Do it for my dogs. I'd take them with me if I could. But they'd freak in New York and they'll freak if I stick them in a kennel. No matter what's wrong between us I'd always make sure your pups are all right If you asked me."

As if I ever would. Besides, the cats were petrified of him. He'd made no secret of the fact that he disliked felines. But he knew I was a sucker for animals of course. Even his. After a decent interval during which I hoped he got good and worried I said, "The first time Howie tries to bother me I'll shoot him in the leg."

He grinned, relieved. "I'll tell him. But I doubt you have anything to worry about. He's already scared shitless of your shepherds. He has never come back here, has he?"

"Not that I know of." Though there was one evening right after dark that both dogs cocked their ears and looked to the edge of the clearing, growling softly, hackles raised. Something was in the bushes that didn't belong. And it was big. I'd gone to the screen door and shouted, "I'm counting to ten and then I'm letting the shepherds out." Immediately, that big *something* crashed away. I'd barricaded both doors all night and the dogs stayed awake guarding, sifting the air for unusual sounds and smells.

"What's with the car?" I asked. "You've always hated SUVs."

He shrugged. "My little Brat quit on me. I lucked into a good deal with this baby. And it's got four wheel drive." He stepped away, adjusting his tie. "I'm catching the next flight out. It's just for a couple of weeks. My mom will want to show me off to the relatives. The prodigal son. And I'm supposed to be there when the will's read. Not that I expect anything. The trust fund I bought my land-share with came from my grandparents. On Mom's side."

As he toddled to the SUV I marveled again at his expensive haircut, expertly razored at the nape of his neck. No one wore their hair that short anymore unless they were going into the military. "I won't forget this," he cried with a final wave, getting in. Then he rolled down his window. "Oh—we reattached the gate cable and set the lock with the old combination. For your convenience. Maybe you could collect my mail for me? Somehow I don't think Howie would be too good at it."

I didn't answer, nor did I wave back or watch him drive off. Stepping to the calendar above the dead phone I blinked and wondered what day it was, what month, what season. It was no use checking. I'd lost my point of reference.

Most likely Paul thought I had died.

CHAPTER 32

I MOVED MY APPLIANCES BACK TO THE KITCHEN the next morning, before it got hot. A good deal of the grass-fed beef roast I'd sliced into minute steaks for myself was no longer inside the freezer. If I'd been smart I'd have wrapped a chain around its door while it was parked at the pump house. The lettuce in the little refrigerator had long since turned to slime, the celery had become limp and bleached. It was time for some shopping.

On the way in I stopped at the auto parts store and bought a locking gas cap. Now that Howie was in charge of Barret's farm truck he'd start looking around for a dependable, nearby, and free source of gasoline. Once I was done grocery shopping I covered the food with a blanket to keep it cool. Then I parked in the biting heat outside of Paul's office. He was not sitting at his much-too-clean desk. I heard the buzz of a television through the door to the back room. I knocked, calling his name. The door flew open. Without warning, Paul pulled me inside, restraining Racket before he could throw himself into my arms. Looking haggard, Paul said, "You haven't heard, have you?"

"Heard what?"

"I forgot. You don't have a TV. Though it's probably on the radio news, too."

"What is?"

He pushed me into a chair and began to channel surf. "There," he said after a few clicks. "This." He increased the volume. On the screen was an enlargement of a photo I'd stuck in Jimmi's suitcase before we drove to the airport. Barret had taken it last year. It showed Jimmi and me, cheek to cheek, smiling, my arm around his shoulders. While I was wondering what that photo was doing on national television it was replaced by a press conference featuring Leroy.

I would have recognized him anywhere with his air of superiority and that odd twisted smile of his, although the muscles he'd so carefully built and nurtured had turned to fat. He was reading from notes, surrounded by cameras and microphones. His monotonous voice was overdubbed by that of a solicitous female newscaster condensing his rambling speech for the viewers. I leaned forward, straining to hear, but although the language was familiar I couldn't understand a word.

"What are they saying?" I asked Paul.

Ashen faced, he recapped for me. "It seems Jimmi has accused the singer Ariel Jordan of molesting him on two occasions when Jimmi stayed in his . . . Oregon vacation home. Leroy is suing Ariel. And you."

The scene shifted back to the photo, zeroing in on my smiling face. Bewildered, I heard the newscaster slaughter my name and pepper it with terms like "accessory," "collusion," and "corrupting a minor."

Obviously Leroy had heard that my painting was starting to pay off.

I jumped up and blindly felt my way to the door.

"Stay," Paul said.

"I suppose you believe Leroy? I don't see Jimmi at his side."

"He's keeping his meal ticket under wraps," Paul said drily, clamping a hand on my wrist. "In my business you learn to read people. Leroy's a shyster. Ariel wouldn't hurt a fly, let alone a child. But he's got something Leroy wants and Leroy thinks he knows just how to get it."

Some bitter wind was screeching in my ears. Then everything went black. I could feel myself clutching the door knob, swaying. Paul tried to guide me to a chair, but I shook him off, stammering, "I've got to get home."

"Stay in town tonight," he urged. "They've played this scene over and over since yesterday. By now the reporters are on your trail."

"Jimmi wouldn't give them my address!"

"You have a valid driver's license?" Paul asked. "These guys work fast. And pay well for every ounce of dirt they dig up. Jimmi's classmates, maybe. A neighbor who needs extra cash . . ."

"This can't be happening," I pleaded. "Ariel trusted us. What's *he* saying?"

"So far not a thing. He cancelled a couple of shows. No one can find him. His ranch gates are locked. Private security guards are patrolling inside the fence. The reporters can't even confirm that he's in there. Check into a motel, Silvi. Or sleep here."

I glanced at his second-hand convertible couch, feeling a cramp in my back at the thought of its decrepit springs. "My animals!"

Paul sagged. "Of course. Well, hurry on up the mountain then. With any luck you'll beat the horde. I never thought I'd be grateful for Barret's locked gate." He escorted me through the office, steadying me. I stopped at the threshold. "You don't seem surprised that we know Ariel."

He gave a wry laugh. "Oh, I was. But the clues fell into place pretty fast. The white face inside your cabin, glowing in the moonlight. Enoch Foundation *and* Enterprises. A certain Mr. *Rafael* buying all five of your paintings. My hat's off to you for being so close-mouthed. Anyone else would have bragged."

I opened the door and was immediately assaulted by a blast of hot air. Then I felt Racket trying to push out between my legs. I picked him up and held him close. "Ariel was my friend when I desperately needed one," I said. "A sweet soul whose only fault is trusting people who don't deserve it. Before I forget—what happened with Violet?"

His mouth tightened. "Previous convictions. Marijuana possession. Growing. That sort of thing—as if judges and prosecutors don't smoke the stuff themselves, in private. They kept her locked up long enough for Lavender's father to fly up here and spring his little girl from a temporary foster home. He took her down to California with him. Joint custody. I finally got Violet out on bail. She disappeared right afterwards even though she promised to check in with me every day. I only hope she didn't skip."

"She might be sleeping in her truck somewhere away from phones."

He nodded. "I tried to talk Zora into taking her in but she seems to have developed an aversion to Violet. Especially after I mentioned the previous convictions."

"Zora's nice but straight," I said. "She's led a sheltered life. I don't think she can imagine what Violet's going through. And then of course there was Barret, smack in the middle between them. Honestly, I don't think Violet will run. She'll be in touch."

He shrugged. "I sincerely hope so. If Barret wasn't such a miserable bear I'd have offered her the use of my unfinished cabin."

Why did that remark give me a pang? "He probably instructed Howie to take potshots at her if she shows up. I've got to go." I handed him Racket and stepped onto the shaded sidewalk. Unfortunately the shade did not reach as far as Efi.

"Call me when you get home," he said with a frown.

"My phone's dead. Been dead for weeks."

"Ah! So that's why it keeps on ringing and ringing when I call. War games?"

With a hollow laugh, I said, "Obviously you've had experience with Barret's strategies." Climbing into Efi, I quickly rolled both windows down all the way, folded up the sun screen, and, craning my neck, noted with something akin to pleasure that Paul stayed in his doorway, watching me ease into traffic.

THERE was no one on Old Siskiyou Highway where it wound up the mountain. There seldom was in early afternoon. The county road, too, was empty. As was the tortured gravel road leading up to the ridge. Paul was wrong after all. I wasn't that easy to find. This ridge wasn't even on most maps. And maybe the DMV didn't give out private information. Although these days, with the internet . . . Then again, it wasn't as if I was newsworthy. The paparazzi hounding the Emperor of Song were too busy to sniff around for the likes of me.

Or so I thought until Ridge Road wound out of the woods. I had one clear glimpse of the abrupt rise lying ahead with the ditch on one side and a lethal drop on the other. Near the top I spotted a logjam of matchbox size minivans and a black jeep. Tiny arms were gesturing out of car windows. A man the size and shape of Howie was swaggering from car to car, panhandling or auctioning me off to the highest bidder. He stopped, listening to the sound of Efi's engine straining uphill. Raising his greedy hand he gestured directly at me.

Without thinking I slammed the clutch into reverse, backed down until I found a possible turnout, and laboriously inched sideways a few degrees at a time. Already the car at the end of the line was beginning a similar maneuver. Efi's right rear wheel got too close to the ditch, rolled in, and quickly dug a rut for itself. I jumped out and engaged the locknuts, got in again, switched to four wheel drive, and eased out of the ditch. Looking uphill I saw that the last car had completed its turn-around and was recklessly speeding toward me. I disengaged the 4X4 clutch but decided I couldn't afford the few seconds it would have taken for me to climb out again to free the locknuts. Hitting the accelerator, I counted on the little computer in my brain—the one that had logged every curve, every degree of rise and fall of the roads and the highway for years—to come to my rescue. No matter how good the drivers behind me were, I was bound to be better.

The whole time I was racing down the mountain I never looked back though I did glance at the rear view mirror every now and then. Most of the curves were so tight I couldn't even get a peek at what or who was chasing me. When I came to the long straight stretch just before this highway merged with 66, I floored the accelerator, shot across both lanes of the 66, and maneuvered into the tenuous dirt path obscured by brambles, leading to the lake.

I rammed Efi in there until she was hidden by bushes, then got out and sneaked to where I could see through the leaves. And there came my pursuers, down the straight stretch, almost as fast as me, one vehicle after another like a long famished python tracking a sure meal. At the crossing they took a sharp left toward town and sped around the next bend. I waited just long enough to make sure there were no stragglers. Then I backed out and drove in the opposite direction to Ariel's land, reasoning that no one would bother trying to find his vacant Oregon hideaway since he was presumed to be elsewhere. The farmhouse definitely was not on anybody's map. And the road to it was a labyrinth; only the initiated had a chance of coming out at the other end.

Or so I assumed.

BOTH the Chevy and the farmhouse looked derelict and dusty, but I realized almost at once that something was wrong. The car doors, the hood, and the trunk were all open, as was the glove compartment. The seats were slashed. The front door of the house had been forced and stood open. I pushed it wider.

Even before entering I could smell the most recent visitor; he had left a strong musky odor in his wake. I found him in the pantry, standing on his hind legs, trying to scrabble up a shelf. After opening the back door for him, I withdrew into the wrecked living room. The telephone rang. It took me a while to find it. It was an old stationary model, the kind that has a cords attached on both ends, without voice recording equipment of any kind. I meant to pick up the receiver but by then I'd gotten a good look at the mess the police had made and lost heart. They had dismantled everything. Books had been tossed off the shelves, cartons emptied, the couch ripped apart.

While the telephone continued to ring I looked toward the kitchen in time to see a bushy black and white tail, raised high in the air, disappear out the back door. No doubt what had drawn the skunk inside was the food they had dumped out of the freezer. A couple of bags containing frozen cherries had been clawed open and emptied. A carton of ice cream lay on its side, spilling vanilla soup. But the TV dinners and frozen meats were intact and still reasonably hard. The refrigerator, too, had been emptied. Yogurt containers, several shriveled apples, one moldy orange, and a dozen broken eggs lay on the floor beside it. The pantry was in disarray, though I had to blame some of the mess on the skunk. The phone finally stopped ringing.

A quick look through the rest of the house confirmed that they had conducted a thorough raid, slicing, ripping, upending whatever tickled their fancy. In a way it was a relief, for now they would feel no need to return. While I stood staring, unable to take in the full extent of the destruction, the phone began to ring again.

It was entirely possible that the same reporters who had managed to find my home address had found Ariel's number and were testing to see if anyone was there to answer. Hopefully, not even the best of those computer savvy but out-of-state newsmongers would find their way to the farmhouse. The police, I was beginning to realize, had their own covert sources.

I put away my groceries and stepped outside, looking uphill and longing for home. Surely Asa and Marvel were waiting to eat, the cats lining the table, the tips of their tails whipping the air with the first signs of irritation at my continuing absence.

Reason insisted I stay put at least until sundown. Ariel had some flashlights on top of his refrigerator. As soon as it got dark I would brave bears and mountain lions to hike up to where I belonged. The phone stopped ringing for half a minute then started again. I imagined there was something frantic in its tone. I counted thirty rings this time. It took every ounce of resolve I had to keep myself from picking up the receiver. Not until the clamor stopped could I make myself empty my purse onto the counter, smoothing out every crinkled store receipt, movie ticket, grocery list until I found the scrap onto which Ariel had written his mother's private number. I dialed with trepidation, fighting an ever-growing sense of guilt. A man answered, "Jordan residence, Tron speaking." That would be Metatron, Ariel's oldest brother.

"Ariel gave me this number," I said quickly before he could hang up. "He said your mother would pass on a message for me."

"Just a minute." He muffled the receiver and asked an undecipherable question to which he got a muted reply. Then a resonant female voice spoke into the mouth piece. "Yes?" it said. "This is Alicia Jordan. How may I help you?"

Past my chattering teeth, I said, "My name is Silvi. I'm a neighbor of Ariel's, in Oregon."

"Oh, that Silvi," she said. "Haven't you done enough damage already?" Then she hung up.

I had no idea what to do next. A few minutes later the ringing started again. I answered with a guarded "Hello?"

"At last!" Ariel said. "I've been calling and calling. Your number and mine."

Dry mouthed, I said, "My phone's out of order. Remember the strange noises it made last time we talked? It died soon after." A deep sense of shame burned through me. "Look," I went on. "You know I don't have a TV. I just found out an hour ago what Jimmi has done."

"Not Jimmi," Ariel protested. "Leroy. The Jimmi I know has a pure heart as all children do. He was coerced."

"That's no excuse," I said. "He's old enough to say no to something that is utterly wrong."

"He's hungry for his father's approval. He'd probably do most anything to get it."

"Even betray his mother and his friend?"

"Even that."

"It's very bad for you right now, isn't it?"

He gave a toneless laugh. "I've got a first class migraine that won't quit. My back's seized up and so has my voice. All over the world people are trying to get refunds. Even my most loyal fans are beginning to doubt me. I sort of weathered the first accusation although a lot of people are still saying, 'Where there's smoke, there's got to be fire.' This time around, my future is burning to ashes. My career can't survive this one, Silvi." His voice broke as he went on, softly, "Neither can I."

It was all my fault of course. If I'd let Jimmi accompany Ariel on the tour he'd never have gone to Florida. Leroy would never have been able to snare and corrupt him. "Ariel, don't say that!" I cried. "I can still make it all come out right—if I can get Leroy's address. You know people down in L.A. Ask them to hire a detective to track him. He must be going to his lawyer, plotting strategies and signing papers and such. Call me as soon as you get a valid address. I'll do the rest. I promise."

With a tremulous voice he said, "Do you have any idea how many people have broken their promises to me?"

"Yes," I replied. "But that has nothing to do with us. I am exactly who you thought I was. I haven't changed. I won't."

I waited while he thought it over. At last he said, "All right. If you stay in my house so I can reach you. Any reporters outside there?"

"Not a one," I told him, deciding it was the wrong time to mention the raid. "This place is so well hidden even I had trouble finding it today. I almost got lost a couple of times, following the wrong road."

He chuckled. "One of its attractions for me. Listen—the pantry's stocked. There's enough of everything to see you through a long siege. Bring down your animals. They're as welcome as you are. The closet in the spare bedroom is full of disguises for next time you need to go to town."

"Surely this won't go on much longer," I said. "After all, I'm only me."

"You're a pry bar. They need to keep the drama going, you see. For their ratings. One more thing . . . the Chevy. Drive it onto the bridge and lock it up tight. Leave it there. It'll be the next best thing to a gate. And some BEWARE OF DOG signs and GUARD DOGS ON DUTY signs posted along the creek bank would help."

"Good thinking," I said.

"If you get bored you can always watch one of my music videos. Just in case you've ever wondered what it is that I actually do for a living."

"Ouch," I said. "You've noticed I'm not enthralled with pop music. Nothing against your songs but I keep my radio tuned to the classical station. I do like your ballads but not that loud boom-boom stuff."

"Try my latest album."

I wasn't about to tell him I already had. "Call me the minute you get Leroy's address," I repeated. "I'll take it from there."

What I didn't tell him was that I had no clue how I would proceed. Not yet I didn't.

CHAPTER 33

KNOWING THE ANIMALS WERE HUNGRY, I SET OFF for my cabin as soon as it was dark. I brought one of Ariel's flashlights but was afraid to use it. Howie might have spotted the beam, homing in on it and me. I didn't want to risk a nighttime encounter.

I studied the shadowed cabin from the safety of the forest, aided by moonlight. The gate leading into the dog yard was open. For one panicked instance I was afraid Howie had managed to drive the dogs off. But then I saw them, trapped in the cat yard. They could never have gotten in there by themselves. Clearly, someone had wanted them out of the way. When I released them they were trembling. There was no sign of the cats.

Howie had used a hack saw on the padlock I'd fastened to the outside of the kitchen door. So much for Barret's faith in the drifter. If I'd had a phone and the Bear's New York number I would have given him an earful. Then again most likely he was sitting in front of a TV right now, watching my personal life unravel on the nation's TV screens and itching to return the favor.

I stepped into a razed kitchen, realizing almost at once that the destruction I saw went beyond anything Howie might have attempted. It was created by the same force that had trashed Ariel's house although it was likely that Howie had done some gleaning. As I stood wondering how much of the mess piled on the floor could be saved, the cats began to creep out of hiding one by one. They jumped onto the table, nervously flicking their neck fur, twitching their tails, wanting to be fed. I'd brought enough ground turkey for everyone including the dogs.

I began to sort through the chaos but soon gave it up as hopeless. The telephone was gone, taken by the law or by Howie. It was possible Barret had kept his word and arranged to have the line fixed, but I doubted it. There hadn't been enough time. Unlike Ariel's, my machine had a built-in answering device. Maybe that's what the police had been after. In the living room the desk drawers had been pulled out and spilled, my stack of paintings scattered, the futon on my bed slashed, dragged half off the frame and piled high with the clothes that had been hanging in the closet.

With leaden feet I climbed up to Jimmi's room. His mattress was slashed too. His box of CDs had been upended. So had the drawers of his small student desk. His childhood collection of Star Trek ships and action figures, his books—including the entire Baum *Oz* series and *The Little Engine That Could*—had been swept from their shelf of honor. Lifting a corner of the lacerated mattress I saw that the porn magazines were gone.

My home was now hostile territory. I fought the impulse to run. The dumped, thawing meat had to be returned to the freezer. I left out a couple of half-defrosted bags of necks. Sifting through my overturned boxes of hardware supplies and tools I chose the three biggest padlocks I had on hand, removed the keys duct taped to their sides, and snapped the first lock shut on the cat yard gate. The second went on the dog yard gate. The third replaced the sawed lock at the kitchen entrance.

The living room door, latched on the inside, could not be opened from the porch, although a couple of swift kicks might have easily torn it right out of the jamb. I dragged over Asa's heavy recliner and tipped it to lean against the inside of the door. Then I sealed both pet doors and climbed to the loft for cat carriers,

Stillman's revolver, and a box of bullets. The last two items were just where I'd carefully hidden them, in a plugged hole at the end of one of the wooden ceiling beams. I stuffed the gun in my pocket and vowed to hike up here twice every night and morning until I'd carried the last cat to safety.

Five minutes later the two felines who'd finished eating first were inside the carriers. One shared its tight quarters with the chicken necks, the other with the electric meat grinder plus attachments. Assisted by gravity I found it easier to carry my load down to the farmhouse than I'd feared. I shut the cats into Ariel's downstairs bathroom along with a carton I'd filled with dirt. Then the dogs and I went to get the next couple of passengers. This time I brought Ariel's sturdy day pack for my art supplies.

Eventually I managed to transport all the cats. I put their litter boxes on the screened back porch. During the day I let them outside to explore the creek bank and meadow. Since they were used to eating at five p.m., getting them to come into the house before dark was never a problem. In the end I brought down the easel, my sketch books, the paintings I'd cut from their frames, and the huge roll of canvas, glad that due to my creative cowardice I didn't have to worry about smeared oil paints. That roll was the most awkward to carry no matter what angle I tried. It fit nicely onto one of the living room walls. It wasn't until I finished pushing in the last thumb tack along the edge of the canvas that I finally started the cleanup.

As shocked as I was by the carnage I didn't mention it to Ariel when he called. He had enough worries trying to deal with his concerts. A disciplined entertainer since early childhood, he had only cancelled the two, which he made up in the following week. Some of the TV gossip news showed him performing. He looked totally at ease onstage, delivering his songs and the accompanying moves with his usual fervor. The so-called newscasters called him heartless and callous.

But whenever he phoned me he exposed a different side of himself. "I hurt so bad I have to take a handful of pills just to get through my performance," he said in a small, young voice. "I had to fly in my massage therapist so he can loosen my cramping muscles a couple of hours before each show." Silence. Then he added in an even smaller voice, "My entire life, all I ever wanted was to make the world a happier place. I worked hard at it, Silvi. And now everybody hates me, calling me 'ari-fairie' and 'freak.' The word 'bizarre' has become my middle name. And I'm supposed to keep smiling and dancing as if nothing's wrong."

"It'll pass," I told him with more optimism than I had any right to. "Concentrate on your fans. Most of them will keep right on loving you."

"I love them more. And I'm grateful to the ones who're still loyal. But I can't turn on the TV or radio without hearing the most outrageous lies about me. Neither can they. Last night one news show interviewed this fancy woman psychologist in New York. The announcer claimed she was as an expert on pedophiles. She did a thorough job of assassinating my character, starting when I was three. Even though she's never even met me."

Each of his grievances was like a ice pick stabbing my heart. The next day he called at two in the morning and said, "Haters are flooding the internet. They're gathering outside my mother's house and at the ranch gates. A maid I fired last year for stealing me blind got paid by a tabloid to tell the most appalling stories about me and the boys I invited for weekends. Even though they brought their parents with them."

The next time he called he was even more dejected. "I've been getting a lot of death threats, Silvi," he cried. "My life's become a nightmare I can't get out of." I knew exactly how he felt. If he hadn't helped me on the night the void was closing around me I might now be rotting between the madrones, and the puppies and cats turning to slime in their grave. I wished I could think of something to do or say that would make it better for him. But I had no talent for grief counseling. And the ugly truth was that I was part of his problem, not the solution.

Thanks to his state-of-the-art satellite dish I was able to keep up with the news. I cringed when I watched the interview where Leroy slammed Ariel and me as partners in a pre-arranged plot to groom Jimmi for a life of pornography and male prostitution. But I had to admire his cleverness. He was making sure no judge would ever favor me in a custody fight.

As tour de force Leroy read aloud from a passage of a "secret" diary. He claimed it was Jimmi's. The section described in great detail every perverse sexual act Ariel supposedly committed upon my boy. I had no doubt the words were written by Jimmi's hand— nor that they were dictated to him by his money-grubbing unprincipled father. Only God knew what he threatened the child with to get the black-and-white proof he was after.

Their whereabouts remained undiscovered. Soon the fall term would start in California's schools but I doubted that Leroy would enroll Jimmi in any of them, public or private. The man had dodged creditors most of his life; he knew how to get by under society's radar.

"WHY did you settle that law suit with Frankie?" I couldn't help asking Ariel one night although I realized a lot of other people must have asked him the same question before me. "Somebody like Leroy was bound to find the prospect of milking you again irresistible. The moment Jimmi let slip that you were a personal friend of his neither of you stood a chance."

You don't understand. Frankie and I were very close. I loved him like a little brother. How could I let his father force him to perjure himself under oath? Courtrooms are ugly. I've spent many mind numbing hours and days in them all over the world, being sued for anything from alleged copy right violations to child support."

"Oh? You have kids?"

Don't I wish! This last one was just some silly girl's idea of a get-rich scheme. She broke through security in the middle of a performance, climbed on the stage, and kissed me on the lips before they could tear her away. Nine months later she had a baby and sued me for support. Maybe no one ever told her there's a bit more to the birds and the bees than mouth-to-mouth contact.

"Good grief! Does that kind of thing happen a lot?"

Too often to suit me. It's amazing how ferocious some of those sweet looking girls can get.

"Must be hard," I said drily, replaying in my mind's eye his signature bump-and-grind. "But seriously—are you telling me you *want* to have children?"

Of course. More than anything I want to be a dad. I want to choose who with, is all. And I'd like to keep it private.

Do girls chase you a lot?

All the time. But my mother warned me about devious women so I've been careful. And lucky I guess. Anyway, my attorneys said the case with Frankie might drag on for years. I didn't want that for him or for myself. I just wanted the whole mess to go away. So I didn't put up a big enough fuss when the insurance company decided to settle. And I've regretted it ever since.

"Are you planning to handle this case differently?"

I've got to. Though I feel bad for Jimmi.

"Don't. You must speak out. Loud and clear. Hold a news conference of your own, Ariel. Tell the fans you're innocent and determined to prove it. You should have done it already."

I was waiting for Jimmi to gather enough courage to tell the truth.

"What if he can't?"

I promised to find him for you.

"And you will. But right now you've got to defend yourself. I'll be rooting for you."

Not for Jimmi?

"No," I said, feeling a terrible weight in my chest. "I won't be rooting for Jimmi."

THE MEDIA were so skilled at presenting me as a subhuman monster, I had to keep reminding myself that I'd done nothing to be ashamed of. The latest news flash was that the law had raided my house and confiscated the "porn material" Jimmi supposedly claimed Ariel gave him. Who could have leaked that tidbit? Perhaps not even police insiders were immune to gossip rag bribes.

One night I clicked on the TV and saw the announcer's self-important face begin to gloat the moment before he even mentioned Ariel's name. I clicked the set off and decided right there and then to keep it that way. It was much more peaceful to restack the stuff the cops had swept off the library shelves. Ariel was right. Leafing through his photo albums gave me new ideas for the painting.

I discovered a couple of his early music videos under the library couch. They were still wrapped in cellophane and appeared to be untouched. I viewed them on his state-of-the-art wide screen and found them mesmerizing. Although he was handsome in person, made up and costumed he was so beautiful that it actually hurt to watch him perform. It was beyond me why anyone would want to destroy his blazing, one-of-a-kind career. There never was and never would be anyone who could come close to him in talent and style.

After I'd spent the day painting it was my nightly habit to replay those two DVDs and watch him strut through his astounding routines in eye catching costumes. And when I found a box containing tapes of all of his recorded songs, I learned to appreciate even the fastest, loudest hits he made before his awful last album. I always looked forward to the end of the day.

One evening, surrounded by my beastly companions, I began to sense that another human was somewhere in the house. But no matter how fast I swiveled my head I could never catch sight of the person. Then as I was watching one of Ariel's videos something inside of me warmed and shifted and glowed, stretching toward his image. I thought I heard a delighted giggle. Without thinking I put my hands on my belly.

That's when my eyes snapped wide open. When was the last time I had my period? After Stillman died, I'd stopped keeping track—but didn't I have one at the *Trüffelhof* a week before I flew home?

Poor Ariel. What had essentially been an extended hug, the act of an empathic Samarian, was having unforeseen repercussions. Just because he'd forgotten his mother's warning. Once. If he hadn't learned to regret meeting me yet, an accidental pregnancy would surely do it. There was only one way to proceed—and that was to keep it entirely to myself.

*

THAT evening, Barret's Labs came to find us and decided to stay. It was too late to take them back to the Manor and too late to let them hang around outside, so after they ignored my repeated commands to go home I invited them in. The first thing they did was to sit in front of the refrigerator, panting with benign expectation. Barret fed them cheap on-sale kibble. The raw chicken backs I tossed into their gaping maws excited their stunted taste buds. They swallowed the meat with no visible chewing and shamelessly asked for more. I offered them the couch instead and they made themselves comfortable. Asa and Marvel, who'd never had a high opinion of Barret's Labs, followed me to the bedroom.

In the morning the Labs accompanied us on our walk but when I steered them uphill toward the Manor they pressed themselves to the forest floor and refused to move until I changed directions. We hiked to the madrones on a deer trail crowded by poison oak and brambles. There was no sign of any backhoe activity. Yet. Perhaps Gierig had decided it would be wise to finish obliterating Raspberry Hill before starting on this one.

I sat on the swing Paul had tied to the horizontal madrone branch for me and puzzled at the new twist my life was taking. I was never one of those women who don't feel fulfilled unless they replicate themselves. Not that I regretted raising Jimmi but mothering him had cost an immense amount of time and effort, leaving little energy for my painting career.

Delightful as Jimmi had been as a toddler, he was constantly on the move, insisting on my undivided attention. A light sleeper and relentless talker, he was the kind of child who had an unlimited supply of questions for which he wanted immediate answers. Taking care of his ever expanding needs hadn't been easy. I drove him to and from school and helped with his homework. I cooked three meals a day, when left to myself I might have preferred an apple and a slice of buttered bread. I played with him and colored with him and sang to him and spent at least an hour a day on reading him stories. There had been mountains of laundry to lug to the Laundromat every Saturday. Just remembering the heaps of clothes I used to fold and stack and put away could still give me goose bumps.

To my delight he finally grew big enough to fold his own clothes, prepare his own meals, do most of his own homework. Ah, those were sweet times compared to this last rebellious year during which he turned thirteen. In my reveries I used to fast-forward to the day when I would send him off to college. I'd think, "Not much longer. In five, six years I'll have my life back."

His recent defection changed everything and now I was doing exactly what I'd always wanted to do. Way ahead of schedule. How could I possibly give it up to start the entire child raising cycle all over again with a new baby? On the other hand, although I supported every woman's right to choose, I realized that I myself could never have an abortion. But what other options were there?

I knew very well that living in the farmhouse was only a short term solution. Where would I go once Ariel wanted it back? After sampling Barret's latest downside I would never again feel secure on the ridge. Just because he'd recovered his wits this time didn't mean there wouldn't be a next, possibly worse episode during which he would kick me out as easily as he'd evicted everyone else who annoyed him.

Though I grieved over losing Jimmi I had to admit that his absence gave me almost unlimited freedom. I could indulge in shrill whistling, sing loudly off key, and fart without him responding with a disapproving, "Silvi, p-lease!" from upstairs.

True, I wanted the chance to finish the job of raising my boy. I owed it to him— and to myself. It was part of the program. Raising a new baby from scratch was not. Yet here I sat, in a swing on top of the world, with a passenger looking out of my eyes, its brand new mind trustingly locking onto mine. Expecting things.

CHAPTER 34

As I SLEPT WILY NATURE STARTED TO WORK ON ME, breaking down my resistance by drenching my system with mother-hormones. At dinner I knew clearly that I must sacrifice everything for my art. At the following breakfast I inserted an *almost* between *sacrifice* and *everything*.

Hadn't I always regretted the fact that I missed Jimmi's infancy and babyhood? Here was an opportunity to experience what holding a newborn was like, to watch it unfold and become. Maybe it wasn't having a child that was so discouraging—maybe it was being poor in the process. But wasn't my financial status about to change? Ariel and Paul hadn't bought my paintings just to please me. Neither had the two art lovers to whom Dorrie had sold my acrylics. And Ariel certainly hadn't commissioned the big one merely because I was suicidal and he wanted to give me something positive to focus on.

Or had he?

He couldn't have.

THUS, yesterday's problem shrank in the light of the breaking dawn. My improved reasoning was that if I could feed and house two dogs and countless cats surely one small addition to our household would make little difference. Besides, I wouldn't have to drive her—somehow, it felt like a her—to school for the first five years. During that time my reputation as an artist was bound to grow. I'd have a steady flow of commissions. Exhibits. Ads in art magazines. We would all live happily together in a more convenient location where I'd convert the garage into a gallery.

I patted my belly, still flat and trim. "You and me, we'll be all right," I said. "I promise." Maybe this baby was nature's way of hauling me out of the abyss that Jimmi's desertion had plunged me into.

FEEDING the Labs breakfast that morning, I noticed they were still ravenous. And weren't they just a tad thinner than they used to be? What was going on up there? I'd better risk taking them home to find out. Surely even the most stubborn journalists were off covering more important stories by now, preferably on the far side of the continent. I hid the gun in my waistband, left Asa and Marvel in the house, and loaded the Labs into Efi.

The drive up to the high valley was uneventful. When I reached the county road I remembered Barret's request to have me gather his mail. So I rolled up to his dented box. It was full of postal junk. Barret must have subscribed to every catalogue on the market. Sifting out the first class mail I noticed one unusual letter. On the envelope someone had printed, in a wavering unpracticed hand, "To the people who took in Howie. Open at once." The second sentence was underlined. Twice. Carefully, as if it might contain anthrax, I slipped that letter into my jacket and put everything else in a brown paper bag.

I found the ridge gate locked and deserted. Howie was nowhere around. So far so good. I drove down to the Manor. Barret's SUV was not there. No doubt it was still waiting for him in the airport parking lot. The Labs refused to get out of Efi until I grabbed two fistfuls of hides and heaved. Then they led me to their feeding dishes, strangely subdued, their tails between their legs. The dishes were around the back of the house in Barret's moldy basement. They poked their noses at a mixture of kibble and cheap canned dog food. The tops had become crusty and were buzzing with flies. I took the bowls outside, stabbing one of the crusts with a stick. It cracked, revealing a soggy inside that was crawling with maggots. Retching, I dumped the pap behind the nearest bush, aimed the hose at the empty plastic bowls, and let the hard spray scour them clean. Then I scrubbed the Labs' dry, algae-ringed water bucket, filled it with fresh water, carried the bowls to the front porch, and knocked on the door.

No one answered. I pushed it open, calling, "Barret? Howie? Anyone home?" No response. I walked through the kitchen straight to the kibble sack, scooped some into the bowls with an old yogurt container, took a can of dog food off the shelf, found the can opener. As I was cutting the lid I noticed how cluttered the kitchen had become. Not at all the way Barret liked to keep it. The waste basket in the corner was overflowing with odorous trash and squashed beer cans. More of the same, mingling with empty wine jugs, crowded the counter and spilled onto the floor. The only place not covered with the proof of Howe's alcohol addiction was by the telephone. That spot was layered with business cards bearing the logos of cable news shows and gossip rags. With hand-written telephone numbers, dollar signs, and exclamation marks.

Then I heard some small sound coming from upstairs. "Howie?" I said. Still no answer, although I had the distinct impression that someone was holding his breath. My skin crawled. I started to hum hoping it would give me more courage, stirred the canned meat into the kibble, and put down the dishes. Pulling the gun out of my waistband, I made sure it was loaded and crept up the stairs with it, stopping when my head cleared the open trapdoor.

I was expecting a drunk, wasted Howie sprawling on top of Barret's bed. But it was Violet who was hiding under the blankets, long strands of white-blond hair giving her away. There by whose request? "Violet!" I said sternly, stuffing the gun in my pocket. "What are *you* doing here?"

She sat up, blinking her watery eyes at me. "I could say the same thing about you!"

"I found the dogs wandering on the highway," I lied, hoping to keep the location of my hideout a secret. "What the heck's going on? Barret won't like what Howie did to his kitchen. Not one bit."

She had assessed the situation. "Don't look at me," she said with a hint of defiance. "I just got here last night. I've been camping out in the woods till yesterday. Then my pickup wouldn't start. Howie's over there right now trying to fix it."

"And he told you to keep the bed warm for him in the meantime? That's sick."

She tightened her lips. "You should talk. I'm surprised you have the nerve to show your face in public these days. Not after what you and Ariel Jordan did to poor Jimmi. Pedophiles!"

"Oh, shut up!" I cried, climbing up the rest of the stairs. "For your information, no one did anything to Jimmi—except for his father who's no less scummy now than he's ever been. What's gotten into you? Shop lifting. Bed hopping. I saw your truck parked at Gierig's. At his invitation I presume." I pulled the blankets off the bed. She was naked. Small breasted, narrow hipped, her long legs bruised, with every one of her ribs showing, she really did look like an orphan.

Grabbing the blanket back she covered herself with it and said, "John surprised Lavender and me one night when we were using his cabin. He seemed so nice about it. Bringing us takeout. Firing up the hot tub for me. But then I caught him touching Lavender. I stopped him in a heartbeat. Unlike some mothers I could name. Naturally, he threw us out right after and threatened to have me arrested for prostitution along with breaking and entering. The poor never win."

She gave a shuddering sob, then hiccupped a laugh. "If Lavender hadn't gotten so hungry I wouldn't have stolen that food from the co-op. But look—" She rose, slipped on some grubby jeans and a frayed shirt, and rummaged under the bed. Pulling out a battered shoe she peeled back the sole, showing me the two crisp one hundred dollar bills she was hiding underneath. "My granny sent these in her last letter. As soon as my truck's fixed me and Howie are heading for California to get Lavender." She stuffed the money back under the sole, smoothed it, and stepped into the scuffed shoes, feet bare. "We'll be long gone by the time Barret gets home."

"You're going on the road with Howie?" I envisioned rape, chopped off hands, her body buried under old leaves in some forest, Howie making off with her truck.

"He's not so bad," she said. "And he was ready to move on anyway. Barret's been working him too hard. Besides, Oregon gets freezing cold in the winter. Who wants to be homeless up here in the snow?"

"What about your court date?"

She forced a fluttery laugh. "Oh, that was last week. I'm done with this place. My granny said we could use the spare bedroom in her trailer. For a while. Just till we get on our feet."

"You and Howie?"

Her eyes reddened and teared. "Me and Lavender of course. I know she's missing me something awful. I can feel it day and night. She wants her mommy. Her daddy might have better luck with the police than I do but he's always off playing gigs or practicing or drinking." She pointed down the stairs. "I don't know why but I seem to attract addicts."

"Clyde too?"

"It wasn't liquor with him. He was into weed. He was planning to grow it in these woods. That's why he came up here with Lavender and me. Just another loser in a long line. Even with all the money he lucked into. If his father wasn't handling it Clyde would run through it like it was water."

From the top of the ridge came the rattling sound of the farm truck. Her head snapped sideways. She listened. "You better leave. Before Howie remembers his plans for you."

Even with the revolver's weight pressing against my thigh I was beginning to feel vulnerable. But all I said was, "Don't go with him, Violet. You don't know him well enough." Then he came rumbling down the drive, tires spinning gravel. I stepped outside because it seemed safer. At least there was a chance that someone would hear me scream. Surreptitiously, I put a hand on my bulging pocket.

Violet followed me into the yard as Howie got out of the truck. "What do *you* want?" he asked, his voice insolent, his glance scrolling over my body, making me glad I was wearing my sagging burka-adaptation.

"She brought the Labs back," Violet explained. "It's okay. I told her we're taking off as soon as my pickup starts. How did it go?"

He scratched his head, then shook it. "Battery's dead. I don't have a charger. And judging by the oil slick on the alternator, it's dead, too. You've got a serious leak, girl. Guess we'll just have to borrow Barret's old rattle trap."

"You can't do that!" I said sharply.

He showed me the palms of his hands to prove he was harmless. "Only as far as the Greyhound station. You can help him pick it up from there when he comes home tomorrow." He was looking past me at Violet, giving her some sort of signal with his eyes. "You ready to go? I packed up all your stuff from inside your pickup."

She ran limp fingers through her uncombed hair. "I guess. Let's take some food. Barret left everything in his refrigerator to spoil. I'll just be a minute." She went inside.

"What's the rush?" I asked Howie. "Why don't you wait until Barret gets here? So he can at least pay you for the work you did on Stu's cabin."

He stared at me. "Didn't Violet tell you? About the fire?"

"No. What happened?"

"Oh . . . nothing. Nothing much." He glanced uneasily uphill.

From where I stood Stu's cabin looked fine. Then again maybe the long view wasn't adequate. "I think I better go up and see," I said, relieved we'd dodged a bloody showdown that might have ended with him on a slab and me imprisoned for life, especially after the adverse publicity I'd been getting lately.

"Wasn't my fault," he called after me as I got into Efi and drove off. I parked at the bottom of Stu's cement path and rushed up to the cabin. Already I could see what looked like charred wood at the back corner. The inside was scorched black. A bare foam pad on the floor had melted. So had the sleeping bag topping it. The stench was atrocious. But the aluminum beer cans strewn every which way were unscathed, though obviously drinking and smoking hadn't mixed well for Howie. The stairs to the loft were charred but still seemed solid, so I climbed them. There were just a few scorch marks up there. The paint on the plywood floor had blistered but other than that the only bad thing was an overwhelming acrid smell. A spent canister of fire retardant lay forgotten in the far corner.

From down below, the farm truck was shuddering up Barret's drive. My view was blocked by the cabin roof but I could hear Howie stopping beside Efi. Then he cut his engine. By the time it finally dawned on me that I'd left my key in the ignition, Efi was already halfway to the top of the ridge. "Hey!" I yelled, descending the ladder-stairs so fast I nearly slipped. "Stop!" Standing out on the porch I heard Efi idling for a few seconds, probably by the camper. Then her door slammed and Efi eased down the far side. The mountain swallowed what was left of the sound.

Even before I reached the old farm truck I knew Howie had taken the ignition key with him. I wasted a couple of minutes running uphill on Ridge Road, came to my senses, and galloped to the Manor and Barret's phone. It was gone. But Howie had forgotten about the upstairs extension. I dialed Paul's cell from it. Luckily he answered right away. I gasped out what happened.

"She can't leave now," Paul protested. "Her trial's coming up next week. I'll forfeit the bail."

I was getting calmer with each breath. "We'll have to go after them," I said. "Will you come pick me up? If you have a spare gas can you might want to get it filled before you leave Ashland. I'll start walking. And if I get to the old highway before you I'll head for the Siskiyou summit on-ramp."

I TOOK the Labs outside for a toilet break, put them back in hoping they wouldn't need another one anytime soon, and started off. On top of Ridge Road I checked the inside of the camper and was instantly sorry. The claustrophobic space was alive with flies, filled with detritus, some of it wiggling, and smelled like a dumpster. Empty beer cans and wine bottles were heaped at one end.

Paul and I reached the county road at the same time but from opposite directions. There were two red gasoline canisters strapped to the back of his Tacoma. "This may take some time," he said when I climbed onto the passenger seat. "Any idea how much gas was left in your tank?"

I said I couldn't be sure. "They won't get far beyond Shasta Lake," I guessed. "Not a good place to get stuck. No doubt neither of them has a cell phone. Or Triple A."

He grinned, taking the highway uphill in the direction Ariel's Rolls Royce had gone that long ago fateful day. "As long as they stay on I-5 we'll find them."

"Never mind *them*. Just find Efi."

"Well, there *is* that little matter of Violet's bail. She's not bad, Silvi. Misguided. Desperate. But not bad. That Clyde must be a real jerk to leave her without an emergency fund."

"One jerk in a long line," I guessed. I could tell Paul felt just as awkward with me as I felt with him. He kept stealing glances. Finally he said,

"You're looking well."

"I doubt it."

"No, really. All . . . dewy."

I waved the compliment away. "If that's what you're seeing you must have stared at the sun too long on your way out of town. I've been in hiding in Medford at an friend's house. Nobody knows me there."

"You could have called."

"What for? I'm being vilified by the press. And not fit for human company right now."

"I could help you check on your web gallery, for one thing."

I snorted. "You don't really expect anyone to buy a picture from this illicit child-procurer and assistant pedophile, do you? I'll have to change my name. Erase my signature from the paintings, brush in a new one."

He stroked his chin. "Let's see . . . Silvi Randolph. How does that sound?"

"Bad for your lawyering business, that's how."

Keeping his eyes trained on the road, he said, "We could always move to Canada. Or Mexico. Together."

I wondered if the offer would still be good if he knew about the baby. "I didn't marry Stillman. What makes you think I'll marry you?"

"Ouch."

"Don't take it to heart," I said. "But I'm not the damsel-in-distress type. I don't need to be rescued. And I've seen the damage a loveless marriage can do."

"Your parents? Whatever happened between them has nothing to do with us."

I gave him a hard stare. "There is no 'us.' Never will be. Think of me as a nun, Paul. And start paying attention to some of those pretty young women strolling down Main Street. Get on with your life. Besides, I have no intention of leaving Oregon. It's my home. Things will calm down before long. Until they do I'm staying put where I am."

As a rule the people of Ashland were fair and forgiving. But lately, on my errands, I'd seen them whispering about me. That's why I shopped at the co-op at seven in the morning now, when it was deserted, or as near to closing time as I could.

He punched on his radio. It was tuned to the classical station. Isaac Stern was making his violin sing. The tone was so pure I wanted to cry.

In an effort to be friendly, Paul said, "How are your dogs?"

I told him they were fine and asked about his. He described walking Racket along Loop Road one early dawn when a police cruiser happened by. "He was off-leash of course. Before I could snap it on he started chasing the cruiser and when it stopped to avoid running over him he kept circling around it, giving a steady rendition of his blood-curdling war cry. Once I finally caught him the only action the two cops inside were still capable of was getting away as fast as they could."

We laughed together. It felt good. Then Isaac Stern yielded to Schubert's Unfinished Symphony. I'd always been fascinated by that piece. Paul increased the volume and I leaned back, closed my eyes, and allowed myself to become engrossed in the music. It wasn't until Mount Shasta began to dominate the flat landscape around it that I remembered the letter I'd stuffed in my pocket. Upon retrieving it I noticed it wasn't addressed to a specific person, so I tore it open and extracted a hand-written note.

It said:

> Hey there,
>
> A couple of weeks ago my son Howie wrote me a postcard asking me to send him a money-order c/o your address. I don't know who you are but I'd do this for anyone, so here it goes. Howie is one of the sleaziest low-lives any family produced. He lies, he steals, he whores, he drinks away every dollar that finds its way into his pockets. He set our house on fire twice though he claimed it wasn't on purpose. Whatever hard luck story he told you don't believe him. Give him a ride as far away from your house as you can and leave him stranded without a dime. It's the best way to keep you safe. Setting the police on him won't hurt either. He's got a long record. Hope this letter finds you before things start going wrong.
> Sincerely,
> Homer McPharland

"Well, well," Paul said. "Seems Howie's doing us a favor. He could have burned down our forest."

"Almost did." I described the damage to Stu's cabin.

"You have to admit he stole the perfect vehicle for a getaway," Paul said. "Faulty gas gauge and all. A bit inconvenient for us but at least it got us talking to each other again. I've missed your . . . uh . . . platonic company."

I was glad I was wearing that extra large shirt. It did a good job of hiding my incipient belly. For some silly reason his regard mattered to me. Which was why I was more determined than ever to keep the spectacle of my body transforming itself into a blimp strictly private. With a smile that asked silent forgiveness for my previously hostile attitude I said, "What I like about dogs is that they ask no questions, expect no answers, and are always nonjudgmental. They're all I can handle right now." If I renewed our friendship, sooner or later he'd want an explanation. But I didn't feel the slightest desire to justify myself to him or anyone else. For now anyway.

Driving past the turn-off to Weed he said, "Promise you'll call if you need me. Or want me. I'm there for you. Twenty-four seven."

I let a few minutes go by. Then I said, "The main reason I phoned you was because Violet is jumping bail."

Passing Shasta City, he repeated softly, "Twenty-four seven."

We found Efi on the freeway shoulder somewhere past Dunsmuir. Violet was sitting in the cab. Alone. She was fiddling with the radio. It was blaring country music. She didn't recognize us until we got out of Paul's Tacoma. Then she flinched and said, "Howie hitched a ride to the nearest filling station. He took a hundred. I'm sure he'll be back soon."

"There's no nearest anything around here," Paul told her. "What else did he take?"

"His back pack. And a carton of beer."

"What did he leave?"

"Only the empties," she said wearily. "And me."

CHAPTER 35

THE NEXT AFTERNOON, WHEN I DROVE UP to feed Labs, the farm truck had been moved out of the road and the SUV was parked in front of the Manor. Barret was home. The Labs, bursting out of the house ahead of him, greeted me with their former enthusiasm, making me realize just how much they had missed him. He invited me into his newly scrubbed chlorine-scented kitchen looking remarkably jolly for a man who had just cleaned up after a truck jacking bum.

I handed him his downstairs phone, which I'd found in Efi's extra-cab, gave him the bag filled with his mail, and said, "I suppose you've heard about my troubles."

He nodded sagely without speaking, put the phone in its customary spot, and plugged in the cord. Then he upended the bag onto his pristine, bare counter and began sorting.

"The reporters were thick up here for a while," I went on. "I've been bunking in Medford with a friend."

"I figured something like that," he said cheerfully, bundling the junk mail and dropping it into the waste basket.

"And you've probably started suspecting that Howie didn't pan out after all."

He chortled. "I should have known better. I confess the filth waiting for me in here threw me for a loop. But no harm done— except to my pride." He picked up a soil-covered coffee tin, tipping it to show me that it was empty. "He dug up my rainy day fund. Resourceful bastard, wasn't he? I figured he must have skipped yesterday; the food he left on the uppermost plate crowding the sink hadn't had a chance to go crusty yet. Unlike the rest."

I narrated Howie and Violet's misadventure with my pickup ending with, "Paul booked her into a motel room till the trial. I bet he wishes I hadn't called him when she got arrested."

Barret's clean-shaven face rearranged itself into a scowl. "Are you kidding? Randy's not happy unless he's helping somebody out. Compulsive do-gooder. If you ask me there ought to be a 12-step program for suckers like him. At least I only tried being nice to one deadbeat. And never again."

Clearly, he wasn't ready to forgive Paul for having been friendly with Violet. I asked, "I suppose you've found all the damage Howie's done?"

"Probably not." He frowned at the oven door, opened it, gave a hard blink, and slammed it shut. "But then I've only been home a few hours. I did stop at the camper on my way in. That little nightmare's okay since I'm going to junk the piece of crap anyway. And luckily the appalling sight helped desensitize me to the state of my kitchen."

"You checked Stu's place? Howie scorched it."

"Doused to the gills no doubt." Barret sounded much too complacent. "He should have burned that cabin right down to the ground. Yours too while he was at it. As it turns out I've got a multi-million dollar business to run. These miserable little shacks are of no consequence by comparison."

Shocked, I steadied my back against the wall while he explained, "My dad was an all-or-nothing kind of guy. According to his last will and testament either I take over the company and inherit everything he owned or I stay in the Oregon woods to fade into a vicious old age without getting a penny. Which means I've only returned to pack up. Hey, you know anyone interested in adopting a couple of overweight Labs? I can't take them with me."

"Not off-hand. Have you tried Paul?"

He didn't like the suggestion. "I'm thinking of Zora," he said. "I doubt Randy will want to do me any favors. Especially when he finds out who I'm selling out to."

"Who?" I asked, sick with foreboding.

"Why, Gierig of course." He waved a card. "I found his number. Already called him. He's coming over tonight."

"You can't be serious!"

"I kid you not. I see him as a collector. Of land parcels. Mine's going to cost him."

"This is the guy who's ruining our mountain."

He was gazing out of the kitchen window but I could tell from the faraway look in his eyes that it wasn't the mountain he was seeing. A new woman? In New York? That would explain everything. He made a sweeping motion. "What's to ruin? It's nothing but stickers and poison oak and sagebrush anyway."

The man had returned to us brain-washed. "He'll pave it over," I said. "What'll happen to the bears? The squirrels?"

He waggled his brows as if I'd said something funny. "Not to mention the shit-load of rattlers and skunks. And coyotes. And cougars." He nodded at the opposite hillsides. "Most of the wildlife will move over there. In an orderly retreat."

"With Gierig right behind them. He'll buy those slopes next. There'll be no stopping him. In ten years he'll have a town up here. With its own freeway ramps."

He rubbed his hands together with honest enthusiasm. "Some people would call that progress."

I stepped away from him, perplexed. "I don't recognize you anymore."

"We've gone out of synch is all. Life moves faster in New York. I find it exhilarating." He rubbed his jaw. "Say, what got into Jimmi, lying about you like that? After everything you've done for him. Any idiot can see his father's trying to fleece Ariel Jordan." I almost forgave him for everything. Until he said without changing his inflection, "How much time do you figure you'll need to clear out of your cabin? I suspect you won't like your new landlord."

My insides flip-flopped. As soon as they steadied again, I snapped, "Will next weekend be soon enough? What the hell's wrong with you? Some kind of mid life crisis?"

He traced an invisible rainbow with his hands. "I've seen the lights of Manhattan. These woods are bleak by comparison. I'm tired of being depressed."

As usual he put his comfort before anyone else's. My many years as an exemplary tenant ought to have entitled me to some miniscule consideration. "I take it you will return my deposits?" I said coldly.

"Only if you can present me with the receipts. Off the top of my head I don't recall the transaction."

There were no separate receipts. "Don't you remember? You wrote them on the rental agreement."

"What rental agreement?" he said, allowing me to see his growing irritation. It was plain he wasn't going to give me a dime. I remembered thinking that if he shaved off his beard and cut his hair he would look like the sourpuss he was. Yet here he stood, trimmed to the bone, as cheerful as a paid clown. But the meanness was still there, hiding beneath the new jovial image. I had to admit I liked him better at his worst. He went to the door. "Now, if you'll excuse me, I have to go inspect Stu's cabin."

I stayed where I was. "May I use your phone before I leave?"

"No problem," he said with his fake new enthusiasm. "Take your time." He snapped his fingers for the dogs. They came trotting in from the living room and followed him to the yard.

I waited until they were around the bend of the driveway. Then I called Paul to report the newest development. I couldn't risk phoning him from the farmhouse. He might have traced Ariel's number. "Can't *you* buy his land?"

"Are you kidding?" Paul said. "Barret would rather give it to the next drunk who crosses his path."

"Please try."

"I know Barret. But if it makes you feel any better I'll put in an offer. Where can I reach you with the good news?"

"I don't have a phone of my own," I said. That much was true. "*I'll* call *you.*"

"Ah!" he said. "I consider that a promise. Need any help with getting your things out of the cabin?"

"There won't be much left to get out after I build my burn pile. Most everything I own came from Goodwill, the Salvation Army, and the free box."

He laughed. "In the spirit of a cherished ridge-top tradition."

I couldn't make myself laugh along. Losing my cabin and most of my possessions was an unmistakable sign that I was sliding toward homelessness. Like Violet. Or Howie.

ARIEL rang me late, sounding excited. "We've got an address for Leroy," he said. "I had a detective stake out his lawyer's office like you suggested. Next time Leroy showed up the guy followed him home. He waited around to make sure Jimmi's there too. And he is. But I can't guarantee how long they'll stick, so you better hurry— that is if you still want to talk to him."

"You bet I do. I'm leaving first thing in the morning."

"Good luck, Silvi. Remember, be kind. He's just a boy."

"And you remember that I can't do more than try."

The detective had provided some additional information. Leroy worked as a security guard. The night shift, from 10:00 to 6:00. "South central L.A. is not the best place to leave a boy home alone every night." Ariel said. "Jimmi locks himself in and won't answer the door. But he's enrolled in school. Under a fake name. He walks to it every week day morning. The detective thinks your best bet is to catch him then, along his route. Leroy sleeps in but sometimes he gives Jimmi a ride home in the afternoon."

"Great research. Thanks."

"He's a good detective, Silvi. Discreet. And expensive. If you call him when you get down there he'll take you right to the apartments. Please be careful."

*

THERE was no one to stay with the animals of course. The cats were easy; they had their litter boxes inside the house and they loved snoozing. I left them two day's worth of fresh ground necks and two more portions that were hard-frozen. They could nibble at the thawing edges. The dogs came with me along with an ice chest. It was an incessant drive with short rest stops during which I napped behind the steering wheel. Asa and Marvel stayed in the canopy, poking their noses into the cab from time to time, watching the countryside whizz by, and dozing. The closer we got to Southern California, the louder my heart thumped. I had no idea what I would say to Jimmi—or even if I'd get the chance to see him at all.

AFTER I followed the detective to Leroy's address the next morning, I parked around the block in the shade, making sure the canopy was locked. At a quarter to eight I was hiding behind a cluster of squat, fat-trunked palm trees, watching Jimmi come out of the dilapidated apartments across the street swinging a book pack. Needless to say, I was dressed in loose clothes. Not that Jimmi would have noticed a difference.

He wore a tight black stocking cap over his greased and squashed flat hair, sun-glasses, an oversized white t-shirt, and drooping black pants. Hood camouflage. I followed him around the first corner. When we were out of sight of his building I called his name. He stopped in mid stride. Even though he had eschewed motherly hugs for more than a year I gave him one on the spot. His shoulders felt slight and rigid under the shirt.

"You can't make me come with you," he said, his voice rough.

"That's not why I'm here." I fought the urge to pick him up and carry him to Efi, strap him in, and drive him away from everything he held dear on the off-chance that he would come to his senses on the long trip north and turn back into the Jimmi I knew. Unfortunately he was too tall for the maneuver. So I sat down on a bench inside a tinted-glass bus shelter doing my best to ignore the reek of pee and vomit rising from its concrete floor. "You've made your choice. I have to accept that." I patted the space next to me. He sat on the opposite end of the bench, half hanging over the edge. Most of his face was inscrutable behind the shades but his lower lip quivered. I averted my eyes before he could realize that I'd noticed. "Do you know what Leroy has done?"

He gave an elaborate shrug. "My dad needs money. Ariel Jordan's got plenty."

I suppressed an angry retort and said calmly, "Every day for the twelve years you were my son I've taught you to be honest. And just. Do you think destroying Ariel because you want a chunk of his money makes you just?"

"He'll get over it."

"He'll never get over it. After everything that other boy did to him he had the courage to trust you. And you've shown him that you're one in a long row of people eager to betray him."

He stuck out his chin and said, "I didn't do nothing to him."

"Wrong. *He* didn't do anything to *you*. Yet for the simple act of befriending you he is losing a career he spent his life-time building. *And* what's left of his reputation. Have you been watching TV?"

"Our set's busted. The screen still works with the DVD player though. My dad's got loads of movies. Action flicks. And stuff like that."

Knowing Leroy, the "stuff" was X-rated adult entertainment. "Is that how you're spending your evenings?"

He glared. "They're showing me the real world. The one you were so busy keeping me from. I've got a lot of catching up to do."

"Do you even know what your lies have done to us?" When he didn't reply I said, "Let me tell you about it." I explained in vivid detail how the police had ransacked the cabin and the farmhouse and got especially graphic about the destruction they wrought on Ariel's fine library. Nor did I fail to confess how ashamed I was to show my face in Ashland during daylight hours.

"But . . . what do *you* have to do with anything?" he asked, puzzled.

"Don't you know? Leroy is suing me too." Out of the corner of my eye I saw his hand clutch at the bench. Then he deliberately flattened the palm against his thigh. "Somehow," I continued, "he got wind of the fact that I finally sold a few paintings. Now he's planning to take that income away by claiming I was helping Ariel Jordan make a sex slave out of you."

"What does that mean?"

"You know. A boy-prostitute. "

"My dad's saying that about you?"

"Yes."

"Then it must be true." He didn't look convinced.

"You know better," I said, feeling a great sadness descend. "I drove all the way down here to give you my side of the story. It's in your power to destroy a loving human being whose only crime is that he wants to help needy children. People have stopped attending his concerts. His new album isn't getting promoted so it won't sell. The public hates him. The tabloids want him in jail. You're killing him, Jimmi."

"Not me. My dad."

"No. You. Because you are the only one who can stop Leroy and you won't. Are you happy here?"

I pointed to the littered sidewalks, shattered bottles, boarded-up businesses, the clusters of men idling at the next corner.

He stuck out his chin. "These are my people. I'm three quarters black."

"May I remind you that color is only skin deep? You can go anywhere and be anything. Through your own efforts."

He nodded at the men. "Like them, huh?"

"Yes. Except that you have a head start. Don't lose it, Jimmi. It isn't your fault they're standing around day and night with nothing to do. It isn't Ariel Jordan's fault either. He's given away many millions to help the poor, hungry, and sick. Not just in the states, but all over the planet." I slid over and pulled off his shades. Silently I counted to six before he could make himself harden his eyes.

Staring straight into them, I repeated, "You're killing him, Jimmi. Make it stop before it's too late." I wrote Paul's number on a slip of paper, opened his hand, pressed it in his palm, and folded his slack fingers over it. "I'm hard to reach right now, for obvious reasons. But Paul will get a message to me if you need my help. I'll always be there for you. And I'll always care about you no matter what. If you want to come with me right now no one can stop you. If you decide to stay it's okay too."

He tilted his head as if he were actually thinking. "You brought the dogs?"

"Sure. They've been missing you."

I could see his face closing against me. "My dad says dogs are nothing but parasites. Even police dogs like yours. Actually they're worse because they're bred to attack black people. Don't ever turn your back on them. They're dangerous. He says they should be destroyed."

"You're kidding. Asa and Marvel?"

He stood up. "I've always hated those names. Why can't you call them something simple, like Buddy and Cissy? I hate the way they bring dirt in on their paws and the way they shed all over the place. There's not a single dog hair in our apartment. Cat hair either. I'm staying." He stepped into the sunshine. It lent his skin a glimmer of gold. "I was born here. I should have been raised here. This is my home." And then he shouldered his pack and walked away. He didn't turn once. I watched him swagger past the cluster of idlers, watched him round the next corner. And the whole time I was watching he kept Paul's number balled in his fist.

ON SATURDAY I drove to my cabin. Unaired throughout the summer, the stale inside smelled of rancid old bones. I built a burn pile in the yard with our box springs, bed frames, book shelves, table, chairs, the kitchen center aisle I'd once hammered together, the pantry shelves I'd unscrewed from the wall, my home-made counter extension, and Jimmi's desk. I tossed his books on top of the pile, keeping only the Baum collection and *The Little Engine That Could*.

Asa's easy chair, destined for the landfill, was too heavy for me to carry. I rolled it out to the porch, down the steps, and to the truck, wiggling it up and over the tail gate in preparation for my dump run. Then I folded the slit futons, tied them, dragged them over the tail gate too, and squeezed them in beside the chair.

Stacking Jimmi's clothes and sneakers on the chair cushion, I marveled again that a discarded shoe could keep on holding the impression of a boy's foot when the boy who had made it was irretrievably gone. It was almost as if he had died. No, losing him to his father was worse than death. Leroy wouldn't be able to hurt a dead boy but he sure could damage one still living—and change him to something unrecognizable.

Next I stacked my winter clothes, snow boots, art and photography equipment, radios, CDs, tapes, books, and the family albums on and behind the passenger seat. The only item I was leaving inside the house was my metal desk. It wouldn't burn and was too heavy for one person to shift even after I removed all the drawers. While I was sweeping floors, wiping walls, and polishing windows, I was wondering what to do about my small but much cherished refrigerator and freezer. They were the only things I'd bought new and still worked perfectly. But chances were any house I might possibly move to in the near or far future already had a combined unit installed. I decided to come back for them after the dump run and store them on Ariel's back porch for now.

I was upending jars, pouring nuts and various grains over the forest floor for any interested rodents, when Barret's SUV cruised up my driveway. Stocky, grim faced Gierig occupied the passenger seat. The moment he saw the rural tableau lying before him his expression darkened. He climbed out, hands on hips momentarily shifting the jacket he wore away from his waistband to give me a glimpse of his gun. "Isn't she the one always trespassing on top of my mountain? The one with the dog?" he asked Barret, who'd stayed in the car.

"Well. She does have a dog," Barret hedged. "I told you, most everybody does around here."

"No, no, I remember her face. Tracked it with my binoculars. I can't stand that woman. She's the one in the news, right? With the colored boy? And that slime ball singer?"

"Ah," Barret said, the amiable smile he'd painted onto his face congealing fast.

Gierig considered the weather worn cabin, the items on the burn pile, my pre-owned, scratched-up pickup. "Tell her not to bother bringing out the rest of her junk. The first thing my dozer guy's gonna do here is knock down this poor excuse of a hut and crush the remains into sawdust." He considered his watch. "And if she's still around fifteen minutes from now our whole deal's off. Meanwhile we're checking out Paul Randolph's place."

"He's not there," Barret said in a strangled tone after giving me a clandestine, apologetic half smile. Six months ago he would have torn up their agreement and told Gierig to get the hell off his land.

"Fine. That means we can do our snooping in peace," Gierig replied. "That guy's turned out to be one pain-in-the-ass neighbor."

"You're telling me." Barret released the emergency brake. The developer climbed in. They drove on.

Good thing I hadn't brought the dogs. No doubt Gierig would have executed them on the spot.

CHAPTER 36

A FEW MINUTES LATER I SLUNK OFF, LEAVING MY ridge life on the burn pile. Then at the dump I said a hurried good-bye to all I had left of Jimmi. I had the most trouble letting go of his smelly old shoes. I was tempted to pitch out the family albums too, particularly the ones containing pictures of Mam*a*. It was a good thing that she could no longer telephone me. She'd sent me a couple of letters, the address slanted across the envelopes in furious longhand. I'd stuffed them unopened into the glove compartment. Most likely she was demanding to know why I had sabotaged the family reputation by getting my face smeared across the lite-news hemisphere.

Pap*a* was a different matter. I didn't know if he was still on the Alm, but even if he'd returned to the *Trüffelhof* by now he would have remained pleasantly insulated from media sputter. In my answer to the only letter he'd written I had made a point of pretending I was perfectly content with all of his choices and mine.

That afternoon I concentrated on Ariel's painting, feeling numb and weightless. Starting to prepare the canvas made me see just how expensive and time consuming the project was going to be. I decided I would create separate miniatures framed and connected by shadowy forest. I listened to Jimmi's *Jordan Boys hits* to put me in the right mood. On cue, that night Ariel encouraged me to watch his cache of music videos. "I only found a couple," I said. And then I finally admitted that the police had confiscated most of his equipment. After a shocked silence he asked, "Did they take my laptops, too?"

"How many did you have?"

He groaned. "Luckily I backed everything I care about onto jump drives. I bet the cops don't know about my storage unit. If you give me a minute I'll track down the security info so you can get inside. I have copies of everything I've ever done in there, though I understand you can find most of it on YouTube these days. In one of the cartons are a couple of extra laptops I bought in L.A., still sealed in their original boxes. Choose one and keep it. Have you heard my latest album yet?"

"Which one is that?" I asked, feeling cagey.

"Not much of a fan, are you?"

"I am incapable of being anyone's fan."

He chuckled. "I thought so. It's called *Undaunted*. There's a stack of them in the unit, in different colors. Pick your favorite. I really want to know what you think of the album. Especially since you're not a fan."

I hoped he'd forget all about it the next time he called.

On my way to the storage facility the following day, I coordinated the errand with a shopping trip and mail run. I brought home all of Ariel's magnificent short films and viewed them via his big screen entertainment center. The rest of the world might have become satiated with them but to me they were brand new. I couldn't stop watching him perform. Living alone in the country, my nights were long and lonely. Normally I took myself out of my misery by going to sleep at my earliest inclination. But I was so fascinated by his talent that I elected to keep ever later hours. For not only did I replay each film several times; with his help I set up the laptop and learned basic navigation—something Paul had never got around to teaching me. Before long I knew how to turn mine on, connect to the net, and conjure up YouTube. I practiced handling the tricky cursor until it tamed under my finger tips. And then I accessed the interviews Ariel had participated in since he was a small boy.

Each night my viewing left me a bit more puzzled. In every interview, every documentary, every music video, his eyes and face broadcast unabashed love and affection for his audience and an unquenchable eagerness to give all of himself, holding back nothing. No good journalist could possibly think Ariel capable of vile acts of any kind. Yet reporters were constantly misquoting and misinterpreting him. Trusted friends sold him out for a headline, their day of fame, a tabloid bribe.

Scrolling down to the comment section on Google news and under the fan-posted YouTube videos, I was stunned by the rampant emotions Ariel evoked. As expected, the fans were glowing with their praise. What I hadn't been aware of was the cruelty of the haters. Their vicious remarks disturbed me even after I figured out that they were trying to get a rise out of hapless readers with their sleazy bits of attention grabbing verbal garbage. At least on YouTube industrious fans sooner or later got around to reporting the shameful attacks as spam. But the internet "news" gossip media went out of their way to concoct misleading headlines that made Ariel seem bizarre, accompanying their articles with the worst snapshots of him they could find. And they took great pride in concocting odious comments.

For a couple of nights I sent off anonymous rebuttals to the worst of them, hoping to set the record straight. But the avalanche of headlines was unceasing, each outlet copying the same shop-worn information as if they had been the first to report it. On the third night I had to admit that if I were Ariel I'd have slit my wrists a long time ago.

Deciding my need to know his enemies did not outweigh the bad taste their offal left in my mouth, I made the conscious decision to stay away from online news. Instead I researched Ariel's life and works on YouTube, careful to keep my eyes away from the comment section where his fans clashed with his haters. *Mateus Simao Marco* of *Lisboa* had been right—people either loved Ariel passionately or hated him passionately; it seemed there was hardly anyone in our country who was indifferent to him.

There was a particular posting that had me in awe. During one of his most spectacular numbers he'd climbed into a cherry picker basket. It took him up high over the audience. While the camera did a close-up of him singing, a purple-haired skinny girl of no more than fourteen appeared outside the basket seemingly out of nowhere. Spreading her freckled, fanatical, bony arms over the guard-rail, she imprisoned Ariel in a big hug. Evidently she had evaded security to run up the slick metal arm of the picker.

Without missing a note or a beat Ariel grabbed onto the girl, putting her hands firmly onto the railing and anchoring one forearm around her to keep her from falling. Their struggle seemed endless, she letting go of the railing to spread her arms wide as if she could fly, he belting his song while wrapping her fingers around the metal bar again. Since she was standing unsecured outside the platform with barely enough room for her feet, one jerk of the cherry picker, one sudden move, would have plunged her to her death.

At last he finished his song and the picker gently returned them to the stage floor. The girl, fearing separation, clutched onto Ariel with all her might. It took four security guards to pry her loose and carry her off, wildly struggling.

At that point I realized that the baby inside me was paying close attention. I could feel her yearning toward the screen. Soothingly rubbing my belly I replayed the event several times, watching Ariel's competent hands keeping the girl safe. How come this scene had not made it onto the news? Or any of Ariel's many hospital visits showing him enfolding a sick or hurt child in his arms?

When I was good and tired I attempted to listen to *Undaunted* but couldn't get past the third song. To my untrained ear the tracks were too much alike: equally noisy and dense with a heavy bass beat. Try as I might I couldn't decipher more than a couple of words of the lyrics and gave up in disgust, switching my player to *Eine kleine Nachtmusik,* which lulled me to sleep.

"Did you listen to my new album yet?" he'd ask shyly at the end of every conversation we had.

I'd tell him I was too busy with my painting, that I wanted to wait until I had more free time. After a week of my lame excuses he said, uncharacteristically blunt, "You don't like it, do you?"

I didn't want to lie to him outright. "I'm sorry. I just can't get into it. The music's too heavy handed for me. It drowns out the lyrics. I guess I'm more the ballad type."

He was silent for what seemed a long while. Then he said, "I love ballads too. But a lot of my fans want fast dance tunes, Silvi. Maybe that's why I clumped those first three together up front. To get them out of the way. I tell you what—why don't you just skip to the fourth track? You might be surprised."

I did just that after we hung up. In the dark, on the bed, with my eyes closed, I listened to one stunning ballad after another, in my mind's eye seeing the man with the curly dark pony tail wearing a blousy blue flannel shirt half unbuttoned, his porcelain face graced with those unforgettable trademark eyes and topped by bold, sweeping brows. Like a violin played by Itzhak Perlman or Jascha Heifetz, Ariel's voice soared and dipped effortlessly up and down his entire range of three and a half octaves. When the last song ended I programmed for *repeat all* and let the music carry me aloft.

In the morning I clicked on the news just long enough to hear his sister, speaking at a news conference, tell an entourage of reporters that her entire family had long suspected Ariel was a pedophile. "He deserves to go to prison for the rest of his life," Gabby said, preening for the press. "Only then will the world be a safe place for young boys like Jimmi."

In vain I hoped Ariel wouldn't hear about her monstrous betrayal. He called me at noon and wept for a good ten minutes. "I'm only human," he cried. "If you cut me, I bleed. I've been bleeding for a long time now." Then he whispered, as if to himself, "This is more than I can handle. Gabby's just destroyed the little bit of faith I had left. I can't make myself go on tonight. But if I don't everyone will think it's an admission of guilt."

By now I was aware of a classic, playful interview taped with the two of them when they were on the cusp of adulthood. At its end the moderator had asked Ariel what he wanted to accomplish in his life. He said he wanted to be the greatest entertainer of the century and do his best to make people happy. The talentless Gabby, sitting primly beside him, said she wanted to be exactly like him and have everything he had. Her second choice was to become a world famous diva or at least a popular talk show guest. Denouncing her brother was sure to be the ideal launching platform toward the latter ambition.

"I've had it," Ariel confessed, weeping. "I'm done. My life's become too hard for me. I'm on my knees half the day asking God to bring out the truth. And this is what I get. I can't eat or sleep and I can't leave my hotel room because there are paparazzi camping out everywhere. I'm even afraid to touch the phone. Might as well be in prison. Better yet, dead."

"It'll blow over," I promised. "Just hang in there a while longer."

"Why? Jimmi isn't recanting. The D.A. is talking about convening a Grand Jury. The man hates me. There's nothing he wouldn't do to get me convicted. When all I'm trying to do is follow the example of Jesus. You know, *suffer the little children to come onto me.*"

"You want to be like Jesus?"

"Of course. With all my heart. Turning the other cheek and all."

"But Ariel—they *crucified* him!"

"He was a light that shines to this day and will go on shining forever. I used to be able to see him when I closed my eyes. And feel him, too. The only thing I see now is an abyss. God has deserted me, Silvi. Why should I bother sticking around? It's not as if anyone will miss me or need me."

I forgot how religious he was. Even though I heard him say in some of the interviews that God was present in every living thing, I suspected some small part of him clung to the childhood notion of a heavenly father looking down from the clouds. Punishing him for something he didn't do.

"But you haven't even begun to reach your full potential," I protested. "Your fans are waiting for the next stupendous thing you'll do. *They* need you."

"No they don't. Their numbers are dwindling as we speak. And God has taken away the stream of inspiration I've always tapped into. It's gone, Silvi. No more creative visions. No more music playing in my head. You were right, my last album sucks. I've lost the knack. I'm nothing now. To tell you the truth, I wish my heart would just stop beating next time I'm asleep so I wouldn't have to wake up again."

Even telling him how much I'd enjoyed the awesome ballads didn't help. He accused me of praising his work just to console him. The trouble was he'd stopped believing in himself and his future.

What if his heart really stopped beating and he never opened his amazing eyes again?

What would this country and this world be like without Ariel in it? The mere thought paralyzed me. His passing would leave a mind numbing vacuum. I couldn't stand by and let such a tragedy happen, could I? That's why I resolved to distract him from his dark thoughts with *my* truth.

"I know someone who needs you," I began. And then I described the fascination my unborn child had with anything to do with him, how she strained toward the screen when he was on it. "I don't think she came to be with me, Ariel. She's expecting to be your little girl."

Gulping for air, he struggled to absorb what I said. "Hold on— hold on now," he stammered. "What . . . what are you trying to tell me? That you're . . .you're pregnant? With my baby? Are you sure?"

I swallowed my momentary resentment and said slowly, "I know you didn't mean it like it sounded. What happened between us was an accident. There's been no one else."

"I'm sorry," he said quickly. "I wasn't implying . . . I have the utmost . . . Forgive me, it's just that I have to get used . . ." He paused, gave a choked giggle, and then he hummed. I didn't recognize the tune but I gathered he was trying to buy himself a few extra seconds to digest my news. At last he said with obvious misgivings, "I suppose we'll have to get married now."

Visualizing the noose he felt tightening around his neck, I had to laugh. "Sorry, Ariel. But no thanks. I'm not some underage unwed mother too young to fend for herself. I've already raised one child. For me that's enough. I want to be free to paint without interruptions. You on the other hand are aching to be a dad. This baby should be with you. From birth. Why don't you think about it?"

He cleared his throat. "What do you want in return?"

To my surprise I had an answer ready. "Complete anonymity. I hate being in the spotlight. And a legally binding contract. Stating that she is to be unconditionally yours forever and ever. Without strings, without compensations of any kind. In fact if you try to give me anything, anything at all, the deal's off." His generosity was legion. That's why he was always surrounded by "friends" with fool-proof ideas for getting a slice of his pie. I swore to myself I'd never be one of them.

"Can I at least buy you a house?" he asked, testing.

"Absolutely not. But I would appreciate it if you let me stay in this one until your daughter is born. That is, unless you have other plans for it."

His voice warming, he said, "Not that I know of."

There was no doubt in my mind that I was doing the right thing. Now he needed to find the same certainty before this deal could go through. Without anyone's interference. "I don't want to talk you into anything, Ariel. Think it over then let me know tomorrow night what you've decided. We'll take it from there."

"You mean she'll be mine? All mine?" he said, his voice turning eager. "Right from the start?"

"That's the way I see it. Good night."

"But I've already—"

"Tomorrow." I hung up, smiling. It was working. My proposal had made him forget all about his considerable troubles. As I was forgetting mine. Going to sleep that night I could swear the baby was purring. It made me wonder whose idea it actually was.

THE NEXT day the Jordan family gave their own news conference, denying everything Gabby had claimed. Ariel's mother looked into the nearest camera lens and said, "Ever since he was a little boy, Ariel's greatest ambition has been to do everything in his power to make the world a better place. He has always loved children. If he could he would take every hurt child in his arms and fix whatever's wrong with their bodies and lives. May the Lord forgive my misguided daughter. The rest of us stand firmly behind him."

For the first time since the scandal broke the media was forced to report something positive about Ariel. If his family so openly supported him he couldn't be all bad. I was expecting our usual bed time conversation but Ariel rang early in the evening. "Silvi, quick, turn on the TV," he said. "My attorney just called. There's going to be a news flash about Jimmi."

He stayed on the line to listen. Apparently one lone paparazzo had followed our detective's example and staked out the building housing Leroy's shyster-lawyer's office. As soon as he saw Leroy and Jimmi go inside he called headquarters. The rumor spread like wildfire; more paparazzi came, and came, and came. And waited.

And then at last the thick plate glass entry door swung open and Jimmi swaggered outside. By himself. Went straight to the microphones, took off the shades, and jammed them into a deep pocket of his low-riders. Without the shielding sunglasses his hazel eyes looked frightened. He spoke rapidly, fumbling the first sentence a couple of times before he found the courage to say, "You're all wrong about Ariel Jordan. I did spend two nights with him but they weren't anything like what my dad said. Ariel helped me with my homework and fed me TV dinners and ice cream. He showed me some new dance steps. We watched a funny movie together. I drank a couple of huge sodas and ate my way through a big bowl of popcorn. Then I fell asleep on the couch. He woke me when the movie was over, walked me to the guest room, and said good night." He shifted his weight nervously from one foot to the other. "My father made up the rest of the story. He said it wouldn't matter since Ariel's reputation was already ruined and he wouldn't miss a few more millions. Same deal as with the first boy. Same lawyer. And the same shrink."

He turned uneasily to scan the building's facade, then gripped the nearest microphone and said slowly, with effort, almost as if he were reading from a prompter he couldn't quite see, "I want to apologize to Ariel and to my mom for everything they had to suffer because of our lies. Not that I deserve it, but maybe they'll try to forgive me someday for my part in this mess. I—" Glancing over his shoulder, he saw Leroy rush out of the entrance, bawling with rage. Jimmi let go of the mike, pivoted, and raced down the block. Leroy, still limber in spite of his sizeable paunch, chased after my boy. The paparazzi chased Leroy. Then they all disappeared around the corner. The camera focused on the only person left. It was a disheveled female reporter who smoothed her wayward hair and stammered out a quick re-cap while trying to regain her composure.

Ariel sobbed into my ear. When he could speak again he said fervently, "Thank you, God!" And then he asked, "Silvi—does this mean our baby deal is off?"

"Don't be silly," I replied, sobbing too. "I'll have my hands full with Jimmi. I hope."

CHAPTER 37

For THE NEXT FEW DAYS THE NEWS PROGRAMS were full of exclamations and speculations. They played Jimmi's speech over and over again, trying to figure out if he was volunteering the self-incriminating information because of a guilty conscience or because "someone" worth billions had furtively paid him off.

The matter was laid to rest when the first boy who'd accused Ariel of sexual misconduct unaccountably recanted. Frankie had been living anonymously in a foreign country with his spoils. And now he surfaced to confess that his case was a complete fabrication. I remembered the many photos of him splashed across the front pages of newspapers ten years before. He'd grown into a handsome young man. "Jimmi's courage has inspired me to speak out too," he said. "Even though I was only thirteen when my father filed the civil suit, I knew it was wrong. But he threatened and bullied me until I played along. I wish I could set back the clock. With all my heart I apologize for allowing my father and his lawyers to destroy my best friend's reputation and career. My father has already spent his part of the settlement. I am more than willing to give back what is left of mine."

In the ensuing pandemonium Jimmi's revelation was all but forgotten. According to the press Leroy never did catch up to him in that memorable chase. The paparazzi caught up to Leroy, but only long enough to hear him grunt "No comment!" before he sprinted out of sight. Father and son vanished without a trace. Not even Ariel's detective would venture to guess if they were hiding together or in separate locations.

"You've got to find Jimmi for me," I told Ariel the next time he called. "He could be living on the streets. Under a bridge. Or worse." As naïve as my peaceful rural existence had made me, I had a pretty good idea what that "worse" might entail.

"I'll keep the detective on my payroll," Ariel promised. "He'll track him down sooner or later. But Silvi you're not giving Jimmi and yourself enough credit. Obviously you managed to teach him the difference between right and wrong. He's a smart boy. He'll be okay. And he knows where north lies on the I-5."

I knew he meant well but in his state of prolonged euphoria he'd lost touch with the reality of Jimmi's situation. The boy had no money. The police were looking for him. So was his enraged father whose scheme he had squelched. Not to mention the predators roaming the inner and outer cities of greater L.A. who were partial to homeless young boys. And he had no way to contact me other than the slip of paper containing Paul's number which he might or might not have had on him when he decided to put the world on its head.

Ariel's life turned completely around. He agreed to an interview with a prestigious TV news program. His face was dazzling with an inner light as he announced that his record label had committed to funding half a dozen music videos for *Undaunted.* All at once the critics couldn't say enough good things about the album; the CDs melted off the same music store shelves on which they had been gathering dust these past months. Demand far succeeded supply, a situation the record company promised to rectify forthwith. Hungry old and new fans rediscovered his previous work. His world tour once again was sold out in every stadium along the way. *Opus* announced they were issuing a coffee-table volume entitled **THE ENDURING GENIUS OF ARIEL JORDAN.**

Everywhere on the globe the young and old were out on the street dancing to his signature tunes. A new documentary about his dazzling career started production, and Hollywood offered the greatest entertainer of all time an epic movie role. Day after day there were new testimonials from former friends and colleagues who swore they had never doubted his innocence.

Frankie, his self-sacrificing first accuser, received a multi-million dollar book deal for his side of the story. With each phone call Ariel had another triumph to report. Last but not least his attorneys had drawn up the contract I requested. They wanted my mailing address so they could send it to me. They also wanted contact information for my lawyer.

There was only one lawyer I knew and trusted. Without hesitation I gave Ariel Paul's particulars knowing full well that if I went to him with the paperwork it wouldn't matter how loose my shirt and jacket were. He'd know. And he'd judge.

No longer caring whether or not Paul copied down Ariel's number, I called him for a formal appointment the day after I found the contract in my mail box. Using my formal voice. In response, he schooled his own to match my business-like tone.

"Of course I will represent you. In anything. Looking at my calendar I see I have a few minutes open this morning. At ten?"

I told him that would be lovely.

DRIVING into town I noticed that the sky had become engulfed by low hanging clouds. The university area, always a damp spot, was hidden inside marrow-chilling fog. We were well into fall. I wore a water proofed trench coat, the kind that reaches down to the ankles and wraps itself around your calves each time you take a step. I also wore shades and a low angled baseball cap.

Paul's office was more upscale than I remembered. Racket was napping on a dog-sized couch in back of the desk. He startled awake when I walked in, gave an ecstatic yelp, and came dashing to scrabble up the side of my coat, wanting to be picked up. I sank onto a luxurious brown leather armchair, patting my lap. Racket jumped up and licked my face. "I love you, too," I murmured, admiring his once-more stream lined frame, appreciatively running my hands over the proud curves of his back and his rib-cage.

Paul watched our reunion in silence. He wore a well-tailored tan suit, the silk tie matching his eyes. The silver threads in his hair gleamed, adding distinction. His expression was guarded.

"Ariel Jordan and I are working out a contract we both want to be absolutely binding," I began once Racket had calmed down enough to make himself comfortable on top of my thighs. "I don't know if this is your expertise. If it isn't or if you feel uneasy I'd appreciate a referral to someone you hold in high esteem."

Pulling a manila envelope out of my bag I slid it across the desk and leaned back watching Paul extract the papers and scan through the legal gobbledygook. I saw the exact moment the shock at what he was reading began to course through his system. By the time he finished the atmosphere in the room had gone down a few degrees. Or so I imagined.

The clouds had dipped. The sidewalk outside was getting pelted with a spectacular downpour, the kind that left me in awe at the forces intrinsic to gravity and water. "Wow!" I said. "Do you suppose this means the drought is over?" If I had stayed at the farmhouse I'd be celebrating the rain by running outside with the dogs, my head tilted up at the sky, tongue out, getting gloriously soaked.

Paul kept his eyes downcast, shuffling the pages back into order. Buying time? At last he looked at me with an odd little smile. "This has been quite an eventful year for you, hasn't it?"

"No doubt," I said. "It's all due to Jimmi of course. Poor Ariel would never have stopped his Rolls for our first encounter if Jimmi hadn't been standing beside me. And if my boy hadn't deserted me Ariel would not have rushed to my cabin in the middle of the night to help me glue myself back together again. I owe the man. Big time."

He smoothed the papers, though they were as flat as they'd been when he pulled them out of the envelope. "Is that why you're doing this? Because you owe him?"

I crossed my legs, careful not to dislodge the doting Racket, and leisurely folded my hands across his back hoping to broadcast a calm I didn't quite feel. "Not at all. I'm doing it because I want the best for his child. And because Ariel wants very much to be a parent. I've been one. Time for me to move on."

"That doesn't mean you have to give up all rights."

I shifted forward. "Do you think for a minute I would want to be part of the media circus that surrounds him? Become a regular fill-in for the gossip rags? Have reporters calling and snooping at all hours? I came to you because I know I can count on your absolute discretion. And because I am certain you have my best interest at heart. Now the question is how much will it cost me to retain you for this matter?"

He busied himself at his laptop typing something I couldn't see into the search bar. The browser pulled up my website. Paul scrolled down the list of my paintings and stopped when he'd found what he was after. "A couple of these will do nicely," he said. "This one, for starters. Of the woman watering the little wild tree at sunrise. How is your conifer friend doing these days?"

I didn't hide my regret. "I hardly know. Gierig hates my guts. The only time I can cross his vast holdings is in pitch-black. And even then I have to be afraid for my dogs."

"Has he done anything with the tract above the Enoch Foundation acreage?"

The instant the words were out of his mouth I could see understanding dawn in his discerning brown eyes. "Oh," he said. "So that's where you've been hiding out."

"I intend to keep that confidential until I'm back on my feet. What's the second picture you want?"

He leaned back, enjoying himself. "You haven't painted it yet. It's the one where the woman is sitting on a swing between two fabulous madrones. Also at sunrise. That's the time, if I may remind you, when their awesome branches look their best, red-golden skins gleaming, the leaves a translucent bright green."

"It will take a while. I'm still working on a great big one Ariel commissioned." I loved saying that word. It added professional stature. "And with Gierig afoot I don't know how often I can sneak up to sketch the madrones. In any case, you have to promise me something first."

He spread his hands. "Consider it done. What is it?"

"That you will never reveal their location. I presume you mean to hang both pictures in here? To add a bit of class to the neutral egg-shell white walls?"

"Precisely." He pointed at the two not interrupted by windows or walnut cabinets. "Those paintings will make my job so much more pleasant. Although I love doing lawyering work I detest being cooped up in this small cubicle of an office."

"What have you done with the ones you bought in Key Largo?"

His cheeks flushed. "I just got around to putting them up. They're hanging at the foot of my bed. So I can see them before shutting my eyes and when I wake up."

Unable to find anything to say in reply I carried Racket to the doggy couch and gently straightened the blanket folded on top of it before putting him down.

"Any news of Jimmi?" he asked, watching us.

The heaviness that had so briefly lifted settled on me again. "Not a word. That's the other reason I came to see you. It calls for another promise from you."

"Oh?"

"Your cell phone is the only contact number he has. The moment he calls please let me know."

"Better yet, I'll give him the number for the farmhouse. I presume you phoned me from there?"

"You copied it down!"

"Of course!"

We stared at each other. I looked away first, saying, "Then I suppose you'll call when you're ready for me to sign Ariel's contract?"

"For sure."

"In a strictly professional capacity only?"

"Why would I do that?" he said. "There's Jimmi. And Racket. And the two pictures you owe me. We might even meet for a business-type lunch . . ."

I touched my belly. "Hardly."

He raised his hands in capitulation. "The twenty-four seven offer still holds." I went to the door. Racket jumped off the couch and followed me. I picked him up. "Are you taking him with you?" Paul asked, the alarm in his voice the first real emotion he'd allowed himself to show.

I carried the dog back to his little couch. "I love him as much as I ever have. But if you love him more he'll remain yours for good and all."

Looking relieved, Paul said, "I'll give you updates. He's lost all that excess weight. Don't you think?"

"I've never seen him look better." Putting my hand on the door knob, I remembered to ask, "By the way. How did it go for Violet?"

He sighed. "I got her off. Bought her a bus ticket, too."

"Good. I hope she thanked you before she left."

With a wry smile, he shook his head. "Oh she thanked me all right. By cashing it in. She's still around somewhere. In fact I saw her last night. At the brewery. Dining with Gierig."

"Oh my God. After what she told me about him?" I could see him perk his ears.

"What did she tell you?"

Maybe it wasn't even true. Most likely she was a thief *and* a liar. I said, "Never mind." Then I pulled up my hood and walked out. The coat was indeed waterproof. Not even my socks got wet.

THE SNOW came early that year. It stuck. I was glad the farmhouse was on more or less even ground. It made my shopping expeditions so much easier than they used to be when I lived up on the ridge. I only went to town when the produce ran out or the beasts needed more meat. Great chunks of time passed while I kept painting. Ariel's calls became less frequent. I didn't blame him. He was busier than he had ever been. And it was likely he wanted to put some distance between us, afraid the baby, growing and kicking according to nature's schedule, would make me change my mind. Or perhaps he was weaning himself away from me. Per our contract all ties between us would be cut from the time he took possession.

He'd had the biggest guest bedroom on the California ranch remodeled into a nursery. His attorneys were discreetly interviewing prospective nannies without letting them know who their charge might be. And he was emptying toy stores in every city he passed through. It caused little comment in the press; it was something he'd always done.

I was in my element. Hours seemed like minutes to me. Ariel's commission wasn't just something I was painting; it was something I entered, leaving it only when hunger recalled me to the mundane real world. For days on end I talked to no one except the dogs. They got used to my almost constant preoccupation, expanding their excess energy in playful bouts of wrestling, sleeping close together, and watching me work, their expressions benign. Twice a day I took them for long romps. We seldom went uphill. There were many flat trails between the farmhouse and the highway.

Last winter El Nino had kept the weather in the Pacific Northwest unseasonably warm. He was also responsible for the drought that came to us in late spring and stayed through our golden Indian summer. This winter La Nina took over, burying us in more snow than we'd seen in a decade. In the middle of December, and then again in January, the first part of February, and half of March, the snow was so deep that I couldn't navigate the road even with four chained tires. But we had plenty of provisions and the lights only went out twice, both times for less than three hours.

During the last blackout Marvel jumped onto my bed to produce the results of all that playful wrestling—two snub-nosed, very dark pups, one male and one female, both so tiny that they had done little to increase the size of her belly while they were gestating within— although what with Marvel's long hair and my preoccupation it was possible I wouldn't have noticed if she had been pregnant with a litter of ten. She and Asa took care of the infants together, she nursing them, he tongue-bathing them and herding them back to the nest when they got old enough to wander. Often I would place the mewing pups on my belly for an early bond with their human litter mate and soon-to-be lifelong friend.

Ariel's wintry farmhouse kept us all cozy. What I loved best about it was the push button heat. And the fact that he was paying the electric bill. After decades of winters that had me sawing, dragging, splitting and stacking my firewood, I felt I deserved the easy temperature regulated warmth Ariel's largesse provided. By road, the farm was far removed from civilization. And yet it was fairly close to Ralph and Edie's place, though largely inaccessible from that direction due to the barbed wire topped fence, the dense strip of forest, and the vertical creek bed.

On the last day of March Marvel consented to leave the puppies safe in their nest in order to join Asa and me for a brisk hike. Last year this time the buttercups, already well established, were joined by the first purple shooting star. This year we were breaking through deep snow with each step. It was tiring even for the dogs. They ate lumps of ice to quench their thirst. We passed rusted, bullet riddled signs nailed to tree skeletons that read, *Trespassers will be shot.* No doubt this used to be pot growing backcountry before our region's helicopter surveillance program was funded.

This particular morning we were on a trail I didn't remember having been on before. At last we encountered two trim black Labs. They snuffled, whipping their rear ends with enthusiasm, smelling Asa and Marvel from top to bottom. Someone was whistling for them. They paid no heed. Then an elegant young woman stepped into the path, her auburn hair long and silk-smooth. I almost didn't recognize Zora. Her face had slimmed considerably. So had the rest of her though it was hard to tell how much since she was wearing a puffy down coat.

"Silvi?" she said. "What are *you* doing here?"

I zipped my own puffy down coat down a bit in an effort to give myself a straight silhouette, unwound my thick mile-long woolen shawl, held it artfully in front of me, and fanned myself with its fringed ends, asking, "Are those your dogs?"

"Barret's. I took them in. He mentioned the pound."

"You did wonders with them. They look like puppies again."

"It's something called *barf diet*. Mostly raw meaty bones."

"You should send Barret a snapshot. He always claimed his vet said Labs were supposed to be fat."

She shrugged carelessly. "Barret, shmarret. I don't know what I ever saw in him."

"You're looking pretty trim yourself," I said. "A new woman."

She grinned. "It's Conny's fault. We're into ballroom dancing. He's living with me now. Tries out his lines on me first. Boy can he act."

She didn't seem to notice anything different about me. Perhaps she thought fat-bellied women were the norm. "I'm glad I turned out to be wrong about Ariel Jordan," she said. "Conny set me straight long before . . . before Jimmi . . . " She touched my sleeve. "I'm so sorry. Have you heard from him yet?"

The day was turning rapidly darker. More snow was expected. "Not a word."

"That's tough. You moved, didn't you? Maybe he doesn't know how to reach you. Don't you have a friend in common he might have called? From happier times?"

I thought of Dorrie and dismissed the notion at once. "I gave him Paul's number. He must have lost it." The idea that Jimmi might be desperately looking for me only made me feel worse. But according to the detective I should be glad he hadn't shown up in any morgue, hospital, or detention facility. Yet.

Zora gave a dry chuckle. "Do you know, that scumbag Gierig came around and said his wife had fallen in love with my chalet and just had to have it. He had the nerve to pull out his check book. I tried to sic the dogs on him but they only leaned against his knees asking to be petted. It freaked him out though. That and the fact that Conny came out of the kitchen rolling his eyes, swinging a big cast iron frying pan, and quoting Othello." She half-turned. "You've never been to my farm, have you? It's up there a ways. Cross fenced for horses and dogs. I won't start getting cows until the last bit of snow is gone. Come over for coffee."

If I didn't want her to get wise to my condition her invitation would have to wait a while."Sometime," I said. "But not right now. The sky's about to fall." The yellow-cast clouds were lowering fast, advancing a cutting wind. Flakes danced all around us, ever faster, denser. "Winter storm warning," I said. "You better go home while you can still see the hands in front of your face."

We went off in opposite directions.

THAT NIGHT I tossed around a lot. No matter what position I assumed sleep kept eluding me. At three a.m. I jumped up and went to the phone, dialing Dorrie's number. Before I could apologize for the early call she exclaimed, "Silvi—thank God you called. Jimmi's been trying to reach you for weeks."

Heart pounding, I eased myself onto the couch. "Where is he?"

"I don't know! He calls from a pay phone. Collect. Asking for your new number, wanting to know if you still live on the mountain. Every time the operator announces his call it's from a different city. The first one was Bakersfield. The second Fresno. The third Stockton. I think he's hitchhiking, Silvi."

"Or riding the freight trains," I said, my throat going dry. "He'll freeze to death before he gets halfway up the first mountain. The snow is wicked this year. What happened to him after Leroy chased him? Did he say?"

"At first he slept in parks. When he got cold and hungry and desperate enough he risked going to Leroy's mother. She took him in, kept him hidden in a back room, and fed him up. But in the end Leroy called her from around the corner to ask if he could hole up at her house for a while. As he was walking up to the front door the woman snuck Jimmi out the rear with all the cash she had in her cookie jar and told him to go home to Oregon. Of course she's old and hasn't been on a Greyhound in years. She didn't give him nearly enough for the fare. He decided to make his own way and save the money for food. But he's getting scared, Silvi. Your old phone's disconnected and so is your landlord's. He lost the slip of paper you gave him when you came down to L.A. Now he doesn't know where to go."

Without hesitation I gave her the numbers for the farmhouse, Paul's office, and his cell. "Next time he calls you tell him to stay put. I'll drive down to wherever he is and pick him up. I have a question."

"What?"

"How come you didn't send him the balance he needed for a bus ticket?"

She sputtered, "What do you take me for? I offered but he never stays on the phone long enough to work something out. I'm afraid he thinks I'm going to tell Leroy where to find him. My own fault. That whole Ariel Jordan fiasco could have been avoided if I had kept Leroy out of Jimmi's life. I swear to you, to my dying day I'll never—"

"Yeah well," I said, cutting her off. "There are always plenty of *ifs* to go around, aren't there? But I'm tired of blaming. You give him my message. Remember to tell him that I'm waiting to hear from him. And eager to see him. No questions asked."

I didn't cry till after I hung up. Once I started I couldn't stop, couldn't help wondering who'd get here first, Jimmi or his almost-sister, or if by chance they would both arrive at the same time.

AFTER Ariel had regained his status as Emperor of Song I brought home more of his music and movies from the storage unit. The selection was vast. If I had wanted I could have watched movies all day and night long. While I worked I liked listening to Ariel's stuff, especially the ballads. But what gave me the greatest pleasure were his protest songs. He had recorded some for every album. The title track of *Undaunted* was one of the latest. They were not only raunchy with emotion but rich with chocolaty layers of sound, one on top of another, now blending, now swirling around each other. On much of his songs he sang every part, background vocals and all, in dizzying, free-for-all harmonious arrangements that made me laugh in spite of my gnawing fear for Jimmi.

According to my calculations I was due in April but as that month arrived nothing shifted except for the snow. It plopped like an slushy ambush from the roof and the trees. Snow grenades. The creek, a stone's throw away, defrosted and rose, grumbling. My gait had become a waddle. Afraid of eye-witnesses and medical records, I had never seen a doctor, not even in Medford. But Ariel, in his wisdom and uncommon thirst for all knowledge, had a shelf full of books pertaining to pregnancy and childbirth. Lamaze and all. And I kept up with my yoga breathing and the *asanas*, though from month to month I had to modify the postures.

As my condition advanced I did less shopping at the co-op where I might run into someone I knew, switching to one of the more anonymous chain stores. It carried an uninspired selection of organic produce and meat but had the advantage of being open most of the night. Ariel called the first Sunday of April, trying to keep a mounting impatience out of his voice. I reminded him nature works at her own speed. He had just finished filming the music video for the *Undaunted* song and said he had sent me an advance copy.

"Overnight delivery. Check for it in the morning. How are the pups?"

I filled him in on the latest installment of their rapid development. According to our calculations they would be ready to go around the same time the baby was supposed to be born. "It couldn't be better. God must have arranged the dates Himself," Ariel said.

From their birth I had taken frequent snapshots for the scrap book Ariel had asked me to start. "They're real fluffy now," I told him. "And their coats have started to lighten."

"That's great. I can hardly wait to see them for myself." Ariel paused, continuing with barely disguised apprehension, "Look, Silvi, even though you signed the papers and everything and my lawyers made me promise not to do this—I just want you to know you're not stuck with the promise you made to me when you knew I was down and out. If you want to change your mind I'll tear up the papers with my own hands. Don't go ahead if you're not absolutely sure."

In that moment I realized just how much I loved him. "The same goes for me," I told him, tears of gratitude scalding my eyes. "Your name's been cleared. You're on top of the charts. Women are throwing themselves at you left, right, and center. If you've changed *your* mind, I'll tear up *my* copies and send *you* the shreds."

"Are you kidding?" he cried. "I'm already talking to Melody. Every day."

"Who's Melody?"

"Melody Rafaela Jordan. Our little angel."

I started to correct him with, "*Your* angel, you mean," but the pronoun got stuck in my throat. The one he'd used was so much nicer. I let it ring in my ears until it faded of its own accord. Then I said, "I suppose the detective hasn't had any luck yet in Sacramento?" It was where the expert predicted Jimmi was heading next. Ariel had dispatched the man to the sprawling capital, where he unobtrusively hung around the Greyhound station, freeway on-ramps, the freight yards, and nearby overpasses and parks.

"Not yet," Ariel admitted. "But it's only a matter of time. From now on I'm calling you twice a day. If you don't mind."

Although I was beginning to feel like a slow baking pound-cake he was continuously pricking for doneness, I didn't mind in the least. For one thing, I loved our talks. For another, he always ended the conversations by singing a song to the baby. That night was no exception. As usual, his tender ballad filled me with awe. Inside me Melody shifted, testing her vocal cords. They weren't quite ripe enough to join the refrain.

A few nights later La Nina decided to stage a spectacular exit. She started with an enormous layer of additional snow which lay innocently sparkling at predawn when I shone my flashlight out of the window. It snowed big fat flakes for three days although it never got very cold. And then La Nina brought on a rain-storm that turned the snow to mush, overwhelming the creek whose sound took on a threatening note. The cottonwoods framing its banks bent double. The oak trees next to the house were creaking ominously. Looking uphill I saw that the forest canopy was a wildly convulsing giant green wave. I could hear things snapping and crashing. The thud of a particularly big tree falling somewhere close shook the ground like an earthquake. Asa hid behind the couch and Marvel looked at me as if asking for permission to be scared. I didn't give it. I was pleased to note that the puppies showed not the smallest sign of fear.

It seemed a perfect time to unwrap the *Undaunted* video. It had been waiting for me in a special pouch inside my PMB last time I drove into town. I loaded it into the entertainment center, making sure to turn the volume all the way up. That had been part of Ariel's dedication. "To Silvi, with all my love. Please turn the speakers to the max to get every nuance of sound." Little did he know how much I detested loud pop music. Remembering the heavy handed bass line of this particular tune I had the terrible suspicion I was in for an uncomfortable five minutes.

But I was wrong. For one thing his speakers were state of the art, separating out each distinct tone. For another the music managed to muffle the awful noise of La Nina's furious farewell. As the cheeky, spit-in-the-wind notes of *Undaunted* wrapped themselves around the dogs and me I was captivated by the images unfolding on the big screen. Wearing a bright yellow, half unbuttoned shirt and his famous flooding pants Ariel was belting full force while executing some spectacular new dance steps he must have secretly practiced for months. In intercutting scenes he alternately played drums, a keyboard, and the oddest mix of home-made instruments I ever saw.

He and his band were having so much fun making music it was infectious. Before I knew what I was doing I was up on my feet, singing and wiggling along with the beat. Then Marvel decided to sing too and Asa began matching my dance steps, becoming so overwhelmed by enthusiasm that he nipped at my butt.

Every now and then the set would shift to a rugged beach where, in the distance, a man was walking with his two dogs and a small child. The child and the dogs were dancing around the man and in and out of the surf. The dogs were long-coated German shepherds. The child was a lovely, straight haired, latte-toned girl. At the end, as the music wound down, they were standing on a rolling dune covered with tall golden grass blades that stirred in the evening wind. The sky was aglow. The man and the girl were holding hands. The dogs sat close beside them, all four figures dark against a backdrop of fluorescent, ever-deepening turquoise. The scene left me speechless.

OVERNIGHT, the creek breached its banks but it never rose higher than the pilings that anchored the farmhouse. Then it made itself a new channel on the far side of the pastures and left us alone. Ashland was not as lucky. Ashland Creek, coming from Lithia Park, overran the plaza and put it under water. JPR radio reported that many hillside basements had sprung leaks as the underground water level rose to unprecedented heights. Interrupting an evening music program, the mayor came on to say that the town's drinking water had become contaminated and was no longer safe. Whole sections of road were washed out.

My phone service capitulated, but only for a couple of hours. As Paul told me later, when he stepped outside he found that the city streets had become rivers. He tried to call me to make sure I was all right but couldn't get through. Knowing that a creek ran just below the farmhouse he jumped in his truck and decided to come to the rescue. He got as far as the golf course. Across the street a house standing close to Neill Creek was half under water; the yard had become a small lake. He wrestled with himself. His impulse was to go ahead, damn my desire for privacy. But he reasoned this wouldn't be any different from the last time he came running, when I'd opened my door just long enough to tell him to leave. Besides, hadn't he tried to find the farmhouse once before and gotten lost?

He called again. This time the phone rang. And rang. Then he went home.

CHAPTER 38

NATURALLY MELODY CHOSE TO BE BORN THAT windswept night. The theories I had ingested from the birthing books bore absolutely no resemblance to the actual event. If I could have I would have put my belly down on the couch and walked away from the mind-numbing cramps. In between pains I was searching through every bag, pocket and drawer for Ariel's mother's number. I remembered only that I had put it in some easy-to-find place.

My first moan brought the dogs running, their eyes round with distress. I put them and the pups, who were in an exploratory mood, in Ariel's comfortable office at the opposite end of the house to keep them from losing faith in my coping abilities. Then I shut myself in the bathroom, biting a towel to muffle my moans. Somewhere on the other side of the door the telephone rang. I barely noticed. Catching a glimpse of my twisted face in the mirror I said, "Get a grip, Silvi. Women have been doing this job since Eve ate the apple. Think third world delivery. Alone. In some field."

The storm was rattling the clapboard siding. The phone stopped ringing. The rattling grew louder. Something hit the roof, scraped over the gutter, and thundered to the ground right outside my window. One of the oaks. Feeling claustrophobic, I went back to the living room for my copious birthing-notes, where I'd written,

Breathe! It's the fear that hurts, not the pains!

"Take your time, Melody," I said. "Slow and easy."

As a child I'd often overheard Mam**a**, presiding over *Kaffee und Kuchen,* regale her coffee-klatch friends with the details of her two excruciating labors and deliveries, starting round robin discussions of childbearing hardships in which every woman present sought to out-brag the others. Right there and then I promised myself I would never join that particular club.

Suffice it to say Melody was successfully born on a dark and stormy night. Sometime in the middle of proceedings Ariel called. "This is it," I said. "The sooner you get here, the better."

He chartered a private jet.

Once Melody finally consented to slide into the world I washed and dressed her in the second-hand outfit I'd bought from Goodwill, complete with receiving blanket. Only the disposable diapers were new. The whole time I was bending over her she looked steadily up at me with her limpid blue eyes. They were as discerning as an adult's. I put her in the dresser drawer I'd prepared, felt my way along walls and furniture, and let the dogs come into the living room. Asa and Marvel followed their noses and the puppies followed Marvel. When I'd made my way to the couch the two big shepherds were already standing over the drawer, solemnly gazing at the baby, their faces incredibly gentle, their tails swishing a welcome.

The cats, who considered the service porch their private domain and seldom came to the rest of the house, made their own pilgrimage to the couch, sitting on cushions, surrounding the drawer, gazing at Melody looking out at them from her makeshift bed.

I had given birth to the sound of classical music, but JPR went off the air from two to six a.m. leaving nothing but white noise on its band width. I awoke to the sound of John Gierig's name spoken by the morning newscaster while he was reading a short eulogy.

According to an eye witness the mountainside above the million dollar cabin, softened by the deluge, gave way and flattened the house as if it had been built of toothpicks. Gierig was trapped under the falling ceiling. His house guest, who escaped serious injury, hiked to a neighbor to alert authorities. She left before sheriff and rescue vehicles arrived. Gierig's wife, asleep in their Ashland residence, was awakened by a phone call from a local reporter but refused to comment on the tragedy.

Melody's thin mewl came at the same instant someone started pounding on our front door. Asa and Marvel dashed to it looking pleased. "Silvi!" Paul's voice called. "Are you all right? There's a huge tree lying across your yard!" I felt my way to the latch I'd installed the day after I'd moved in and undid it. Paul tumbled in carrying Racket. They were soaked. "Your bridge is flooded!" he said accusingly as if I'd orchestrated it to keep him away. "And there's a locked Chevy parked on it, blocking the way. I had to walk in." He put Racket on the floor and went to Melody's drawer. "Wow!" he said. "I forgot how tiny they are in the beginning. Ariel called me when his plane touched down in New York. He wanted mc to comc hclp you with labor and all."

"We did fine," I said, sinking onto the couch.

"So I see. He'll call again when he gets to Medford. To find out if it's safe to drive in. Which it isn't." Abruptly he stared at the big canvas tacked to the wall. "Good grief," he said, moving forward. "How long did it take you?"

"Months," I said. "You think Ariel will like it?"

He peered at my rendition of Blossom Lane. "If he doesn't *I'll* buy it. I made an offer on a house a while back. As far as I know, escrow's about to close. Knock on wood. It has a wall that's exactly the right size for this painting."

"A house? Is that right?" I said, hardly listening. "Congratulations. There's your picture." I nodded at the easel from which the two gilded madrones shone, their trunks massive, the leaves fragile. "It's only half done."

He studied the composition. "I'll say. You haven't put in the most important part yet. The woman on the swing. But take your time. I am a patient man." Carefully, he lifted Melody out of the drawer and placed her on my chest.

Even though every instinct told me I would regret it later I couldn't resist putting an arm around her. "Is it still raining?"

"You bet. Old Siskiyou Highway has become a mad river. It's not much better in this flat backcountry, except here the rain has made a network of lakes. I got lost five times. Half the roads dead-end, the other half are washed out. You don't mind if I borrow a couple of towels for Racket and me, do you? Then I'll make us something to eat."

"Melody and I aren't hungry," I said, automatically stroking the baby's back. "But I bet the dogs are."

He put the towel dried Chihuahua on the couch by my feet, covering both of us with a blanket. Shivering, Racket pressed himself against my calves. Paul fed the animals and brought me a tray holding some toast, two soft boiled eggs, and a cup of steaming tea. When I declined again, he took the baby from me, hauled me into a sitting position, and placed the tray on my lap. "Got to get your strength back. You look like hell," he told me, tenderly rewrapping Melody. "Gosh, this brings back memories—I used to be a pretty handy dad." He carried her around the room, crooning a lullaby. He had a pleasant, deep voice. She was looking at him with the same seriousness with which she'd considered me. But soon she closed her eyes and Paul laid her in her drawer.

"If you would take the dogs out for a toilet break I'd be obliged," I murmured. "Not that I couldn't do it myself if I had to."

He groused, "I'm quite aware that you don't need anybody for anything, but as long as I'm here I *would* like to make myself useful." He preceded them out and I tried to stay awake long enough to watch them come in again, but I was as tired as a newborn and gladly gave in to sleep. I resurfaced just long enough to hear the phone ring and Paul's answering murmur. Afterwards he made a bunch of homey little sounds that made me feel safe—rattling dishes, clinking silverware, scraping pots, low-volume music. It wasn't until Melody stirred that I roused enough to open my eyes.

Paul brought her to me freshly diapered. Greedily my arm closed around her again, making me feel like a junkie getting a much needed fix. "Ariel called from Medford," he explained with a relieved smile. "Turns out he brought a whole layette. Bottles, formula and all. He's thought everything through." Hovering over me, he hesitated and said, "That doesn't mean you can't change your mind. If you want to. No one would blame you."

"I'm not the type to renege," I told him. "The whole thing was my idea in the first place. Nobody twisted my arm. You should have heard how excited Ariel was when I brought it up."

"Still is."

"You don't really think I'd take this away from him now."

With a lawyerly frown, he said slowly, "I would support you every step of the way."

But my mind was made up. "Forget it, Paul. This is Ariel's baby not mine. All those months she was growing inside me she was yearning for him. I'm not kidding. I think she'd be royally pissed if she had to live with me. Particularly since I won't have a place to stay after this. I promised him I'd be out of here a couple of weeks after she was born. It's only fair."

He indicated Ariel's painting. "You have any idea how much this is worth?"

"Ariel and I haven't discussed it."

"Six, seven months of labor, at least. Not to mention all the material, which must have strained your puny budget. Let me broker a deal for you."

"Why? You're getting the madrones for merely shuffling a few papers."

He laughed. "Okay. I'll shut up." He sat in the armchair, crossing his long legs. "Any news about Jimmi?"

"No," I said, immediately saddened. "Not yet. In a way, I'm glad. I don't want him mixed up in any of this. It's too big of a secret for a boy to have to keep. I'd rather he didn't know."

He studied Melody's face. "My girls looked like cooked lobsters when they were born. Yelled like somebody had dunked them in a deep-fry basket. This one's got a peaceful face. I'd love to see her grow up."

I stretched, careful not to disturb Racket. "Oh, but you will. From a safe distance. I only hope getting exposed to the press from an early age will make her immune. Did you hear about Gierig?"

He nodded. "You thinking what I'm thinking?"

"The eye witness? Violet."

"An unlucky woman. Keeps putting her faith in the wrong men."

"I put mine in no man."

He grinned. "Why? You have better men to put your faith in." He took my hand, holding it lightly. "Listen up. Ariel's renting a chopper. Get ready—he'll be here any minute."

He left me alone with the baby. I could hear the puppies snuffling around in the kitchen. Paul had placed a board across the bottom of the door to keep them from getting underfoot. Asa and Marvel were watching them from this side of the barrier. The proud but practical mother was avoiding their needle-sharp teeth.

I asked Paul to outfit my biggest cat carrier with old towels. A few minutes later I heard the chopper drone overhead. He went outside with my car keys to move Efi out of harm's way. While he was gone I tightened my hold on Melody, memorizing her flawless face, her ever watchful serene eyes. "I will always love you," I whispered. "From afar."

The chopper noise increased. I could hear the propellers spinning. And then Ariel walked into the room, bringing with him a cold gust of air. "Poor oak," he said. "It was the biggest one. Two hundred years old. At least. It's blocking half of the yard. We had to land in the pasture." He was wearing makeup to cover his translucent skin, a ski cap, heavy sideburns along with a pencil-thin mustache, the horn rims, and hillbilly overalls under a bulky coat. There was a baby sling wrapped around his neck like a scarf. When he took off the glasses and smiled not even the opaque makeup mask could keep his inner glow from lighting the room. Melody tilted her face in his direction. Her doll sized arms waved to and fro.

I placed a hand on the top of her pretty round head. And then I blessed her.

Ariel leaned the thin attaché case he'd been carrying against the wall next to the front door and began to move slowly toward us. Until he spied the painting. It compelled him across the room. But after the first few steps in its direction he restrained himself and approached the couch instead. "May I hold her?" he asked. When I lifted her up I could feel my arms trembling. He took her from me. Her infant eyes had already tuned me out. I was forgotten.

He held her close. A tear trickled down his face, washing a runnel through his powder. Impulsively he stooped to put his cheek next to mine, smearing the tear onto my skin. "Are you sure you want to go through with our deal?"

"You two are made for each other."

He squeezed his eyes shut. His lips moved in silent prayer. Then he said, "I will always be thankful."

Paul came into the house, his eyes wide with undisguisable admiration. "I love your new album," he gushed, enthusiastically pumping Ariel's hand. "I listen to it every night when I go to bed. Can't get enough of it. I really think you've come into your own with this one. It's a classic." Then he cleared his throat and said, trying for a more detached, professional tone, "I put our copies of the contract on the table so you can sign them off. You brought yours?"

Ariel straightened and acknowledged Paul's words with a small bow and a blinding smile. Then he took the attaché case to the table, pulled out a folder, and put it in Paul's hands, all the while keeping a firm hold on the baby. "The puppies?" he asked.

"I'll get them." Paul tossed the folder onto the table and stepped over the barrier into the kitchen.

I nodded at our painting. "Well, Ariel, what do you think?"

Ariel took his daughter to the canvas, studying the many miniature scenes in the mountain forest. He and Melody were featured in each one. In some, they were toddlers together. In another he was an old man and she a grown woman, holding a child of her own. It had given me profound solace to picture Melody in various stages of growing up. In the scene I liked best Jimmi and I were included. Four German shepherds lay in the background, guarding. The cherubs hovering over the group were the friends I imagined Melody would make as she moved through her life.

Ariel said in a hushed tone, "Pure magic. Like I've just teleported into the woods. I wish I could take it with me."

Everything was right there. Exactly how I wanted it to be. The peak, the forest, Blossom Lane, the wildlife. I'd chosen spring time, with melting patches of snow, the first flowers and leftover autumn leaves. It was a happy wood, a thriving place, each stroke brushed on with love so that the entire composition was a tapestry of that most splendid of emotions. It would go with Melody to surround her, to surround them both, embracing and succoring them through whatever lay ahead. The entire tapestry was my final and never-ending benediction.

Ariel came to stand before me, steepling his hands and making a deep bow. His eyes shone. Then he pulled out his check book and asked, "How much?"

I found it hard to speak. "It's a gift," I said. "Of love. For Melody and her daddy. I'll send it to you as soon as you are done with the last leg of your tour."

"I can't let you—"

"You better!"

I could hear Paul's cell phone ringing in the kitchen. "Hello?" he murmured. "Yes? Speaking."

Ariel's eyes swam in tears. "All right then," he said with an odd little smile, stuffing the checkbook away. He went on to examine the madrones, exclaiming, "Oh God! My two favorite trees. I used to visit them before sunup. Can I buy—"

"That picture is for Paul. In lieu of legal fees."

He feathered a finger up the smooth trunks."I loved climbing them. You can get pretty high because the boughs are so strong. From the top you can see all the way down the mountain to every part of this valley, everything laid out like a living, three-dimensional map. I'll always miss the madrones. And the farm. And you."

My insides did an elevator-drop. I thought, "Don't go!" What I actually said was, "You're never coming back, are you?" Some unexamined place inside me had hoped to glimpse Melody every now and then. And him. From the madrones.

He looked at the floor and then directly at me. "There's no point now that I've blown my cover. Before too long the paparazzi would find me. You have no idea what that's like."

"I had a taste of it," I said. "And I can't blame you for selling the place. I'll be out at the end of the month."

"Take your time. There's no rush."

I hesitated, then asked, "What did you do with your Subaru?"

"As far as I know it's still at the Medford airport. I've been paying a small fortune in parking fees." He fished for his wallet. "I've got the pink slip right here, if you want it."

"No, thanks," I said. "But I know someone who does."

PAUL came in with the cat carrier. The puppies were already inside it. Asa and Marvel were tracking them, noses high. When he put the carrier on the arm chair, the dogs lay down beside it. Paul sorted through the contracts and handed Ariel a pen. Ariel signed the final copies. So did I. Paul witnessed our signatures, then slid half the pages into the attaché case. Outside, the chopper motor was still running.

Ariel reached into the carrier, rubbing first one pup, then the other. "Melody's best friends. Gee they're cute. Still kind of dark, though. I don't see much red in their coats."

"You wait. Asa and Marvel looked just like them at that age." I remembered the beach scenes from the *Undaunted* DVD. "Where did you get the little girl you had in the video, and the dogs?"

He grinned, giving me a final close-up of his excellent teeth. "I told you, I have loads of nieces and nephews and cousins of all sizes. And I rented the shepherds just for the film. I figured those scenes would prepare my fans, so that when I announce Melody's arrival the day after tomorrow it won't come as a complete shock." With a practiced hand, he put Melody in the baby sling. "Look for the clip. It'll probably be on the six o'clock news."

Paul, pacing the floor empty handed, seemed to be wrestling with some anxious private thoughts. He picked up the attaché case and said, "Let me see you out, Ariel. The pilot's waiting. I'll carry the pups."

"Okay." Ariel wrapped his open coat around the baby and then wrapped his arms around the coat. Our eyes met for the last time. "Good-bye, Silvi. I hope the universe gives you everything you want." And then he was gone, taking all the light with him.

In the resulting gloom, a shadowy Paul stood before me, suddenly somber. "We need to talk. About that—"

"Not now." I curled onto my side, pressing against the upholstery, hiding my face. "Don't keep Ariel waiting."

"In a few minutes then." He picked up the carrier.

"No," I whimpered. "Don't! Go on home. I need to be left alone for a couple of days."

"But I—"

"Can't you see? I'm broken right now! Go!"

Nodding, he set the carrier out on the porch and shouted for Racket who zipped out from under the blanket and jumped into his arms. Paul shut the door. Marvel looked at it, then at me, and whined softly. Asa began to bay. I'd never heard him make that sound before. Putting a pillow over my face, I pressed its ends over my ears. I kept them there until the noise lifted away.

It left behind an airless void and deafening silence.

CHAPTER 39

TWO MORNINGS LATER I SCROLLED DOWN my internet gallery and discovered that every painting on display had a big yellow SOLD sticker under it. I called Paul for clarification.

"I didn't know you bought a computer," he said after a cordial greeting. "You want to handle the website by yourself from now on?"

"I'm not good enough yet. In fact, I don't even know enough to access my own email account. Who bought all those paintings all of a sudden?"

"Sorry, I'm in a meeting. Let's discuss it over soup and a sandwich. At noon? Our usual place?"

Suspecting he was putting me off just so he would get that "business-type lunch" he'd suggested earlier, I said, "I'll try to work you into my schedule."

"Bring the dogs. If you're up for a little walk afterwards, that is."

Although it was only nine a.m., I put them in Efi and eased her away from her mucky parking spot. During the rains the puddle in front of the door had become a pond. Ariel hadn't been exaggerating

when he said the storm-felled centurion oak was occupying most of
the front yard. Its tremendous boughs reached past the second story
all the way to the roof gutter. The twigs were covered with buds that
would never unfurl.

I had made plans. First off I wanted to see the damage La Nina
had done to Gierig's villa and to his ridge-top land. The creek had
gone down, leaving debris lying across the bridge. I cleared the
biggest pieces from around the Chevy, propped up the hood,
reconnected the battery cables, and started the engine. It was a well-
practiced procedure by now. Although it had become unnecessary it
still made me feel safer to drive the car back onto the bridge once I'd
maneuvered Efi across.

Turning onto Old Siskiyou Highway I saw it was covered with
mud. Boulders of various shapes and sizes, along with dead tree
branches, lay strewn along the tarmac. But already a road crew was
out with machinery scraping up the residue.

I'd never been up the tarred access road that started behind
Gierig's fancy mailbox. Ascending, it wound around Strawberry Hill
to the other side. When I came to the top of the rise I saw that the
clear-cut slope, sliding down, had buried most of Gierig's driveway
along with his cabin. Rescue personnel had carried away his corpse,
put up warning tapes, and gone on to other tasks.

I released the dogs and pulled two old mop handles out of the
canopy. They had been drafted to become hiking sticks; my legs
were still rubbery. Worse came to worst I'd keel over, rest, and
scrabble up again. Slowly, I skirted the twisted, mud-engulfed
wreckage of splintered walls, roof sections, porch railings. Off to the
right a deer trail would take me to the logging skid where Marvel
had found the skunk and Gierig had almost found us. Looking
straight ahead along the road he had carved into the mountain, I had
a good view of the beheaded Raspberry Hill, the crime hidden
behind a rim of conifers.

That road and the other two he had surfaced with the peak's
bedrock had been washed away during the storm leaving a muddle
of potholes, furrows, and rocks. The ditches the bulldozer dug were
filled in with the soggy remains of the banks the machine had so

diligently denuded. I couldn't go far; wet clay clung to the bottoms of my shoes in ever thicker clumps that refused to be scraped off. I wondered what Gierig's widow would do with her tainted inheritance.

The dogs watched me with sorrowful eyes, their paws clay covered, their bellies spattered with mud. "Let's go to the truck," I said. "You'll like our next stop better."

I TOOK the old highway to the county road and drove up to what used to be Barret's land. He and I had patched the unstable lane every summer except for the last and kept the ditch clear. Other than a couple of small breaches that could easily be mended Ridge Road was in good shape. Every trace of the cable-gate Howie had guarded was gone. So was the battered camper. Stu's cabin had been felled by the dozer, pushed into a pile, and burnt after the fire season ended. All that was left of more than a quarter century's habitation was a charred spot and chunky home-made cement pilings.

The stretch from Stu's cabin to mine had always been risky during the wet months. I had expected as much. Switching into low drive, I cruised at less than 5 mph up and down the undulations, past the pump house—still intact—and past what, in better times, had been my home. An involuntary glance showed me that it, too, had been reduced to ashes. Among the rubble lay what was left of the box springs and my two prized possessions, the little chest freezer and the under-the-counter refrigerator, both equally mangled and covered with soot. Even the dog fence was gone.

Putting on mental blinders, I continued on toward Paul's land. Since he never did get around to grading and graveling his part of the road, it was the hardest to maneuver. When my tires spun even in low drive I was sure I'd have to get out and put on my chains to gain traction. But then Efi prevailed.

The abandoned cabin, once the worst of the lot, looked remarkably solid. Before Barret ousted him, Paul had finished installing the new insulation, repairing the windows, replacing the warped doors and half of the porch, and patching the roof. With any luck it had remained dry inside. I drove up to the remodeled steps, climbed them, and tried the front entrance. It was latched from within. I walked around to the kitchen door and pushed my way in. The inside air was frigid but not damp. "Violet!" I called, looking up to the loft. "It's me. Silvi."

Just then, I heard the front door clicking shut. The dogs started yapping. Efi's left door squeaked the way it usually did when I opened it in damp weather. Running out, I found Violet sitting behind the steering wheel wishing I'd left the key in the ignition. "It's no use," I said. "I don't make the same mistake twice."

She was unkempt, smelly, cold. Her lips were blue, her large marble eyes glassy with tears. "Go back to California, Violet," I said. "Go home."

She rubbed at her dirt-streaked cheeks. "Easy for you to say. Even if Clyde's truck wasn't busted, I wouldn't have enough money for gas. Most likely I'd never make it as far as Yreka."

"Your granny?"

"She gave all she could spare. Thanks to Howie it wasn't enough."

"And the cash you got for the ticket Paul gave you?"

"It melted away. Food gets expensive when you don't have a stove."

It's what I had expected. "Move over," I said. "I'm taking you to Medford. Ariel left you his car. I'm supplying your traveling fund. The rest is up to you." I gave her the pink slip he'd signed off.

She hiccupped a final sob and then her face began to flush a warm pink. "You'd do that for me? After the way I acted? Why?"

"Because," I said, gently helping her over the gear shafts to the passenger seat so I could climb in, "Lavender needs you and you need Lavender."

MISSION accomplished, I drove straight from the Medford airport to downtown Ashland to meet Paul. Ashland Creek had returned to its banks, but it would take some time before all the damage could be repaired. Volunteers were still busy shoveling creek mud out of the basements of plaza shops. Since I was a bit early I decided to check my mail box. It held a letter from Pap*a*. Judging by its shape and thickness I guessed it contained an invitation. I was right. He and Soferl were announcing their upcoming July wedding. I had to admire their nerve.

"That gives you plenty of warning," he had written in his excellent script. *"We expect you and Jimmi to help us celebrate. Bring your friend."* With relief I realized he had no idea what I'd been going through. I found myself longing to have another look at Grandfather's paintings and wondered how much it would cost me to bring along two German shepherds. But without my boy it was an impossible plan. There was a P.S. at the end of the card. It said, *"Josef wants you to know that his chocolate was effective in overcoming the shyness gene."*

PAUL was already sitting at "our" table when I walked into the restaurant. The sun was shining. The air was fresh but spring-time mild. He was wearing white slacks and a crisp, sage-green shirt with rolled up sleeves. It was my favorite color. With the matching jacket he had slung over the back of his chair, he looked the epitome of a high priced attorney-at-law. The two young women at the corner table were preening and whispering about him and when I approached they gave me a what-could-he-possibly-see-in-you glare.

But to my satisfaction he saw only me. "Good," he said with a welcoming smile, pulling out the chair across from his, "You have some color in your cheeks today. I've ordered our usual. If that's okay."

I sat down feeling awkward and shy. "Just soup, thank you." I had no appetite but was thirsty enough to empty my glass of ice water in one long gulp. "So—what's up with the gallery?"

He signaled the waiter, changed my order, and said in a low voice, shifting closer, "I'll get to that directly. But first . . . I had a long chat with . . . Mr. Rafael. In the chopper. He invited me to ride to the Medford airport with him. Long story short, he hired me as administrator for the Enoch Foundation. To buy the mountain." He beamed with delight, toning it down and adding, "Gierig's widow

saw the unmitigated disaster John created up there and couldn't wait
to sell out. I cinched the deal by showing her all the before-and-after
snapshots you took. She was in my office this morning when you
phoned. It seems she can hardly wait to leave our town *and* our
state."

The information was totally unexpected. I found it hard to
absorb. "Back up, Paul. Did you say he bought Gierig's part of the
mountain? From the widow? What for?"

"Actually, I let him buy my land first, but not until he showed
me the list he'd made on his flight from New York. He insisted that I
keep the cabin. As my field office." With a jubilant smile, Paul
leaned even closer.   "He's determined to restore Raspberry Hill to
its natural state, Silvi." He counted off Ariel's list with his fingers.
"To erase every man-made road, ditch and bank. Re-form and
reforest the peak. Plant baby conifers on the slope where your little
ancestor tree stands. Negotiate with the Nature Conservancy. Get
permanent easements from our neighbors. Turn the farmhouse into
an overnight nature camp for school kids. Build a music retreat on
Barret's land complete with small cabins, converting the Manor into
sound proofed studios. And, last but not least, purchase your entire
stock of paintings for his California ranch. He's quite an art buff,
you see. In his opinion—and mine—the paintings were seriously
underpriced. When he insisted on paying what they're actually worth
I couldn't exactly argue with him. Especially since he was right."
Paul was obviously enjoying himself.

I, on the other hand, was experiencing a good-news overload.
"Wait a minute!" I whispered, outraged, "according to our contract
he can't pay me a dime for giving up Melody!"

Paul grinned. "He didn't. He merely purchased a bunch of
paintings that were for sale to the general public at an internet
gallery. There was nothing in your contract to prohibit a transaction
like that. And he's deeding the mountain to the Nature Conservancy.
You'll have to move of course."

"Of course," I muttered, trying to balance my innate fear of
homelessness with a rising sense of exaltation, "I already told him I
would."

The waiter unloaded our tray. Paul chewed through his roast beef sandwich with gusto while I made only a listless attempt at spooning my soup. "And now for my own smidgen of news," he continued. "Remember me telling you about the house I'm buying? Well, escrow finally closed and I've started to move in. Five minutes from Main Street, Silvi. It has a little studio off to the side. With a couple of rooms on top. I'm thinking of renting it out. To you, maybe. Care to look?"

Seeing a glimmer of hope, I said, "Your truck or mine?"

WE TOOK Efi because she was more secure for the dogs; his Tacoma had no canopy. He directed me up the loop road. I assumed we were taking a short cut across town. Instead he asked me to stop at the apple farm. The For Sale sign at the gate had a SOLD plate screwed across it. He got out, opened the gate, and closed it behind us.

"*You* bought *this*?" I asked, cruising down the pleasantly winding driveway toward the pretty stone house. "How can you possibly afford it? You're the guy who's been sleeping on a lumpy couch in the back room of his humble office."

With a chuckle he said, "I'm sorry if I gave you the wrong impression, but I never said I was poor. Actually, what with my savings and my share of the New York property my ex recently sold I was able to afford a hefty down payment. The rest, I'm afraid, is still to be earned. Rumor has it attorneys make good money in these parts. I don't mind bunking rough but my girls do. They're visiting this summer."

I drove past the house, the picturesque, filled-to-the-brim pond, the weeping willow beside it, and parked in front of the studio. Before I could get out Paul had already opened the hatch. Asa and Marvel spilled onto the ground, noses high, scenting. "I thought they might want to stretch their legs," he said. "The fence is escape-proof. I checked every inch." He pointed to the pasture where three thin sway-backed brown horses stood leisurely grazing the emerging spring grass. "I hope your dogs won't object to my little herd. I've adopted some of Zora's rescues. She thinks they'll fill out nicely."

The dogs made a bee line for the nags, trying to figure out which of their ends did what. Meanwhile Racket, who had recognized the sound of Efi's engine, was whooping from inside the house. Then he came streaking across the lawn to greet me, ran circles around the pups, and led them off to explore. "After you," Paul said, inviting me into the studio.

It was a well-designed space, fully furnished, with a kitchenette and a small bath. There were triple glazed floor-to-ceiling windows all around making it seem as if there was no barrier between me and the drooping willow on one side, the young redwood on the other, and the watershed forest rising behind. In the summer the windows would stay open to let the breezes flow through. "I'm going to build a wraparound deck for this little gem in my spare time," Paul volunteered. "I'll appreciate any help I can get."

The two upstairs rooms were tiny, a twin bed in each. If Jimmi ever came back to me he could have them both.

"I'd sleep on the couch," I said. "Near the dogs. We're used to being together."

"Of course." Paul pulled a form out of a kitchen drawer. "Here's one of the rental applications." He brought it to me with a pen. "Take your time filling it out." He placed it on the coffee table and sat on one side of the couch.

I sat at the other, fingering the pen. "How much is the rent?"

He gave a careless shrug. "Reasonable, considering. The realtor suggested eight hundred and fifty a month."

Impossible. I could never afford it.

"It's the going rate," he explained. "And you *can* afford it. As soon as you deposit Ariel's generous check for the paintings into your bank account."

"On the ridge I was paying three hundred and fifty."

"For an under-wired drafty old dump with a twenty-five-year-old outhouse. This place has a state of the art bathroom and climate control."

Did I really expect a special deal just because we used to be neighbors? More to the point, did I want him to live no more than a shouting distance away?

"Or," he said, watching me closely, "You could move in with me. We could get married. I'm sure Racket wouldn't mind."

I laughed at his little joke. Then I pushed the application away. "Sorry, Paul. I think you better post an ad in the newspaper. Or on the co-op bulletin board. I guarantee you'll soon have your pick of flush tenants. I'll scrounge around for something more . . . lived in."

He put his hand on mine, suddenly serious. "Hear me out. You may not have noticed but I'm deeply in love with you. Have been from the time I saw your picture of my cabin in Key Largo." The reverence in his voice prickled my skin.

Overwhelmed, I pulled away, scooting sideways till my hip collided with the arm rest. "I like you, Paul. But I'm not in love with you."

"Yet," he said, letting his hand drop to the couch.

"Do I look like an attorney's wife?" I asked, pointing at my face. "You want someone more . . . glossy."

He gave a fake yawn. "Been there, done that."

"Some nice little wife," I continued, unmoved, "who adores wearing makeup and cooking and cleaning and shopping. All I want to do is—"

"Paint. I know. That's why I bought this place. So you'd have your own studio. And because you worship the land. We'll get a housekeeper of course. And I don't care what you do or don't do to your dear face."

"Then there's Jimmi," I said, groping for a more reasonable objection. "How would he fit into your equation?"

"Ah." He leaned back, his intelligent eyes on high alert. "We're coming to my final revelation of the day. If you're ready."

"For what?" I could feel my gut tie itself shut. If the news had been good surely he would have told me at the beginning instead of the end.

"While you and Ariel were saying your good-byes in the living room," he began calmly, "I stayed out of the way in the kitchen. That's when Jimmi called my cell, since he'd tried the other two numbers without getting through. I made him promise he'd stay put in Redding—somehow, he had managed to elude the detective in

Sacramento. I knew if I told you where he was you'd insist on driving down there right away, birth or no birth, no matter how weak you were feeling. So I said you had a bad case of the flu and that I'd come to get him instead." He grinned. "Ariel insisted on hiring the helicopter for our rescue operation. Jimmi got a ride he'll never forget. He's here now. In the house. A little worse for wear but nothing that can't be fixed with a bit of love and a lot of patience."

He moved closer, reclaiming my hand. Stunned as I was, I let him keep it. "I want to adopt him, Silvi," he said urgently. "Now that his name has been smeared all over the media he needs a new one. A fresh start. And a real family. We could be that family, you and me and Jimmi. And the dogs. And the horses."

"And the cats?"

"Especially the cats."

The road to a man's heart might lead through his stomach, but the way to this woman's was through her son. I was hooked. "I'm not in love with you," I repeated, no longer sure I believed it myself. "But over these past months I've learned to trust and appreciate you more than I can say. You're an exceptionally fine man." I found the courage to meet his astute gaze. "I'd be devastated if you stepped out of my life. So I guess the answer is—"

There was a timid knock on the leaded-glass door. Through its swirls I could see the shape of a boy. "Come in," I called out. He did. Walking straight into my open arms, he made the world stop wobbling and slid it smoothly back into its natural groove. Those hazel eyes. The creamy brown skin. That soft cloud of hair.

He simply said, "Hi, Mom. I'm home."

Looking over his gaunt shoulder into Paul's moistening eyes, I mouthed a distinct "Yes!"

Let the pheromones flow.

Stillman would have been pleased.

THE THREE of us cooked spaghetti for dinner that evening. We ate it amidst companionable small-talk floating comfortably around our table. Afterwards we took our bowls of honey-vanilla ice cream to sit in front of Paul's TV. He tried to find a station that carried Ariel's announcement. But we were too late.

What we got instead was an image of the Emperor of Song dressed in his finest military regalia but without his usual shades. He was standing on a high up balcony on the far side of the globe, tiny Melody in his arms. Beaming, he offered her to the world, looking directly at me as if to say, "Here we are, as happy as you have made us." In that instant I felt that all my beloveds were in the room with me.

For the two seconds she dangled over the railing the whole world stopped breathing. Not me. I focused on Ariel's capable hands holding her as firmly as he'd held the crazy fan on the cherry picker.

And then, for an instant, I thought I saw her invisible wings.